LETTING GO

Letting Go

A novel
by

CLAUDIA PIEPENBURG

BOOKS

Adelaide Books
New York / Lisbon
2020

LETTING GO

A novel

By Claudia Piepenburg

Published by Adelaide Books, New York / Lisbon
adelaidebooks.org

Editor-in-Chief
Stevan V. Nikolic

For any information, please address Adelaide Books
at info@adelaidebooks.org

or write to:

Adelaide Books
244 Fifth Ave. Suite D27
New York, NY, 10001

ISBN: 978-1-952570-99-5

Printed in the United States of America

For Mike, finally... it is written

Chapter 1

Less than two minutes into my conversation with Sam, I catch myself wishing he were calling to tell me that Dad's dead. Dad being dead is preferable to what I know is coming, and what part I'll have to play in all of it. Considering Sam's condition and the fact that he's who he is and despite his best intentions, there's little he can do, and as for George—neither one of us has heard from him in years. For all we know, George is the one who's dead. So, it's going to be left to me to handle—just like old times.

"He's getting bad. He's scared. I can see it in his eyes. There's no denying it anymore. He's losing it."

"Losing it?" I ask, and half-laugh half-snort as the oh-so-pleasant life I'm living begins to recede from view, as if someone were slowly pulling a warm quilt off my body on a cold winter's day. "Losing it? Losing what, exactly?"

"You know what I mean, Charlie. Losing it as in—well, he can't find things. Sometimes he can't find the right words. He can't find his keys. He can't find his day-planner. How much longer until he can't find the house anymore? And he's so angry much of the time, he blows up over the most unimportant things."

Sam sounds tired. He sounds beat-up and downhearted and I detect just the slightest bit of exasperation in his voice. Of course I really can't blame him for that. When I left for

California five years ago I made a promise to myself to never have any contact with Dad again. Sam yes of course, Dad no. It's a promise I've kept because it's good to never break promises, even when they're just to yourself and even when keeping them makes you feel a little wrong-headed, a little selfish and stubborn and more than a little guilty.

"How often do you see him?" I ask, hoping that Sam will tell me he visits with Dad infrequently, only once a month or so, figuring that if he doesn't see him often, when he does any changes in Dad's behavior will be more obvious.

"I get over there at least once a week. Peter drives me. He waits in the car, but if I'm staying for more than an hour, Peter drives around or goes shopping."

It's the melancholy in Sam's voice that makes me wish he weren't over two thousand miles away. How does he do it? How did he ever forgive and forget? If he were here, I'd hug him right now.

"That's probably a good idea, Peter not sticking around. If Dad's getting mad a lot, I'd hate to see the fireworks if your boyfriend was sitting in the living room trying to play nicey-nice. Don't see the three of you tossing down a few cold ones."

"That's getting to be a problem too, tossing down a few beers. He's drinking more than ever. It can't be good for him, not that it ever was, but now with the dementia, Alzheimer's whatever the hell it is, his diet is mostly wine, Scotch and crappy snacks like chips and cookies."

I want to cry, but I don't.

Poor Sam—having to deal with this alone and all because of me. Because I was so determined to leave him and Dad, just like Mom and George did.

I visualize Sam: dark-eyed, dark-haired, and handsome, missing one arm and one leg. "Hey, it could be worse, Charlie" he had said the first time I saw him in the rehab center when he'd returned stateside. "Lost the left arm and right leg. I'm better balanced this way, would have spent my days listing to only the right or left if I was missing an arm and leg on the same side."

By the time Dad and I got back to the car that awful day in 1971, I was as crumpled, wet and wasted as the tissues I was using to mop my eyes and my nose. But Dad's face had been smooth and dry, all hard geometric angles, and when I'd looked into his eyes there wasn't anyone there.

"Are you asking me to move back?" I feel the guilt gnawing at me. Little nips over and over, like some alien creature chewing. A creature eating at me from the inside out.

Please, please Sam. Don't say "yes".

"No, I'm not. I don't think so."

"You know I can't, Sam. I've got a life here now."

"I know, I know. I don't want you to feel guilty."

"I don't," I say, the gnawing making my stomach ache.

"That's good, 'cause you shouldn't. I'm probably being overly dramatic, anyway. Hey, what else would you expect from a gay guy in a wheelchair with one arm and one leg who lives with his boyfriend in a house that was once a brothel and warehouse for rum runners during prohibition."

"Which speaking of, how are the renovations going?" I ask, grateful for the change-up in topic and tone.

"They're coming along, little by little. Peter's a genius. I come up with the ideas for how I want things to look, but he's the one who makes it real, just like I imagined."

"You sure lucked-out with Peter. Your own private therapist who knows the difference between an Allen wrench and a screwdriver," and the second the words "lucked-out" become air-borne I knock my knuckles, hard, against my temples and think:

What kind of idiot are you, Charlie? Lucked-out? Yeah, right. Sam sure is the lucky one. Had to lose an arm and a leg in Vietnam so he could meet the love-of-his-life in a military hospital, the physical therapist that turned out to be Mr. Right.

Before Sam has time to respond, Cindy, my roommate and best friend since kindergarten, emerges from her bedroom, in her "lets get the party started" outfit: tight black leather mini-skirt, red tights, zebra print blouse, denim jacket and red and black beaded hoops hanging from her earlobes nearly to her collarbone. She glares at me, raises her eyebrows, points at her watch and mouths: "We have to leave. Now."

Bless your heart, Cindy. You've rescued me again.

"Hey, Sam, you know I didn't mean that you're, you know, lucky like being in a wheelchair doesn't mean you're not lucky or anything. I mean, lucky you guys found each other. You know, that kind of lucky."

Just shut the fuck up, Charlie. Stop digging the hole any deeper.

"Sam, I have to go. Cindy and I are going to be late for a party if we don't leave right now. I'll call you next week, I promise."

"Tell her I said hi. You girls have fun. Sayonara." A squeaking pursed-lips sound like wind escaping from a balloon as he kisses the air and he's gone.

Cindy doesn't say anything; she just stares at me, waiting for me to speak first. Twenty-two years after our first meeting over a shared nap mat in our kindergarten class, I know that no one understands me better. And right now I know she understands that I'm in the "why can't I stop myself from saying the wrong thing" and "I'm really unhappy now" mode.

"That was Sam."

"I know."

"He said hi. And he said that Dad isn't doing too well." If I cry my eyeliner is going to end up all over my cheeks and then

I'll have to go back into the bathroom to fix my face, and we'll definitely be late for the party.

Keep it together, Charlie. You haven't talked to Dad in the past five years and you know that most of the time you think that you hate him. So why was it hard just to say the word Dad without feeling like you're going to start bawling like a baby? Shit—if only Sam had called to say he was dead. Maybe that gnawing would go away.

"Then we need to get you to this party. Pronto! There's this guy who's gonna be there that I want you to meet. He's a friend of Matt's brother. I've met him three or four times. I like him. You'll like him, too."

I smirk and roll my eyes, but per usual Cindy pretends not to notice.

"You're twenty-seven, Charlie. We can't live together forever. You know Matt's been talking about me moving in with him. I'm seriously thinking about it. But I can't leave you all by yourself, what the hell would you do?"

"I'd be fine, and I could stay up late every night and eat whatever I wanted for dinner. I wouldn't have you cooing over me always telling me to stop eating stuff that's bad for me."

Undaunted Cindy tosses my fuzzy blue sweater at my head and waits for me to put it on; pulls my green, gold, blue and red striped knit skull cap over my close-cropped Irish setter red hair; hangs my purse over my shoulder; and pushes me out the door.

"We're going to have a blast tonight, Charlie. You're gonna love this guy. I just know it. Everything's going to be great. Lets not think about anything bad or sad for the rest of the night, okay? We're gonna have a blast."

And off we go into the cool Southern California night. It's party time.

Chapter 2

When we arrive at the party people are slowly drifting in and drifting back out again, like smoke riding on still air, onto the deck overlooking the canyon where twenty or so are inhaling joints and drinking peach schnapps and beer, the pungent scent of the weed blending provocatively with the sweet smell of the night jasmine circling up the redwood footers that anchor the deck into the ground.

Cindy and I have been to lots of parties at the house, at least four just in the past few months. We've heard the rumors that this is the house that the Mamas and the Papas lived in for a brief time in the 60s, but I don't think so. I'm sure that they lived in another house, on another street, probably close-by but not this one. I prefer the romanticism of this being the home where Graham Nash had written "*Our House*" while living there with Joni Mitchell. But I'm also intrigued by the thought that Jim Morrison might have had wild animal-like sex there, while under the influence of some of the strongest psychotropic drugs in the history of mankind.

Not that I don't know that Nash and Mitchell and every other musician or artist who lived in Laurel Canyon hadn't enhanced their creativity with massive amounts of drugs and had made love on a regular basis, but for me there's a clear line of demarcation between love and romance and unbridled passion and mind-blowing sex. Perhaps it's because up to this point in my life, I haven't experienced any of those things.

Doug Wilson, the creative director at the small boutique ad agency where Cindy works as a copywriter, rents the house; no one knows who actually owns it. All those hippies and musicians rented these houses, too. Lately though the neighborhood has started to change, it's becoming gentrified. Families are buying the homes and moving in as permanent residents, and a few of the smaller, funky cabins have been torn down, replaced by five thousand square foot mansions reeking with pretention.

When Cindy and I talk to people who've lived around here for a long time, what they tell us is that things really started going south when four drug dealers were murdered in '81, three years ago. Of course drugs were always a big part of the culture, but in the late 70s the drugs, sex and rock and roll vibe took a sharp turn into something more sinister and scary. The welcoming *'come on people now, smile on your brother, everybody get together and love one another'* feeling seemed archaic and quaint. Cindy thinks that when Sid Vicious (we've often laughed over the delicious irony of his name) stabbed his girlfriend to death in '78 is when the ugliness finally won out.

But I'm not so sure about that. I've told her on more than one occasion, usually when I'm high, that I believe the agitation and divisiveness started as the Vietnam War was ending, and everyone in the country, not just those crazy college kids and worthless good-for-nothing hippies, but older, mature people like grandmothers for god's sake, came to the realization that all those guys had suffered and given their lives for nothing.

I tell her that I think that everyone felt so damn guilty about those wasted lives they took it out on the guys who did make it home, and blamed music and movies for the anger and violence that had replaced the sense of peace and coming together. Talk about ugly—guilt is a soul-gutting emotion. I know this all too well.

Cindy ditched me about ten seconds after we walked in the door. I figure she's gone to find the wonderful guy who I'm going to fall madly in lust with and will want to screw within ten minutes of meeting him, but we'll have to move quickly. It's critical that potential fuck-mates stake out their tryst accommodations early in the evening, there're a limited number of beds in the house.

No, I'm wrong. Mr. Wonderful obviously hasn't shown up yet because Cindy is walking toward me with two red plastic glasses in hand, foam is dripping out of one of them all over her hand and onto the sleeve of the denim jacket that's been soaked over the past several years in a lot more beer than liquid detergent. Matt is following her; he likes to stay behind Cindy when she walks. I know he's just watching her ass. Cindy does know how to work it.

"Here, I got you a beer."

"Thanks, I can see that. I can also see, or not see as the case may be, that Mr. Wonderful hasn't shown up. Hi Matt."

"Hi, Charlotte."

"When are you going to start calling me Charlie, Matt? Please, really. I've known you for five years now. Call me Charlie."

He does this on purpose, I know. It's just as easy to say Charlie as Charlotte, in fact it takes a little less time, like maybe one-one hundredth of a nano-second. I think Matt is a little odd but Cindy loves him, so what can I say? I've never loved anyone. I've just had a lot of unfulfilling sex with guys I really don't like very much, and afterwards I never like myself much, either—all those couplings ending up being rather pathetic, meaningless draws.

Cindy on the other hand, Cindy is the one who gets (or thinks she does) the whole love thing. She has been with only two men in her entire twenty-seven years. John Davison was the first, the guy she started dating when we were freshmen in high school. They dated all four years and then right on through college. Cindy and I were both smart enough to get into the University of Michigan. John's grades weren't quite as good, but somehow he managed to get accepted, so off we went, the three of us.

It was heaven, blissful, nearly perfect (at least in Cindy's mind) up until graduation day. I had been planning on saying "so long" to the Midwest within seventy-two hours after hearing "*Pomp and Circumstance*", but Cindy had a different (heavenly, blissful, nearly perfect) future in Michigan in mind, which was terribly sad for her because John's future didn't include Cindy.

Turned out that John had been sleeping with another woman since sophomore year at U of M. The day after graduation he told Cindy that the mystery woman was pregnant, and they were getting married. Cindy spent the next twenty-four hours sitting in her bed in her old room at home, eating chocolate ice cream out of the container and drinking beer. I came by a few times to deliver more Baskin Robbins and Stroh's. I was never invited to stay.

Three days post-commencement we loaded up her new Volkswagen Beetle (a graduation gift from her dad, who being a Ford Motor Company exec agreed to buy it for her only because we were leaving the home of the big three automakers and wouldn't embarrass and shame him by driving around in a foreign car) and drove west to Southern California: Los Angeles in particular, Hollywood to be more specific. She got a job at the ad agency within the first week after our arrival. Matt Sanders was the account manager who sat in a cubicle across from hers. It only took Cindy two weeks to fall in love for the second time in her life.

Cindy is staring at me and pointing at her head, then at mine. "Take off that hat" she orders.

"No, my hair looks like shit. I miss my curls."

"You didn't have curls, you had frizz. I told you not to try that home perm. God, what a disaster that was. Your hair looks adorable short."

"I hate it, I look like a ten year-old. All my sex appeal is gone."

"Take it off right now and look at yourself in the mirror."

I do what I'm told, and Cindy and I turn to look into a huge rectangular gold-framed mirror leaning up against the opposite wall. The thing must weight a ton. I wonder how anyone ever got it up here.

There we are, ourselves reflected back at us. (Matt has turned too; it's so obvious now that he's staring at Cindy's butt, even though at this point in time it isn't moving.) I'm shorter than her, only five-foot-four to her elegant five-eight, and I'm carrying at least fifteen pounds more. Her boobs fit perfectly into an espresso cup, mine are better suited to a large mug. Cindy has long thick dark hair that just grazes her shoulders and bangs she refuses to cut until they brush against her lashes. My reddish-gold hair used to be long too, not straight but wavy, now it's just straight and flat up against my head like a little cap. My eyes are washed-out blue that sometimes look gray. Cindy's are so dark they're almost black. My features are soft: my cheeks still plumpish as if my baby fat decided to stick around to try out adulthood. Cindy's face is angular; she's elegant from top to bottom. Our physical selves are as different from one another as our psyches—we're the perfect foils—set apart in every way, but as good forever friends as any two people could be.

A few bodies just crossed behind us, the mirror is so big it reflects quite a wide expanse of floor and wall space. A couple walk by, she's leaning in towards him and he's pulled his torso back so far he looks like he's sway-backed. It's definitely argument time, these two started early. And that's when I see him.

He's heading for the door, so I can't quite see his face. His hair is brownish. He's not too short and not too tall. His shoulders are broad and his waist slim. His jeans accentuate the athletic roundness of his butt, and I feel a desperate longing to lie in my bed with him, both of us naked. Simultaneously I feel a desperate longing to talk to him for hours, something I've never cared to do or have done, with lovers in my past—knowing somehow that both options are not only within the realm of possibility, they're actually going to happen.

And suddenly a memory, wrenched free from its mooring, floats to the surface of my mind—Dad telling me that he fell in love with Mom at first sight, the moment he saw her standing alone by the punch bowl at a high school dance.

So this is what it's like, love at first sight. This is how it happens.

I grab Cindy's hand, twist her around and ask:

"Who is that man?"

He's on his way out so Cindy doesn't have long to size him up, but she recognizes him just as the door shuts.

"Oh, him, that's Terry Mitchell from accounting. I'm not surprised he isn't sticking around. The administrative folks have their own more tepid parties that us creative types luckily aren't invited to. But hey, don't bother with him. Erik should be here anytime now. I've told him all about you, he can't wait to meet you. You'll like him Charlie. I think he might be—you know—*the one*."

I don't tell her that *the one* has just walked out the door.

Chapter 3

The party was three weeks ago. Terry and I have our first date tonight, but it wasn't easy getting to this point. First I had to deal with the Erik situation. Erik who didn't show up until after 10:00, and followed me around as if he'd given up drinking for Lent, it was now Easter and I was an ice-cold beer. Within the first ten minutes of our introduction (his palm had been too dry when he shook my hand) we moved to the deck where we shared a joint (which wasn't necessary, the haze was so thick out there that all we had to do was step outside and breathe in) he nibbled on my ear (I wished that my hair had still been long, access would have been much more difficult) and suggested, no not suggested as much as crassly insinuated, that we were meant to be together and we needed to affirm his certainty by having sex as soon as possible, perhaps with a pre-coitus line of cocaine to jump-start the process.

"Sorry, Erik" I'd said in my most 'what's a woman to do' voice. "I've got really bad cramps. You know…cramps." When I was still having cramps two weeks later Erik finally stopped calling.

Initially Cindy was shocked. "Really, Charlie. Really? You aren't interested in Erik, but you want to meet Terry. Are you kidding me?" But she eventually came around.

"OK, I get it. You think he's the one, but you saw him just once for about ten seconds and as far as we know, he never saw you at all. Don't you think it might be a good idea for the two of you to meet, like face-to-face, kind of—oh, I don't know—maybe coincidentally?"

So, I coincidentally showed up at Cindy's office for lunch two weeks after the party. Terry's a runner; he runs three miles at lunch everyday. My timing was perfect. I was walking south on Figueroa, about twenty feet away from the entrance to Cindy's office building when I saw him running north towards me. Cindy had told me that if I came by after 12:30 chances were good that I'd bump into him, and even though I'd seen him only in profile, I knew it was Terry.

He's not classically handsome, not like my twin brothers or even our dad (in photos taken on his wedding day Dad is as compelling to look at as Mom). Terry's head is nicely shaped, rounded; no 'cone head', I got squeezed coming out of the womb look, and it isn't too big for his body. In fact, his head, torso and all four limbs are in ideal proportion, as if he'd been designed by an artist with the perfectionist tendencies of an engineer. His hair is brown, not light or dark, a soft shade that will wear well as he ages and gray begins to creep in. He has blue eyes, again soft; the pupils flecked, under ambient lighting, with just the tiniest glimmer of gold. A long, straight nose that's narrow at the top, widens slightly in the middle and turns up at the tip. His lips are full, the top evenly matching the bottom. The muscles in his shoulders, upper arms, thighs and calves are well-defined; he's not body-builder muscular, but real body, real man, no drugs involved muscular.

We arrived at the building's front door at the same time.

"After you" he'd said, as he held the heavy glass door open for me. He smelled musky and intense, leathery like a racehorse that hadn't cooled-down. A mix of sweat, warm skin, and Aramis cologne.

"Do you work here?" His voice was deep, masculine and sexy. Even though he was asking a question there was no rise at the end where the question mark would be.

"No, I work at Warner Brothers. But my best friend Cindy Andersen does. I'm meeting her for lunch."

"Say hi to Cindy. Enjoy your lunch." He smiled as he walked away.

You're not a puppy, Charlie I'd thought. Don't follow him.

Oh, but I so wanted to.

Two days later I returned for another lunch date with Cindy, and casually met Terry again just as he was finishing his run. We both laughed at the outrageous coincidence. That time I told him I remembered seeing him at the party at Doug Wilson's the month before, and then I said the classic 'You aren't really going to say that are you?' line: "We need to stop meeting like this." That's when we decided that not only were we not going to stop coincidentally meeting; we planned a meeting for the next night. A Friday. He'd pick me up at 7:00. We'd get Chinese.

It's 6:55 Friday night and I've already changed clothes three times. Each time I emerge from my bedroom wearing something different Cindy tells me that I look perfect, and each time I shake my head and tell her why what I have on isn't going to work: "Too sexy, too demure, too boring."

I don't think she's being as honest with me as usual, telling me I look perfect when I know I don't. Nothing's ever perfect; she's said it herself many times (the John situation having driven that point home all too well). I think she keeps telling me so because she's still not too sure about my dating Terry anyway, and figures that it isn't going to make any difference one way or another.

I have yet to tell her how hearing his voice makes me smile. How I love that when he smiles, his whole face beams, from his hairline all the way to his chin. I have yet to tell her that I think I'm in love with a man I've spoken to for a grand total of five minutes.

By the time Terry arrives, promptly at 7:00 as I'd expected from a numbers guy, I've settled on a simple white blouse and black jacket with padded shoulders and my favorite pair of Calvin Klein's. He's in jeans and a Polo sweater, and that animal musky smell is embedded in every molecule of air that floats around him.

Cindy pops out of the bedroom to wave "bye"; Matt's due to arrive in a few minutes. She hasn't yet decided if they're going to stay or go to his place, although I know that she's leaning toward leaving so they won't be here when she figures I'll return dejected and heartsick, well before 10:00, a carton of chocolate ice cream in hand, sufficiently chastened into accepting the reality that love at first sight only happens in movies, and when it happens for real it doesn't end well anyway. Mom left and Dad spent the rest of his life searching for her at the bottom of a bottle.

Terry's car turns out to be a surprise—it's a black Camaro. I'd been expecting something a little more safe and staid from a guy who works in accounting, maybe an Accord or even a Civic. An even bigger surprise is his suggestion that instead of eating at the restaurant we pick up the food and take it back to his place.

"Chinese just doesn't seem right unless it's carry-out, agreed?"

I agree and half-an-hour later we're sitting on the dark blue leather sofa in his tiny one-bedroom apartment eating chow mien off Desert Rose dinner plates that he tells me were a gift from his mother when he graduated from college.

"Kind of girly I know—the plates. But mom insisted. She said I couldn't be serving any potential daughters-in-law off plastic or paper plates. She collected them for years. Guess she always figured that one day she'd have a daughter of her own to give them to."

"So she never did?"

"Yes, and no. I'm the oldest. I've got a younger brother, his name's Paul. And yeah, there was a girl… her name was Sara. She died when she was ten, some kind of blood disease. I'm really glad I have them now…the dishes I mean."

"Does your mom come over for dinner a lot to make sure you're taking good care of them?"

As soon as the words leave my mouth I worry I've asked the wrong question, in the wrong way. *Charlie, you're implying that he can't be trusted to take care of the dishes. Don't stick your foot in it.*

Terry's silent for a few seconds, then looks at me with an expression of regret and unfathomable sadness, liquid pooling along his lower lids.

"No, she doesn't come here. She has…she has issues. Severe depression. Mom's gotten worse over the years, even with the medication. She doesn't always take it like she should. She says it turns her into a zombie. But sometimes I can still make her smile. And those are good days. Those are really good days."

His tears vanish as quickly as they appeared. He smiles, I see that glint of gold in his blue eyes, and I know that it's his mother's wide smile lifting his cheeks.

It occurs to me that Terry has just shared something very personal, I'm expected to reciprocate, and I'm hopelessly unprepared. Unprepared because I seldom if ever have serious conversations with any of the men I end up having sex with, and because I realize that he needs to know about my life, but I'm ashamed and embarrassed at how dysfunctional my family is, and I don't want him to think less of me because of it. This is all new territory for me, a whole new world of emotional give and take that I've never experienced before.

But I don't have long to ponder how I'm going to introduce my family to Terry because he sets his container of food on the antique trunk pulling double duty as a coffee table, and takes my face in his hands. He pulls me in close to him and the closer we get the more things start to blur, even as they're simultaneously becoming clear. I just have a sense of what he looks like now, and what he smells like and what his lips feel like when he presses them to mine.

It all happens faster than I'd had imagined it would. His soft blue eyes and I see those sparkles of gold, and then they're closed, and I smell his skin, and it's powerful and musky and male, and his lips taste aromatic and sweet, and they're so soft, and his tongue is as sweet as his lips and it's exploring the inside of my mouth with such a fervor and passion that it's as if it's trying to escape from his mouth and move into mine forever, and I'm sinking back into the sofa, and now his hands are moving down my neck, and I'm pressing against him, and I move my hands up and encircle the back of his head and pull him in even closer to me, his tongue further inside my mouth, and I move my hands around his skull loving the roundness of it, and his hands move further south and I go to another place, a place I've never been before, a place that I know I want to go to again and again and again.

It's two, three or maybe even four hours later. I have no concept of time and I have no intention of ruining the moment by pulling myself up off the bed to look at the clock radio on the bedside table. Terry and I lay beside each other, his right arm under my head, I'm turned slightly in toward him with my right arm draped across his chest. I think both of us might have drifted off for a few minutes, he might still be asleep. His breastbone rises and falls steadily, and I can feel his heart, thump…thump…thump, beating against my open palm.

"Hi, kiddo." He's not asleep after all.

"Hi."

"Did you think we would end up here?"

"Here? You mean in bed?"

"Yeah."

How am I supposed to respond? Yeah, of course because that's pretty much my MO. I always have sex the first night I'm with a guy. To tell you the truth, Terry, I sleep around quite a bit. I feel empty afterwards, but I do it anyway.

"I did. Did you?"

"Yeah. It was pretty amazing—you're pretty amazing." Terry rolls over onto me, licks the corners of my lips, then my ears, returns to my lips and kisses them— once, twice, three times. His fingertips roll over my nipples, then he slides a finger gently into me and I'm so wet that at first I hardly feel it, and he's moving his finger, then two fingers in and out, and I whisper in his ear and then he's deep inside me again, and as each wave rolls and rolls and rolls over me I think: *No ice cream for you tonight, Charlie. No ice cream tonight. Tonight's different. It's a night unlike any other.*

Chapter 4

It's Christmas Eve. I'd been so excited when I told Cindy two night's ago that I'd be spending tonight with Terry and his family.

"I'm spending the Christmas holiday with Terry." The words had flowed out of my mouth like a fine French wine being slowly poured into a crystal decanter.

For the past five years, since Cindy and I moved to California, we've have spent the holidays together—Cindy, Matt, thirty or so of his family members—and me. Extended family doesn't begin to describe the vast array of individuals who I've eaten ham, turkey and oyster dressing with; drank too much champagne with; sung *Auld Lang Syne* with; played the dictionary game with; drank too much wine with; argued over politics with; argued over religion (or lack thereof) with; even kissed under the mistletoe when I was too drunk to realize until the next unhappy morning that the uncle, or maybe a twice-removed cousin, who stuck his tongue in my mouth and rolled it around like a dentist probing for sore spots was the same person who was patting my groin under the table while extolling the virtues of trickle down economics. The fact that the creepy old uncle cliché come to life was attempting to sell me on the merits of an economic policy that I believe to be a modern day fairy tale, a particularly cruel and shameful one at that, while feeling me up beneath my plate full of turkey, dressing, mashed potatoes and cranberry sauce, somehow made the experience even more sordid.

The holidays with Cindy, Matt and et al have been nothing short of uncomfortable, outrageous, sad and really quite lonely—at least for me. I'm the outsider, the interloper, the single orphan single girl on Christmas and New Year's Eve. So dear sweet Cindy always brings me along. Tag-along Charlie, that's me.

"Why, hello Charlotte. So nice to see you—again," Matt's mother's sister, or maybe she's his father's aunt; I don't remember and don't care, smiling tepidly at me and quickly walking away to refill her wine glass, removing herself from my general vicinity so fast one would think I have a rare type of female heterosexual AIDS. Those sorts of non-greetings have become de rigueur among the Sanders', and countless other surnames that I can't begin to remember, clan.

"Oh, Charlie. We're all going to miss you. I'll miss you, Matt will miss you, everyone…."as her words trailed off Cindy had realized she was in the middle of a fairly big lie, and she knows too well that she can't get away with lying to me.

I could have saved her, finished off her sentence by saying: "All the perverts will miss you," but I wasn't sure that she'd find it funny or even appreciate the sarcasm. I wouldn't have found it funny either, that is up until the moment when Terry invited me to share Christmas Eve and Christmas Day with him, his parents and brother and sister-in-law. I'd been in such a state of happiness that all my recollections of Christmases spent with that oftentimes-mordant group had been edited from my mind like scenes cut from a movie after the director reviewed the dailies.

Terry's parents have returned from church and Gloria (Terry's mom) lays out a spread of French bread, and various hard and softened cheeses, crackers, sliced turkey and prosciutto, four different kinds of olives, unshelled walnuts, cashews, rum balls and sugar cookies shaped like stars and pine trees.

The six of us loop around the table: Gloria, Harold (Terry's dad), Paul and his wife Barbara, Terry and I, stacking up treats on our plates, talking and laughing. Harold breaks into a rather mangled version of *Let It Snow*, which makes us all laugh even harder because his singing is horrible and there's not going to be snow in Santa Monica tonight, or any other night this winter for that matter. We move into the contemporary living room, highlighted by a fifteen-foot pine tree covered in hundreds of twinkling white lights; the tree out-shining the city lights framed inside the panel of windows that make up one wall. The feasting begins.

Half an hour later I'm pleasantly bloated, not so full though that I couldn't eat a few more rum balls, and I have an eggnog headache that pairs perfectly with what's going on in my stomach. Terry has belched, indiscreetly, a few times. I know he's experiencing the same culinary conundrum as I am. Should I have more prosciutto or maybe more sugar cookies, another glass of eggnog perhaps? And he's smiling crazily at me, has been all evening. No man has ever smiled at me like this, not ever. A wide grin that spreads across and widens his face from ear to ear, and I've caught him humming under his breath. I can't quite make out the tune but I think it has something to do with sleigh bells ringing. He's certainly one happy guy.

And then, when I can't imagine how the evening could be any more delightful, Gloria stands up and says: "It's time to go to the theater."

Perfection to panic in five seconds—I feel like I'm in a tampon ad.

The theater. Good lord, I was so happy that we weren't going to church so I didn't have to dress for that and now I find out that I should be dressed for the theater.

My eyes dart around the room like a lizard searching out prey, settling for a second or two on the non-church goers in the room.

Paul's wife isn't all that dressed-up. She's in black, but she seems like the kind of woman who wears black most of the time anyway, and not 'cause it's slimming. She must weigh ninety pounds max. And Paul's got jeans on. *Yeah, he's wearing a sports coat but who wears jeans to the theater?*

I was with Terry when he was dressing, as well as undressing, this evening so I know that he's not wearing what I would consider to be appropriate stage-viewing attire: a sweater layered with stripes in every color on the Pantone chart and stonewashed Guess jeans. Even Paul's jeans aren't stonewashed.

And it's at that very second, when I've reached the conclusion that we're going to some avant-garde theater in a library or maybe in an old gas station in Studio City, that Terry grabs my hand and whispers in my ear: "This is the best part of Christmas Eve. It's the saddest, too. But it's still the best part. It's our tradition. It's special, particularly for mom."

Hand-in-hand, Terry and I follow Gloria, Harold, Paul and Barbara down a long hallway to—the theater. Their in-house theater, complete with a huge screen that fills most of the entire far wall, red carpeting and two rows of eight black leather seats with high backs and wide arm rests, just like at the movies.

I've always known that people watch movies in their houses, especially people in Hollywood. There was even a rumor going around when I was growing up on the island that someone had a movie screen at home. I never found out who, or if it was true. But this is the first time I've seen one up close and personal. I'm as excited as a kid at an amusement park for the first time.

Terry's dad is a producer, not a movie producer but a television producer. The second time we were together, after much prodding on my part, Terry reluctantly rattled off the names of some of the shows that made it to the small screen courtesy of Harold's money, imagination and influence. I was impressed. I had been even more impressed by Terry's reticence in parting with the information. Terry's proud of his dad, rightfully so, but not because of his three Emmy's.

"Dad only invests in projects that mean something, you know, dramas that make people think. That reflect what's wrong in society and what we can do to make things right. He's never been much of a sitcom kind of guy. Except for *All in the Family.* Dad's really good, he's no Norman Lear but he's cool with that."

I had kissed Terry, delicately right on the tip of his nose, when he spoke of his dad that way and decided that I was as much in love with the elder Mr. Mitchell (who I hadn't yet met) as I was with the younger.

And now here I am, the younger Mr. Mitchell beside me, his hand resting on my thigh, and the older Mr. Mitchell in the back of the theater making noise, rigging something up, creating whirring sounds behind us and then saying "And now ladies and gentleman. For your Christmas Eve viewing pleasure..."

The screen before us is illuminated with a scene of a main street in a small town, a long time ago. Snow is falling. We see a sign welcoming us to Bedford Falls. We hear voices, people praying. A man's voice: "I owe everything to George Bailey. Help him, dear father." And a woman prays: "Joseph, Jesus and Mary. Help my friend Mr. Bailey."

Terry's father moves as if wings, rather than legs, propel him into the seat next to his wife, who covers her face with her hands and begins to weep.

Four hours later, well after midnight I'm sure although I haven't looked at the clock, Terry and I are snuggled, nose-to-nose and toes-to-toes in his bed. We've made love a few times, dozed off for a few minutes and we're awake again. The evening's been beautiful, joyful, loving and sad.

Terry's mom cried throughout *It's A Wonderful Life,* yet despite her tears I hadn't felt a sense of burdening sadness, the kind that weighs on a person so heavily they're unable to function. Instead each member of the Mitchell family had taken on a piece of Gloria's grief and wrapped themselves in it, finding solace and comfort in sharing their familial sadness and love.

Harold kept his arm around his wife's shoulders throughout the showing, and a few times he'd turned towards her and wiped her wet face with his hand. Harold, Terry and Paul didn't cry during the film, but in the final two minutes, when the ornament rang on the Bailey's Christmas tree, each of them reached underneath their seats and pulled out a tiny silver bell. As Zulu said: "Look, daddy. Teacher says, every time a bell rings an angel gets his wings," they rang the bells in unison, then presented them to Gloria, who graciously smiled as tears flowed in rivulets to her mouth and fell, silent drop-by-drop, from her chin to her collarbone.

"I had a wonderful time tonight," I've pulled far enough away from Terry's face to see him clearly. "Loved Paul, he's just like you, only younger. Barbara is beautiful but she's not a snob. And your parents—your parents are really special."

"They all loved you, too. I could tell. I'm so glad you came with me, Charlie. I'm glad the evening was as wonderful for you as it was for me."

If you only knew; I could have gotten sick and thrown up all over myself and it still would have been a couple hundred times better than the last five Christmas Eve's have been.

"*It's A Wonderful Life* obviously has a special meaning for your family, especially your mom."

Terry's silent for a few seconds and when he does speak his voice is flat, emotionless.

"It was my sister Sara's favorite movie, that and *The Wizard of Oz.* We watched *It's A Wonderful Life* every Christmas, as a family. We'd all be eating cookies when it started but by the time it was finished only Sara was still munching away. She was always so thin, even after all those cookies."

He stops and kisses me, just softly on the corner of my mouth.

"The part Sara loved best, besides when Jimmy Stewart puts Zulu's petals back on her flower, was the ending when the bell rang on the tree. The Christmas Sara was five Dad said that she should have her own bell to ring, so he got her one and the year after that and the year after that. Every Christmas until she was ten, because she didn't make it to that Christmas; she died in April. The bells that we ring are the bells dad bought for her all those years."

We're both quiet. Quieter than library quiet: a reverent sort of quiet, like the way people are still when they're standing by a casket. My dad's parents died before I was even born so I don't have much experience with funerals, except for when everyone's favorite teacher died when I was a junior. I remember how strange it was to not hear all the jocks mouthing-off and trying to sound cool and sexy, and the girls weren't rolling their eyes at them and laughing too loudly. Instead we all stood around with a 'what does this mean' look on our faces, and when we spoke, we whispered. I never heard a guy, certainly not a big football player, whisper before, and the last time I'd whispered, or heard another girl whisper, I think we were in junior high.

This is definitely a time for whispering, which I do:

"Is your mom's—does her—is she depressed, on medication because…?" I'm not communicating well, not at all. My heart is beating fast although I'm talking very slowly and just now my stomach has started to make strange noises like there's a small angry animal being born in there, and I pray, even though I'm not sure I believe in God, that all the eggnog, cookies, meat and wine doesn't return for a curtain call.

"Was mom depressed before Sara died? Yes, she was."

Terry props himself up on his elbow and smiles his mom's smile at me.

"From what Dad's told Paul and me, mom was depressed even back in high school. That's where they met, when they were sophomores at Hollywood High. Mom and dad are an anomaly, a Hollywood couple who've been together ever since they were teenagers. I think dad thought that maybe he could make her better, that his love for her would heal her. But that only works in the movies."

I so want to say: "Well, I understand depression Terry. You're not the only one. I understand, I really do."

But I can't, not quite yet. It's not the right time. How I'll know when it's right, I'm not sure yet but I will, when that moment comes. Up to this point Terry only knows a few details about my family. He knows that I grew up on Grosse Ile, an island in the Detroit River. He knows that I have an older homosexual brother who was badly wounded in Vietnam. That his twin went to Canada rather than Khe Sanh. That my mother left us when I was six. And that I have no contact with our alcoholic, chronically unhappy Dad, who's now losing his mind, or at least his memories. Dad, the reason I 'get' depression.

My response is so inadequate I wish I'd kept quiet: "If I could only help but I… I'm sorry."

"It's okay, it is. Eventually you learn what moments don't really matter and what ones do, and those are the ones you hold on to. Sometimes even the most seemingly insignificant moments mean the most. Like the sound of a bell ringing."

Terry kisses me again, a long soft kiss that's more comforting than passionate.

"Let's get some sleep. Merry Christmas, Charlie."

Chapter 5

Christmas morning, 1984. It's 8:30, a very reasonable, adult-like time to be awake and looking forward to all the excitement to come. I lie very still for a few moments and revel in it. How amazed I am that this is even happening. With Terry still asleep by my side, one arm flung up over his face and the other nudged up against my left hip, I engage in a bit of Christmases past reminiscing.

Every Christmas Eve mom made sure I was in bed by 8:00. And every Christmas Eve, until I was six, I would get up after midnight, believing that I was going to catch Santa in the act of delivering presents to all the good little boys and girls in the world.

I'd be up a little after 1:00, sneaking out of my room, dodging toys strewn around all over the floor, then out the door and down the hallway, padding along in my bare feet. Past everyone's bedroom, as quietly as I could because by that time I was running not walking and running is noisier. You have to be quick if you're going to find Santa spreading packages out under the tree. But by the time I got downstairs, he had always already been to our house.

When I was three and four I wanted to find him there because I wanted to ask him if he had liked the cookies mom and I had left out. But when I was five I wanted to ask him if he could come by more often, because the day that he brought presents, was a happier day in our house, maybe even the happiest.

On the days when Santa wasn't coming, Dad came home from work late. I was usually in bed when he got home. Sometimes I would hear mom talking loudly to him, not yelling (mom never ever yelled at anyone) but talking loudly as if she were scolding a dog that had peed on the carpeting. I never could quite hear how Dad responded to her, maybe because he never said anything or because he was tired. That's what I believed for a long time.

"Your dad is very tired," is what mom used to tell us: Sam, George and me. "He's a very busy man. It's not easy running a company. A lot of people depend on your dad. So that's why he's so tired. Don't bother him when he gets home. Leave him alone."

It worried me that Dad was always so tired. Once, right after I turned six, I asked mom if maybe he was sick. A sister of one of Cindy and my classmates in first grade had died. She had been in fourth grade and had gotten very tired and couldn't play with her friends anymore and then she died. I was scared that Dad was going to get sick and die, too.

"No, no Charlie. Your dad isn't sick, he's just tired." But she hadn't answered me right away.

I guess Sam and George were used to the idea of Dad being tired, and getting home so late every night. They were eight years older than me, and by the time I was old enough to worry about Dad, they didn't seem to care. I sometimes wondered if they ever had cared, maybe they did when they were little like me. Once when I asked George if he wasn't worried that Dad might be sick or something, George laughed at me, not in a mean-like way, but he still laughed.

"Oh, Charlie. Don't be silly. There's nothing wrong with him. He's just being a man, that's all."

I liked the man Dad was on Christmas Day. He was my favorite man then.

When Sam, George and I came downstairs in the morning (me for the second time) Dad was always sitting in his big leather chair, holding a cup of coffee. He was smiling, sitting there waiting for us as if where he was right then, at that moment, was the only place on earth he wanted to be. He didn't look tired at all. Mom was in the kitchen. We smelled cinnamon and bacon and coffee. When she heard us she came out and said:

"Time to open one present, just one, before breakfast."

Every year it was the same, and every year it was good and special and we were a happy family.

Family! It's almost noon in Michigan. I should have called Sam by now.

"Terry, Terry. Wake up. I need to use your phone," I shake his shoulder and kiss him on his right eyelid.

Terry takes a shower while I dial Sam's number. Peter answers: "Hello, and Merry Christmas. Peter here."

I love listening to Peter. He's from England. His enticing accent more than makes up for his bad teeth. I know that one of the reasons Sam fell in with Peter wasn't because of his mouthful of pearly whites, because they're certainly not.

"Perfect teeth really aren't all that important at home," Peter explained to me soon after we had met. "We English don't care if our children's teeth are as straight as the steps on a ladder or train tracks. There are more important things than straight white teeth, Charlie."

I'm unconvinced by his defense of his mother country's seeming disregard for dental perfection, but I still find him to be disarmingly charming and sexy in a sweet, homosexual way. And although I haven't seen him in five years, that charm and sexiness (although I can't quite understand how I can find him to be so attractive while my brother does, too) hasn't abated. I haven't heard his voice in a long time. Hearing it on Christmas Day, especially this Christmas Day when everything in my life has finally come together, feels good. Peter is the love of Sam's life and Terry's the love of mine.

"Hi Peter. So good to hear your voice. Merry Christmas to you. What have you and my brother done today so far to celebrate?"

"We made love when we woke up, had brunch and then Sam called your dad. I was going to take him over there today so Sam could give him a present."

Was going to take him over there. Suddenly I'm not feeling as warm and fuzzy as I was just a minute ago.

"So, what—Sam's not going to see Dad today? It's Christmas." My throat is starting to close up.

"No, I don't think so, Charlie. Your dad told him not to come. He was already drunk when Sam called."

I don't know how I'm going to get another word out, I feel like my windpipe has constricted to the size of a straw.

"How's Sam doing? Is he there now? Can I talk to him?"

Peter pushes out an extended sigh, not one for dramatic effect; he's not a showy gay guy.

"I'll let Sam tell you, Charlie. He's coming down the hall now. Merry Christmas again. I hope you're happy. Here's your brother."

Sam and I haven't talked since September, when I called him on his birthday. I love talking to my brother but we only talk a few times a year because that's all I can manage. Our conversations always start out on a high note but it isn't too long before they go off-key and I invariably take the blame, at least in my mind, for the dissonance. I know it's my fault. I'm the one who left.

I hear the sound of Sam's wheelchair rolling across the wood floor, and Peter's distant voice as he drops the receiver: "It's Charlie."

"Charlie. Hi, Merry Christmas." Over the last few years my dear brother has become less practiced in hiding his feelings. The day has ceased to be merry, clearly just as much for him as for me.

"Oh, Sam. What happened? What happened with Dad? Why doesn't he want you to come over?" *I hate the stinging feeling right before the tears finally spill.*

I hear what sounds like someone trying to talk while they're gargling. Is Sam crying, too?

"I'd bought him a sweater, just a sweater that's all. A blue sweater. I called him an hour ago and told him that I'd be over at two to give him his present. He was drunk. He yelled at me." Sam coughs once, again and then clears his throat.

"He yelled at me, Charlie. He told me that he didn't want a present from his fag son. It's been a long time since I've heard that. He said that he doesn't want to see me again. Not ever again. I'm a fucking homo is what he said."

I'm not going to ask Sam today if he wants me to come back, not like I did six months ago. Today I know what his answer will be. Six months ago we had both danced around the subject, shifting adroitly as one would expect from long-commiserating siblings. But today there isn't going to be any dancing.

I don't hear water running in the shower anymore. Terry has stopped singing Christmas carols over the sound of the spray.

"Sam, I'm so sorry." It's just occurred to me that Dad really is sick, which I suppose I've known all along. "I'm coming back. Soon. I'm not sure exactly when, but I'm coming back. Back home."

Terry's come into the room. Even with my back to the doorway I can smell soap, a warm fresh water scent, and his aftershave; sweet and leathery. "Hey, babe. How's Sam?"

As I turn toward him, slowly, like a music box ballerina whose song is winding down, tears drop into the corners of my lips, upturned into a fake half-smile.

"Sam? He's good. Sam's home. He's home, celebrating Christmas."

Chapter 6

It's funny, isn't it? No, funny isn't the right word at all, so it's funny that people use that word when they say, invariably whenever things change, especially when they turn bad: "Funny, isn't it that just a few hours ago I was as happy as I've ever been in my life and now I'm so unhappy I can't remember how happy I was when everything was different." Funny is most definitely the wrong word. There's nothing funny about the emotions I'm feeling.

But I'm doing a damn good job of keeping what's going on inside me from revealing itself. Except for the tears that Terry saw when he walked into the living room, but I'd been able to convince him that I was crying only because it was Christmas and I missed Sam. I'm wearing a mask and I'm hiding behind it.

The play-acting continues during the drive to Terry's parents. Terry singing carols (like his father, he couldn't carry a tune even if he took lessons from Pavarotti) most of the way down nearly traffic-free Wilshire Boulevard, occasionally asking me to join in, helps me maintain the disguise.

Between our off-key last two stanzas of *O Holy Night* 'and Terry's karaoke sing-along with David Bowie's version of *Little Drummer Boy* playing on the radio, I tell him that even after five Christmases in California, I still get as excited as a first-grader when I see garlands of lights strung on palm trees.

"I called Sam my first Christmas here and went on and on about how different it is in California. How the only snow is on top of the mountains and red bougainvillea growing wild is even more beautiful than all the poinsettias people buy in stores back east. And then I bragged that all of the poinsettias sold everywhere come from California anyway, and told him it was sixty-five degrees and he said it was thirty-two there and that's when I realized that I was being obnoxious."

Terry chuckles. "He forgave you, I know."

"Yeah, of course he did. Sam forgives everyone. He's that kind of guy. He's not one to ever hold a grudge, not Sam."

This isn't the time, Charlie. Don't go there, not yet. It's Christmas day. Let it go for now.

We've arrived at the Mitchell's. The trip took even less time than last night. The City of Angels citizens' Christmas gift to themselves: unclogged freeways and side streets. No blaring horns. No middle finger salutes. Enjoy it today, people. Tomorrow the mania takes up where it left off.

I'm looking in the rearview mirror, putting on fresh lipstick as Terry reaches in the back seat to grab the two grocery bags filled with presents he brought for his parents and Paul and Barbara.

"Uh, oh."

Harold is walking down the driveway toward the car. I know instinctively that something's wrong. Mr. Mitchell is disheveled, his hair sticking up around his ears, looking like it hasn't been combed since I saw him last night. He obviously hasn't shaved since yesterday morning. He's wearing sweat pants and a Hollywood High School sweatshirt. There are flip-flops on his feet, and a markedly dour expression on his face that makes my stress level rise even higher than it already is. I feel like I'm watching a surgeon walking from the operating room to deliver bad news. I want to put my hands to my ears, close my eyes and back away, but I'm trapped.

"What babe?" Terry turns his head to look at me and then, as he sees his dad: "Oh, shit. This doesn't look good."

Harold taps on the driver's side window and Terry rolls it down.

"Hi son, Charlie. Merry Christmas." He tilts his head sideways, toward the house. "Your mom isn't having a good day, buddy. I tried calling you earlier to tell you not to come over but the line was busy. When I called back there was no answer. Sorry you drove over here for nothing."

"Hey, Dad. Not for nothing. I've got presents for you and Mom. I've got presents for Paul and Barbara, too. But I guess they're not here, huh?"

"They got here early, came a little before eight. Your mom hadn't gotten up yet. She's still not up. Refuses to get out of bed. They're gone now. I'm sorry."

Thirty minutes later, and Terry and I are sitting in a Chinese restaurant on Vermont Street, in the heart of Los Feliz. Unsurprisingly it's the only place open on Christmas day, except for hotel restaurants that have been booked for months. Surprisingly Harold told Terry before we headed out in search of a meal that he could probably 'make a few calls' and get us into the Beverly Wilshire Hotel for brunch. Terry had hugged his dad and politely refused.

"Dad, don't. You know you don't want to do that. And you don't need to do that. We had last night, all of us together. Charlie and I will be fine. We'll find someplace to eat. Let it go Dad, let it go," he'd said. I loved Terry more at that moment than I could fathom.

We've ordered shrimp dumplings, pot stickers, meatballs, ribs and noodles. Tea has been poured, and I feel as if I'm watching the two of us from afar, like we're actors in a movie and I'm sitting in the audience way in the back, close to the projection room. The reason I've chosen to sit at the rear of the theater is so I can make a quick exit when what I'm seeing on screen makes me uncomfortable.

"So, this is okay, isn't it? We love Chinese anyway. Reminds me of our first date." Terry's smile is wan, forced, which is a new look for him.

"Yeah. Sure." My fake smile mimics his. So soon—is it time already for me to start shuffling around in my seat, swiveling my head, looking for the red exit sign?

He reaches across the table, my hands are in my lap but I raise both of them back and up and in sliding my right hand towards his I hit my cup, which tips and I'm looking at a tea puddle spreading across the white tablecloth.

It feels like hundreds of tiny tear-filled balloons are pressing against the back of my eyeball. I feel them back there, pushing to the point of bursting and when they do…

It's not about the tea. It's about what you know is coming. What you've known has been coming for months, but you kept pushing it away. A little further away each time. But isn't your mind circular? Your head round? You push thoughts away and eventually they come back around again.

"No crying over spilt tea," I say as I dab with my napkin at the ochre spot. "And look. The stain seems to be forming the shape of a lotus flower. Not a coincidence, there's probably something in the fabric to make liquids follow that pattern."

Terry's timing is perfect; he picks up his cue like a pro. "The lotus flower is on our table. That one over there," his thumb points to the table kitty-cornered to ours, "someone spills tea or soup there, and the stain comes out in the shape of a dragon."

"Confucius." I point to the table behind him.

"Hah. Mao Tse Tung," to the table on our right.

"And the table next to that one—The Great Wall."

He pauses. "This isn't quite how I expected Christmas Day would turn out." Terry's astute enough to know that the spilled tea theme has gone on just long enough to release the tension and set-up the next scene.

"No—I mean yes. This isn't what I envisioned either."

"So, we make the most of it."

It's time.

"Terry—things aren't good with my dad."

He squeezes my hand tighter. "You haven't told me much about him. He drinks too much. That's all you've said."

"There's more."

"How much more?" Our hands are sweaty.

"It wasn't easy growing up, sometimes. Not all the time. Christmas was always the most fun. We were happy on Christmas, the whole family. But the rest of the time…not so much. Once I got to be seven or so I was old enough to understand that things weren't as they should be."

Terry looks away, back, and then away again; it's all over in a few seconds. The gold-flecked orbs of blue moving back and forth as if he'd experienced a momentary ocular tic.

"Who's to say what should be, Charlie? What people think should be and what actually is can often be two very different things. I believe I understand that."

"Yeah, I know. But the thing is, there's a lot of love in your parent's house. Between your mom and dad. And you and your mom, and you and your dad. You love them."

"Sure, I love them. They're my parents."

"And it's easy, isn't it? It's uncompromising unconditional love. It's easy for you, right?"

"Easy? I don't know that love and easy are words that belong side-by-side. Natural maybe. I think natural is the better word. The way things are meant to be."

Jeez. That sounds like something I'd say out loud and be sorry for it later. Natural. So, in other words, I'm not. I'm unnatural.

"Then, okay. Natural, the way things are meant to be. But I just don't feel that kind of love for my dad, okay? It doesn't come easily for me, or naturally, either. He's not a nice man."

Terry flinches, it's over so fast I barely feel it but it happened. An involuntary movement, the tendons in his hand contracting like a rubber band being snapped.

"He didn't…?" The words come out deep and guttural, almost a growl.

"Oh, god Terry. No, no nothing like that. No. Dad's just an alcoholic bigoted homophobe who hates his own son because that son has sex with men instead of women. But other than that, he's a great guy. Great guy."

Terry's lips form a rosebud shape as he lets out a shallow breath. "That's a tough one."

"Oh, you have no idea. There's more. You probably don't remember the riots in Detroit in sixty-seven. You lived here and like me you were only ten."

"Well, I do kind of. Two years earlier were the Watts riots. Even though I was only in third grade I was aware of what was going on when they happened. Dad made a point of talking to Paul and me about those things, explaining why black people felt they had to take to the streets to be heard. He told us they weren't allowed to live in nice neighborhoods even though a lot of them had fought in World War II and were fighting in Vietnam. He said that they were just as hard working as white people but employers didn't want to hire them."

"My situation was a bit different. There are two bridges linking the island to the mainland. One's what we call the 'free bridge' and the other one's a toll bridge. When the riots started Dad shut down his company for four days, even though it wasn't in Detroit, and he tried to get the residents on the island to raise the bridges so no one could cross them. I remember him standing in front of the TV, holding a bottle of vodka, yelling: 'Goddamn niggers. Goddamn fucking niggers. They aren't coming here. Not across our bridges, they're not.'"

I'm shaking, my body and my voice. I've never said those words out loud. Never said 'that' word out loud. I'm ashamed and disgusted with my dad. Humiliated by my association with him. Humiliated by the life I ran away from. By what I put up with before I did.

After mom left I took care of him. Made him dinner almost every night when I got older. Cleaned up after him. Tried to make him laugh. Listened to his awful stories about how bad the war was. How even though he got injured badly he was never a hero like his brother Howard who got killed over there. "Heroes are the ones who don't come back. Heroes are the ones who die," he used to tell me. Grade school. Junior high. High school. All those years, listening to his stories.

Terry doesn't let go. He's holding on to my hands so tightly I think my fingers might fuse together.

"Hey, that generation. Your dad's generation, a lot of them thought...think that way. That's just how they are. They grew up in a different time that's all."

"Nice try. You and I are the same age. I think our dads are, too."

"You got me there. But Charlie, people have their prejudices."

My fingers are getting numb; it's a relief to loosen my grip and Terry responds accordingly.

"Prejudice is bad. It's bad enough. But then there's Sam." I've pulled my hands back off the table now; they're clenched together in my lap. I've stopped leaning in, hoping that by straightening my spine I'll have the strength to continue.

"I was twelve on the first of December nineteen-sixty-nine. The night of the Vietnam draft lottery. I don't remember if we knew ahead of time that it was going to be televised. They broke in to *Mayberry RFD,* I remember that. We were all watching: Dad, Sam, George and me. Sam and George were twenty. They never sat around and watched TV with Dad and me, so I guess they all knew it was going to be televised, but I didn't."

I grab and pull at the folded over fingertips of my opposite hand again and again. Right hand fingers grab and tug at the left, trying to pry them open and flat. Then the left grabs at the right.

"It didn't take long to draw the first date, maybe a couple of minutes. I'm not sure. For Sam and George it must have seemed like an hour. September fourteenth: that's what the guy said when he unrolled the piece of paper. God—it all seems so antiquated now. A piece of rolled up paper, with a bunch of other pieces of rolled up paper thrown into a big glass bowl. Kind of like drawing Bingo numbers, I guess. Rolled up pieces of paper with a date on each one. No letter 'I' or letter 'O' but someone's birthdate. A birthdate. That's all."

Left grabbing right, then right grabbing left, my hands are dry now.

"Sam and George's birthday is September fourteenth."

I'm leaning in again, and so is Terry. We're both bent over at the waist, torsos pushed against the table.

"Sitting here now I can remember exactly how it felt in the room when he said September fourteenth. There were four of us there, in that room; hearts beating, lungs breathing, brains working. But when we heard that date read out loud, for just a few seconds, a brief flash of time—I felt like I was the only person in the room. Suddenly Sam, George and Dad were gone. Their hearts stopped beating, their lungs stopped breathing, and their brains stopped working. They were just gone. It was so quiet that I looked behind me to where they were sitting, thinking that there wouldn't be anyone there."

A young Chinese girl, surely no older than six, sitting at the Confucius table behind Terry to the right of his shoulder is looking at me, smiling. She's with her parents and a much older brother. Mom and Dad and brother look very serious, almost angry, no one is talking to anyone else but the girl is oblivious to their seeming displeasure and crankiness. Her smile widens and then she crosses her eyes and sticks out her tongue.

"But they were there, of course. The room had felt so empty and then suddenly it filled up again. Filled up with a kind of energy that made me feel like my eardrums might burst. Bad energy, destructive energy kind of like a monstrous hurricane. Dad stood up. I remember the sound of the ice cubes tinkling against each other in his glass. He pointed to Sam and said 'You're going. You're the one who's going. The fag son goes to Vietnam. They won't take both of you. So, you're the one who's going.'"

The girl is mimicking a clown now: alternating between an almost maniacal grin that spreads across the bottom of her small face in a pink slash and a downtrodden, lips turned pouty and eyes squeezed almost-shut facade.

No, not a clown, not exactly. She's pretending to be a Janus mask, but what would a six-year-old know about comedy versus tragedy? Maybe what she learned from a clown.

"And so that's what happened to Sam. Sam came back with half of his limbs missing because he's the one who went. Because Dad made him go. If George had gone, it wouldn't have happened to him because that's not how it works. It would have been different for him. George would have come back the same as he was when he left and Sam would have stayed at home and had a much different life. But because of Dad, he never got the chance. Everything changed for Sam."

The waitress is rolling a cart towards our table, plates of steaming food atop it. Our Christmas dinner is here. It's time for eating now, not talking, which is perfect timing because I've said all I want to say—for today.

Chapter 7

The flight back to Michigan is an experience I'm observing as if I'm seated in an imaginary floating theater, higher up in the air than the plane. I'm in the audience again, watching the protagonist as she stares out the window, looking at the world below her move at a pace that's both imperceptibly slow and heartbreakingly fast.

The cool blue of the Pacific meeting the sun-bleached Los Angeles sky at the horizon, eventually melds into glaring brightness. Spring snow sprinkled like mounds of sugar on the tops of the San Gabriel Mountains. Harsh desert, looking like a vast bedspread made of sandpaper, tufted here and there with shadows of forms struggling to survive against the brutal aridness. The ancient granite of the Rockies, slumbering under heaping quilts of near-blinding white. The plains, one gigantic checkerboard spread out for miles; perfectly square farms, plots of land some with pieces in the center, not red and black but the muddy-green circles of irrigation pivots. And finally, the Midwest displaying its fresh young greenness tree after tree after tree, on and on, a never-ending canopy stretching out below, interspersed with small cities and towns in seemingly random clusters as if they'd been dropped there on a whim, connected by rivers and roadways that seem to be intruding on all the pines, oaks and maples.

I wonder when the plane finally touches earth again if at that very moment I'll become grounded too, not watching any longer but stepping back into the role that I've been reluctantly playing ever since Sam's call in late March.

It was a Sunday morning, around nine California time. Terry had spent the night and when the phone rang he was in the kitchen brewing coffee and making sandwiches out of fried eggs nestled between two pieces of white bread that he'd slathered on one side with catsup. (Until I'd met Terry I had no idea that native-born Californians appreciated such a homey Midwest breakfast. Then again, maybe he just told me he liked them because he loved me.) I was still in bed, in a languid post-love making state. When the phone rang it surprised and shook me, the sound made me think of a siren.

"Charlie, it's Sam." But he didn't sound like Sam, at least not the Sam I was used to hearing.

He sounded out of breath, gasping as if he had just run the hundred-yard-dash on no training. And for one brief, fantastical moment a very childish vision had hopscotched through my mind: Sam had regrown his missing leg and he had in fact just run a relay race; Sam, running the anchor leg, carrying the baton in his freshly minted arm. Peter, you're not just an amazing physical therapist, you can also replicate and reattach missing limbs.

"Sam. You sound winded. Like you've been running. What's going on?"

Please tell me that something magical and unbelievable has happened.

"It's Dad. I'm at the house now. He nearly burnt it down, Charlie. The house. He nearly burnt down the house."

So this is how the ending begins.

"What do you mean? Did he start a fire or something?"

"In a manner of speaking, yeah. That's what he did. For some reason known only to him, he decided to build a fire in the fireplace sometime early this morning. It's not that cold here today, forty or so. I don't know why he thought he needed to have a fire. I mean it's March twenty-fourth for God's sake."

The words tumbled out of Sam's mouth like dice from a cup.

"The only reason the house didn't burn down is because John Mason, the guy who lives next door, was backing down his driveway when he saw flames shooting up out of the chimney. That chimney probably hasn't been cleaned in years. John went back in his house and called the fire department and then came over here and started pounding on the front door."

"Was Dad even at home, or had he built the fire and then left?"

"No, he was home. But I don't know if that was better than if he'd left and forgotten about it. John said dad answered the door after he'd pounded on it for nearly three minutes. Dad had been drinking and he was still in his pajamas. There was soot all over them, and all over Dad's face and hands."

Before I responded I thought: this is going to be the most difficult thing you'll ever do.

"He's okay though, Dad is, right? Why the soot? He didn't get burned or anything, did he?"

"No, he's not burned. Just confused. I don't know why the soot's all over him. Maybe he was digging around in the old ashes before he lit the fire. He's been crying on and off since we got here. Saying that he's an old fool, that he doesn't even know how that fire got in there. He keeps saying it: 'I don't know how that fire got in there.'"

That's when I'd heard voices in the background. Peter's I recognized immediately: "It's okay Mr. Carpenter. Please Mr. Carpenter. It's going to be okay."

But the other voice was foreign to me. Not only because I hadn't spoken to my father in over five years, but also because the voice was garbled and blubbery yet simultaneously robotic and monotone. The person speaking was clearly confused and frightened and remorseful, but his ability to express that emotion wasn't translating to his speech. It wasn't the voice of anyone I remembered. It was the voice of a stranger.

"Don't know how that fire got there. Don't know where it came from. Don't think I made it. Maybe I did. I don't remember. Don't know how that fire got there."

Hearing Peter talking to Dad, trying to console him, I'd wondered if Dad even knew who Peter was. Surely he couldn't; he'd never stand for that: his son's lover in his house, talking gently to him, perhaps even touching him. But I put the thought away, figuring that I'd have time enough to become familiar with Dad's discombobulated world in the not-too-distant future.

"Sam," I said sotto voce, as if by doing so my words could be taken back in case I felt the need to do so; I could make-believe that because I'd spoken so softly my words were never heard. "I'll have to give two weeks notice. Matt will probably move into the apartment with Cindy. They've wanted to move in together for months. I guess I'll stay at the house?"

"You'll find that it hasn't changed much. In fact, it hasn't changed at all. Your room is exactly as you left it when you moved to California. The furniture and other stuff you left behind, it's all still there."

"And Mom's room. Did he ever clear her room out? I asked, even though I knew what the answer would be.

"All still there. He keeps the door shut."

The vision of dust bunnies the size of real rabbits sprung across my mind and for a few seconds I entertained the idea of vocalizing my cartoon-like fantasy, but Sam's next words shut me up.

"Get here soon, Charlie. Dad—I—we, we need you here."

And so, here I am. Back in Michigan, after five years gone. I feel like a bird that spent days pecking its way out of the shell, weeks gobbling up mush from mom's gullet, lost my pin feathers, finally got pushed off a branch and found out that I could fly on my own, and now I've returned to the nest—pasting the pieces of the shell back together, leaving a space open so I can crawl back in before the shell closes up around me again.

Sam and Peter meet me at Detroit Metropolitan Airport; Sam standing proudly at the gate on his prosthetic leg, the leg that I wasn't aware he'd acquired. He hasn't replaced the missing arm, explaining to me as we walk to baggage claim that having two feet is far more important than having a phony replacement arm with a hand on the end that since he was right-handed, he would never use much anyway.

"It's so green here. I'd forgotten how green it is in the spring," I say as we drive south from the airport toward the bridge to the island.

"Yeah, I guess we kind of take that for granted, the seasons changing and all. Things greening-up. You guys don't really have that out there, do you?" Sam asks.

"We have seasons. Fire and flood, that's what people say our seasons are."

Peter snorts as if soda has gone up his nose; coming from him even those noises sound sophisticated and classy. "Fire and flood? Good lord, that doesn't sound very pleasant. Have you suffered through any plagues of locusts since you've been there? What about frogs falling from the sky?"

Sitting in the backseat I watch as, with his right hand, Sam reaches across his torso and pokes Peter's side ever so gently with his forefinger. Then he turns to grin at me.

"I apologize for Peter's jealousy, which he displays in satirical form. I mean he comes from England for God's sake, hence his consistent pallor. What does he know about fantastic weather? Nothing, which is why he needs to taunt you for coming from a place where it's beautiful all the time."

When are we going to start talking about the important stuff? How much longer can we use the weather as a diversionary tactic to keep us from talking about what really matters? I gave up a lot—I gave up everything. I gave up love. I gave up the life I had planned out so carefully for myself to come back here. So, we need to talk about that.

It's as if Sam has read my mind. The grin disappears as quickly as it blossomed.

"The company, Charlie, Dad's company. I don't know how much longer he can continue to run it. Jeez, I worry about him even driving to the office anymore, let alone actually being responsible for all those people who work for him. It's scary to think about him driving, even scarier to think about him managing a whole fucking company. I don't know how he does it anymore. Maybe it's all just rote memory. Shit, I don't know. I do know that it keeps me awake at night."

"He isn't going to step down of his own volition. You know that, Sam. Have there been problems that you know of?"

"Really? How would I know? We never talk for very long and if I ask him about work he always says: 'Same old, same old.' That's it. He might think that everything's the same, but I doubt that it is. How can it be? He's not the same."

Before I can respond *We are the World* starts playing on the radio and Peter promptly changes the station and says: "I liked that song the first fifty times I heard it but it's getting somewhat old now."

"No kidding," Sam agrees as he hums along to the final bars of *One More Night.* When it's finished playing the deejay proclaims: "Now for the most popular and important song in the country right now": pianos and violins build-up to a crescendo and then Lionel Ritchie's syrupy vocals begin: "There comes a time..."

"Fifty-one and counting," Peter laughs and Sam and I join in because really at this point, what else is there to do? And that's how it goes for the next half hour, the three of us laughing and joking, until we reach West Jefferson and turn onto Grosse Ile Parkway.

"Not much change around here since you left five years ago," Sam says as Peter steers the blue Pontiac Grand Prix across the free bridge. "Let me clarify that, not much change on the island itself."

We've turned and are heading down West River Road now and my stomach is flip-flopping, my mouth is parched because I've been breathing with it open ever since we left the airport parking lot, sucking in air like I'm in a room with walls slowly closing in around me.

"Here we are," Peter and Sam say in unison, and through eyes misted over with tears I see the big white house with black shutters, the wide porch with its ubiquitous swing and red front door. It looks the same as I remember it looking on June 18, 1979, the day Cindy and I let our old lives go and embraced new ones. There was no going back we'd thought at the time. Not ever.

But now here I am—returned, standing in the brick driveway feeling like my presence there is being advertised to the entire neighborhood by a giant 'look who's back' neon sign blinking over my head, my brain accusing me of being a stranger while my heart is purring 'welcome home' inside my chest.

And as I look more carefully I see that the house doesn't look exactly the same. There are quite a few dead plants around the house, daffodils and crocuses that should be in bloom are dry and spindly; the grass is pock-marked with irregular patches of brown and yellow; the eaves need painting, as does the front door; one of the shutters is hanging just a little off-kilter; the wrought iron front step railing has vanished; and the smudged soot line ringing the top two rows of bricks on the chimney suggest to anyone who's paying attention that whoever lives in this house has stopped caring about how it looks.

"Go on in, Dad's waiting for you," Sam says. "Peter will get your suitcases, we'll be behind you. Dad can't wait to see his daughter, the big-time Hollywood actress."

"What are you talking about?"

I turn to confront Sam, and for one brief moment I envision myself bolting right past him, running across the road, diving into the water, swimming to the mainland, taking a cab to the airport and flying back to California. "Sam, I'm not an actress. You know that. I mean, that's what I wanted to be when I moved to California but it never happened. Reading scripts at Warner Brothers, that's what I do. You know that. Where did Dad get such an idea?"

Sam wraps his arm around my waist and whispers: "Welcome to our world, Charlie."

Chapter 8

"So, how are things with your dad?" Terry asked me when I called him twenty-four hours after I'd arrived. "Is he as confused as you'd expected? Is he really bad?"

"Well, as far as Dad's concerned, I should have won my first Oscar by now. Somehow he's got it into his head that I became a famous actress when I moved to Hollywood and he doesn't understand why he hasn't seen me in any movies. Of course the fact that he doesn't go to movies is irrelevant."

When I walked in the door that day, Sam following several steps behind, Dad was sitting in the living room with a book of crossword puzzles on his lap. I wondered how he could possibly be working the puzzle because the room was dark, the heavy drapes shutting out the spring sun, except for one narrow shaft of bright light peeking between two of the panels, pointing downward and across the dingy threadbare carpet, as if to highlight the fact that the inside of the house needed care as much as the outside.

It didn't take long for me to realize that it made no difference how dark the room was, because Dad wasn't actually doing the crossword puzzle, anyway. When he stood up the book fell off his lap but there was no pencil to accompany it as it fell to the floor: just a lonely book of puzzles—puzzles that would never be solved.

"Dad, it's me, Charlie," I said as Sam walked past and pulled apart the drapes covering the large picture window across from me, darkening Dad's face for a few seconds as the bright light poured into the room from behind him. Whether he was smiling at that very moment or not I don't know, but by the time we were close enough to touch, a tentative hug, which evolved from a mushy and uncomfortable handshake, he was grinning; a grin that seemed almost phony, a facial expression fraught with hyperbole, too wide and expressive to be real.

"There she is, there she is. My daughter, the big-time actress," he said as the embrace retreated into an arms-length grasp, his fingers tight across my shoulders. "So, what big-time movies have you been in?"

I was just about to explain that acting wasn't paying my bills when Sam caught my attention, shaking his head from side-to-side and mouthing the words: "Play along."

"Well, Dad, I haven't had a lot of big parts yet. Small roles, I've been in small, you know—bit parts."

"In what movies? Maybe that one about the Commie doctor? Didn't see it because of the damn Communists. But I'll go see it now if you're in it."

Even though *Dr. Zhivago* had come out twenty years before, when I was only eight, I followed my brother's lead: "Yeah, Dad. *Dr. Zhivago.* I played Julie Christie's friend. I got to say a few lines. It was very exciting working with her, and with Omar Sharif." I'd immediately regretted saying the foreign name.

"Sharif, Sharif? Omar Sharif?" he said, and his hands sprang away from my body as if he had opened a package of meat and discovered that it was spoiled.

"An Arab? A goddamn raghead? Arab? You in a movie with a goddamn Arab raghead?" and Sam came forward then, placed his hands around Dad's shoulders and led him back to the chair, saying: "Dad: it's all right, it's okay. Charlie didn't have any scenes with the real Mr. Sharif. He was sick when Charlie was filming. She did her scenes with a stand-in who wasn't an Arab at all. He was an English guy."

It took Dad a minute or two to calm down and when he did, he looked at me with eyes that despite their seeming depth, like deep dark pools rising up from a subterranean source, were in reality shallow, lacking in substance, and said: "An English guy. Hah! Like his boyfriend, your brother's boyfriend. Sam's a fucking fag, you know."

And he grinned, winked, picked up the crossword puzzle book off the floor, sat back in the chair, placed the book on his lap and was silent.

It's been six weeks since I came back, and while some things have changed, primarily the condition of the house since I hired painters, a handyman and a cleaning service, Dad's behavior remains the same. At least, as I tell Terry and Cindy when we talk (Terry everyday, Cindy once a week or so), Dad doesn't seem to be getting worse.

"He follows the same routine, day after day. I've gotten into a routine now, too." I told Cindy last night. "Since I took that job working part-time in the bookstore, the only night I don't make dinner for us is Thursday because I get home too late. That's when he goes to Martinelli's to eat. Just like he's been doing for years."

"After all this time, does the staff call out his name like Norm on *Cheers* when he walks in the door?

"I guess I'm going to find out tomorrow. I switched nights with Daphne so I can go to dinner with him. He wants to introduce his famous actress daughter to the waitress. The same damn waitress has been serving him dinner for something like the last twelve years. Crazy."

"Well, there's crazy and then there's crazy. Why don't you just explain to him that you've never been in any movies? I mean, what could be the harm in that?" Cindy asked, and I'd felt a pang of anger, a sharp jab like the tingling pain you feel when you hit your elbow on the corner of a table: unexpected, jarring and deeply hurtful.

You don't understand, Cindy, I'd thought. I'm angry with you because you don't, even though I know that it's not your fault. You've always understood everything, or I thought that you did. I'm angry because I'm here and you're in California living with Matt and you're happy and you don't know what I'm going through and now you're making jokes about it and it hurts me because this isn't something that I can joke about. I miss Terry, I miss my job, I miss California, I miss you. I miss the life I had, the life I wanted. I had to let it all go and you don't understand. You don't understand and I'm alone here. I'm isolated. I'm living with a stranger, who I'm a stranger to.

Those feelings, feelings I didn't—couldn't—share with Cindy last night before I cut short our conversation, are still swirling in my head tonight as Dad and I drive to Martinelli's. Initially he was reluctant to let me drive.

"I know my way there, damn it. I drive to work every goddamn day. You think I'm going to get in an accident and get us killed? Is that what you think?"

"No, Dad I don't think you're going to cause an accident. I just thought that you might like to have someone else drive for a change."

"You want to drive me around like your chauffeur drives you?"

"Yes, Dad. I'd like to drive for a change. I never get to in Hollywood."

"Okay then. But just this once."

I sent him back to his bedroom twice to change his clothes. When he walked in the living room the first time he was wearing the heavy flannel plaid shirt, red sports coat and wool suit pants that he'd worn to the office. When I suggested that he might be dressed too warmly for early June, he returned wearing madras shorts and a bright green golf shirt. We finally settled on khaki's, a short-sleeve shirt and a cotton sweater; unfortunately he misplaced his belt (according to him all his belts are missing: "All those goddamn belts keep getting lost. I have to keep buying more") so the khaki's settled in well below his waist and he kept pulling at them as he walked across the room.

He hasn't said anything since we got in the car. I probably have the radio turned up too loud, but it's not easy to carry on a conversation, much easier letting pop artists' musings fill the void. I've noticed though that occasionally he hums along, but the humming doesn't last the length of the song, eventually he starts blowing air out of his mouth: "Whoof, whoof, whoof", again and again like he's trying to breathe life into a small animal or a baby.

This isn't going too badly. He seems content just sitting there. I don't have to try to make conversation. Maybe dinner is going to turn out okay.

"Those goddamn drivers. All of them. They all drive so goddamn fast. Where is everyone going in such a big goddamned hurry?"

The words a torrent rushing from his mouth, at a decibel level loud enough to drown out Tears for Fears proclamation that all of us want to rule the world, so sudden and virulent that I come close to slamming down the brake pedal for fear that he's having some sort of attack.

"Dad, what drivers? People aren't driving that fast. Everyone's going the speed limit from what I can see. You should see how fast people drive in California. This is nothing, really."

It's six-thirty on a Thursday night, what passes for rush hour here is over. I'm maneuvering the car through the five or six blocks that make up the entirety of downtown Trenton; there aren't a lot of cars on the road. To me it's quietly boringly peaceful, such a change from the shrill but alive busyness and bustle of Los Angeles.

I wonder what this world looks like to Dad, does he see things as they really are, do his eyes see what mine do, but once the sights make it to his brain is that where the distortions begin, or do his eyes see a fun-house world from the moment he opens them every morning until they close at night because his befuddled mind is one step ahead, having already laid out all the distorted scenes?

Thankfully Martinelli's is on the next corner, and Dad hasn't said anything else since the outburst. I pull the '78 black Buick Riviera (*might as well be driving a tank, I miss my Civic, hope that tattooist I sold it to isn't driving the hell out of it)* into the parking lot.

"Dad, we're here." He appears to be sleeping but the second I shut off the ignition I hear "Whoof, whoof, whoof", softer than before.

He opens his eyes, stares at me through irises so dark, large and vacant I would swear he's high and says: "I don't park in this spot."

Wondering how he knows where we're parked since he's looked only at me since opening his eyes, I ask: "Would you like me to move the car, Dad?"

"No, it can stay here. But this isn't the usual spot, that's all. It can stay here though," and before I have time to undo my seatbelt he's opened his door and is heading for the entrance.

Martinelli's is pretty much as I had envisioned it would be. A throw-back sort of place. The main dining room holds eight round tables (only two of them occupied) each one accompanied by chairs for four; the tables dressed in vinyl red and white checked tablecloths with a single plastic flower in a clear glass vinegar cruet in the center of each one; four (empty) booths with fake red leather seats and white square Formica-topped tables, line the rear of the room, looking as if they belong in a different restaurant altogether; a silent juke-box in the far left corner; black and white photos, some of them autographed, lined up like marchers in a 'Most Famous Italian Celebrities Parade' on the wall to our right: Dean Martin, Frank Sinatra, Tony Bennett, Frankie Avalon, Eydie Gorme, Gina Lollobrigida and Sophia Loren; black and white linoleum tiled floor; a mural of what I presume is the countryside surrounding Rome or maybe Florence covering the left wall that looks like it might have been a Paint-by-Numbers project; non-mural walls painted a distressingly putrid shade of yellowish-green; and an ersatz wood hostess dais standing six feet or so from the front door. Not a salad bar to be seen.

There's an entrance to a smaller room, the bar, to the left of the dais. Elvis crooning *Love Me Tender* is emanating from the very dark and very smoky interior. There's a low hum, murmuring coming from the people sitting at the bar. Even though I can't see them, I'm certain that there are more people in there than in the restaurant.

A hostess has yet to appear, which makes no difference to Dad. In the twenty seconds or so that it takes me to size up the venue, he makes a beeline for the booth that's the farthest from the kitchen, the no-man's land location. I follow like a visitor from another country eager to please my gracious host.

I've barely had time to slide across the seat cushion, my buttocks encountering a few divots along the way where the foam filler has flattened to half the depth of a short stack of pancakes, when, as if she'd been hiding under the floor behind a trap door, waiting for us to arrive, our waitress appears.

"Al, so nice to see you. How's life treating yah today? And this must be Charlie. Such a masculine nickname for a lovely feminine woman," she says as she pumps my hand up and down with, considering the compliment, what I find to be rather ironic male vigor. "My name's Rebecca, but I'm known as Becky." Our hands separate and at the same time we both laugh and point to the nametag on her blouse.

"Really, I thought your name might be Margaret or Jennifer," I joke. "My given name's Charlotte. But I go by Charlie because when I was first learning to talk I had trouble saying my own name. For some reason it always came out sounding more like Charlie, so it stuck. Truthfully, I prefer Charlie, anyway."

Becky's plump cheeks puff out even more as she opens her mouth to speak, and turn from pale pink to red, the reddest red I've ever seen. She looks like her body temperature just went up ten degrees.

"A rose by any other name…" and as she turns to walk toward the bar she looks over her shoulder and calls out: "Gin martini, up with two olives on its way. And for you, Charlie, I'm thinking the house red."

I watch her as she strides purposefully across the room, as if fetching our drinks is the most critical thing she could be doing at this very moment and wonder: *How did she know I'd want the house red? She seems so easy to talk to. Did dad ever confide in her? She's been serving him dinner and drinks all these years. Did he ever tell her how he felt about anything? How does she feel about the way he is now? I wonder if she misses the man he used to be.*

Chapter 9

Thanksgiving was one week away when I started having panic attacks. Although I've never had a panic attack before, I felt quite sure that what I'd been experiencing for several days were full-blown "Here, let me prescribe something for you" panic attacks. I knew I was suffering because I wanted a normal Thanksgiving holiday, like everyone else. Roast turkey, dressing, mashed potatoes, cranberry sauce, pumpkin pie and smiling, loving, happy people gathered around the table. How difficult could it be to achieve such familial order and community?

Pretty damn difficult as it turns out.

When I first mentioned the idea to Sam, right after Halloween (which evolved into a nightmarish evening because Dad insisted on buying bags and bags of candy to give to children who never came to the door because all of the kids in the neighborhood have grown up, so by 8:00 he was crying and saying that he didn't understand why children don't trick or treat these days) I sensed, and wasn't surprised, that initially the concept wasn't appealing.

"You want to what?" he asked.

"You heard me. I want to have Thanksgiving dinner here, at the house. I'll roast a turkey and make dressing and potatoes. The whole Thanksgiving package. You and Peter can bring something, maybe pumpkin pie. It'll be fun." I knew I sounded far too chirpy and upbeat, but I was trying.

"Whoa. You want Peter and me there—together? Oh, Charlie. I'm not so sure."

"I know you're worried about how Dad will be but I think it'll be okay. I really do. Dad's been around Peter in the past year, more than once. When he almost burnt down the house Peter was here and the day you guys brought me in from the airport. Dad didn't go off on Peter either time. From what I could tell that day I came back, I don't think Dad even knew who Peter was."

I could tell by his silence that Sam was considering the possibly that this plan might actually work.

"But what if Dad has too much to drink and gets belligerent?"

"I won't let him drink too much. And besides, lately he falls asleep early most nights. He doesn't sleep in the bedroom now, just falls asleep in that old leather chair in the den."

"Does he still wake up screaming sometimes?"

"Yeah, it happens a lot. I'd only been back for a few days the first time I heard him screaming in his sleep. Even though my bedroom door was closed I heard him, from all the way downstairs. I ran down the steps, scared to death, worried about what I would find when I got down there. But he had already fallen back asleep. I know now what to expect. He's having nightmares, there's nothing I can do."

Discussing Dad's sleeping disorders wasn't helping me make my case. "Please, Sam. Lets do this, okay? The four of us, lets try to have a real Thanksgiving together."

Sam finally agreed to attend, with Peter. They'd bring pumpkin pie and a couple bottles of wine. And for the next few weeks I felt confident that my plan was brilliant. I would be the ideal hostess, the most loving, caring and forgiving daughter and sister on the planet, or at least on the island. The intuitive and sensitive favorite child, and remarkable sister, who would bring my loved ones together; would bridge the divide; would heal old wounds; would make those I loved love one another. What a wonderful role I'd created for myself to play.

It didn't take long for my carefully scripted plans to go awry. The weekend before Thanksgiving the woman I hired to clean abruptly quit. She said that she had a sick child to care for, but I think that Dad might have said something to her that made her angry, or hurt, or maybe even scared. Even though she's white, after the second time she came to clean Dad told me that he thought she was half-black, and he said that he knew she had gone into Mom's room "To steal things", despite the fact that the room was always locked.

On the following Monday evening Dad told me that he would be going to Martinelli's for Thanksgiving dinner, "Like always."

"Dad, Martinelli's isn't open on Thanksgiving." I'd replied.

"You're wrong. It is. I went there last year."

"Okay, Dad," over these last few months I'd learned to agree with him on nearly everything he says. "Maybe you did go there last year. But this year Martinelli's isn't going to be open. They're closing down so that people like Becky, you know, Becky your favorite waitress can spend time with her family."

"She has a family? I don't think so."

"Yes, she does. The last time we were there she told us that she has a son. She'd like to be with her son for the holiday. Just like you're going to be with your son and your daughter. It's going to be nice. A nice day."

"I have two sons. One of them isn't a homo," he'd said, the first time I heard him refer to George in months. "Who's coming? The homo or the other one?"

For a few moments the thought of my contacting George began to blunder across the right side of my brain, on its way to the left where it would be summarily tossed out for being too irrational, romantic and idealistic.

"Sam is coming, Dad. You—we –none of us has seen George in a long time. He lives in Canada. I don't think he'll be able to make it.

"My son, Sam…" I saw a flicker of acknowledgement in his dark eyes. Something leapt up, lit up, like a match burning just long enough to light the candle before being snuffed out. "We should call him Samuel now. He's a man. That's what his mother said: Samuel is a man's name. But is he a man? He's a fag, you know. Can we call him Samuel even if he's a fag?"

We're supposed to refer to Sam as Samuel now that he's all grown up? I was learning this for the first time, but mom had left when I was only six and I never heard anyone call him by any name other than the shortened version. Even Sam doesn't call himself Samuel.

I'd wondered then about my own name. Maybe the story I'd been told all these years, that I go by Charlie instead of Charlotte because I couldn't pronounce Charlotte correctly isn't true. Thinking such things is unsettling.

"I've never heard Sam called anything but Sam. But we'll ask him when he comes for Thanksgiving if he would like to be called Samuel since he's an adult." I sidestepped the "Can a homosexual man be a real man?" query altogether.

The Tuesday before the holiday began on a downslide and continued its descent to the bottom as the day progressed. A little after nine that morning I received a call from Ray

Thomas, the vice-president of Dad's company. He wished me a nice Thanksgiving, and then requested that Sam and I meet with him to talk about "The situation with your dad" as soon as possible after the long weekend. After his call I discovered, although I wasn't searching, that panic attacks include rather unpleasant stomach distress.

In the late afternoon I made lasagna for dinner, and when, after baking in what was supposedly a three hundred fifty degree oven for over an hour, the mozzarella still hadn't melted but languished across the top of the lukewarm sauce and even less warm noodles looking exactly as it did right out of the package: taunting dollops of creamy white milk curds, I realized that the thirty-year-old oven no longer heated to the set temperature. Roasting a turkey in that stove wasn't going to happen.

But it was after Dad and I ate our hastily pulled-together dinner of macaroni and cheese, from the box, that I began to think that trying to do the right thing never is the right thing. Just because someone is being a good person, doesn't mean that the karmic gods will necessarily cut him or her any slack.

Cindy called. We hadn't talked for a few days, so her call couldn't have come at a better time. Everything was going to shit and I needed to share it with someone. I planned on calling Terry later that night but with him I wasn't going to despair. Our conversations still had that sexual and emotional tension that didn't include, or allow for, complaining. We were too busy reaffirming our longings and desires, the love that wouldn't be dampened, not by the passage of time or distance or mundane problems like discovering a few days before a Thanksgiving dinner that could turn out to be a disaster anyway that for starters, the oven didn't work.

"Charlie. Hi, it's me. Guess what?"

Cindy sounded more exuberant than I'd ever heard her. Tightly-wound yet ready to burst like a ripe watermelon; even more giddy than when she told me what it had been like having sex with John for the first time. The wildly inventive metaphors she'd used to describe his penis were so unforgettable, so imaginative and revealing, that I was never able to look at John again without wanting to either laugh or ask him if I could have a look for myself.

"Hi. Guess what—what? Can you give me a clue here? Category? Animal, vegetable, mineral—anything?" How people are supposed to respond when asked that rhetorical question is something I've always wondered about. I've asked the question myself, many times, knowing that the person being asked couldn't possibly know the answer.

"I'm going to see you at Thanksgiving, me and Matt, too. We're going to be on the island. We come in tomorrow. I wasn't going to tell you. I thought we'd just show up sometime Thanksgiving night or Friday morning but I wasn't sure what you're doing to celebrate so I figured I'd better let you know ahead of time."

Although I knew that Cindy said quite a few words during those twenty-five or thirty seconds, I heard only six of them: "Me and Matt. On the island." I knew exactly what those words meant. They were words shaped like miniature daggers, six nasty little daggers being lobbed at me by those miserable karmic gods. I knew too that the next words wouldn't be daggers—they'd be sabers. Tiny daggers hurt—sabers kill.

"We're engaged, Charlie. Matt's meeting my whole family for the first time. I'm so excited. We're so excited. I can't wait to show you my ring, it's crazy beautiful."

Loving someone and being happy for their happiness, while simultaneously hating being happy for their happiness creates a dissonance in one's brain. It's not easy to hold two such conflicting emotions in your head without sounding bitchy and half-insane, particularly if you verbalize those feelings before carefully considering your word choice. Wisely, I waited to respond and Cindy jumped into the deafening silence.

"I know what you're thinking," (no, you really have no idea and don't want to know, I'd thought) "We're going to have a big wedding, here in California and of course you'd be my maid-of-honor but don't worry. You can save your money. Sometime in December, I think between Christmas and New Year's we're getting married in Vegas. You can fly out for that, to be a witness. But no big wedding…" and I'd waited for the sound of the saber to slice through the air before it fell… 'swoosh'…"I'm pregnant, Charlie."

Chapter 10

Peter didn't stay for dinner today, but the turkey he roasted did. He and Sam arrived at 1:00, in a car filled with food and drink: twenty-two pound perfectly browned bird, sweet potato casserole, three pumpkin pies and several bottles of wine. Once we'd hauled everything into the kitchen Peter announced that he was sorry but he wouldn't be partaking of the meal, the meal that he prepared nearly half the food for. Partake is a word most people seldom use, but most people aren't Peter. The word slipped off his tongue like sweet soft butter being spread across a warm scone.

"I'd love to partake of this magnificent feast today, Charlie. You know how much I want to. But I've given it much thought over the past day or so and I've decided that it would be more appropriate for just the three of you, the family, to spend this first Thanksgiving together in some time, no interlopers anywhere to be seen."

"Oh, Peter. No, please—stay. My God, you roasted the turkey. You have to eat your own turkey for heavens sake," I said, while thinking that it's a rare day when you hear the words 'partake' and 'interloper' spoken in a span of less than thirty seconds.

Sam was busying himself with the foil covering the aforementioned bird, attempting to tuck it down around the drumsticks as if he were putting a fitted sheet on a mattress, not an easy task to accomplish with only one hand. Although he was trying his best to keep me from looking at his face, I'd seen the expression he wore there when he first walked in. A mask with two opposing sides, expressing both disappointment and relief.

"Sam. Can't you convince your other, better half to stay?" I asked, knowing that the question was moot; the decision had been made.

The day had begun with some bloodletting.

"Can I help?" Dad asked when he walked into the kitchen early that morning, and before I could answer he took the peeler from my hand, then grabbed for the potato I was holding and began slicing away at it as if it was a head and he was carving off the scalp. He attacked it with such intensity and ferocity that within thirty seconds or so, he'd chopped off a piece of skin shaped like an oval from his left forefinger. In the short time it took me to retrieve a Band-Aid from the bathroom, he managed to shove handfuls of bloodied potato peelings down the garbage disposal, which thankfully, he hadn't yet switched on.

"How about this, Dad?" I said as I took hold of his wrist and held his bleeding finger under cold water. "I'm going to put this Band-Aid on so you'll stop bleeding, and then you can set the table. Would you like to do that? I'd like you to; it would be a big help to me if you set the table."

I've become parent, teacher, older sister, therapist, 'calmer-in-chief.'

Dad stared at me with a sheepish and confused half-grin on his face as I dried off his hand and wrapped the Band-Aid around the end of his finger, and I thought how much he reminded me of a rambunctious kid named Eddie who was in fourth grade with Cindy and me. Eddie was always hurting himself. He seldom got through recess without performing a maneuver as drastic as falling off the jungle gym or sustaining some type of knee or elbow-scraping injury because his physical body seemed to always be at odds with what was going on in his mind; his brain always a few steps ahead of his arms, hands, legs and feet. Except in Dad's case, it's the brain lagging behind the body. He displayed the same innocence and wonder as Eddie used to when he would bruise his shoulder or bloody his lip: 'Look…I hurt myself' but, unlike Eddie, Dad didn't quite grasp what part he played in the injury occurring.

Once the bleeding stopped I led Dad to the sideboard in the dining room where earlier I'd laid out plates, silverware, glasses and napkins for four. I figured that setting the table would be a much safer activity for him to engage in than kitchen tasks, despite the fact that place settings involve knives. Unfortunately I was wrong.

When I left Dad to get back to work in the kitchen he was hovered over the tableware looking like an archeologist examining rare items discovered in a dig. Less than a minute later he began to yell, and I heard a sound no one wants to hear the morning of a carefully-scripted holiday dinner: glasses clattering and china breaking.

The desire to scream myself, to swear and cry and throw up my hands and run out of the house was so strong that I snatched the closest soft item nearby: a dishtowel, and bit into it hard, until the feeling subsided.

"Goddamn it. Goddamn it all to hell. Goddamn fucking dishes. God damn it all. I can't do anything right."

"Dad, what happened? Are you okay?" As I slowly walked back into the room I fought against any shrillness or accusatory tone in my voice. And when I saw him standing at the table, looking like a small child who knew he'd done something bad, waiting to be punished, my emotions hopscotched from frustration and anger to sadness and compassion.

I had no clue as to how he managed to break two plates and a glass in such a short period of time, within just the two-foot parameter between the sideboard and table. But he did, and he was angry and crying because of it. This is a good lesson in not letting little things upset me I thought. They're just plates and glasses. There are eight more plates in the sideboard. Don't worry yourself over porcelain.

"It's okay, Dad. It's just fine. We've got more dishes. Let me clean up, it won't take long. And in the meantime, why don't you go in the den and watch TV? I'll bet the Macy's Thanksgiving Day parade will be on soon."

I took hold of his arm, which was rigid instead of shaking as I had expected it would be, and walked him away from the mess on and around the table. His limp was more pronounced, and he was humming an unintelligible tune as we made our way toward the den.

"This is going to be such a nice day, Dad. All of us together for Thanksgiving. We haven't had Thanksgiving dinner together for a long time. Don't worry about the dishes."

Dad spent most of the rest of the day in the den, alternating between watching television, pretending to read and napping. At around 11:00 I poked my head in the door and asked him if he wanted an egg sandwich to tide him over until dinner, which he refused, telling me that he wanted to be "Good and hungry for that turkey." Close to noon he snuck into the kitchen, quiet as a cat stalking a mouse, surreptitiously opened a cabinet, took out a glass and filled it with wine from the carafe I'd left out on the counter to breathe. I pretended

I never saw him, keeping busy snapping off the ends of green beans, but as he walked out of the kitchen I said: "It's five o'clock somewhere, Dad" and he turned back to look at me, all wide-eyed, kind of ashamed but alternatively somehow proud, the way a teenage boy feeling-up his girlfriend would react if his father unexpectedly walked into the room and caught him in the act. Dad smiled, winked and kept on walking, wine glass in hand.

I filled his wineglass once more before Sam and Peter arrived, and Sam took the carafe with him when he went into the den to visit with Dad, leaving Peter and I to sort out both the gastronomic delights and our emotions. By the time the three of us sat down to eat, Dad had drank at least a glass more than I wanted him to, but we were engaged in a delicate balancing act: weighing the consequences of his keeping occupied by drinking wine and sitting still, in one place, versus his wreaking havoc attempting to help with the preparations. The potential consequences arising out of the first scenario seemed preferable to those we'd already experienced.

At least that's what I had thought then, but now that we're in the throes of our 'first Thanksgiving Day dinner as a family in years', I'm not so sure.

"You know Rock Hudson was a fag, right? Pretty funny. Big handsome man like that. Making all those movies with Doris Day. Even was married." Dad takes another sip of wine and looks at me across the table. Although Sam's sitting cater-cornered to his right, he's behaving as if Sam suddenly became invisible.

"Yes, Dad. I know he was a gay man. Sam, how about some more casserole?" I ask, giving him a look of desperation and panic.

Damn! Everything had been going so well. Dad and Sam spent a long time together in the den. With Peter not being here

I figured Dad would be okay. I didn't think he'd forget that Sam's gay but I thought I'd be the foil, with me around Dad wouldn't be mean.

"Gay? Hah! Why do people say that? Gay? Men having sex with other men is something that makes you gay, like happy? I'll bet Mr. Hudson wasn't so gay when he got sick. What is it? That homo disease? Something about being aided? He sure must have needed some aid when his dick rotted and fell off."

I breathe in the suddenly sour and polluted air, way deep down to the bottom of my lungs and let it leech out—slowly, as if I'm meditating in a sewer.

Please, Sam, please say something. But what can you say to counter the words coming out of Dad's mouth? Is this why your mind has turned on you, Dad? Are you paying for the unnaturalness of not loving your own flesh and blood? Have all the synapses in your brain become clogged up with the hatred and anger? Maybe the brain needs love to function properly, without love it stops working right. If the heart doesn't love, the brain begins to deteriorate.

"Well, if Sam doesn't want more, I do. Pass that casserole down my way."

Sam and I look at each other, eyebrows lifted and mouths open as if we're getting ready to say: "What?" as we wait for the next tirade.

But it seems that the vituperation has passed as quickly as it blew into existence, like a violent windstorm that suddenly appears, wipes out an entire town and dissipates back up into the sky.

"Say, Dad," Sam's voice is calm and steady. "Why don't you finish up the casserole and the little bit of turkey left on your plate and lets go watch the Lions play. It should be a good game. They're playing the Jets."

"Can I take my plate with me?"

"Sure, Dad. In fact, I'll take my plate with me, too. We can finish up in there. And by halftime we should be ready for some pie. How's that sound?"

Dad grins at Sam, winks and with less than a steady hand, pulls himself to his feet and then reaches for his plate with one hand, the wineglass with the other. I sense a minor disaster in the making.

"Here Dad." I'm at his side so fast I'm surprised I don't trip. "I'll take your plate and glass. You guys go on in the den and watch the game. I'll clean everything up. You go watch some football."

"Football." Dad's lower lip trembles. "Football. I used to play football. So did my brother, my brother Howard. He was a better player than me, Howard was. He died in the war."

I watch Sam and Dad as they walk into the den, thinking how similar they appear on the surface. Dark hair (although Dad's is streaked with silver now along his temples); dark eyes; strong, handsome faces; bodies that have retained some of their muscular physicality despite the damage they've suffered. Both limping, listing just a bit, but on opposite sides: father and son, connected in ways that transcend the vagaries of the mind.

Dad has been asleep for at least an hour. He didn't make it to the end of the third quarter; he never got that piece of pumpkin pie. But there are two-and-a-half pies left so he isn't going to go without. We'll be eating pumpkin pie for days. He also didn't get to see the Lions rout the Jets 31 to 20, which according to Sam is a very big deal since the Jets are in the play-offs. Dad snored, ear-numbingly loudly, for several minutes, shortly after his chin dropped onto his collarbone. When he heard the first nasally outburst, Sam turned up the volume on the television, took the half-full glass out of Dad's hand so the wine wouldn't spill on his lap and covered Dad's legs with a hideous red, white and blue checkered quilt that has lived in the den for as long as I can remember. Sometimes it's easier for people to express their love for someone when that someone isn't aware of what they're doing.

Peter has returned; he came back half-an-hour ago. He ate a plateful of his own turkey, dressing and sweet potato casserole, along with my green beans, mashed potatoes and gravy. He had two pieces of pie and one glass of wine, while Sam and I have drank at least three apiece. We've moved to the living room, the three of us forming an equilateral triangle: me on the sofa and Peter and Sam sitting in club chairs facing me, sharing another bottle of Cabernet, and I'm feeling sloppy and sentimental and mellow.

"What a Thanksgiving, huh?" I say as I sit up and pour from the bottle on the coffee table, lie back down, stretch my legs out over the sofa arms and prop up my body on one elbow, balancing the glass in the opposite hand. The sofa's upholstered in a print that could have been made into drapes or a dress someone's grandmother would wear to go to church. "I was worried there for awhile. I didn't think Dad would make it through the day without slicing off a finger or demanding that you leave the house, Sam."

"Yeah, things got a bit dicey there for a minute when he brought up Rock Hudson."

"Rock Hudson? Not a surprise, I suppose. I imagine a whole lot of people will be discussing him in the months to come," Peter chimes in. "Rock Hudson: the man's man. The handsome sexy guy who always got the girl. Virile and masculine. The last person you'd expect to be homosexual. He had a lot of people fooled, poor guy. Living a lie all those years, pretending to be straight."

Sam clears his throat and squirms, ever so slightly, in his seat.

"It's not like you—me—it's not like we're exactly advertising who we are," he says, then clears his throat again.

"No, you're correct. We don't share with a lot of people the fact that we're two homosexual men who cohabitate. What I'm referring to is the fact that for oh, the last thirty years or so, people have assumed that Rock Hudson was a straight, heterosexual male. And then he died of AIDS."

Partake, interloper and cohabitate in one evening. Peter, you're a delight.

"He had to do that, Peter. He never could have had a career as a leading man, acting alongside Doris Day and Elizabeth Taylor. If anyone had known he was gay, he would have been drummed out of Hollywood."

"I'm aware of that. It's just that sometimes—oh, I don't know. Sometimes the assumptions we make, and the scenarios we create to make those assumptions real. When it's all said and done, are the misrepresentations and misunderstandings really for the best, for anyone involved? Maybe everyone should be transparent and upfront at the outset."

This conversation is getting way too serious. All in all the day was pretty good. Dad and Sam got along okay, and there wasn't too much blood. We need to talk about something that's less upsetting. This is winding-down time, not winding-up.

Suddenly, unexpectedly, Peter lifts himself up from his chair, all six foot three of him, strides towards the sofa, stopping on his way to pour another glass of wine, gives me a nudge and when I sit up he slides in beside me. We're now shoulder-to-shoulder, and face-to-face.

"So, Charlie on the delivery run this morning Sam and I were saying that we thought it might be fun to look at family photographs today. He says he hasn't seen them in years."

Our faces are so close that I can see every stain on his dull gray teeth. Much of Peter's physical appearance is dull, and gray: from his washed-out 'I'm always just getting over the flu' complexion to his thinning hair the color of bleached-out corn silk—except for his eyes. Peter's eyes are blue, deep azure blue; a blue so cool that they're warm; a blue in such stark contrast to the rest of his virtually no-color face that they should be inside a different head.

I plant a kiss on his pallid cheek: "Great idea! Simply wonderful idea. I'm pretty sure all of the photos are in that old trunk in the corner. Please help me pull it over here so it's more centrally located. Then pour Sam another glass of wine, he looks parched, poor child." And together Peter and I pull the metal-strapped trunk closer to the coffee table.

The photos are arranged, layered in the trunk as if they'd been deposited there by an ancient civilization, each layer representing a milestone in the society's advancement, slow decline and eventual decay. The bottom two layers are made up of leather-bound photo albums. Five have the same title neatly printed on a label taped on the front cover: 'Alfred & Maggie, Our Early Years, 1938-1944'. Three are titled: 'Alfred & Maggie, Before the Twins, 1946-1949'. The albums in layers two and three have heavy cardboard covers rather than leather. They're titled 'The Twins, Sam & George, 1949-1956'. Two albums with covers coated in plastic printed in a garish psychedelic flower pattern make up the last tier. They're the ones devoted to me: 'Charlotte (Charlie), 1957-1962. And scattered over everything, like so much detritus, are twenty to thirty loose photos: random shots of Sam, George and me together; a few of them out-of-focus, none featuring either mom or dad, and none taken later than 1963.

I don't remember ever seeing these photos, any of them. Mom and Dad's wedding photographs used to be around the house, I recall seeing those when I was very young. They were so beautiful; they looked so happy and so much in love. These photos, the ones from the bottom of the trunk, go back even further in time. They're teenagers, looking into one another's eyes in several of them as if they have just discovered the secret to life: "Yes, this is what it's all about, you two. You figured it out. What you're experiencing no one has ever experienced before you, and no one ever will. What you have is special."

Terry, I miss you so much right now. I wish you could be here. I want to introduce you to my family, as they were. My Mom and Dad: stopped still, forever, not moving, suspended in time. Before Sam and George, before me. Just them, the two of them. What they were like when they were young and in love. Like the two of us. God, I miss you.

Sam's crying, just a little. He's looking at pictures of him and George dressed in Halloween costumes, they're both policemen. He runs the index finger of his only hand over another photo, this one a Polaroid of the two of them dressed as Zorro, plastic swords drawn.

"You know, those Zorro swords had chalk on the ends. The tips of the swords were chalk, so you could make the 'Z' signs on walls. That used to drive Mom crazy, us drawing 'Z's' all over the house. It was only chalk though, so it cleaned right up."

"Do you ever hear from him, from George? Do you ever hear from him at all?" I ask, hoping his answer will be different from what I know it's going to be.

"No. I think the last time was maybe—oh, I don't know. Peter? Was it Christmas the year Charlie was a freshman in college?"

His question obviously a rhetorical one as he doesn't wait for an answer, and Peter just shrugs his broad shoulders and picks up one of the 'pre-twins' albums.

"I guess maybe, whenever it was, he was still feeling guilty. The thing is, I never blamed him, you know. It had nothing to do with him; it was the damn luck of the draw. But when it happened like it did, I guess George just got scared. So he left for Canada, and that was that. Dad never got over it. First Mom leaving, then his favorite son, the one who wasn't gay. I never got over it, either. We all lost a lot in those years."

"Look at this one," Peter holds the album out, opened midway through. "Look at how beautiful your mom was in all of these photographs, even when she was pregnant. Hugely pregnant with Sam and George. Beautiful even in those ugly maternity dresses women wore back then. Like the one that looks like a giant checkerboard sack."

Sam joins Peter and me on the sofa. All three of us "Ooh and ah" over Mom's loveliness, and make wise-cracks about the reasoning behind covering a woman's swollen belly with fabrics imprinted with patterns guaranteed to make her look even fatter.

"Obviously Dad was thrilled when Mom was pregnant, "an observation that I know isn't necessary. "Three pages of photos of her, dressed in those hideous maternity tops. I sure hope for her sake that the clothes were better looking when she was carrying me."

"So, lets see the final result, who emerged from underneath that purple and blue floral nightmare," Peter says as he opens Sam and George's pictorial biography. "Oh, my. Look at all that dark hair. You were a looker even at one week, Sam. Although I'm not sure which baby you are and which one's your brother."

As Sam identifies himself to Peter, "That's me in Mom's arms, I was a little bit larger from the time we were born," I grab my album and open the bad acid trip cover.

And there I am: with Mom and Dad and Sam and George in the front yard—and I'm at least two months old. No photos of Mom pregnant, not a gaudy maternity top to be seen. No pictures of me as a newborn, with Mom and Dad cooing and making gaga faces over me. It's as if I skipped over the growing in my mother's stomach part of becoming a human being. I feel cold, then very warm and sweaty and then cold again.

The phone rings and I jump up so quickly that wine splashes out of Peter's glass.

What difference does it make? Wine on that ugly sofa, it will blend right in. What difference does it make? What difference does it make that there aren't any pictures of Mom pregnant with me? Maybe they got burned up or something. Or maybe Dad wasn't so thrilled with her being pregnant the second time around. Maybe the maternity dresses were even more ugly then, so she didn't want any pictures. Who am I kidding? You can't burn up photos that never existed.

I know Terry's the person who's calling, right on time, as promised.

So, how's this call going to go?

Hi Terry. What? I sound different, really? Well, maybe it's because I'm not sure anymore who Charlie really is. I've had one hell of a Thanksgiving, Terry. Interloper, indeed.

Chapter 11

"Your father is no longer capable of running his company."

Ray Thomas speaks in a flat, timid monotone at odds with the temerity of his words. He fidgets in his seat, and sinks down into it, as if he'd like it to somehow swallow him whole. He's a small man, probably no taller than five-foot seven, bald except for a few lone strings of gray above his ears, round brown eyes that appear to be lidless and a plump red face. He looks like a baby who someone mistakenly sat with the adults, a tiny person who'll continue sliding down until he's under the table.

Right now, if I were the Charlie of three days ago, I'd be nudging Sam's leg with mine, beneath the tablecloth so Ray wouldn't see it happening.

"Are you kidding me?' is what I'd be communicating to Sam, who'd understand. "This guy is the vice-president? Any minute now he might ask us for permission to go to the bathroom."

But I don't nudge Sam, because I'm not that Charlie, and I'm not sure that the Charlie who I really am would behave like that. Because it's the Monday after Thanksgiving, the day that I learned that I've been pretending to be someone I'm not for these past twenty-eight years.

When I spoke with Terry Thanksgiving night our conversation was boringly benign. I didn't once mention that he was talking to an imposter. We discussed how dinner had turned out: "Not as disastrous as it could have been", I bragged; what the day with his mom and dad had been like: short, since Paul and Barbara spent the holiday in Oregon at her parent's house and his mother went to bed not long after the meal; what I thought about the weather: "I'm missing the California warmth", I'd said, "it's getting cooler here but I'd forgotten how pretty the fall colors are"; and when he planned to fly in for Christmas: "I'm coming in on Monday the twenty-third. I can stay until the twenty-ninth. I took the whole week off."

At some point during our conversation I might have said: "Maybe when you get here a month from now I'll have found out who my real parents are, so at least I'll know who I really am by then," but I didn't.

And on Friday I didn't mention anything to Cindy about my newly discovered back-story. I might have said: "Hey, Cindy. Guess what? I'm not the daughter of Alfred and Maggie Carpenter. I belonged to someone else, someone who gave me away, but I don't know who that person was or why they didn't want me," but I didn't.

Instead I joked and laughed with Matt and Cindy and her mom and dad at the Anderson's house, making sure that I let Mr. Anderson know that I was getting quite a kick out of his "California and all its sinners and tiny Japanese cars sinking into the ocean after the next big earthquake" references. I didn't have to pretend to be impressed by Cindy's engagement ring, at nearly a full carat it deserved all the accolades being bestowed on it, but as the evening wore on I found that continuing to be mesmerized by the big brilliant rock on her finger, and having to wax poetic about it whenever the conversation lagged, was beginning to wear me down. So, I got very drunk on red wine and at midnight I threw up all over the moss green rug circling the base of the toilet in the Anderson's powder room. Who puts a rug around the bottom of a toilet, anyway? I'd thought as I watched in horror, but with some fascination, as the viscous liquid splattered like blood red rain onto a newly sprouted spring lawn.

"I've essentially been running the company for the past year or so."

Ray's droning reminds me of the hum of a buzz saw that's in another room, where someone's using it to chop the legs off furniture or cut the house into pieces. It's a not-quite-far-enough-away sound that annoys and seems never-ending.

"Al—your dad—he started making mistakes and forgetting things years ago but we were able to work around it, you know?"

I'm assuming this is a rhetorical question, Mr. Thomas. I certainly would have no idea of my dad's state-of-mind over the past years. But obviously his memory wasn't exactly stellar at any time in his adult life because he neglected to let me know that I'm not his biological daughter. That's kind of an important thing to forget. But I don't know how you could have worked around that.

"Since around the holidays last year I've pretty much taken over. I deal with all of our vendors, all our customers and I try to maintain good relations with the employees. It isn't easy, I can tell you that. Since Donna left our employ five years ago, Al has gone through five secretaries. Five."

Ray puts some weight behind the word "five", there's inflection in his voice, he says the word as if it has such significance that it bears repeating—which he does.

"Five, five secretaries in five years. Donna was with us—with Al—for nearly seventeen years. But she couldn't take it anymore. Al's—your dad's outbursts, his forgetfulness and confusion. The new girls, they don't know what to think when he yells at them because he wonders why vendors aren't calling him back. He blames them for that even though I've explained to him over and over again that I take care of our most important vendors now so he can relax a little more, but he still gets pissed, excuse me, gets angry."

Ray's becoming more confident the longer he talks. At this rate he'll sound like a Dale Carnegie graduate in the next five minutes.

"So, Mr. Thomas what are you saying we should do?" Sam asks, turns to look at me, nods and looks back at Ray again.

"Well, you two, and your brother, there's a twin brother, correct, will be happy to learn that we do have suitors," and his bright pink lips spread into a contented smile reminiscent of the satisfied expression a baby makes when peeing in its diaper.

Suitors? I have a sudden vision of myself as a senior in high school, onstage playing Laura in *The Glass Menagerie* listening to my pretend stage mother chattering about her gentlemen callers.

"Two companies, both German, have expressed an interest in purchasing AlMag. The company's done very well over the years, and people in the solvents industry have taken notice. We've done—your dad has done well. Weathered the recession in fifty-eight, you know that was only eight years after he started the company, and we got through the big downturn that started in seventy-three and then again in eighty-one: the oil crisis and all the Iranian mess."

Ray pauses, takes a deep breath and finishes with: "Al's a smart man. He surrounded himself with good people over the years. Damn good people. I've—well, all of us—helped make him the success he is today."

I'm wondering if he expects Sam and I to stand and give him a round of applause when our waitress arrives. I'd hoped that maybe Becky was working tonight; I'd wanted to talk to her without Dad around. When Ray said that he wanted to meet us here because he knew Dad doesn't come in on Mondays, I'd agreed that it would be an excellent idea, partly because I knew Dad wouldn't find out, and partly because I wanted to thank her personally and privately for the attention she's paid to Dad all these years. But the skinny almond-eyed girl with dyed black hair and braces on her upper teeth asking us if we'd like to order drinks isn't Becky.

I order the house red, so does Sam, and Ray orders a martini, with two olives not one. Ray also asks our waitress Desiree (her name strikes me as being simultaneously pretentious and slutty) to bring an anti-pasta platter, which is worrisome because I know that pasta fagioli, angel hair with marinara sauce, garlic bread and cannoli's will follow; food and drink to fortify us as we plot out Dad's future, while the only future, in fact the only past, present and future that I'm concerned about now is mine.

Where did I come from? Will I ever find out? Who am I... really?

Tonight's the first time I've seen Sam since Thanksgiving. I didn't have an opportunity that evening to bring up the subject of my being a biological misfit; Dad's night terrors abruptly ended the evening. While I was in the den trying to pacify Dad and get him back to sleep, Sam and Peter put the albums back in the trunk and went home.

I've got so many questions for Sam; questions that I know will birth even more questions. Questions such as: "Don't you think it's strange that there aren't any photos of Mom pregnant with me?" will lead to: "Do you remember seeing Mom pregnant?" and I'll follow with: "Do you remember when Mom went into the hospital to have me, and when she came home with me?"

I know Sam was only eight when I was born, but he should remember those things, shouldn't he? What else am I supposed to do? I probably can't depend on Dad to be of much help. He never told me anything up to this point in my life. Why would he start now? Besides, he probably can't remember much of anything, anyway.

"What we—what you—have to do is convince your father that he needs to sell the company," Ray makes a disgusting sucking sound as he slurps his martini. "That's all on the two, or three of you. He needs to understand that it's best for everyone if he sells, gets out now before something happens that might make AlMag less attractive—if you know what I mean?" He cocks a barely visible eyebrow, a match to his barely visible eyelid.

"Less attractive, how exactly?" Sam will do most of the talking this evening. I'm too caught up in my own drama to fully appreciate the seriousness of Dad's situation, and anyway, it seems so simple to me, what we need to do.

In the next few days Sam and I will sit down with Dad and explain to him that it's probably time for him to retire. We'll tell him that he'll make a lot of money from selling his company. We'll tell him how nice it will be for him to not have to drive into the office everyday. We'll tell him that he can vacation down in Florida now if he wants to, can get out of the cold Michigan winters. We will not tell him that Germans want to buy AlMag, but better Germans than Japanese. The horrors of Okinawa, the place where he nearly lost his leg, the place where over one hundred fifty thousand men lost their lives, are forever imprinted on Dad's brain. Maybe the suitors have American-sounding names. One way or another, it will all work out.

Chapter 12

"Terry, you know how much I've been looking forward to Christmas, your being here. We haven't been together in so long. I miss you so much…"

I'm rambling, something I promised myself I wouldn't do, let words tumble out of my mouth as if I'm five, lying about who smeared the lipstick on mom's new mohair sweater.

"How long has it been? Seven months? Yes, seven very long months. God—it seems so much longer than that. I've been so excited thinking about Christmas, about seeing you again."

"So why am I getting the feeling that you may be excited about seeing me, but it isn't going to happen?" Terry's questions still sound more like statements of fact than an inquiry, even when he's talking on the phone and doesn't have the advantage of body language illustrating his intent.

"Terry, you can't come for Christmas. I can't see you, much as I want to. It's not good here."

The torrent of tears that follow my declaration reinforce my fear and anxiety that any level of maturity I thought I'd achieved over the past few months by coming back here to take care of Dad, has somehow been sucked right out of me, or at least temporarily misplaced. I'm not a rational, clear-thinking, levelheaded adult. I'm nothing but a silly, snot-nosed kid who sobs uncontrollably because in my little egocentric world things aren't going my way.

"I'm a mess. I'm a fucking lousy mess. My life's a mess. It's all a mess. This isn't what I thought my life was going to be like. It's all so sad and confusing and hard and I don't know who I am anymore, or what the hell I'm even doing here."

The words pour out of me, just like my tears, all flowing like a lake that's been freed. A lake that was once held back by a dam, but the dam broke and now there's hell to pay downstream. I'm not even sure that Terry understood what I said; I'm blubbering so much I sound like I'm talking through scuba gear, underwater, bubbles flowing up to the surface as I mouth unintelligible words.

"Charlie. What are you talking about? When you left here I knew for sure that what I'd believed all along was true: you're a loving woman, a devoted daughter and you're strong. You're doing the right thing. You're such a good person, that's why I love you. I wish you were with me, but you're where you need to be. At least for now."

More disgusting, embarrassing slobbering and then: "There's just this one thing though, I'm not my father's daughter."

"No, of course you're not. Your dad isn't perfect. He isn't the man you'd like him to be. He's bigoted, he drinks too much, and he's got a lot of bitterness and anger inside him. You're not like that; you're not like that at all. Your dad's a lucky man to have a daughter like you to take care of him."

"But that's the thing, Terry. I'm not his daughter." And I wait for the significance, for the outlandish reality of my words to sink in.

Silence across a telephone line reverberates with implications, assumptions and contradictory feelings. Is the person being spoken to not speaking because they don't know how to respond, or because they know how to respond but don't want to say the words out loud or because they think that if they wait long enough the speaker will come to their rescue and bring up another topic or, better yet, say: "Hey, I was just joking around when I—you know—said what I just said."

In this case I realize that all three scenarios are in play. The quiet space vibrates in waves, like hot air shimmering upwards from the sidewalk on a skin-blistering August day.

"Terry?"

"Yeah, I'm here."

I know you are, but why is it that I suddenly feel like you really aren't?

"He's not my dad, Terry. Not my biological Dad, anyway. So of course my mom wasn't my biological mom, either. It's pretty fucked-up, learning this when you're closer to thirty than twenty."

"God, Charlie. When did you find out?"

"Dad more or less confirmed in his own confused and convoluted way a couple days ago what I got slapped in the face with on Thanksgiving. It's been a weird and strange and surreal past several days."

Actually I'm not being totally honest with Terry as to how I found out that I have or had, parents or a parent somewhere who for whatever reason decided that I wasn't worth keeping. I learned the truth because I snooped, what I've convinced myself that anyone in my situation would do. It's my life after all, even if it's been a phony one for the majority of it.

A week after Thanksgiving I found the key to Mom's bedroom, unlocked the door, walked in like I belonged there, started opening up dresser drawers whose insides hadn't been exposed to daylight for over two decades and that's where Dad found me: crouched down on the floor over the bottom drawer of Maggie Carpenter's imposing old oak dresser, holding onto something, a piece of paper, a document that I'd found there—the incriminating legal document that encompassed the entirety of my life in the two words typed in Times New Roman centered at the top: Adoption Agreement.

What I did next is another reason why I'm ashamed, why I can't tell Terry the truth; especially not after he's commended me for being such an exemplary daughter. Because that's something that I surely am not—a loving devoted daughter, flesh and blood child or otherwise. A loving devoted daughter doesn't stand up, turn and face her psychologically, neurologically and physically damaged father, flesh and blood or otherwise, and scream at him, eyes wide and face contorted like a hideous mask, the mask of a demon, the face of a monster.

"What the fuck is this? What the fuck is this? When were you going to tell me? You were never going to, were you? What is this? Where do I come from? Who am I? Who the hell am I?

That look on his face—I'll never forget. Not ever. No one had been in her room since she had left in 1963, a few days after the nation's young, handsome, brilliant president had been gunned down under the Dallas sun. I'd been six when he was murdered and Maggie went away, and now, even now I can remember the crying and dark silences and how the television was on all the time but I couldn't watch any of my programs because all that kept coming out of the screen were the same pictures over and over again, and I didn't really understand what I was seeing and I didn't understand why I couldn't watch *The Flintstones* and *Mr. Rogers Neighborhood,* and so I'd asked Alfred to explain it to me.

And that look, the expression he wore when he tried to explain to a six-year-old why grown-ups all over the country, all over the world, felt like they might never laugh and feel quite so happy and secure again, certainly not the way a six-year-old is happy and secure, and the look I saw just a few days ago when I screamed at him in her room—what I saw on his face those two times—will stay burned into my brain forever like a miserable scar. The first time, in 1963, the sadness and despair and shock and confusion that cluttered his face weren't my fault, but two days ago, in 1985, they were.

"What is this?" I'd screamed it again, knowing all the while exactly what it was.

"It's…" and he'd stopped, just outside the door, as if by entering he might invoke some terrible curse to inflict him. "It's—it's. What does it say? What does it say? Why are you in here? This is your mother's room."

"My mother! My mother! She wasn't my mother. You know she wasn't my mother. You knew and you kept it a secret all these years."

He began to cry, his face scrunched up so tightly that his shuttered eyes and turned-down mouth looked like mirror images. His shoulders jerked up and down, over and over again as he sobbed, as if something monstrous and ugly inside of him was throwing him from side-to-side as it tried to push its way out.

I could have stopped then, could have reached out and consoled him; could have stopped thinking about myself and behaved like the person Terry thinks he's in love with—but I didn't. I couldn't let go; I hung on and gave it one last shot, drove home my point with merciless precision.

"And now it's too late for you to explain. Your mind is gone now. You couldn't remember any details even if they were written down for you. You're an old man with an old, dying mind and you're no help to me. You're no help to me at all."

Psychologically, emotionally, physically—there should have been no part of him capable of responding. He was the child, beaten down and abused, unable to defend himself against adult cruelty and malice.

Yet…"We were going to tell you. Your mother and me. We were going to tell you when you were older. You'd understand when you were older"…he managed to sputter out before he turned his back to me and walked away, muttering: "…when you were older. When you were older."

But I don't plan on telling Terry any of this, which is why I know I have to end our conversation as soon as possible. I've spoken all my lines; it's time for my exit.

"Terry, this is a really difficult time. A really difficult time. Dad and I—we—we need some time, just the two of us, you know. He's getting more upset, more forgetful, angry and confused. He may have to stop working."

"Babe, I understand. I'll stay here for Christmas. I'll be warmer, right? I'm a California boy. Spending Christmas in Michigan I'd have been surly and disagreeable 'cause of freezing my ass off. We'll see each other soon, I promise."

And as I hang up the receiver I know that promises so easily made are so often just as easily broken. Not because the person making the promise doesn't mean what they say, not because they don't have the best intentions or because they're unaware of the significance of their words. No, the reason that promises are often easily broken is because life gets in the way.

Chapter 13

We have good days and bad days, Dad and I. The good days aren't really all that good, but they're so much better than the bad days that there are times a good day might be deemed spectacular compared to the twenty-four hours that preceded it.

Dad was forced to retire two days after I called Terry to tell him that I was an unknown entity who wouldn't be able to entertain him at Christmas. Ray's martini-fueled prescience had, unfortunately, proven to be accurate.

Somehow, even though he wasn't supposed to be interacting with anyone other than immediate office staff, Dad had placed an order for AlMag's oldest, and best, customer. Not only did he order the wrong solvent, he ordered ten times what the customer needed. When Ray told Dad that he had made a mistake, in fact more than just one, Dad started screaming loudly enough for everyone within earshot to hear that he wasn't the one who had made mistakes. The mistakes, according to him, were all made by the: "Fucking new buyer over there—that young kid who doesn't know what the hell he's doing."

His tirade continued as he marched into the warehouse and began berating the supervisor, Reggie Good, a barrel-chested, hard-working black man of fifty-four who had been with the company for thirty years; a blatantly illogical and unfair act considering that Reggie had merely shipped what he was told to.

Reggie took it for awhile, sat at his desk, eyes cast downward at his tuna sandwich (Ray told Sam and I later that Dad's modus operandi was to yell at and scold employees when they were on their lunch hour); but when Dad began to call him a "good for nothing, lazy nigger" Reggie lifted his six-feet-four inch frame off the chair and told Dad that if he didn't stop using that word, he might have to punch him in the face, and then Reggie said: "And after that, I'll walk right out this door and never come back here again."

Sam and I both arrived at AlMag at the same time that day. Peter dropped Sam off, gave us both hugs and told us that he wished he could be of more support. "This is a tough one, kids. This is a tough one," he said as his vibrant blue eyes glinted with tears.

Another image I'll never forget: Dad sitting in a chair in Ray's office, facing Ray across his desk; shoulders rounded, so slumped that he looked like a hunchback, staring at his shoes. Neither were speaking when Sam and I came in, but as soon as we came across the threshold Dad turned to look at us and said: "They're taking away my life."

Sam drew in a deep breath and made a choking noise; I knew he was seconds away from tears. But when Dad spoke again: "Don't let them do this. Don't let them take away my life," Sam mustered-up strength from his sorrow.

He limped over to Dad, faced him, put his hand on Dad's shoulder and said: "Dad, no one is taking away your life. You're starting a whole new one. A whole new life. What a lucky man you are." Authoritative, the rough edges rounded with compassion and empathy.

It wasn't a pleasant leave-taking. No one came by Dad's office to say good-bye, there weren't any parties with cake, balloons and banners strung across the room reading: "Enjoy your retirement. We're going to miss you" and "You're not retiring—you're going golfing." As the three of us walked Dad out to the car, Ray said that Donna had heard the news and mentioned that she'd like to come by to see Dad one more time, but Ray explained that he told her it might be best if she let it go, at least for the time being.

"Maybe you can pop in for dinner at Martinelli's a couple months from now after Al's gotten used to being retired. He'll be there for sure and he'd be happy to see you then," Ray told her.

The drive from the office to the house seemed to take two hours, although I know it was only twenty minutes. Dad sat in the passenger seat and Sam huddled in the back seat, directly behind him, occasionally reaching out to touch Dad's back. Sam didn't speak and neither did I. But Dad did—over and over again. Five words, he repeated, five words like a chant: "You're taking away my life."

That was seven months ago. Because our time together vacillates between so awful that I cry myself to sleep at night (on those days I look at my watch every few minutes, thinking with each glance that surely an hour has passed since I last turned my wrist) to the occasional day when neither one of us has a melt-down and we carry on lucid conversations, that seven months has stretched into a lifetime. A merciless life that seems like it will never end. The passage of time has lost all meaning. I know that time is passing only because the good days are fewer and fewer while the bad days metastasize, gobbling them up like a cancerous ogre eating away at Dad's memories and identity.

Cindy had her baby. I don't remember how old it is, maybe a month, maybe two. And I really don't remember if it's a boy or a girl, although I think it's a boy. She called me the day the baby was born; I do remember that we didn't talk long. She was so happy; I remember how happy she sounded. And then she said that she was sorry, and I didn't understand what she was sorry about. She had just had a baby with the man she once told me she couldn't imagine ever not having in her life. What did she have to be sorry about? I haven't talked to her since that call; that's probably why I'm not sure how old her boy or girl is. She's busy. Taking care of a baby, being responsible for another human being is the most arduous task a person can take on.

Terry calls every so often, but not as much as he once did. I suppose he wishes that I would call him once in awhile. Why is it always left up to me to be the one to call, I'm sure that's what he wonders. I do consider calling him sometimes, on the good days. A day that Dad and I took a long walk for instance, and Dad walked even faster than me so I had to hurry to catch up and he noticed the world around him and commented on it ("Look at that cute little dog sitting in the window at the house over there" or "I think it's going to rain soon") Sometimes I think about calling Terry on days like that—but then I think: "Why?"

Today began as a good day.

"I want to go visit the navy base. I want to go with you and George," Dad declared a little after 7:00, shortly after finishing his second cup of coffee and bowl of cereal.

He stopped eating his usual eggs and bacon breakfast months ago, insisting that nothing tastes the same as it used to, "...because people are putting dangerous drugs in the food now." He has yet to identify who "the people" are. The muscles in his face are slack, his jowls hang loose like a turkey's neck and his clothes don't fit; everything is far too big. He's disappearing: both his mind and body.

"I'll have to ask George if he wants to go, Dad. He may have something to do today."

I know of course that we're talking about Sam but Dad started confusing Sam for George the day we drove him away from AlMag for the last time. When we got to the house Dad said to Sam: "George, why are you doing this? Why are you taking away my life?" And then his eyes had widened and he stared at Sam as if he were seeing him for the first time, and asked: "What happened to your arm, George? Where did it go?"

Sam and I have accepted the fact that for Dad Sam is gone, rubbed-out like a charcoal drawing, as if he never existed. We pretend that he's George, the way I played along when Dad thought that I was a movie star, which he seldom mentions anymore. The last time he brought it up was a month or two ago when we were watching *On the Waterfront*, one of his favorite movies, and mid-way through he turned and said to me: "I had a daughter once who was an actress. She could have been in this movie. She was just as good and pretty as that saint woman." He was quiet for a few minutes and then he looked at me with eyes as black and lifeless as coal, and asked: "Are you her?"

The naval air station closed in 1969. It's a municipal airport now, but in Dad's mind it's still a working military installation. This will be the third time we've gone for 'a visit.' The first time Dad wondered why there weren't more people in military dress, and was disappointed to find out that I couldn't get him in to see the commanding officer so he could complain about "...the young people in the military today who don't even have enough respect for their country to wear a uniform."

The second time he brought his camera with him, and last year's day planner, so he could document through photos and his notes how the new generation of military leaders disrespected their country.

Dad writes nearly everything down now: the name of a movie he just watched so he'll remember the title the next time; what he had for breakfast, lunch and dinner; what board game we tried playing before he grew frustrated and quit; the name of a dog we met on a walk (not the owner's name, just the dog's); how far it is from the house to the mainland across the free bridge. It's his way of identifying and making real and permanent what's most important in his disordered life, names and numbers written down in his own hand, on pages protected by a well-worn black leather cover.

Sam didn't have anything more important to do on this glorious June day than to spend it with Dad and me at the old naval base. It's the kind of early summer day in the Midwest that makes you forget that winter ever happened. A warm languid breeze caresses our faces as we get out of the car, the trees look like they could topple under the weight of all the brilliant green leaves weighing down their branches and the sky is a white-washed blue.

"We'll just walk around a little bit Dad and look at the planes and then how about if Sam—if George and you and I go have lunch at that new restaurant that just opened that's on the water?" I ask as Dad starts walking toward one of the hangars. He doesn't respond.

"Dad?" Sam calls out as he tries to catch up with him. "Dad, wait up. I'll walk with you to wherever you're going. Just wait up."

Clearly Dad has no intention of waiting up or responding; he's on a singular mission that Sam and I aren't a part of. I can tell that Sam's in distress, his prosthetic leg won't allow him to move much faster than a very slow jog, and despite his age, illness and his own wounds, Dad is moving at a fairly quick pace. He has at least a twenty-foot head start, so I run to catch up with him.

"Dad, Dad. Wait for me. For George and me. Don't be in such a hurry. We've got time."

When he turns and looks at me I see something on his face that I haven't seen in weeks, if not months: emotion. For a while now I've seen only two expressions on Dad's face, a mask-like grin and a rigid blank stare. But not today—today Dad's energized; he has a reason to be alive, he must accomplish something and he's giddy with anticipation at doing so.

"I'm going to see the commander today: the commanding general. I'm going to tell him that Howard isn't the one who's going. I'm going in his place. They can't take Howard. I'm going to fight those bastard Japs."

Howard? Good lord, what do I do now? What do I say?

"Dad. Dad. There isn't a war going on now. Dad. Howard—your brother Howard isn't alive anymore." I'm at his side now, reaching out to grab hold of his arm, thinking that this isn't acting that I'm capable of.

"What do you mean, isn't alive? What do you know? Susan—his fiancée—she's planning a big wedding. They're going to Niagara Falls on their honeymoon."

A man in a one-piece denim jumpsuit, carrying a socket wrench, is rounding the corner of the nearest hangar; he's obviously a mechanic, probably working on one of the planes. Dad sees him too, and although what the man's wearing doesn't come close to resembling a uniform, Dad reacts as if he's come face-to-face with a kindred soul, a fellow military man who'll help him in his quest to save Howard from going off to war.

"Captain. Can I have a word, please?"

From his response and the look on his cherub-cheeked face, the man appears to be both annoyed and amused. "Hey buddy. What are you talking about? Who do you think I am? Captain? Hah! Captain of what? Never got as far as private. Hey buddy—who are you, anyway?"

"I—I—I'm Gunnery Sargent Alfred George Carpenter, sir. Reporting for duty. Reporting for duty, sir. A bit maimed, but I'm A-OK. Reporting for duty, sir. I'm replacing George. George—he's named for me. Alfred, middle name: George, Carpenter. I'm replacing George. George can't go. He can't go. George has a fiancée, Susan. They have to get married."

Dad pauses, and the man who I know is named David because I'm close enough to him now to read the embroidered letters stitched over his heart, smiles at me with such understanding and empathy that I would kiss him if I wasn't in love with someone else.

"Okay, buddy. Okay. I get it. Sure. I get it. George isn't going to go. You will. We'll take care of that. Okay? We'll see to it, buddy. We'll make sure that you go, not George."

I wish now that when Dad said he wanted to go to the naval base I would have made some excuse as to why we couldn't. I wish that I had suggested we go on a picnic, instead. I wish that he'd agreed to the change in plans. I wish that I wasn't here. I wish that everything was different—but it isn't. Wishing is for kids. Wishing is for Disney movies. Wishing gets you nothing but heartbreak, because just wishing—doesn't make things real.

"George? Is it George? I had a son named George. Did he go? I don't know. But what about Howard? Howard's the one. Howard's the one. I have to go so Howard won't die."

He pauses again, glances at David, me, his eyes linger for a full twenty seconds or so on Sam before returning to David.

"Gunnery Sargent Alfred George Carpenter, sir. Reporting for duty. Reporting for duty, sir. I'm replacing Howard. Howard can't go. I'm replacing Howard. George is here. I'm just a confused old man. George is here. He's standing right here."

Chapter 14

Today is my thirtieth birthday, and today Dad died. That these two events occurred on the same day is a coincidence that I accept, along with the accompanying irony. A thirtieth birthday is a milestone, for the person turning thirty and for their parents. How many times have you heard a mother or father say: "Boy, nothing like your kid turning thirty to make you feel old."

Thirty—a milestone for me most definitely, but not in the way I'd imagined and hoped for. I'd always envisioned myself being in an entirely different place, both literally and figuratively, when at one minute after twelve on November 1, 1987 I metamorphosed from an impetuous quasi adult into the real deal; mature and responsible, comfortable in my own skin, sure of myself and my place in the world. But instead I'm an orphan, and I know it isn't exactly true but I feel like this is the second time I've been orphaned in my life. It doesn't seem fair.

Dad had no idea of course that he died on such an important day in my life. He no longer knew who I was, and even if he had he wouldn't have known what happened on the day I was born anyway, because he wasn't there. Why celebrate an occasion that you weren't privy to? He never knew if my mother had an easy labor or a hard one. He never knew if there was a man there that day, but I imagined that there had been. My real father, my dream-father who in my imagination had told my real mom that he couldn't marry her but he'd be there when I was born because that was what responsible men did. Dad never knew what mom said to me when she held me to her breast just minutes after I came into the world. In my dreams, my imagined dream-mother told me that I was the most beautiful thing she'd ever seen, then she pressed her warm lips to my moist forehead and whispered: "I love you and I'll never let you go." Another promise.

Dad had been living (just existing really) in a nursing home for two months before he died. Sam and I decided soon after Dad moved out of the house that we weren't going to have a funeral or memorial service for him. No one had come to see him after he retired, except for dear sweet devoted Donna who had shown up at Martinelli's for dinner one night but stayed only long enough for Dad to ask her what her name was over and over again before she left, her weeping twisting her body like a piece of dough being molded into a pretzel as she walked out the door. We figured that if people didn't care enough to visit Dad when he was alive, why would they want to pretend that they'd cared by showing up after he was dead. It wouldn't make Sam and I feel any better.

Dad would die. We'd have him cremated; his ashes interred in the burial plot he'd purchased in the late fifties: a dual gravesite, one side reserved for Maggie. We'd plant two flags next to the headstone: one American, one Marine Corps and we'd walk away. End of story.

But stories don't always end so neatly. All the loose ends aren't necessarily pulled together by the next-to-last scene. Because even though Dad chose my thirtieth birthday to finally mercifully let go, I'm not holding it against him. I'm not begrudging him that one last ill-timed act. When he drew his final breath wasn't his choice, and over the last year I'd grown closer to him. I'd discovered the person Alfred was, even as that person was irrevocably slipping away. I got to know him, as I was losing him and as he was losing himself. And that's the irony of it all.

I'd found more than just the documentation attesting to my once-secret backstory in Maggie's room that day. I'd found letters. There were six letters in all: four just one page, two double that, writing on both sides. All six were written to Maggie, from Alfred when he was away fighting in the war to end all wars. Reading those letters I learned who Alfred Carpenter was, and who he wanted to be. For her, for Maggie, the woman he promised he would grow old with and would love until his soul left his body.

It's been almost two years now, since that first Thanksgiving back in Michigan, when Sam and Peter and I had looked at all the old photos and I'd seen the ones of who I grew up believing were my real Mom and Dad, and I'd wanted to share the find with Terry, wanted Terry to see that my parents were like everyone else's. They'd been young once and in love and Alfred wasn't an angry homophobic racist and alcoholic, and Maggie had loved him and back then, when they were young, she wasn't thinking about leaving him, not ever. But after reading his letters to her I realized that the photographs were only what their name implies: snapshots. Just a brief view, a moment in time, one second captured forever that would never, ever represent or explain the totality of a love affair—not the way words can. In Alfred letters to Maggie, I learned who he really was, and I came to love him for it.

So, that's why, as Sam and I leave the nursing home for the last time I say: "Sam, we'll have Dad cremated like we've always planned and we're not going to have a funeral or ceremony, like we've always planned not to. But, what about having a memorial dinner at Martinelli's? I think some people would come, don't you?"

And Sam turns to me, wipes the tears away from my cheeks with his only hand and replies: "I think that's a wonderful idea. Dad would love it."

Chapter 15

People came. There weren't enough mourners to fill Martinelli's main dining room, but there were enough that Mr. Martinelli's son, Nick Martinelli Junior who'd taken over managing the restaurant after his dad died last year, told me half-an-hour ago as we were saying good-bye to everyone that he didn't regret closing the dining room to regular customers because "Just for this one night, it's okay. My dad, he loved your dad. Your dad ate here for many years. Dad used to say that if Alfred didn't come in as usual, he knew that something was up. You know, my dad and your dad, they were in the war. Not together, but they both fought. So they understood each other. They knew what it was like—living with—all of that. My dad, he loved your father. It's good we honor him tonight. Paisan, he was paisan."

Sam and I had made sure guests understood that the memorial, as it were, was a sit-down dinner, so everyone brought spouses or girlfriends. Ray and his wife came, Donna and her live-in boyfriend and even a few vendors, which would have surprised Dad and might even have made him happy, even though he wouldn't have shown it. John Mason, the next-door-neighbor and his new blonde trophy wife showed up, along with one of the Mason daughters who I figured came just so she could keep an eye on the inappropriate step-mom who was young enough to be her older sister. But it was the sight of Reggie Good walking in the door of Martinelli's for what I'm certain was the first time in his life, Mrs. Good at his side, that caused me to involuntarily let out a sob so loud that everyone in the room looked at me as if I'd shouted out "fire" or "help" or "fuck" or all three one right after another.

"Mr. Good, Mr. Good" I'd said as I trotted over to the couple, hands outstretched, thinking all the while *what an apropos name.*

"Mr. Good. I'm so happy you came. Sam and I, we're so happy you came. And you must be Mrs. Good?" I knew she was, of course; I just loved saying their surname out loud.

"Yes, Ms. Carpenter. This is my wife, Elfie. Elfie, this is Ms. Carpenter. Alfred Carpenter's daughter. His only daughter, am I right, Ms. Carpenter? And that fine looking man over there, Elfie, that's Mr. Carpenter's son." With one sweep of his huge hand, Reggie Good introduced us, and I knew at that moment that what I'd thought was true, wasn't. The relationship between Alfred Carpenter and Reggie Good wasn't at all what I'd imagined it to be.

"Mr. Carpenter—your dad—he gave me a job. My first job, first real job. Not counting them times I worked in a drugstore when I was a kid."

So proud Reggie Good had been, his already massive chest puffed-up even more. He'd looked over at Elfie who held on to his arm as if it was a life-vest keeping her afloat; her shiny eyes locked onto him like a star-struck teenager.

"I was a kind of good-for-nothing kid growing up. Always getting into trouble. Petty stuff. Smoking and drinking and all. Not too bad, not 'til I started hanging with some really rough characters. Nearly broke my ma's heart. Ended up serving one year in the Wayne County jail. Broke into a house with some of them boys. We didn't steal much. Pawned what we stole—got fifty bucks for the stuff. Ended up in jail for fifty dollars worth of shit."

His eyes gleamed wet as he described his transformation from ex-con to provider, a stable working man and husband. The husband who to this day could still make his wife swoon.

"I was almost twenty-four when I got out of the clinker. Twenty-four year old black man who'd never had a real job and had just got out of jail. Wasn't nobody going to hire me? My ma said I should go to work at Ford. I said to her, ma nobody's gonna hire me. There's enough colored boys who ain't been in jail wanting to work at the plant. I was real depressed, Ms. Carpenter, Mr. Carpenter. I sure was depressed. And then I met your dad."

One, just one, perfectly globular tear slid down his cheek.

"I was in that drugstore one day, the one I used to work at. I was buying a soda pop. Your dad came in. He bought a bottle of pop too, and some Tootsie Rolls. He started telling the cashier that he was in the neighborhood 'cause he was meeting with a customer. Then your dad started talking about the war, telling him, the cashier I mean, how he was on Okinawa. How he got hurt real bad there. But how he made it back and started up a business of his own. How his Dad, your granddad Ms. Carpenter, Mr. Carpenter, would have been proud of him, making something important of his self. He said he was always looking for good workers. And then he looked over and saw me standing by the cooler."

One more tear. I waited for a deluge, but it never came. Reggie Good is as strong a man as he looks.

"When he saw me he asked me right off if I'd been in the war, too. And I said no, sir. I didn't go; I was too young. But my big brother did, my big brother Clarence did. And I told your dad that day that my brother Clarence was a big hero in our neighborhood 'cause he killed lots of Germans, and he'd came home with medals. And that's when your dad asked me if I was working anywheres and I told him 'no sir' and he asked me if I wanted a job."

Sam had moved closer to me, his hand gripping my arm as tightly as I knew Elfie was holding onto Reggie's.

"And the thing is, Ms. Carpenter, Mr. Carpenter, your dad didn't never ask me if I'd been in prison or nothing. He didn't never ask me if I'd ever smoked dope or drank too much, or if I'd broke into someone's house and stole their cheap old silverware. No sir, he didn't ask me none of those questions. He just asked me—Reggie Good—if I wanted a job."

"I'm sorry, Reggie. I'm so sorry—you know—sorry for the things Dad said to you before he retired. I'm truly sorry."

And Reggie Good, true to his name, gathered me and Sam both up in his arms and in his fine deep voice said: "No, Ms. Carpenter. No, no. Your dad was a good man. He was a good man. He couldn't help his self towards the end you know. He couldn't help his self. He didn't mean nothing with those things he said. I knew that. I might have left after he said those things. I might have even punched him, just 'cause it hurt me to hear those words. But I would have come back the next day, the very next day. He gave me a job, my very first job. He made me a man."

It's almost 10:30. Everyone's left, except for the Martinelli's crew. Reggie and Elfie were the last to leave. Reggie hugged Sam and me again, and when he held me he whispered in my ear: "Your dad's with the angels now, Ms. Carpenter. He's with the angels and he ain't confused and mean no more. "Cause he don't forget stuff no more. He remembers everything now, and him and the angels—they be talking all night and all day 'bout the stuff he knows."

I'm emotionally drained and so is Sam. I can tell because he's been misty-eyed for the last hour and his limp is worse. He and Peter are lingering now out of obligation.

"Hey, guys, why don't you go on home. I'll stay and settle up with Nick Jr. We've had a long day…" but before I can finish, Becky strides out of the bar.

She's been serving all evening—drinks and food, hustling from kitchen to dining room to bar to dining room and back to kitchen again, in control the entire time, not missing a beat. She'd had help from the Desiree of the braces (which oddly have moved from her top teeth to the bottom) and dyed hair, but it was Becky who'd made sure that the anti- pasta was chilled, the pasta was steaming, and the glasses were never empty.

"Charlie, Sam, Peter, quite a night, huh? Al would have been quite pleased with the turnout I think. It sure kept me busy, all that running back and forth. But I was happy to do it, very happy to do it. Wish though there would have been more time for me to talk to you this evening," she says as she places an unopened bottle of very expensive cabernet on the table and stares directly into my eyes.

"Becky, are you planning on sharing?" Sam's question startles me. *I really thought he was ready to go home.*

"Sure am, that's why I brought over this bottle; it's on the house, compliments of Nick Jr. Peter, would you mind getting four glasses from the bar. I'm about run-ragged carrying trays and plates all night. I'm not as young as I look" she replies, the last few words spoken rather coyly, and even though in the last twenty seconds she's addressed both Sam and Peter, I have the feeling that she's playing to an audience of only one—me.

As soon as Peter gets up and heads for the bar, Becky slides into the chair he was sitting on, the one right next to mine, plops her elbows down on the table and sighs: "If I could somehow get them up that high and if I didn't care if I came off looking like some sort of savage who just came out of a cave, I'd put my feet up on the table so the blood could drain back into them. Damn! My feet do hurt like hell."

No surprise, Sam—emotionally spent, one real leg, one fake leg that I know is rubbing up against what's left of his other once real leg and causing him excruciating pain, makes a move before I do. He hobbles over to the table next to ours, snags a chair, and drags it to Becky's side.

"Put your feet up here, it's not like anyone's going to be sitting here for the next twelve hours or so."

"You're a doll, a real sweetheart, Sam. Thanks, and yes, here's Peter, with glasses. You're the men of the hour, you two. Of the hour—shit—men of the day, men of the year."

Peter uncorks the bottle, pours each of us a quarter of a glass and Becky focuses on me—again.

"Your brother, George. Does he know about his dad?"

"Sam tried. Right Sam?" I answer as I tilt my head in Sam's direction.

"Yeah, I called him. I called the last number I had, up in Alberta somewhere. But it was disconnected."

"No luck reaching him by mail?" Becky asks

"Went that route, too. Sent him a letter the same day. To the address I'd had I guess as long as I'd had the phone number. Ironically it came back today: moved. Left no forwarding address. Guess brother George is in the wind."

Shit. I didn't know about the letter. Poor Sam. I'm really not too sure that this is the conversation we should be having right now. And with Becky, for god's sake. Yeah, she waited on

Dad for years and she's pretty cool for her age, but shit—she's just a waitress.

"That's a tough one, damn, that's a tough one. He's flesh and blood. He's flesh and blood," the last four words trail off and I wonder if she's going to cry, and then she says: "Well, what's that mean for the inheritance?"

She's already emptied her glass and motions to Peter with her forefinger to pour what I translate as a "schooch more".

Inheritance? What the hell? Is this why she wanted us to hang around and have a drink with her? Does she know something we don't? Did Dad leave money to her? Was she more than just a waitress?

Since I'm executor, it's my turn to speak. Until I moved back to Michigan there was no executor; in fact, there'd been no will. Perhaps Dad had thought he would live forever, or Maggie would come back and she'd handle everything, she'd make everything right, or maybe he didn't want to leave anything to a gay son and a daughter who wasn't really his, despite the fact that he had a piece of paper that said otherwise. No matter the reason, while Dad was still cognizant enough to understand the importance of making sure that everything you'd worked for your entire life didn't end up being battled over in a courtroom, I'd convinced him to draw one up.

"Well, Becky. I'm the executor. We're pretty set there...as far as the inheritance. What Dad got from selling AlMag is worth a lot, a whole lot. And he had money in the bank. Jeez! He sure was frugal. And he owned stocks and yeah...we're pretty well set. It's gonna take some time to get it all squared away since George is AWOL but everything's more or less copacetic. The house is paid for. No debts. Shit, I don't think Dad ever owed anyone anything—well at least not up until he started forgetting stuff. But hey, everything's cool."

You're rambling, Charlie. You're rambling. She's not your nemesis. She's just a waitress.

"So, are you going back to California then, Charlie?"

"No, Becky. No, I'm not going back to California. I have so much to deal with, with the will and all. It's going to take time, lots of time. I'm staying in the house. Sam and Peter are here. I'm staying here."

"You still working at the bookstore?"

"I am. They've been really good about giving me time off when things got dicey with Dad. Now that…now that he's gone I'm going to work more hours. And I'm thinking about maybe teaching a few drama classes at one of the community colleges."

"You're moving forward with your life, Charlie. That's good. Making plans. You're young, there's so much life left for you to experience. So much life…"

Becky's voice trails off and I'm not sure if it's the fact that she's tired, she gulped down the wine too fast on an empty stomach (I didn't see her eat anything all night unless she was nibbling on breadsticks whenever she went into the kitchen to pick up platters of food), she misses Dad more than might be expected of a waitress who just served a guy dinner several nights a week for years, or maybe it's something else entirely.

Maybe she's sick herself, she's sick and dying and she's getting all maudlin and what are Sam and Peter and I supposed to do about it because we really don't know her all that well even though it would be sad if she's ill, and so it's probably time to call it a night because Sam and Peter and I need to go home and sleep.

"I have a son, Charlie. I think I may have mentioned him to you and your dad sometime in the past."

What? This is what this is all about? Jeez! Is her son the one who's sick or dying?

Sam and Peter have yet to say a word. They're as quiet as two kids huddled together at the top of the stairs listening to the adults having a party in the living room. ("Don't breathe, Peter. Don't make a sound." "I won't Sam. I'll be as quiet as a mouse.")

They're both looking at me with the most earnest, and anticipatory, expressions. I know exactly what they're thinking; the words might as well be drawn in crayon across their faces, and what I'm thinking and what they're thinking are two very different things.

She has a son, Charlie, a son. Probably close to your age.

"I do remember that you mentioned your son. What about him?" I flick the question out like it's an irritating insect I'm shooing off my shoulder.

Could I have been any more abrupt? Sure. I could have said: "I really don't give a damn about your son, Becky. And it's time for me to go home and get some much-needed sleep. I'm thirty, I've recently buried the man who I thought was my real father, I'm stuck in a place I left a long time ago having to start my life all over again and I haven't heard anything from the man I love more than anything in the world for over a year. So, Becky—I really don't care to hear about your son."

"Well, I thought that it might be nice for you and Kevin to meet. There's only two years age difference between the two of you. I think you'll like him."

Still no sound from the other side of the table, but Sam kicks me in the shin with his fake leg (at the same time as Peter discreetly punches him in the side), raises his eyebrows in fake surprise, widens his mouth into a "we're having some fun now grin", and I think:

Who am I, and what's to become of me?

Chapter 15

Two weeks have passed since Dad's memorial. During that time I've learned that having a will is a very good thing, but in the long run it would be better if people died and didn't leave anything to anybody because lawyers, even if you like and trust them, do charge by the hour; and that Cindy is more fertile than I ever imagined.

Yesterday she called to tell me that she's pregnant, again, with what will be her third and fourth child. Cindy is having twins—a seemingly welcome addition to not-quite-two Matt Junior and his five-month old sister, Crystal. I'm alternately happy for her because she's happy, but also confounded and bewildered by the news. I've no idea how she copes. Just the thought of having four children under the age of three living in the same house with me makes me want to curl up in a ball and weep.

Of course Cindy was always one to love completely, to lose herself in love, whether to John or to Matt, so I guess it makes sense that she'd be raising a brood who she can love forever, who'll love her back. She must love her children just as completely, even more so than she ever loved John, than she loves Matt now—they're part of her after all.

But I wonder if love like that is affected by the laws of diminishing returns—the more children she has, will she love each one just a little bit less than the one before? How much love is available to parcel out? And will the twins, because they're coming into the world at almost the same time get an equal share? Or will the one who's born first, say two minutes ahead of its sibling, get an extra little smidgen of Cindy's all-encompassing and unconditional affection? And what about Matt? Will there be any love left for him?

I feel a headache coming on, thinking about all this. Although what's making my temples ache is probably not the contemplation as much as it is the fact that I've drank one full glass of red wine in the last half-hour and started on the second. Tonight's the 'big night', and I'm so nervous I didn't eat anything all day. Tonight I'm meeting Kevin.

The night of Dad's memorial Becky had been so persuasive about the two of us meeting that I couldn't back out. And it hadn't helped that Sam, and even Peter, had bought into the whole concept with such gusto that one would have thought they were junior high school girls planning a slumber party where boys were being snuck in. But Becky did give me a two-week reprieve.

"You've been through an awful lot these past few years, Charlie. I know how hard this has been on you, so why don't we wait a few weeks, until, Friday the twentieth? You need some time to regroup. I'll plan on working that night; we'll meet here. How's that sound?"

At the time it hadn't sounded too bad. There are worse things than being introduced to someone for the first time for reasons that you suspect might portend a possible romantic or sexual entanglement but you're not sure, by someone you barely know who you suspect, but you're not sure, might have had a romantic or even sexual entanglement with the man who, up until you were almost thirty, you thought was your biological father. I suppose there are worse things than that, but I can't think of one right now, because as the past two weeks have zipped by like a Japanese bullet train (cleaning out drawers and closets, taking things to the Goodwill, closing accounts and talking to attorneys make a day seem like four hours instead of twenty-four) I've discovered that I'm less sure about the idea of meeting Becky's son. I do like the name Kevin, but that's certainly not enough reason to want to meet him.

I agreed to it though, so here I am, behaving like a woman who's never been in a situation like this in her life. Drinking wine ostensibly to moisten my dry mouth, changing clothes a couple of times because I have absolutely no idea what Kevin's like, what he's into, what he expects me to look like.

And suddenly it's 1984 all over again and I keep coming out of the bedroom with a different outfit on and Cindy is smiling at my Charlie jitters and very soon Terry's going to drive up in his black Camaro and my world is going to change over a plate of take-out Chinese food.

Oh, Terry. I miss you. And sometimes, more often than not lately, I wish that I'd never even met you. All that talk about better to have loved and lost—I don't know. I think that's a bunch of bullshit. 'Cause it's hard, it's really hard to have lost what you loved. When you love something, what purpose could there be to ever losing it? What lesson could anyone ever learn from that? Whoever came up with that saying was some kind of sadist who was never in love.

Nick Junior greets me as I walk in; a smile on his face big enough to shove a couple of meatballs through and still have room left for a cannoli.

"Ms. Carpenter, Ms. Carpenter. It's so good to see you. Not quite such a sad occasion this time, huh?" He says as he escorts me to the bar, which is empty except for the ruddy-faced, red-haired, not-quite-chubby but almost, youngish-looking man ordering a drink from the clearly bored peroxide-blonde bartender, and Becky, who's sitting at a table facing the door.

She's up and at my side before I have time to say 'hi."

"Oh, Charlie. I'm so happy, so happy that we can finally get together. I'm just so happy—you can't imagine how this makes me feel. I could hardly wait this past two weeks, I felt sometimes like I was going to burst. But I had to give you some time. You needed time for yourself…all you've been through and everything…"

And a few thoughts pop into my head—she's rambling and that guy standing at the bar is most definitely not Alfred Carpenter's son so I can ditch that scenario, but Becky is most definitely his mother and because of the way she's rambling, and his coloring and build and then, when he turns to look at me through his almost gray eyes, the bar is dark but I know those eyes are pale blue, pale blue that sometimes look gray—I know.

It takes less than ten seconds to reach him and two seconds to decide between a handshake and a hug. I choose the hug, so my words are muffled in his shoulders, as if I'm talking into a pillow.

"Hi brother."

"Hi sis. Is it okay to call you sis? You are older than me." His voice is rich and multi-layered, like a sweet dense cake with frosting on every tier and a big hunk of creamy chocolate hidden in the middle.

With that voice he must have women falling in love with him right and left.

"Sis is fine with me, but you can always call me Charlie."

Before Kevin can respond Becky joins us, kisses Kevin on the right cheek, me on my left and says to the bartender, who looks as if he's just accidently wandered into a sub-titled foreign film:

"Derek, whatever my son ordered, cancel it. And pull out that bottle of Rancia Reserva, classic Chianti. You know which one. And bring us the good glasses, you know which ones I mean." Derek instantly comes alive, perhaps hoping that the evening isn't going to be so uninteresting after all.

"Come, sit." Becky's in control, she's in her element and loving every second of it. All Kevin and I can do is follow her lead—she is our mother, after all. She sits across from us, Kevin's on my left.

"So, Charlie. It didn't take you long to figure things out."

"Intuition, I guess. But intuition that I only acquired when I walked in here and saw Kevin. The way he looks—kinda like me—like he could be my brother and all, I mean he looks more like me than my brother Sam does, and then you rambling on and on, and setting this meeting up in the first place and oh, yeah, did I mention the rambling on and on, which like me I'm guessing you do in many situations, whether you're nervous or scared or tired or upset or…"

"Eager for her children to finally meet? Eager for her daughter to know that I'm her mother?"

"Yeah, a situation pretty much like that."

"You and I are so much alike, Charlie. All these years, apart and yet they're so many similarities. The first time you came in here with your Dad, when you moved back—I saw it then. But I couldn't…"

Kevin's laugh is as captivating as his voice. "So, are the two of you going to ramble on the rest of the night, with all due respect to Led Zeppelin, or can I get in a word or two?"

"Kevin, my son, the professor—I relinquish the floor to you." Becky smiles at Kevin with the sort of beaming "my child is the most handsome smartest person on the planet and you'd better agree with me" expression I've ever seen.

He turns his body in the chair so he's facing me, rising up off the seat before settling back down just on the edge. "I've been waiting for this for a long time, too…meeting you. For years I didn't think it would ever happen. I knew you were out there somewhere, my big sister, but I didn't know where."

With an unsteady hand, the bartender, smiling now and much more animated, sits a tray on our table. He looks relieved, and rather proud of himself, that the three crystal glasses and bottle of wine atop it made it as far as they did without crashing to the floor. I'm not surprised when his hand shakes as he twists the corkscrew, and Becky puts her hand over his and slowly peels his fingers off the lever.

"I'll handle this, Derek. Thanks." As he ambles back to the bar I hope, for his sake, that Derek has a day job.

The bottle opened, Becky carefully pours each of us half a glass and says:

"A toast. A toast to my children. Together finally, after all these years. Charlie and Kevin, my children. My loves."

I can't believe this is really happening.

"I know you've got lots and lots of questions, Charlie. We don't have to answer them all tonight, but I'm pretty sure there's one big one you want to have answered first thing." Becky smiles at me over the top of her glass.

"Yes, there is. Actually, it's a two-parter. First part: why did you give me up? Second part: who's my biological dad, and who's Kevin's?"

A look passes between Becky and Kevin that I can't discern, and I wonder how long they've been rehearsing their responses. Her head tilts forward, a cue so slight I almost miss it, and Kevin sits his glass down, and grabs ahold of my empty left hand.

"I'll answer part two, sis—Charlie. You're probably thinking that you and I are stepsiblings, and it would make sense if you thought that. But, the thing is—we have the same dad."

And I'm supposed to be excited about this? This is supposed to be good news? Yeah, it's great that you and I share the exact same set of parents, great news. Really fucking amazing great news. I want to jump up and down just hearing it. But I never got to know our parents 'cause I was given away. Given away like a puppy you bring home from the pound that chews up the carpets so you end up taking him back. That's me, a bad puppy.

Despite the fact that I'm experiencing a wave of nausea that threatens to wash up on the table, red and angry and ugly, I manage to speak without sounding like I'm holding back a tsunami of emotion.

"I don't understand."

Amazing—I'm not rambling.

"You're really confused now, aren't you? I'm so sorry my girl, my baby, I'm so sorry." As Becky begins to cry I notice that nothing's melting off of her face, the heavy foundation is gone and so are the false eyelashes. She looks younger, her face is virtually wrinkle-free, she's much prettier than I've ever seen her, even with tears flowing down her cheeks and sliding off the end of her nose.

"I…I…I've b…been thinking about this n…night for such a…a long time. Imagining h…h…how wonderful it w…would b…be. Never thinking h…how you'd react."

"Mom, mom," Kevin pulls a handkerchief out of his tweed sport-coat pocket, and I wait.

Wait for the mother who gave me away to explain why she did.

Kevin takes another sip of wine, so do I. Becky wipes her eyes, blows her nose and empties her glass.

"I was sixteen when you were born, still in high school obviously. And so was your dad, Jim. We'd gone through school together ever since kindergarten. When we were in sixth grade Jim asked me to marry him. I said yes and then we agreed that we should wait until we were a little older."

She refills her glass, calls Derek over to the table, orders two plates of fried calamari and turns back to Kevin and me with a tepid smile.

"Some reinforcements, you know? I think all three of us could use a little food. There isn't going to be time tonight to go all the way through to dessert, but we'll probably get as far as the anti-pasta."

I want to get as far as why you gave away your first-born child. Why you gave away your baby girl. And if we're eating tiramisu by that time, if that's how long it takes—so be it.

"Jim's Dad, your grandfather, had been a colonel in the army. A big deal, he'd graduated from West Point and Jim knew all the time he was growing up, from the time he was a little boy, that he'd follow his dad into the military."

Becky smiles at Kevin, who I know has probably heard this story again and again. I can't help but wonder if hearing it like this, with his sister sitting beside him who's hearing it for the very first time, if it sounds somehow fresh and new.

"His life had been planned out for him since the moment he was born. Jim was an only child. He was more than just a twinkle in his father's eye. Jim was his father's legacy. My getting pregnant—with you—didn't quite fit into his dad's plan."

Becky pauses. It occurs to me that I should say something; after all she isn't giving a soliloquy or a eulogy.

"Did you think about—an abortion?"

Charlie, there isn't a worse question you could have asked. If she says "yes" she's going to feel awful about it, and you'll feel even worse. And if she lies and says "no", and she'd have to be lying, she'll feel awful about lying to protect you from feeling bad. Why the hell did you ask her that?

I'm vaguely comforted by the fact that Becky doesn't hesitate to answer.

"Yes, I thought about it—for a day or so. Who wouldn't? I was a sophomore in high school. I had plans to go to college. My boyfriend since we were five was going to go to West Point when we graduated. We were going to get married. Of course I did."

Kevin stands, gives me a quick peck on the cheek and announces that it's time for him to relieve himself.

"Be back in a flash," he says, but I have a feeling that he's going to take a lot longer in the restroom than usual. He might even wander into the kitchen to talk to Nick Junior for awhile; maybe strike up a conversation with a few of the diners on his way back to the bar, or play guidance counselor to Derek.

"But I couldn't do it," she continues as if she hadn't been interrupted. "Jim and I were in love. You were conceived from that love, it felt so wrong to destroy something that love had created. Jim didn't want me to. And I—we, were Catholic at least back then, so that figured into the equation. We decided that I'd have you and our lives would go forward as planned."

Thinking about the weight of that decision, the sureness of it, the youthful optimism that life would go on without a hitch, I feel alternately respectful and unworthy.

"Jim's dad never did come around, he didn't believe that we could make it work—and of course he turned out to be correct. But for a while it did. My parents, your grandparents, did their best to help. They babysat during the day, watched you when I was doing homework. Dad, your granddad, loved you so much, Charlie. That was his name: Charlie. People would ask me if Charlie wasn't short for Charlotte, and I'd say 'no, her name's just Charlie. Her name is Charlie, she's named for her grandpa.'"

No tiramisu ever tasted as sweet.

Chapter 16

In hindsight, looking back two years ago I never should have told Sam in a phone conversation the night I got home from Martinelli's that I'd learned that Becky was my mother, which meant that Kevin wasn't a potential brother-in-law but was in fact, my biological brother. Needless to say, the denouement came as quite a shock, since up until that evening I'd never told Sam that I'd suspected I was adopted.

Dealing with Dad's illness, trying to make it through each day; wishing sometimes that on one of those days Dad wouldn't wake up in the morning and then feeling so guilty for thinking it that I could hardly look at my reflection in the mirror. I was carrying more than enough emotional baggage for one person. Perhaps I should have opened up to Sam sooner, should have relieved some of the burden I carried, but it never felt like the right time, there was never a moment when I thought: Ah, hah—today is the day that I confide in Sam. Today's the day that I tell him I'm not the person he thinks I am, that I'm really not his sister at all.

So Sam was unprepared for my revelations on many levels. It was evident in his voice, and as much as it hurt me to realize how much I'd hurt him, there was no taking the words back.

Perhaps if I hadn't been so excited, so eager to share my news. If I'd given myself more time to think about exactly how

I was going to tell him; if I'd only waited a few days, or even a week, until I saw him again. But, in the same way I'd spoken to Dad when I found the adoption papers in Maggie's bedroom, my emotions too quickly left my heart where they should have stayed buried and quiet, and took up residence in my mouth, where they took on life and sound, and hurt the ones I loved most. With Dad, the words my emotions breathed life into never should have been spoken; with Sam the words should have taken on a different tenor, and come at a different time. Figuring out the right timing is one of my shortcomings.

But I like to think that I've grown up quite a bit since the late Fall of 1987. I'm learning how to be an adult, finally, by behaving like one. Not that I always want to; it's so much safer, so much more comfortable, so much easier when you never have to change roles.

Moving from childhood to being a teenager isn't such a difficult transition. People expect certain behaviors at each of those life stages, and they react accordingly. When you're a child people expect you to perform silly, selfish, adorable acts, which they'll "ooh" and "ah" over and ask: "Have you ever seen a cuter kid in all your life?" And when you're a teenager those same people expect that you'll perform rather stupid, often selfish and frequently self-incriminating acts, which they'll shake their heads over and ask: "Teenagers—what are you gonna do?"

But transitioning from an older teen to adulthood—that's when everything gets complicated. Because people, even the people who love you, don't think you're adorable anymore and they don't think there's an excuse for your behavior. You no longer get a pass because now you're one of them. And you're expected to behave like them. You're expected to be responsible; to pay attention to other people's feelings; to stop thinking about yourself and what you want; to be aware of what you say and how you say it—filter always filter. To disguise your real feelings, if necessary, to avoid creating dissension; to understand the seriousness of not just your life, but life in general. To understand that life isn't easy and you just make it harder when you don't take on the role you refused to accept that you were auditioning for all along.

So, that's why I chose to tell Sam first, rather than Mom or Kevin, that I'm getting married. I told him last night, at his house, just the two of us; Peter was out of town at a conference. I arrived at 7:00 with a bottle of 92-point red; admired Peter's latest handiwork: a British elm dining room table (seating for twelve) that took him two years to design and build; marveled at Sam's new technologically-advanced leg that's so comfortable and so much like the one he lost that he declared he might start training to run a marathon; and when I knew that this time was the right time, I opened the bottle, poured each of us a glass and suggested we sit in the glass-walled sun room at the back of house, to watch the harvest moon admiring its golden face mirrored on the inky surface of the Detroit river.

"I've got some big news. I want you to be the first to know."

"Sid is retiring, finally, and he's letting you take over Book City? That would be great, with all the competition from Barnes and Noble, the only way that store will survive is to have someone young, with fresh ideas, running the place."

I chuckled and then sipped.

"No such luck. Ever since I started working there Sid has said that he's going out feet-first. And I must admit, the competition thing is proving to be good for business. Sid's looking out for our loyal customers, most of them have been buying their books there for twenty years. He's going to put in a coffee stand, near the back of the store so people can have a cup while they read. Don't count Sid out. No—my news has nothing to do with work. It's bigger than that. I'm getting married, Sam. Finally—I'm getting married."

Just saying those three words out loud, for the first time in my life, made me feel like I had finally attained a level of maturity equal to my time on earth, even if it wasn't necessarily true.

"Wow! Charlie, wow! That's great, great news. You know, Peter and I were just talking the other night about your personal life. I said that I've always felt bad that you had to leave California and move back here to take care of Dad. You were in love out there. I know that. What was his name? Larry or…?"

"Terry, his name was—well his name is, he's alive as far as I know. His name is Terry. And yeah, I loved him but that was a long time ago. A lot has happened since I came back."

"I never asked. I'm sorry that I never asked you about him." Sam's expression of remorse was heartfelt and real.

"You're forgiven, it's not that there wasn't anything going on in our lives at the time. Our relationship ended with a whimper. He finally stopped calling."

"What happened to him, do you ever hear anything?"

No chuckle and I gulped instead.

"Yeah. I heard. Last year Cindy told me that Terry married the daughter of a movie producer." My stomach flopped and twisted around like a fish that's been pulled onto a deck, the same way it had the day Cindy told me about the nuptials.

"And now you're the one getting married. So, who's the lucky guy? Tell me everything about him."

For the next several minutes Sam and I bantered back and forth, as I responded to his relentless questions, lobbed at me like snowballs being thrown by a rambunctious eighth-grader.

"So, what's his name?"

"Richard—don't ever call me Dick—Alexander."

A fine red spray exploded from Sam's nose.

"Oh, I love it. Really? Richard—don't ever call me Dick—Alexander. Did he tell you that the first time you met?"

"Yeah. He made it quite clear that being called Dick was something he wouldn't put up with."

"Well I'll certainly keep that in mind when I meet him. Where'd you two meet?"

"At Book City. He's been buying books there for years."

"When did you meet?"

"Six months ago."

Six months spoken out-loud hadn't sounded right. Marrying someone you'd known for just six months; it seemed needy and grasping. I'd felt a pang of desperation and a fleeting longing to be twenty years younger so I wouldn't have to be second-guessing grown-up decisions.

"He must have swept you off your feet I guess. That's good, that's good. What does Mr. "Don't Ever Call Me Dick" do for a living?"

Sam had clearly been enjoying himself. My decision to tell him first had been a wise one.

"He teaches at Wyandotte High School. Math. He's been there for almost eighteen years."

"Ah, a high school teacher. Might be part of the reason why he doesn't want to go by the shortened version of his name. Eighteen years, so he's a few years older than you?"

"He's forty. And yes, to answer the question that's coming next: he's been married before."

"Widowed, I hope not. Divorced then?"

"Divorced. It was tough on him. They'd been high school sweethearts and dated through college. They got married the day after graduation. But things didn't work out."

I had no intention of sharing more details about Richard's ill-fated marriage, thinking that Sam didn't need to know that my soon-to-be-husband's former spouse started having affairs only a few months after their honeymoon, several with men she met through her job as a stewardess, and one who was more familiar: Richard's best friend. Richard had cried as he told me how the enormity of the deception had been like a monstrous black hole that sucked him in and tore him to shreds, and as I'd listened and tried, unsuccessfully, to console him, I'd remembered Cindy's response to John's not too dissimilar deceit. Man is the much weaker sex, I'd thought at the time.

But Sam, perceptive as always, had readily accepted the short explanation and moved on.

"Does he have kids?"

"No, they were only married for a few years. Not long enough to have kids, I guess."

"Does he want them? Do you?"

"We haven't talked about it."

As soon as the words came out of my mouth I knew that I sounded foolish, naïve and maybe even a bit delusional.

"Don't you think you should?"

"Sure. We will, we will."

"When? Before the wedding, or after?"

I sensed that the look I gave him negated much of the goodwill I'd managed to restore in the preceding half-hour.

"Speaking of the wedding, we aren't going to have a big ceremony. I'll have you and Peter of course. And Mom and Kevin. I'm calling Cindy tomorrow to ask her if she'll stand-up for me. Maybe she'd like the break from the kids. Matt can stay with them in California and she can spend some quiet time with her mom and dad. I'll ask Sid and his wife and Daphne and her boyfriend and maybe one other person from Book City. Richard's Mom is coming, even though she's a staunch Catholic who's still trying to get over the fact that he's divorced from his first wife. His Dad died a few years ago. I'm not sure who else he wants to be there."

Sam looked tired, his smile vague and indifferent as if he was trying to recall an incident worth smiling about.

"When and where's this going to take place?"

"Soon, as in before the start of the holiday season. Early November at the Unitarian Church in Wyandotte, at least I think that's where it's happening. Richard's taking care of the ceremony part. I'm tasked with arranging for the dinner afterwards."

"Which will be at Martinelli's, am I right?"

"Well, yes. I mean, why not? Martinelli's has become the go-to spot to wine and dine our way through life's milestones—it only seems appropriate. Becky—Mom, hasn't been there for a couple years. She'd wanted to stop working at Martinelli's for a long time. She only stayed on when Dad bragged to her one night that his daughter Charlie was going to California to become a famous movie actress. She asked him to bring in a picture of me, and it was one of the ones taken on the front lawn, right after Dad and Maggie had adopted me. So, she continued to work a few nights a week, just so she could talk to Dad, to find out what I was up to. Of course he didn't have a lot to say since I didn't communicate with him at all and half the time what Dad told her didn't make any sense. She told me that he insisted that I'd been in *On the Waterfront* and *Best Years of Our Lives.* Once I finally found out who I was, who she was and Kevin—she was more than ready to head out the door. Waitressing isn't easy when you're pushing fifty."

It occurred to me that this was the first time I'd broached the subject of Mom's life when talking to Sam. For the past two years I'd felt guilty about saying too much. Sam had become the orphan, and I was the much-loved first child who'd been lost and then found.

Sam filled our glasses and looked at me straight on, not quite smiling but regarding me inquisitively as if I were someone he was meeting for the first time, someone he wasn't quite sure about but was willing to extend an opening to.

"We've never talked much about—Becky."

"Do you want to know?"

"Of course I do. If I'm going to be spending time with her at your wedding I should know pertinent details about her life. To me, she was always just the waitress at Martinelli's, the one who waited on Dad for years and was kind to us at his memorial. Who I thought was trying to fix you up with her son. It was my choice not to spend the last few holidays with you three; Becky, Kevin and you. I figured that you needed time with your mom and brother, to get to know them. For you I suppose that life has been strange, spending separate time with Becky and Kevin, and then time with Peter and me. Maybe it's time to enlarge and unite the two circles."

My heart fluttered and then soared—thinking about all of us: Sam, Peter, Mom, Kevin, Richard and me as one unit—a family with a conflicted past and a harmonious future. Not unlike all families.

"She's kind of a remarkable woman. No, not kind of—she *is* a remarkable woman."

"Tell me."

Up until then I hadn't had the opportunity to divulge much about my mother's life to anyone, not even Cindy. She and Matt haven't been back to the island since their engagement, raising their brood takes up all their time and money. Her parents, despite her father's feeble, and obvious disingenuous protestations, make the trek to California at least once a year instead. Cindy calls a few times a month, but from the moment I pick up the phone I can hear at least one child whining or crying in the background; our conversations seldom last longer than ten minutes, and more often than not consist of Cindy complaining about the kids passing around childhood diseases like pink-eye, asking about the weather in Michigan and gloating over the weather in California. And although Sid and Daphne are close friends, our work-time talk revolves around our fascination with, and respect for, a reading public who make best sellers out of works as diverse as *The Silence of the Lambs* and *A Brief History of Time*, in the same year.

Sam didn't ask any more questions; he let me speak almost without interruption. I explained to him how Mom and Jim had known ever since they were very young that they'd get married when they grew up. That Mom got pregnant with me when she was only sixteen and she had tried to keep me, even though Jim's father thought it was a terrible idea. How Mom's parents, my grandparents, had helped out, watched me while Mom was in school and babysat in the evenings when Mom was doing homework. But when my grandfather, Charlie, who I was named for, had a heart attack and became disabled, his wife had to take care of him, and it was all too much trying to take care of me, too, and so Mom gave me up for adoption when I was two months old.

"How hard that must have been, I can't even imagine" Sam said. I'd been grateful for the chance to draw breath and compose myself.

"Mom said that it was the hardest thing she ever had to do in her life, up until that point, anyway. Burying her husband was harder."

"I'm sorry, Charlie. I had a feeling that there was no longer a father in the picture, but he's dead—your dad. I'm sorry."

I'd felt then like the unluckiest daughter in the world. Losing two fathers: one who I never met, never got to know, and one who I finally came to know only as he was slowly fading away.

"He died in February of nineteen sixty-eight, in the Tet Offensive. He was a second lieutenant. He'd graduated from West Point, just like his dad. Kevin was eight when Jim died. So, Kevin remembers him—a little."

"Your mom must have lots of photos."

"Oh, yes. Yes. He was a gentle, sweet-faced man and little boy. His face was as sweet when he was ten as it was when he was twenty. Do you remember *The Man from U.N.C.L.E:* The TV show in the sixties? Jim looked like Robert Vaughn, the star, such a sweet, kind face. I wondered after I saw his photos how, like you, such a gentle man could have gone to Vietnam. Mom told me about how he used to pick flowers for her on the way home from school. He'd have a bunch of them in his hand and they'd be starting to wilt and he'd give them to her and say: 'for my princess.' I wondered if even though he knew that he had to kill people because the country was at war, he never reconciled it in his mind. It's what he was trained to do, but how does a man who gave flowers to his princess kill people?"

"He didn't want to kill anyone. None of us did. War turns everything we know about what's right and what's wrong upside down. The world as we know it loses all clarity. It's like you're living in a carnival fun house with the mirrors that bend everything into crazy distorted shapes. "

"Yeah, like a carnival fun house—without the fun. It was so hard for Mom after Jim died. I can't even imagine how hard it was. So hard that she told me once, when it was just the two of us together, that she had thought about killing herself. But then she realized how selfish that would be. She had Kevin; she had a son who she had to take care of. So, she went back to school. She enrolled at Wayne State and started working a few nights a week at Martinelli's."

The bottle emptied, Sam had gone to the kitchen to see if he could "rustle up some more red" and I stretched out on the sofa and watched as the glorious gold moon's twin visages grew smaller but no less bright—one inching higher above the horizon, the other a brilliant bright orb floating peacefully on the water.

Lying there I'd wondered who else was looking up at the same sky, at the same moon. Maybe someone on this side of the island or someone on the mainland, each of us seeing it from a slightly different perspective. And if I shifted my position, if I sat up or walked down to the river's edge, my perspective would be different too from what it was before I moved. If I shut my eyes, held them like that for a minute and opened them again, I'd see the moon and its reflection differently than I did five seconds before. I held my left hand up to the sky, then my right, blocking out the moon's face each time, and each time I took my hand away, something had changed. The change was nearly imperceptible, but it had happened. There had been change, and it happened with such subtlety that I didn't see it happen—but it did.

I woke this morning, still sprawled out on the sofa, empty wine glass on the floor.

"Morning, sunshine", Sam said as he brought me a mug filled with coffee. "By the time I came back with another bottle, you'd fallen asleep. You had such a sweet smile on your face. Now I know where that sweet smile comes from."

Chapter 17

Today is one of those Midwest in-between fall and winter days that make people long for a beautiful beach in the Caribbean or Florida. The sky's the color of skim milk, the brittle leaves that haven't yet blown off the trees are the color of old clay that's been drying for weeks, the sun's a pale pasty yellow circle that's barely distinguishable against the milky blue backdrop and the short tufts of brown grass on lawns appear to be begging to be smothered in white so they can get on with the business of dying.

It's chilly, not quite cold enough yet to wear a heavy winter coat but there's a crispness in the air that portends of frigid temperatures to come; the dynamic fall colors are a faded memory. These few weeks are like living in nature's waiting room, the place where nothing's happening while everyone waits for something more substantial and magical like the first snowfall. It's a limbo sort of time, so wishy-washy and bland that people can hardly wait for winter to come because at least winter makes a statement.

"I'm sure glad you didn't wait until it got really cold to get married," Cindy says as I pull out of the parking lot at Detroit Metropolitan Airport. "At least they're a few leaves left and the ground isn't covered in six inches of snow."

"Just for you, Cindy. Just for you." I grin as I step on the gas and merge the robin's egg blue 1967 Mercedes Benz 250SL onto the acceleration lane.

I bought the car a few months after Dad died, my gift to myself for all I'd been through. I toyed with the idea of buying a Mustang, or even a Corvette but instead I'd decided that it was my prerogative to purchase a classy German car. I no longer had to worry about Dad disapproving, and as I'd told Sam: "You can't argue with German engineering. Cindy still drives that VW she got when we graduated. Says she'll drive it until the wheels fall off, which will probably never happen."

"I doubt it but thanks, anyway. Amazing how your blood really does get thinned-out when you've lived somewhere warm for a long time. Can you believe it? Ten years, Charlie. It's been ten years since we left here and moved to California. So much has happened to us since then, it makes my head spin."

"Mine too. Not much has happened on the island though, it isn't much different from last time you were here, which was…"

"When Matt and I got engaged." Traffic is slowing to a crawl, there must be an accident on I-94 so I don't want to turn to look at her, but from the way Matt's name dissolves on her tongue like an afterthought, I sense that my head isn't going to stop spinning anytime soon.

"Yeah, that was some fun at your mom and dad's that night. Remember how drunk I got? Jeez, I could never do that now, and I wouldn't want to."

She doesn't respond and since we're stopped, there's nothing but brake lights ahead, I look over at her, first at her hands and then her face. The gold wedding band and huge diamond are still there, but Cindy's face is so expressionless that I wonder if she's suddenly gone into a trance, or maybe she's meditating.

"Cindy—what's going on?"

"I'm having an affair."

My thoughts explode into my brain like a carelessly placed stick of dynamite. *Are you kidding? Talk about upstaging my wedding. An affair. When do you have the time?*

I know I should filter what I say, should tread carefully, but Cindy and I go back way too long for me to worry about pissing her off.

"Did you plan on telling me before my wedding? So this is what I'll be thinking about when I repeat my vows? Fuck—Cindy. Really? You've got four kids for God's sake—where do you find time to screw someone other than your husband?"

Her laugh isn't something I expected, and even though it's shocking I find it oddly comforting.

You'll never change, Cindy. Who but you could laugh when you've just confessed that you're having an affair? And it is kind of funny, that last question I asked. It sounds like the line from a movie.

So I laugh too and we sit there the two of us, in a classy German import, surrounded by American cars, on a freeway winding through the heart of the Motor City, none of us going anywhere, laughing over the revelation that a mother of four who has been in love with only two men in her entire life is now having an affair, and her best friend since forever who has been with more men than the number of years she's lived on earth, is getting married for the first time in her life and is scared shitless about it because she knows she isn't in love, and we keep laughing until we're both crying and although I feel so sorry for the people up ahead who've been in an accident, I can't help but be a little grateful that it happened and I hope that no one is badly hurt, but we need time to just sit here a little longer.

"I need Kleenex." Cindy wipes her eyes with her fingers.

"There's some in the glove box. I need one, too."

Faces dried, we hear the high-pitched wail of a siren.

Damn! Why did I think what I did about the accident? I didn't mean it, I really didn't mean it. I'm going to feel like hell tomorrow if I read in the paper that someone died.

"I hope everyone's okay, hope nobody's hurt too bad up ahead." Cindy looks like she's ready to cry again but not from laughing too hard.

"I think they have to call an ambulance whenever there's an accident. You know, just to be safe. And maybe that's not an ambulance, it might just be a police car."

"That's true. Looks like we're gonna be here for a while though. I'm sure glad I peed before we left the airport."

"Me, too" I say, although just thinking that we might be stuck in the car for an indefinite length of time is beginning to put pressure on my bladder.

The police car screams past us on the shoulder.

"Lets hope that's it," Cindy says as she nods her head toward the window. "I guess you want details, huh? Sorry I sprung it on you like that. While I was in the plane I was trying to think of the best way, and the best time, to tell you."

"Details, yeah—that would be nice. First question: who? Second question: why?"

"A doctor in the kids' pediatrician's office. He's not their doctor. That wouldn't be cool."

"Not hardly."

"And why? 'Cause it's exciting."

"That's it? Because it's exciting? What's the most exciting part—the sex or the sneaking around?"

I'm being snarky and bitchy, and I don't care. This isn't how today was supposed to go. I don't know what to do with all of this, how do I process it?

"The sex: that's exciting. The sneaking around: that's scary and it makes me sad and I don't like it. Sneaking around—it hurts, it hurts." She starts to cry again: sad and guilty tears, real ones. Tears that show up without an introduction and can't be held back because they express what they mean and mean what they express.

I hand her my used Kleenex, it's just damp, hers is a balled-up wad of white no bigger than a marble, and the box is empty.

"Shit! I'm so sorry, Cindy. I'm sorry. I mean, with the kids and all and trying to pretend, keeping it a secret. I'm sorry."

She blows her nose and I wish that traffic would start moving.

"Do you love him?"

Cindy answers quickly so I know she's telling the truth.

"No, I don't love him. But until I met Carl I'd been with only two men in my life. And until I met Carl all I had to look forward to everyday was changing diapers, wiping snot off noses and vomit off chins, putting on Band-Aids, cleaning crayon drawings off cabinets, doing loads of laundry, fixing lunches that got smeared all over shirts and thrown against walls, trying not to yell and hoping for five minutes—just five minutes to put my feet up and close my eyes. Now—once a week—I have something else to look forward to. That keeps me sane."

We both turn our heads at the wailing sound; another police car flashes by.

"I'm a good mother, Charlie. I love my children. I'd die for them. I love everything about them, and I love that they love me back, unconditionally. I gave life to them and, at least for now, they need me. And I love that, too. But sometimes—sometimes the neediness becomes a terrible burden because you realize, after awhile, that they're innocent and pure and they need you because in their minds you're perfect, you're on this earth to give, give, give to them—but you're not perfect and there are times when you wish they weren't there, just for a little while and when you think that it makes you feel so guilty that you wish you could just spit it out like something rotten and spoiled…the guilt. But you can't."

She pauses and clicks her tongue against the back of her teeth.

"The thing is—when I'm with Carl, when I should be feeling guilty—I'm not. That's the crazy thing, Charlie. I'm not. Because when we're together all I'm thinking about is how I feel, how I feel right then. Because he tells me that I'm beautiful, stretch marks and all, and he makes love to me so sweetly that sometimes I think he thinks I'm going to break in two. And for that hour or two I know that I'm still Cindy, mother of four and wife, but I'm the one who's needy. I'm the one who needs taking care of. I'm the one who needs to hear that my saggy breasts are perfect—yeah, my breasts sag now, and that he hates to wash away my smell after we've made love. I'm the one who's getting her needs met—and it feels so good, it feels so damn good, to be the one being given to, rather than the one doing all the giving."

I'd turned the volume on the radio half-way down when we started talking, but the muffled static-like noise filling the air is annoying, so I reach out, turn the knob to the right, and have to stifle a giggle when I hear… *if you don't know me by now…*

Perfect timing. Whoever penned those lyrics had it right: we never really know anyone, do we? Not even people we've known most of our lives.

"I understand, Cindy. I understand."

Of course I don't understand—I don't understand at all but this is what a best friend says.

The cars in front of us begin to move and Cindy isn't crying anymore and suddenly, for just a few seconds, one bright beam of sunlight pierces through the gray overhead.

Chapter 18

"His first wife, Sandra, she was a lovely woman. You know, they were together for many years before they married. All through high school and then college, those two. They were the perfect couple. And when they did get married—they did it in the church—the Catholic Church. You know, he was an altar boy for many years. Many years. A good Catholic boy."

My new husband's mother and I were introduced only half-an-hour ago. Gertrude didn't make it to the ceremony, but she showed up at Martinelli's very shortly after the wedding party did, and in the last thirty minutes since arriving she's drank almost an entire bottle of Cabernet by herself. Richard had warned me: "Mom has a mind of her own and she isn't afraid to say what she thinks."

"He's such a good boy. He was always such a good boy. And that Sandra, the two of them together, you should have seen them. Well—I'm sorry—I guess I shouldn't be telling you that, should I? You're the new one, after all. I never thought a son of mine would get divorced. No son of mine. I should be a grandmother by now. They would have had such beautiful babies. He's forty now, you know. It's well past time for him to have sired children, well past time. His father was only twenty-one. Twenty-one, and now his son is forty already without a child of his own and getting married again. In a Unitarian Church. His father is rolling over in his grave. I know it—he's rolling over."

I chuckle a little as I think: rolling over where he is now is probably preferable to rolling over and finding you lying next to him in bed. And why haven't you said Richard's name once since you've been talking about him? He does have a name. What's with all the pronouns?

"I'm sure you would have been a wonderful grandmother to Richard's child," I say his name so loudly that Richard, who's standing at least ten-feet away talking to Sam and Peter, looks over at me and waves. "You know, I really need to talk to some more people so I'm going to leave you now. I think we have a few more bottles of Cabernet, but you might have to switch from an Italian to one from California. Enjoy the evening, Gertrude."

Did you notice the way I used two proper nouns in the last ten seconds? It can be done. And I'll have a little discussion with Derek. You're cut-off from the good stuff, Gertrude.

"Well, I just barely got here. I'm your mother-in-law you know. You shouldn't just walk off and leave me. I don't know anyone. Sandra always entertained me. I don't know why Dick ever let her get away."

Hah! And there's the reason he never wants to be called Dick.

"...It used to be called *Girl Talk,* but I finally got them to change it to *Woman Talk,* which I'm still not enamored with but it's better than the reference to a female child under the age of sixteen. Maybe because I was pregnant when I was sixteen, I've always believed that once a girl reaches that age she's a woman."

Mom is leaning in toward Cindy, speaking softly as if she's sharing a secret. They're engaged in a typical 'wedding reception, meeting someone for the first time conversation.' Cindy asked Mom what she does for a living and now Mom's giving her the lowdown.

"Mind if I join you?" I say as I plop myself down in a chair on the other side of the table.

"Charlie, your mom was just telling me about her newspaper column. That's so cool. So much creative talent in your family, mom's a writer and your brother's a professor of comparative literature no less. Wow! Good genes, you're working with some good genes, girl."

"Yeah," I respond and look over my shoulder to make sure that Sam's too far away to have heard her. "Definitely some creative genes at work, that's for sure. Explains why I always wanted to be an actress, or if that didn't pan out, a writer."

"She's got the talent for writing, my girl. And she just may get her chance. Do you want to tell Cindy about our foundation, or can I? I'm so excited about it. Kevin's the only one who knows besides you and me. We just have to tell someone else. Who better than your best friend since you were kids?"

Mom's doing her usual babbling, which never ceases to amuse me while simultaneously reminding me that I'm one half of a doppelganger.

"Why don't you start Mom and if I think you've missed anything, I'll jump in."

Turning toward Cindy Mom holds her hands together as if she's either about to say a prayer or begin a game of paddy-cake.

"Well, as you may have guessed I'm not getting rich writing a column on women's issues for *The Detroit Free Press.* I mean not that I ever wanted to be rich, that was never one of my goals. But ever since Jerry's mother died—I've been sort of rich."

Cindy raises an eyebrow, then her wineglass and tilts it toward Mom.

"A toast: to being rich even if you never wanted to."

Mom's rosy cheeks (I've encouraged her to wear just blush rather than foundation because her skin is so lovely and foundation settles into the few creases and lines she does have) bloom even rosier, and the redness spreads out and down, all the way to the square neckline of her deep green satin dress. Her tell has always been the color of her facial skin as it deepens—her sympathetic nervous system on full-bore.

"Oh, Cindy, you embarrass me. Honestly, I'm embarrassed about money. My family didn't have a lot when I was growing up and now that I have it, it makes me feel sometimes like I'm a stranger to myself. Does that make sense? But, what the hell? Yes, I'm—we're going to do good things with it, aren't we, Charlie?" She raises her glass to meet Cindy's, they clink their glasses together, from across the table I raise mine, and Mom takes a deep sip and an even deeper breath.

Sweet mother of mine, you're only warming up. The stage is yours.

"Alice, Charlie's paternal grandmother, left Kevin and I quite a bit of money, which she inherited from her husband Larry. Charlie's grandfather invested wisely over the years. He had his military retirement and then another retirement from General Motors, but those two income sources paled in comparison to the wealth he amassed over the years in stocks and bonds. When Alice died, everything went to us."

Richard is waving at me again, and motioning me over. He's still talking to Sam and Peter, the three of them standing in a semi-circle, with Richard occupying the midpoint of the arc.

My God, he is short isn't he? It's so obvious seeing him standing there like that, with Peter and Sam on either side like bookends flanking one very pint-sized book.

Not that Richard's shortness was an issue when we met, he's at least four inches taller than me and he dresses in more tailored simple (rather bland) clothing, no wild patterns, not even his ties; nothing to call attention to himself and his lack of manly tallness. In fact, nothing was an issue when we met because he came into Book City ten times, ten times when he deliberately sought me out and asked me specific questions about specific books, ten times that I met him and the moment he walked out the door he was gone from my mind as well as my sight. Richard 'Don't Ever Call Me Dick' Alexander made no impression on me at all those ten times, so his lack of height wasn't relevant.

When he'd finally mustered up the courage to ask me if I wanted to "...Have a cup of coffee sometime, or maybe even a drink?" I noticed, finally, that he wasn't a tall man, but since I'm not a tall woman and I'd decided within five seconds after he opened his mouth to agree to go for coffee, figuring that an hour conversation over a cup of java would be the first and last time I'd ever see him again, his lack of height just didn't matter, and besides we'd be sitting, anyway.

But somehow, by some inexplicable means, he'd managed to charm me over a large latte, and coffee meet-ups led to a glass of wine after work, which led to our first dinner together and that dinner led to another dinner and after two months of spending two evenings a week eating a meal at a local upscale restaurant, we'd ended up in his large four-poster bed in the rather tiny bedroom of his circa 1925 house on Riverside Drive in Trenton.

It hadn't been bad: the sex. But it wasn't exactly stellar, either. Still, it had been so long since I'd slept with anyone that I'd welcomed the opportunity to just make sure that I could still feel something. I had, but not as much as I inadvertently led Richard to believe. After he'd climaxed, I hadn't, but at least he'd taken his time getting there and the foreplay had lasted long enough that I had believed for a minute or two that I might actually have an orgasm, I'd begun to cry.

"Oh, what's this my sweet girl. What's this? Tears? My darling, my sweet girl—tears."

Good god, I'd thought. He thinks he's such a wonderful lover that he's made me cry. Why do men make such a big deal out of that: making a woman cry? We cry for all sorts of reasons and sometimes, but not often, we cry because making love is such a transcendent experience that we feel like we are truly one, one person with the person we're making love to. I cried with Terry more than once. But this, with Richard, wasn't one of those times. The difference is as distinct as an oasis and the desert that surrounds it. I was only crying because it was a release, a release of all the tension and anxiety and pain and guilt and sadness I've been holding onto for a long time. That's all it was, strictly physical, no emotion involved.

But now I'm married to him, the prematurely graying, brown-eyed and blue-eyed (heterochromia being an 'interesting gift' he'd explained on our first coffee date, "I'm the David Bowie of Wyandotte High School), fit for his age (he plays tennis and golf in the summer and skis in the winter) high school math teacher who wants to take me to the Greek Isles on a 'real honeymoon' when school's out for winter break and who always makes me feel loved but not enough, never enough, to make me cry ever again.

"Excuse me for a minute while I go talk to my husband."

The two words feel soft and squishy and more than a little unreal.

"I'll be right back. Don't finish up this conversation until I can be in on it," I say to Mom and Cindy.

As I walk toward him I wonder: he surely doesn't want to leave already, does he? God, I hope not.

He does though. I watch with some embarrassment as Richard abruptly marches away from Sam and Peter mid-conversation (a social faux pas I've seen him exhibit on more than one occasion, unfortunately Richard's attention span sometimes mimics his leg height), takes ahold of my arm when we meet and whispers in my ear:

"Ready to go, my sweet girl? I've arranged for champagne and caviar at the Westin."

No, not really. Does everyone who just got married get this same feeling of what the hell did I just do?

"Richard, it's early yet. It's not even nine. I was in the middle of a conversation with Mom and Cindy that I'd like to get back to. Cindy and I haven't seen each other in a long time. Can we stay just a little longer?"

God! I sound like a child, begging like that.

"Of course we can stay longer. We have the rest of the night and the night after that and the night after that..." Richard's high cheekbones widen across his face as his lips turn upward into what I know he hopes is a sexy but to me seems silly, smile. "And then in a few weeks we'll be sailing the seas around Greece. Just think. You and me and all those Greek nights."

I am thinking about it, and I'm thinking that some life decisions are better left undecided. Not deciding, inaction is a decision in and of itself. One that could lead to different, perhaps better outcomes. I need to keep that in mind in the future.

Chapter 19

Richard and I never made it to the Greek Isles. The closest we got to Greece was last weekend after we'd left the hospital; we had dinner in Greektown. Winter break began on Friday the fifteenth of December; we were supposed to fly to New York City on Saturday and then on to Greece Monday morning. Monday morning two weeks ago.

"We'll spend Saturday night in the Big Apple. There's a wonderful little Italian restaurant off the beaten path I want to take you to. Sandra and I used to go there whenever we were in the city," he'd said as he was planning the trip.

Knowing that he wanted to begin our honeymoon by going to a favorite restaurant haunted by the memories of an unfaithful spouse (I presumed he'd want us to order the same wine they always drank, the same pasta they always ate) I'd felt sad, disregarded and non-committal all at the same time. The non-committal reaction was the strongest of the three. I knew I should tell him that I would prefer we go somewhere else, but the more he mentioned it, the less I cared.

How appropriate, I'd thought. Starting off a marriage that's being entered into for reasons that neither one of us can explain, or justify, by having dinner at a place where the promiscuous ex-wife's name will be spoken more often than grazie.

But I'll never know how wonderful the spaghetti carbonara is there, or how much Sandra loved the cannoli. Saturday morning two weeks ago, Gertrude had a heart attack. He got the call at 5:00, thirty minutes before we were to leave for the airport. Richard's face went white, entirely white, blanched like a piece of leather that had been lying out in the desert sun for months. And I'd thought that I'd been treated indifferently earlier, in less than a minute I was downgraded from co-star to background actor.

Gertrude's coming home today—to our home. She's been in the hospital for sixteen days and, according to her doctors, she can't live alone, at least not for the foreseeable future.

"It's going to be fine, my sweet girl. It's going to be fine," Richard says as we back out of the garage. In the last few days, since he's realized that Gertrude will survive, 'sweet girl' has crept back into his speech. He's more attentive, more like the Richard of old. Mom's starring role seems to be coming to an end, and I may get a shot at stepping in. I wish I were more excited about it.

"She'll stay downstairs in the room off the living room; she can use the add-on bathroom down there. So you don't have to worry that she'll be living on the same floor as our bedroom." He puts his hand on my thigh and squeezes tight.

"Oh, that's good," I murmur.

"You're being so wonderful about this, sweet girl. So wonderful, and so understanding. It's perfect, having that parlor where she can live. She may be my mother but I sure don't want her sleeping in the room next to us. I draw the line at that, because as soon as we get her back here and all squared-away, I want us to start working on making a baby. I know I've been inattentive lately but with Mom being in the hospital I couldn't focus on her *and* us. Now I can. Mom's going to love being a grandmother."

Stop the car! I want to get out. And when I get out I'm going to run away just as fast and as far as I can.

"Wow, Richard. That came out of the blue. We've been married only six weeks."

Yeah, we should have talked about this before but we didn't. So you really think this is a good time to bring it up? On the way to the hospital to pick up your domineering, obnoxious, narrow-minded mother who's going to be living with us until she dies?

"Well, I know that of course. And maybe we should have talked about this earlier. But I kind of figured, you know, that you'd be ready by now. I mean—you're over thirty and your best friend has a bunch of kids and I'm forty and there's really no point in waiting—is there?"

We're a block from the hospital. I need to push this conversation off for another time.

"With your mom living with us, things have changed some, don't you think? We need to think about her needs, at least for a while. She'll require a lot of attention. Let's give it a few months before we talk about it again. Deal?"

He squeezes my thigh again so tightly that I squirm and let out an exasperated: "Ouch."

"Sorry, sorry—I didn't mean to hurt you. But you're just so understanding about everything, I know I'm repeating myself, but you are. You're just so wonderful, Charlie. We'll wait until spring to talk about a baby again."

And as he pulls the car into the visitor's lot I think:

That's the first time he's spoken my name out loud since we said our vows.

Chapter 20

"So do you think I should change anything in the mission statement?"

I've finished my rigatoni but Mom's dawdling over hers. She'll probably take most of it home; lately she's been complaining about the narrow belt of fat that's attached itself around her hips.

("Seriously, Charlie. Wait until you're my age. I swear, all I have to do is walk by the freezer at the grocery and all the calories in the containers of chocolate ice cream somehow fly out and attach themselves to my waistline.")

"No, you don't need to change anything. It's perfect. I love it. "Mom pokes at the rapidly congealing pasta on her plate, then moves a few squares from one side to the other as if all they need is a change in location to become more appetizing and less fattening.

"Ladies, can I interest you in another glass of wine?" Derek flashes his straight, glinting white teeth at us as he deftly swipes my plate off the table, glances at Mom's, and raises an eyebrow when he looks back at her. "I take it Becky you'd like a carry-out container?"

Derek was promoted to waiter several weeks ago, and those of us who knew him in his earlier role as a bartender are pleased with how well he's doing in his new role. He's much more animated now, tossing off glib bon mots and one-liners as he works the room delivering dishes piled high with spaghetti and meatballs, sometimes stopping to pat the top of a child's head as he tells him or her a silly joke, while simultaneously filling the parents' wine glasses from a bottle held in the other hand.

Observing his transformation, it came as no surprise to Mom and me to learn that Derek's under-graduate degree is in early childhood education. He teaches at a Montessori preschool; for the last year and-a-half he's been working toward a second degree in child psychology, and he told us at this year's New Year's Eve party (while masterfully juggling a tray covered with champagne glasses) that he's going to a clown camp in Wisconsin for a few days this summer: "For the experience you know, I mean, what could be more fun than spending your day learning how to clown around?"

"Sure, we'll have another and yes, I'm going to need a take-out box. And Derek, when you come back I want to run something by you, get your opinion on the mission statement we've come up with," Mom says as she nods at me while he removes her plate.

The foundation, thank heaven for the foundation. The time required to birth 'Play Time, Changing Lives Through Art' into being takes up the majority of my non-sleeping hours. Between working at Book City; meetings with our attorney to discuss particulars about setting up a non-profit; meetings with Mom at Martinelli's to talk about the mission statement, the vision statement, the ways the foundation will positively impact so many young lives, there isn't much time left for me to coddle or entertain Gertrude. Play Time's already having a positive impact on my life.

My grandmother, Alice would be proud. Mom reminds me of that fact nearly every time we meet. Alice had wanted to have another baby within a year after my dad's birth, but although she tried well into her late thirties to get pregnant again, Jim would forever be an only child.

It was Alice's love for children and her inability to have the large family she'd always dreamed of that drew her to volunteering at a homeless shelter in Detroit; which led to her organizing fund-raisers to raise money to give the resident children gifts at Christmas and on their birthdays; which led to her creating a team of women who regularly took small groups of kids to the downtown library or the Fisher Theater; which led to her setting up a separate trust fund to be managed by Mom that would be for the sole purpose of funding a foundation to provide a creative outlet, primarily acting and writing, for disadvantaged children within the Detroit city limits.

Children would be encouraged to write, cast and direct plays about their lives, nothing being off-limits. If a child's parents drank too much or were using drugs, or if the child was experiencing psychological or physical abuse at home, writing about it and then acting it out would serve as a vehicle for him or her to, hopefully, work through some of the pain and come to an understanding that he or she wasn't alone in facing life situations that could seem unbearable, unbelievable and unrelenting.

"Just the writing it down, putting it on paper and then taking that to the stage and acting it out, can help a child feel that she's understood. That someone else sharing the same stage is going through the same thing, that someone sitting in the audience is thinking: *yes that happens in my family, too*—what a difference that will make for these kids. Knowing that they're not alone" is the way Mom first described the foundation to me. "Those were the words your grandmother used when she told me about her vision. I was hooked immediately." As was I.

I'm sitting facing the front door, so I see Richard first, striding across the room as if he's approaching a lectern, preparing to belt out instructions for the most difficult algebra test in high school history. When I wave my three middle fingers, Mom turns to look at him and before he reaches our table I see her smile fade.

"What are you doing here?" He isn't screaming, but the decibel level is just high enough to make a few of the diners seated near us look our way.

"Hi, Richard. What do you mean, what am I doing here? Mom and I are obviously having dinner. We're talking about 'Play Time'. I've been working on the mission statement."

"Why aren't you at home with my mom? You knew I had after-school meetings tonight." Although he isn't speaking any louder, the ferocity in his eyes makes me wish that he would just go ahead and yell. I'd prefer his anger not go unvented for much longer.

"Richard, you know that Mom and I have dinner together every Tuesday night, this isn't a big surprise. You might have mentioned that you had a meeting tonight, I don't remember. But really—your mom isn't an invalid. She's not bedridden; she seems to be getting along quite well, actually. She's been living with us for almost a year now and I have to tell you, she doesn't seem to be all that sick to me. Not anymore."

In an instant Richard deflates, all the fire and fight drains out of him and, as if on cue, Derek appears with a bottle of wine, displays his orthodontic masterpiece and says: "Oh, Mr. Alexander, so good to see you. Your wife and mother-in-law were just going to have another glass of wine, and perhaps some dessert. May I pour a glass for you, too?"

Richard stares at me, then at Mom and back to me again, looking at us as if we're two strangers who've shown up at the front door, claiming to be sisters who he hasn't seen in years, which is odd because he doesn't have siblings.

"No, no, thank you. I don't need any wine. I'm going back to the house now. I'll see *you* there later then," he says, his bi-colored eyes staring into mine, and for one brief second I sense his desperation, his need, but it flickers out as he turns and walks away.

"Thanks, Derek. I'll pour the wine. And the couple seated at the booth in the corner behind you are trying to get your attention," Mom says as she shoos him away, and whispers to me: "We'll get his opinion on the mission statement later."

I'm not sure if I should be relieved or concerned that we're going to talk about what just happened.

Mom's never asked outright but she knows that this marriage wasn't exactly conceived in heaven. What do I tell her when she asks questions that I don't know the answers to myself?

"Things aren't going well—are they?"

Bam! Right out of the box. At least this one I know the answer to.

"No, not especially with his mom living with us. She's been there for ten months now. She's not easy."

"I seem to remember that she didn't show up for the ceremony, right?"

"Right. Couldn't seem to get herself together in time to make it. But she did manage to make it here. I know Derek remembers her. She berated him for pouring her cheap wine."

"So, Mom's not a gem—I get that. What about you and Richard? If you could take Mom out of the equation, and one of these days she will be one way or another, how do the two of you look?"

Shit! Now's when I'm going to start looking like the fool that I am. The questions only get tougher from here on.

"We're...we're..."

"You're what? Happy. Not happy. Still in the honeymoon phase. Already wishing you'd never gotten married. Two out of four, maybe? But which two?"

"You missed your calling, Mom. You should have been a prosecuting attorney."

"Just asking, sweetheart."

"Two out of four. And the least appealing of the four," I answer, and slowly sip my wine.

Her blue-gray eyes narrow and she nibbles at the inside of her left cheek. "You made a big mistake, didn't you Charlie?"

I feel like I'm in fourth grade, being scolded by my teacher. "Charlie, you were wrong to smear paste on the floor so Eddie would step in it, weren't you?"

But who am I supposed to apologize to this time? Myself?

"I did, Mom. I—we—we made a mistake."

But I feel like screaming: it isn't all my fault. I'm not taking all the blame. He wanted to get married, and heaven help me, he wants to have a kid. A baby. He wants us to make a baby. 'Make a baby.' God—I hate that phrase. I hate that damn phrase. It still makes me feel like I'm in elementary school. Sorry, Mr. Alexander, can't make a baby today. Forgot to bring all my materials for paper mache. No baby-making today. Can't even draw one, I broke all my crayons.

"Mistakes aren't the end of the world, Charlie. We all make them. We wouldn't be human if we didn't. That's the beauty of being sentient creatures, we feel. And when we feel that something is wrong, that we've done something that we shouldn't have, we have the ability to make it right. We have that choice as humans. We can stay or we can let go and move on, make a change. It's our choice."

"He wants us to have a kid. He's been bugging me about it for months. I'm lying to him, Mom. I lie to him every single night when we go to bed because even though he doesn't ask, I know that he thinks I went off the pill not long after Gertrude came to live with us. I never did. I never went off the pill. I never will. Not as long as I'm with him, anyway."

Mom smiles, and doesn't look at me as she begins spooning cold rigatoni into a Styrofoam box.

"It sounds to me like you've already started to let go."

I smile back, even though she doesn't see it and take another sip of wine.

Chapter 21

Luckily Richard chose a public space to tell me the news that he's going to be a father. If he had told me at the house, if we were sitting on the sofa now rather than across from each other in a booth at Martinelli's, I wouldn't have the luxury of being able to pinch my thighs under the table in order to maintain a pained expression on my face.

He's crying again, which forces me to apply a little more pressure to my right leg. His blubbering is both remarkable in its honesty and repellent for the same reason.

"I'm—I'm s, s, so sorry. So, s, so sorry."

"I know you are."

"B, b, but the thing is—the thing is—I, I knew that it wasn't you. It wasn't y, y, your fault we couldn't have a b, b, baby."

If you can't get through this without stammering over every other word, we'll be here all night.

As if he read my mind, Richard dries his wet face with a napkin and then vigorously blows his nose.

"After Mom moved into the assisted living facility we really tried—didn't we?"

Oh, yes we certainly did. I could draw a perfect rendering of the bedroom ceiling. I know where every crack is. Where it looks like a shingle might have come loose on the roof and some water's leaked in.

"I had such high hopes. But after three years I knew that it had to be me. You told me that the doctor said you were fine. I knew it had to be me."

I so want to say: "So that's why you decided, 'What the hell', I might as well go ahead and fuck someone else".

I under-estimated you. You surprise me and I thank you for it.

But now's not the time to act grateful. I need to play the role of the deceived wife. I pinch a little harder this time.

"Who is she, Richard?"

"A former student."

Well of course she's a former student. We've now veered off into soap opera territory.

"As in how former? She's not a freshman in college, is she?"

He stares at me, his mouth hanging open as if he's trying to piece together a jigsaw puzzle depicting a black circle, cut into ten thousand pieces, then his lips form a wide 'O'.

"Oh my God! No, no—she's been out of college for two years now. She teaches at a junior high in Bloomfield Hills, but lives downriver. She can't afford to live where she teaches."

"I take it you two kept in touch after she graduated from high school?"

"Yes. She got in touch with me after her first semester at Michigan State. She told me that it was because of me that she learned to love math. And it was because of me that she decided she wanted to be a teacher. Because of me."

Looking at Richard's face I feel a rush of conflicting emotions cascading over me: sadness, guilt, regret, pity, joy and relief. I pull my hands out from under the table and place his sweating palms against mine. He doesn't move for a few seconds and then our fingers intertwine.

"Richard, I forgive you. I know I've been distant for a long time now. The foundation takes up so much of my time, between that and managing Book City since Sid died, I haven't been a very attentive wife. I'm sorry for that."

I could burst out crying right now and I could burst into song and start dancing around the room. I'd sing that song they play on the oldies station: "Two Face Have I."

"Do you want to see a picture of her?" Richard asks, pulling his hands from mine and reaching into his back pocket.

I force myself to keep from laughing and give my thigh another quick pinch.

Richard retrieves his old, very worn brown leather wallet (the new one I bought him for Christmas two years ago sits unused in his upper dresser drawer), reaches into the side pocket that holds cash, pulls out a photograph and places it in my hand. His soft smile suggests that we're sharing in some sort of transfiguring moment, that the photo is a magic amulet that will change both of our lives.

The pale, yellow-haired, green-eyed woman smiling shyly at me as if she has a secret that she'll never share, at least not unless she's coaxed for a minute or two, looks familiar. It doesn't take long for Richard to jog my memory.

"She looks a lot like Sandra, doesn't she?"

If I remember nothing else about the past nearly five years I've spent with you, I'll always remember how naively inept you were at understanding anyone's feelings other than your own.

"Yeah, she does. She looks quite a bit like Sandra. At least from what I remember Sandra looking like. You did show me quite a few photos of her, of Sandra. Yeah, this girl—this woman, does look like her. What's her name?"

"Debbie. Well, Deborah, actually. But everyone, including me, calls her Debbie."

"Debbie, and even Deborah, those are both very nice names. So, you want a divorce so you two can get married before the baby comes, right?"

"Well—yes. Yes, that's what I want. My sweet girl, you're so understanding. Debbie was worried. She was so worried that you'd be really angry and you'd create a scene and you'd say that you were never ever going to divorce me and everything would be a mess. And I kept telling her no. Not Charlie. She's not like that. Charlie will understand."

Congratulations, Richard. I believe those were the fifth and sixth times you said my name out-loud since we met.

"Of course we'll get a divorce. I want this baby to be born into a two-parent family. He, or she, needs to start out right, with a mom and a dad and grandparents, too. I'm guessing that Debbie's parents are still alive?"

"Yes, they're very happy about this. And of course my mother. My mother is overjoyed. Over the moon as she likes to say. She's over the moon."

"They all know?"

"Well—yes. I mean—Debbie's parents think that I'm already divorced. They think I've been divorced for awhile."

Five seconds of silence stretches out like an invisible net ready to capture anything reasonable that might be said in the next few minutes and send the words off to be slaughtered.

"As in how long?"

"Years," the word pops out of his mouth as easily as spitting out a piece of gum.

"Years. Many years? Years longer than you and I've even been married? Debbie's parents don't even know about me, do they? The only marriage they know about is the one to Sandra, am I right?"

Richard's shiny innocent 'Aren't I still a good little boy' smile has faded; it's been replaced by a puzzled, but still 'little boy' frown. "You're right. We, Debbie and I, thought it would be better if they didn't know that I'd been married twice. I guess we'd prefer that they never find out."

Good lord, Richard. You're the most obtuse person I've ever known. Ironic considering you teach math.

"I wouldn't worry about that, they'll never find out from me. And your mom— has she known all along? About the affair I mean?"

Why did I bother asking that question? I know what the answer's going to be.

"She's known for a while. You know that Mom…"

"Never liked me. Never liked me from the very beginning because I wasn't Sandra. And when it turned out that I couldn't get pregnant, she liked me even less, if that's even possible. Isn't that what you were going to say?"

Shit! He's crying again. Lets just put this to bed now. I have to get out of here.

"Richard, I'll meet with my attorney tomorrow. I should be the one to file since you're the one who had the affair. What I'd like to happen now is for you to stay here for another forty-five minutes or so. Give me time to go to the house to pick up my personal stuff. I'll stay with Sam and Peter until I can figure out where I want to live. We'll talk again in a few days. How does that sound?"

On the way to the island I start to think about Terry. Maybe it's because there are two boxes and a suitcase in the trunk filled with toiletries, underwear and three days worth of clothing, reminding me of how little-by-little, one toothbrush, box of tampons and one pair of jeans at a time, I moved into Terry's world. I haven't thought about him for a long time, at least not while doing something as mundane as driving. But I'd often thought of Terry when Richard was on top of me.

What if? What if Dad hadn't gotten sick? What if he hadn't gone to war? Did he get dementia because of what happened to him there? Or did Maggie's leaving destroy his mind? Did he get sick because of what happened to Sam? Did his guilt make him go mad? Or would his mind have left him anyway? But he wasn't my real dad. So what if someone else had adopted me? What if a nice normal loving couple had adopted me and they'd stayed together and even if he had gotten sick she, being the wonderful wife that she was, would have taken care of him? What if when I left the island I only came back to spend holidays with my loving parents? And what if one of those holidays I'd brought Terry home and we'd announced our engagement and then had a big wedding and now I'd be a mother? But—if someone else had adopted me, I wouldn't be the person I am today. Maybe someone would have adopted me who lived in a completely different state. Then what would have happened? Where would I be now? Who would I be now?

The quotation: "You cannot step into the same river twice, for other waters are continually flowing on," suddenly comes to mind and I pull off to the side of the road. I'm only a block from Sam's house but there's no rush in my getting there. I know it will make a difference, ultimately, if I arrive in three minutes, or if I show up in three days, but there's nothing I can do about it because that's the way life is. Life isn't bounded by parameters of time—time is like a liquid flowing through a sieve. Sometimes the holes are bigger, sometimes they're smaller but eventually time flows through them, and when it does, everything changes again.

So my decision to stop is already shaping and changing my future but that isn't something that I can dwell on, because time will continue to flow—and right now I need to cry.

Chapter 22

I turned forty less than a month ago. Turning forty is one of life's benchmarks that's simultaneously incomprehensible and so not unexpected, that I laugh whenever I catch a glimpse of myself in a mirror and think 'you don't look a day over thirty', followed by 'so why the hell does forty seem so much older'?

Perhaps it's because I have to assume that at forty, unlike thirty, my lifespan is now halved. Ten years makes such a difference when considered in the timeframe of the entirety of one's life. Ten years seems like, and is, a very long time. A very long time that passes very quickly, and when it's passed, when you've transitioned through your thirties and you realize that you're at the midpoint of the time you have left you're faced with the reality of being in a new role—a role that arrives bearing a moniker that people often find distressing, depressing and even frightening—middle-age.

Or maybe it's just me who feels that way. When we talk Cindy never mentions her age, and she turned forty a month before me. But Cindy has a lot going on in her life. The kids are all in school; she's got parent/teacher conferences and piano lessons and football practice; and they have two dogs, one of whom got hit by a truck last year and had to have one of its legs amputated; so there's all that to deal with. And she stopped seeing Carl about the same time as the dog got hurt, which is something that we've talked about very little other than her telling me the affair was over, so I don't know if she thought that it was time she settled down and behaved like a middle-aged mother is supposed to and that's why she ended it. I think that might be the reason, but she hasn't said why, so it's just a guess.

It's not like my life isn't busy, and full. Mom tells me that often, and she made a point of reminding me when all of us got together at Sam and Peter's three weeks ago Saturday to celebrate my descent into darkness, which is what I half-jokingly referred to my birthday as, before she made quite the fervent point of setting me straight.

"Descent into darkness?" she growled at me and gnawed ferociously at the inside of the softest part of her cheek. "Charlie, that's not in the least bit funny. I know you're trying to be funny because you think that turning forty is some kind of disaster that there's no escaping from, but really, it isn't funny. You're forty. You're forty now, you're maturing and your life is so full. You're so lucky. Descent into darkness, my ass!" and everyone at the table had laughed, particularly Alyssa, Kevin's daughter who giggled rather than laughed, as five-year-olds do and then blurted out:

"Grandma said a baddie! Grandma said a baddie!"

"I'm going to take Alyssa out for a short walk before it gets too dark and cold. Come, Alyssa, let's get your coat and hat on, sweetie," my sister-in-law Janet said as she picked her daughter up off the chair, and the two of them wandered into Sam and Peter's wood-paneled living room to search for Alyssa's outerwear and coax the men's arthritic nearly blind golden retriever, Elton, into joining them on their excursion.

"Well, I do find descent into darkness a little amusing," Kevin said but followed it with: "However, all hyperbole aside,

I have to agree with Mom that things are going pretty damn well for you."

"That's because you've got three years before you'll find yourself looking into the face of the abyss," I countered. "Come on Sam, Peter. Back me up guys, please. You've been here. Didn't forty feel a whole hell of a lot older than thirty? I mean—this is middle-age for god's sake!"

Peter spoke first: "And where, my dearest, did you get the idea that forty is middle-aged?"

"Well, first. I don't think you've ever referred to me as "my dearest", not once ever before. So, there you go, that's proof right there. "My dearest"—what kind of salutation is that? One reserved strictly for middle-aged women! And, I looked up the definition in Merriman-Webster. Middle age, the years spanning forty-to-sixty. Proof enough for me."

Peter faked a crestfallen expression; he rolled his lower lip out, narrowed his eyes, then reached over and gently punched my forearm. "I was being facetious, an attempt, obviously a poor one, at humor. Of course I've never referred to you as "my dearest" before. You weren't middle-aged until now."

He held out his hands as if he were offering himself up in some sacrificial ritual, looked plaintively at Mom, Kevin and Sam and asked: "Is it the British humor thing? Is it because I'm British that she doesn't get it?" and we all laughed again, and I began to feel a bit foolish.

Foolish because I remembered what it had felt like, or what I remembered it had felt like, when I turned thirty. I didn't know who I was when I began my third decade. I became an orphan that day, a woman with a past unknown to me. There was my remembered past, and then there was my past that I had no memories of. Just a blink of an eyelid, really, two short months of my life that were lost, not even a photograph to ground me, to prove that I'd even existed.

"Okay, you're right. All of you—I know you're in agreement on this Sam, even though you haven't said anything yet."

"I figured you'd come around and realize how superficial you're being," he replied, nodding his head. "First, you have us. We're quite the special extended family, I believe. And you and Becky have created something remarkable with 'Play Time', really remarkable. How many articles has the *Free Press* published about the foundation and the two of you? At least fifteen or twenty over the past few years? You're helping so many kids, changing so many lives. Your mom's right—and now that Alyssa has left I believe that what Becky said bears repeating: descent into darkness, my ass!"

It was about that time that I began to imagine myself as a female Jimmy Stewart in a remake of Frank Capra's Christmas classic. And because remembering the film and the part it played in Terry's family's life, and mine when he and I were together, I began to cry, and everyone sitting around me, who had been expecting to join me again in laughter, had looked somewhat bewildered until Mom reached out and patted my hand and said: "Ass does sound better coming from your mother. I believe that a woman swearing has so much more impact than when a man does. But it's nothing to cry about." And then we did laugh.

Tonight I'm crying again. It's the Saturday before Thanksgiving and I'm watching *It's A Wonderful Life* on the VHS tape I gifted myself shortly after Richard and I divorced (surely the most amicable parting in the history of ending relationships that never should have been entered into in the first place). Watching the film, alone, at the start of the holiday season is only a two-year tradition for me but it's one that I cherish.

Jimmy Stewart's lips are pressed against Donna Reed's forehead, and he's holding the phone and they're both pretending that they're listening to Frank Albertson (playing Sam Wainwright) when in reality they're listening to their hearts beating and the sound is getting so loud that it's going to drown out Albertson's voice and in another thirty seconds Reed is going to tell him that "it's the chance of a lifetime" and Stewart is going to grab her by the shoulders and one of the most innocently sensual and romantic kisses to ever grace the silver screen is going to happen—and my phone is ringing.

Damn! Who's calling me at eleven o'clock on a Saturday night? Obviously someone who knows that I'm going to be home.

I hit the pause button.

"Charlotte? Hi, sorry to be calling so late but I figured you might still be up. It's Matt."

"Hi back. No problem, I'm up. What's going on—everything okay?"

In the short silence that follows I hear my own heart beating.

"Can you come out here—to California? It's Cindy." I hear a breathy sound coming from him like the flapping of a bird's wings.

"What about Cindy?"

God, I think. Did she go back to Carl and did Matt find out about it? Or maybe she found someone else, she's seeing someone else and Matt found out about him. I hope to hell that's what it is. God—that's a horrible thing to think.

"She's sick. She has breast cancer. She's having surgery next Tuesday. The Tuesday before Thanksgiving—huh!" The sound of a man crying is plainly simply and crushingly sad.

This can't be happening. She called me on my birthday. That was only three weeks ago. I shouldn't have answered the phone.

"We just talked, not that long ago. Three weeks ago—on my birthday. She didn't say anything then."

"She didn't know. She'd had a mammogram only a few days before. We didn't have the results yet. The doctor's think that surgery, and chemo afterwards is going to get rid of it. That's what they think. That's what we're hoping for."

"Where is she right now, Matt? Can I talk to her?"

Another silence that stretches out longer than I'm comfortable with.

"She's at a school thing…"

On a Saturday night?

"She doesn't know I'm calling you, Charlotte. Can you come?"

And just when everyone who loves me had convinced me that turning forty hadn't been such a calamity after all. I guess this is what life is: lurching from one crisis to another, relishing the infrequent periods of calm in between.

"Yes, of course I'll come. I'll check on flights first thing tomorrow morning. I can probably get something that'll have me in California by Monday afternoon."

Is it so wrong that I'm thinking 'what might the chances be that you'll run into Terry while you're there'? Yeah— it's wrong and selfish and insensitive but that doesn't stop me from thinking it.

Matt clears his throat, whispers "thanks", the line goes dead and I press play.

Chapter 23

"Cindy's mom gets in tomorrow. She'll stay for a week, maybe more. It depends on if Cindy's going to need the chemo and how long it's going to take for her to recover from the surgery." Matt pulls the white Chrysler Town and Country mini-van out of remote lot 'C' and heads toward the North-405 freeway.

"I know you guys can use the help, even though the kids are growing up. I mean, it's not like the kids are babies anymore—they don't need someone changing their diapers and I'm sure that Cindy isn't doing loads of laundry like she used to when they were younger, and mealtimes aren't as crazy with them—you know—throwing up and all that—but still having someone around to help out, taking them to after school activities, someone like her mom—well..."

Stop babbling for God's sakes. You sound ridiculous. Those kids haven't been throwing their food around in years. Just shut up and look out the window, enjoy the scenery and let Matt talk.

I stare through the glass at the ubiquitous business district that could be anywhere in the country, auto repair shops, hair and nail salons, and ethnic restaurants.

But I'm not just anywhere, I'm sure not in Michigan anymore. Too long gone, I guess. I'd forgotten how different it is.

It's the seventy-foot date palms swaying languorously behind strip malls, beckoning to anyone driving or walking by to visit one of the shops below to get a tattoo or the best burrito north of Tijuana; the ruby-red bougainvillea creeping up the sides of the storefronts; the acacia trees' yellow buds primed to burst open in a few weeks; and the sky whose blueness provides a brilliant backdrop for the vivid white/yellow late Fall sun.

When I left the house six hours ago it was thirty-six degrees, drizzling just enough to make the roads scary slick and the few leaves left on the trees looked abandoned. This is a nice change of scene. It's good to be back.

What if I saw Terry right now? Driving by in a black Camaro? Do they still make Camaros? Maybe he'd be driving a Porsche or a BMW. But his wife would be with him, they'd be laughing at something funny he'd said and he'd turn his head and see me and he'd stop laughing and…

"Cindy's already in the hospital. She needed to get in this morning to have more blood work done. She was resting when I left. As much as it's possible to rest when you're facing what she is."

I wonder if I should ask if he's told her yet that I'm here. Or should I wait for him to tell me that she knows.

Matt sighs. It's a deep sigh expressing any number of feelings that I can only guess at: fear, disbelief, sadness, and even perhaps confusion. Like an emotional soup: all the feelings floating around in a stock of psychological and physical exhaustion.

"I told her last night that I was picking you up this morning."

"Was she happy to hear that? You know—it hurt me that she didn't let me know about the surgery. I don't quite understand why that is."

He sighs again and grips the steering wheel so tightly his knuckles turn white.

Maybe we should stop somewhere—I'm not sure I want to be on the freeway with him right now…

"Do you want to stop for a cup of coffee?"

Before I can respond, Matt whips the wheel sharply to the right, pulls the mini-van into a nearly empty McDonald's parking lot, turns off the ignition and hollers over his shoulder as he strides towards the front door: "What do you take in it?"

I haven't had time to figure out if the sole patron sitting in the booth at the front window: a dark-bearded sunken-eyed man wearing a bright red ski cap, who looks to be fifty but could be half that, is homeless, mentally ill, perhaps both or just an out-of-work actor, when Matt appears, holding two coffee cups and slides into the booth seat across from me. Fingers trembling, he hands me a cup and looks at me through eyes misted over with tears.

"I couldn't understand it, either—not at first," he says, picking up our conversation from the car as deftly as someone reciting a soliloquy after being interrupted by a heckler.

"Not at first?" My coffee's too hot and he added sugar, which I never use, but I flash him a quizzical expression to match my question and take another sip.

"I mean, she was so funny about it. Not funny as in hah, hah funny, but funny as in she acted so differently than she should have if everything was—you know—normal. Like it should be."

I realize that I'm privy to an internal monologue. He's talking to himself, not me.

"I asked her, right away. I asked her when you were coming out here. As soon as we got the results I asked her. Because I knew she would want you to be here, her best friend since kindergarten. But she told me that she'd decided that she'd get through it, the surgery and the chemo and all first—and then—if everything turned out okay, then she'd tell you. Doesn't that seem a little funny to you? It does to me."

He's answered his own question, so I remain silent.

"I'd suspected something for a long time. I knew that something was wrong."

"What do you mean, Matt? You thought that she had cancer? You thought she had cancer before she was even diagnosed?"

He stares at me with eyes suddenly so clear and bright they could be piercing my body like a laser, shining right through me, illuminating everything inside.

"She had an affair, didn't she? Cindy slept with someone else—didn't she?"

"Good God, Matt—no! No!" I surprise myself with how quickly I react.

Liars always take their time to answer—that's their tell. That's what gives them away every time. I'm a liar but I'm a better actor. Should I be unremorseful or ashamed?

Like the looks on Dad's face, the ones I'll never forget, the ones I wish I could— Matt's face I'll also remember forever, and in this case, will be grateful that I do. His dark brown eyes shining wide, a child-like innocence and trust in his wide, toothy smile, that beams an as yet unspoken thankfulness across the table.

"She didn't. She would have told you if she had. She would have—wouldn't she? That's something that women share, I know that. She didn't sleep around. No affair. Oh, Charlotte, I love her so much. I love her so much. Everything's going to be okay now. I know it—everything's going to be okay."

I'm definitely unremorseful.

Chapter 24

Cindy has a private room, which is good because neither one of us would want this conversation to go on within earshot of a sick stranger. We both started sobbing the moment I walked in, but it hasn't taken long for Cindy to recover and adopt an entirely different emotional stance. She's stoic as a British Royal Guard at Buckingham Palace.

"Who would have thought? Who would have ever thought?" Cindy motions for me to sit in the chair closest to the bed. "No cancer in my family, not my mom or her mom or either one of my aunts. No one, not a single damn case of cancer in any woman on my side of the family going back as far anyone can remember. No one. I'm being punished."

Her eyes are flat, betraying no emotion. Her face pale, ever so slightly pinched at the lips like there's something else she wants to say but she refuses to let it pass.

"No, you're not Cindy. You're not being punished. People don't get sick because of anything they did. People don't get sick because of their behavior."

Cindy laughs, a little too loudly and makes a strange nasal snickering noise when she's finished; the sound is more unpleasant than if she were vomiting or passing gas.

"I loved the way Carl loved my breasts. Hah! Tiny little things that they were— are. Even after four kids they're still tiny. Not that Matt didn't, love them I mean, because—he did. But after awhile I guess they just weren't all that interesting anymore. They were the only ones he had to look at for all those years. How could I have made them more exciting—pasted tassels to them and danced around?"

Knowing she's asking a rhetorical question, I let it hang in the air for a few seconds, just long enough for her to answer.

"He—Matt might have liked that. Maybe I would have liked it, too. We'll never get to know now though, will we? You're wrong, Charlie, people get sick and they die all the time because of their behavior. Smokers get lung cancer. People who eat too much meat get colon cancer. People who are out in the sun too much get skin cancer. You're wrong. People pay—they pay for what they've done."

"People don't get cancer because they had an affair."

Her eyes are teary again, glinting, the pupils wide and wet.

"Just what makes you so sure? You don't know, Charlie. You don't know what I've suffered."

But, you chose to have the affair. No one forced you. You chose to act on your feelings. I feel guilty that these thoughts dare to scamper out into the open expanse of my mind—but thoughts are so uncontrollable, they appear of their own volition and once they've made their entrance they're not easily banished back into the shadows.

"You're right, I don't."

"I didn't want you to come because I was afraid that Matt would bring it up to you. When the two of you were alone. I was afraid that he'd start asking you all kinds of questions."

Cindy grabs a tissue and blows her nose. Then she laughs again, even louder this time.

How is it possible for laughter to sound venomous?

"He knows, doesn't he? Matt knows. After I ended it with Carl I knew that that wasn't the end, it was just the beginning. Because I wasn't the same Cindy, so Matt wasn't the same Matt. Everything had changed. We were starting over, but not in a good way. When the doctor told me it was stage two and I came home and told Matt I could see it in his eyes, he was thinking that karma's a bitch."

"No, Cindy. No! This time you're wrong. You're so wrong. He loves you Cindy, loves you more than you could ever imagine. And—he has no idea that you had an affair. None. Zero. He doesn't know. We never talked about it. All we talked about is how worried he is about you. That's all."

That was way too much, Charlie. It's hard not to feel a little ashamed carrying on like that. That's my tell—blabbering on and on—such an obvious lie.

She balls up the Kleenex and throws it hard. It goes only as far as a tissue can travel, just to the metal footboard.

"I want to believe you, Charlie. You don't know how much I want to believe you."

"You have to believe me. You really don't have a choice. I've been your best friend for nearly four decades. I wouldn't lie to you, Cindy. You have to let this go, and then you have to get better."

I'm as unremorseful, and as ashamed as I'll ever be—ever.

Chapter 25

The changeover to the new millennium is wreaking havoc in most peoples' lives. I know that indigenous tribes living on remote tropical islands aren't affected one way or another by this monumental occurrence that the media has hyped to the civilized world for the past three hundred sixty-five days. No, for them the sun will rise in the east as always two days from now on the first of January in the year 2000, and they'll go about their daily lives: the men hunting; the women cooking what the hunters have returned home with; the children playing with toys they've fashioned out of bamboo or some exotic wood; elders patiently watching over the youngsters as they frolic in the sand—and soon the children will sit where the grandparents do, watching their grandchildren and great-grandchildren experiencing the simple pleasures of youth and life. Sun illuminating faces, warm water bathing toes, sticks thrown and retrieved, braids tugged at and gentle laughter filling the air.

But for the rest of us—Y2K is a disaster looming up ahead, one that we seemingly can't avoid. The entire industrialized technologically-wired world is enslaved to nerdy guys wearing black-rimmed glasses, downing twenty cups of coffee a day while furiously tapping on keyboards, trying to save the majority of the human race from a destruction of its own short-sighted making.

Closing Book City doesn't really have anything to do with the impending loss of our ability to cash checks, being in a plane that falls from the sky, finding oneself at a stoplight that's gone black or all the popcorn being popped in microwaves around the country simultaneously imploding at one-minute after midnight on January first, but I suppose that in a way, it does. We've entered a new world, everything around us is changing at a pace that seems impossible to maintain and nothing seems as simple as it used to be. And all because of two numbers. Who could ever have imagined? Obviously very few did.

"You're closing because of that dang YMCA2 thing, aren't you? Because on January first none of the cash registers will work—am I right?" Betty Jackson asks as she lovingly deposits her newly minted copies of *Hearts in Atlantis, The Greatest Generation* and *'Tis* in her red foil-trimmed Book City holiday shopping bag.

Betty has been shopping here since Sid opened the store the year I was born. Her purchases, four to six books a month, have seen her through two marriages; the divorce from one husband and the death of another; the loss of one child to a car accident; two children marrying; four grandchildren being born; the divorce of one of the grandchildren's mothers; her own diagnosis of colon cancer, in remission for three years and a disdain for all things new, strange, untested and too complex to fathom.

"No, Betty. It has nothing to do with YMCA2," (I've found it best never to correct her, in the same way I never corrected Dad) I begin, but then I say: "Well—actually it does have something to do with it, in a roundabout way."

"How's that? And don't make it so confusing that I can't understand what you're trying to say. I get so sick of those announcers on the television, those people with their smug dolled-up faces and all the women with their blonde hair and whiny voices trying to scare us. And when they try to explain to us whey we should be scared, does anyone understand it? Does anyone? I hardly think so." She pulls her thin nearly white lips into a straight line.

"Don't feel bad, Betty. We're all confused by what's going on. I don't think it's right that the media's trying to scare us; everything's going to be all right, I'm sure. They're a lot of really smart people working on this…"

"A whole lot smarter than you and me. And boy, they sure let us know that, don't they? So smug they are."

"I suppose with good reason. We just have to trust them. But as I was explaining…"

"I'm right, aren't I? None of the cash registers will open anymore. The dang front door probably won't open anymore, will it? Isn't it hooked up to some kind of computer-thingy? That dang bell goes off every time it opens."

"The cash registers, and the front door, will work—would work just fine. The problem is that there hasn't been much money going into those registers lately."

If you only knew the truth, dear sweet Betty. We've been operating in the red for the past year. I've tried, I've tried very hard to keep it open, subsidizing it with money from Dad's estate, but it's time to stop beating my head against the wall. The big box chains have done us in. We can't make it. We haven't been making it for a long time.

"You mean that no one's shopping here anymore?" She looks around, verifying her statement, then back at me. "People are going to that other store, that big huge one in the mall. The one where I don't know the people who work there and everything's so bright and cheery and phony. It's all phony to me. I went in there once..." her voice trails off and I wonder if she's going to apologize. "Didn't like it from the moment I walked in. I felt like everyone was watching me, and it was easy to watch me because the aisles are so big. Everything's so spread out and just so—different. I couldn't find anything, I didn't know where to look and I saw a sign that said information, but there were six people waiting in line, and the woman who was supposed to help them had one of those big computer-thingy screens that looks like a TV in front of her face, and I got disgusted and left."

If I could only give you every single book on our shelves, I would.

"What are you doing New Year's Eve, Betty? Have any plans?"

"I'm going over to my daughter's house, babysitting so she can go out with that new man she's seeing. I don't like him at all, he's not friendly and he stares at me funny and when he talks to me he sounds like he's talking to my five-year old granddaughter. I don't think he's good with old people, or children. But I guess she'd rather be with him on the night that everything goes dark rather than with her child. I don't understand young people these days—not even my own flesh and blood."

"Tell you what—why don't you come to Martinelli's before you go over to watch your granddaughter, it's close, isn't it to where she lives? I'll pack up a big box of books from here, I know what ones you'd like and I'll give them to you as a sort of late Christmas present. Even better idea: pick up your granddaughter and bring her with you. Stay for a little while. I have a niece who's only two years older than her, they could play together. Have dinner; you don't have to stay until midnight, my brother and sister-in-law have a sitter for later. It would be fun and you know it's…"

"The last New Year's Eve at Martinelli's. The last anything at Martinelli's."

There's a lump the size of a golf ball in my throat that wasn't there a minute ago.

"That's such a shame that Martinelli's closing. Closing after all those years. I went there with both my husbands, Guy and Eugene. Of course I only get teary-eyed when I think about going there with Gene. Guy and I got in a big fight there once; I don't have good memories of going there with him. But Gene—oh, yes. We had some very good nights there—the two of us. Why does everything eventually go away? Why do things have to change? Just when you're getting used to things as they are."

Please, just keep talking Betty because I can't say anything right now.

"Martinelli's is closing for the same reasons as Book City, am I right? I'm not a stupid old woman. I know what's going on. That fancy-schmancy new restaurant that opened up a few years ago; everyone's going there instead. I went there once, just like I went to that fancy-schmancy bookstore once. I went with my son—to the restaurant— not the bookstore; I went there alone like I told you before. I didn't like it. The waitresses sang songs at peoples' tables; I thought it was embarrassing and tasteless. And then you know what? I went with my son and his family to Chicago once; they just wanted me to go along so I could babysit while they went out and had fun. And while we were there we went out for dinner, and it was exactly the same restaurant as the fancy-schmancy one here. The same singing waitresses and the same too thin spaghetti sauce and just like the bookstore it was all phony and I didn't like it. Didn't like it anymore than I like that bookstore."

You're not a stupid old woman at all, Betty. Wouldn't it be helpful if we all knew, from the moment of our birth, that we should never get used to anything staying the same? Never get too comfortable because just when you've settled in—there's going to be a scene change and some characters will exit and new ones will appear and you'll have to figure out a way to get comfortable again, knowing all the while that nothing's forever—no matter how much you'd like it to be. Wouldn't it be better if we knew that going in? Wouldn't it?

Chapter 26

"Hon? Are you about ready? We're supposed to be there in ten—what *are* you doing?" David says as he emerges from my tiny master bedroom into my similarly miniscule living room where I'm busy placing books of all sizes and cover materials into cardboard boxes.

"Just a few more minutes, see I'm all dressed and ready to go," I say, pointing to my black sweater adorned with braided gold trim at the neckline and around the sleeves. "I need to get this last box of books loaded up for Betty, then if you'll help me carry them to your car, we can leave."

I'm not going to carry a single box to the car; David will be the one doing the heavy lifting. He's like that, which is fine by me; in fact, I like it—I like it quite a lot. That's the way we met just over a year ago, David volunteering to help me move boxes of copier paper and other office supplies from the trunk of my Mercedes to a rental car.

I'd arrived at the repair shop early, ten minutes before seven, for what I thought was the first appointment. The shop's a small one, located just outside the Detroit city limits in Madison Heights. It's small for a couple of reasons: the owner doesn't have a lot of customers and I figure that he wants it small to keep it from being noticed; he's maintaining a low profile. Deutch's Foreign Car Repair is tucked away in a small strip mall off Twelve Mile Road; flanked by a pizza shop that looks like it was long ago crossed off the city's health department inspection list and a comic book shop, owned by a well-muscled heavily tattooed man who rides a Harley.

As I pulled my car into the parking lot I'd been surprised to see another vehicle sitting outside the door marked 'service.' The car was a beauty: bright fire engine red, gleaming like a beacon from some exotic and foreign lighthouse, illuminating the native dreariness around it. A dark-haired man was sitting in the driver's seat.

"Hi," he said as he emerged from the crimson brilliance surrounding him. "You have an appointment this morning too?"

"Yeah, I do, at seven. What time's yours?"

He'd grinned, and his deep brown eyes stayed open, wide and welcoming. There are people who, when they smile, their eyes squeeze shut and disappear; as if the muscles in their faces can't maintain a gleeful expression at both bottom and top. Not so with David—when he smiles his eyes join his mouth in expressing their happiness.

"Seven—oops!"

"But Max has only one mechanic."

"True, but there are two bays and Max is a mechanic himself. I don't think it's going to be a problem. My name's David, by the way." He held out his hand.

During the next hour I learned that David's car is a 1965 Porsche 911, that he's an engineer at Ford, lives in Royal Oak and drives the Porsche only on weekends, in good weather, the majority of the time he drives a Mustang. I also discovered that he's quite the physical type of man, his long arms and legs remarkably strong despite the fact that they match his torso, lean almost to the point of thinness. It took him less than five minutes to empty the trunk, declining my offers to help the entire time. It would be two weeks before I learned that he's married.

"Betty? Betty Jackson, that's who you mean, right? The woman who's been shopping at Book City since it opened?" David's already hoisted one box on his right shoulder.

"Correction: the woman who *shopped* at Book City ever since it opened."

"Shopped. Sorry, Charlie. I know it's been hard on you, these past few weeks. Having to close the store and all." He reaches with his left hand for another box. "I think I can get this one, too."

"Hey—honey, it's New Year's Eve. Don't push it. I don't want you getting a hernia over a couple of boxes. Take them out one at a time to the car, there's only four."

"Okay, okay," he shouts over his shoulder on his way to the garage. "Probably doesn't make much difference, anyway. What's a hernia when the world's coming to an end?"

Walking into Martinelli's I wish the scene were different.

It would be nice, especially tonight, if this was the old Martinelli's: the booths, the mural, the photographs. Of all nights, I wish it looked the way it used to—tonight—the last night.

In an attempt to draw in more customers, Nick Junior redid Martinelli's two years ago, gave it a complete makeover the week of my fortieth birthday. He took out the booths, put in more tables, painted over the mural, replaced the flooring, and packed away all the photos of famous, and infamous, Italian celebrities. When the renovation was complete, Martinelli's looked like any other quasi-Italian restaurant, down to the magnums of red wine hanging in baskets on the walls.

The revamping was a failure. Long-time customers complained that the atmosphere was gone, that despite the fact that the menu hadn't changed Martinelli's without Frank Sinatra staring at you when you twirled your pasta onto your fork, just wasn't the same.

"The food will be the next thing to go! No more handmade cannoli, no more pasta fagioli," is what Nick told me people were saying. He didn't change the menu but it made no difference; many of the old customers were upset and worried that it was going to happen any day, so they stopped coming and new customers never came—they didn't know that Martinelli's existed.

Nick greets us as we walk in, his voice more gravelly than usual. He's wearing a crisp white shirt partially covered with a black satin vest, black bowtie and black trousers.

"Charlie, David! Paisan! Happy New Year's Eve! A big night huh—a very big night! You like how I dress? Looks like a tuxedo, maybe half a tuxedo! Hah!" he kisses me, then David, once on each cheek.

It's going to be a very good night. A big night, just like Nick said. Celebrating a new millennium. That's a big deal—how many people get to do that in their lives?

I look around the room, it's full of people and I realize that we're the last ones to arrive. Even Betty beat us here; she's sitting at a table with her granddaughter and Kevin, Janet and Alyssa. The two girls are shyly eyeing one another but the adults are engaged in conversation; Betty's leaning in toward Kevin, she's smiling sweetly and I get a feeling that at any second she's going to reach over and pat his hand.

She's probably wishing that her daughter were married to someone like my brother. Kevin does have a way of beguiling every woman he meets.

Sam and Peter are in the far corner; Peter's wearing a real tux and doesn't look the least bit out of place, despite the fact he's the only one dressed so formally. Mom's serving drinks with Derek, which also doesn't seem out-of-character. Derek's girlfriend Samantha obviously started imbibing early: Daphne's out-of-sight, possibly in the restroom, so Samantha's trying to coax Daphne's husband into dancing with her, although there isn't any music. John Mason and his no-longer-new trophy wife are already arguing. There're a few other older couples scattered around the room that I've seen dining at Martinelli's over the years. I never got to know them personally, would just smile and nod my head as I passed by their tables; it seems odd and more than a little heartbreaking that tonight I'll finally learn their names, and will never see them again.

No, I was wrong. David and I aren't the very last latecomers—Richard and Debbie just walked in. I know it's them without turning around, I smell Richard's cloying aftershave and hear Debbie's nervous schoolgirl giggle.

I can't believe that I even keep in touch with them, well with Debbie, anyway. But what am I supposed to do? Poor thing—she's often lost, feels out of place, like she took a wrong turn on her way to a very certain and specific destination and ended up somewhere else. Being married to her mentor, the man she looked up to and admired, who turned out to be so different from what she'd thought he'd be. If Richard knew that we've been talking at least once a week ever since their son was born, he'd flip-out. Then again—it's Richard. He probably wouldn't do much of anything.

David pokes gently at my side. "Your ex and his child-bride are here."

Richard has the same look on his face he has every time I've seen him since the divorce: maudlin, with just the slightest hint of math teacher face pragmatism to temper the mawkishness. Debbie's her usual too perky self. I fear the worst because she's obviously already been drinking; alcohol tends to increase one's tendency toward self-deprecation not diminish it.

"Debbie, Richard! So glad you could make it. Quite a night—huh?" I say as I clasp Debbie's hands in mine. They're cold and clammy, I don't hold on for long.

"The world is not going to end tonight. You all realize that, don't you? It's already January first in Australia and other places around the world. This whole thing was just a bunch of hype, that's all." Richard says in a tone so foreboding one would think he had just informed all of us in the Eastern time zone of the United States that our time on earth is limited because Australia did, in fact, suffer a total meltdown of it's electrical grid, as has the entire continent of Europe, and people are already devouring one another in order to stay alive.

"Happy New Year's Eve, Richard. And thanks for the heads-up" I say and reluctantly give him a peck on the cheek. "How's Richard Junior?"

"He's just fine. Such a fine young boy. He's going to be four soon. We can't believe how fast he's growing. Can we, Debbie?" Richard smiles at his Sandra stand-in, who's looking at me as if she wants to get on her hands and knees and crawl away, like a young scared soldier evading enemy fire overhead.

"Yes, growing so fast. He's growing so fast. Pretty soon he'll be a math teacher—just like his daddy." Her eyes plead; I look away.

I wish I could help you I think, but there's nothing I can do. At least you're out of the house tonight, tonight of all nights. I felt so sorry for you when we talked last week and you told me that all you had planned for New Year's Eve was to visit Gertrude in the assisted living facility. This was the least I could do. And the least is all I can do.

Prince would be disappointed. Our behavior this evening isn't living up to his expectations. We're partying like it's 1999, but the celebration isn't all that different from 1998 or any of the other New Year's Eve fests most of us have attended in the past. I'm vaguely recollecting parties where large amounts of marijuana was smoked and cheap beer was drank, and I imagine that others might be too, but those memories seem like something we may have seen in a movie once, behavior we were all witness to—not behavior any of us actually engaged in. I haven't seen anyone 'work it down to the ground', not even Samantha who, once she realized that the musical choices for the evening would be Steve Lawrence rather than Steven Tyler, decided to help Derek serve, so Mom could give her feet a rest.

For the most part, tonight has been an evening of reminiscing about, remembering and then rehashing events in our past lives. The rehashing has led to some interesting conversations, each speaker believing that he or she has recalled an event exactly as it occurred; that the other person or persons involved were only observers, otherwise his, her or their recollections wouldn't be so completely and utterly wrong. "No, no. That's not the way it happened at all," has been bandied about quite often this evening. I've said those words several times in the past few hours, and I'm absolutely sure that what I remember someone else doing, and how I reacted to it, is exactly how it happened.

It's one minute to midnight. Derek and Samantha have handed out the traditional gold and silver party hats shaped like snow cones plus the obnoxious noisemakers that sound like a small boat with a sinus infection pulling up to a dock.

The end and the beginning are getting closer—soon they'll converge.

David reaches out and takes my hand. Everyone in the room is watching the television sitting on the makeshift bar Nick Junior set up in the corner. The sparkling glass ball hovering over the One Times Square building lights up the screen for what won't be the last time, but for those of us here, in this room right now, will be the last time we'll watch its descent with such feelings of awe, apprehension and excitement.

10-9-8-7-5-6-4-3-2-1! The ball explodes into brilliance; the air fills with a cacophony of light and music and the screams of thousands and thousands of people below. We don't speak, not one of us—not for a few seconds. The silly noisemakers are silent, no confetti flies in the air.

And then—horns blaring—champagne corks pop, pop—laughter, subdued at first but getting louder—someone's crying, maybe more than one—silver and gold glitter rises half-way to the ceiling and arcs down, drifting slowly before landing on cheeks and shoulders—David takes me in his arms, kisses me and we don't quite pull apart—our noses are almost touching—all I can see are his dark eyes, there, just his eyes, very open, very wide.

"Happy New Year's, Charlie. Welcome to the new millennium. I love you. I love you."

"Yes, yes."

Chapter 27

The tender brush of David's lips against my eyelids—first the right, then the left, wakens me. A touch so slight, so ephemeral that it might have been the warmth of his breath moving across the bridge of my nose that actually woke me from a sleep so satisfying, so renewing that I'm reluctant to let in the morning light.

"Morning. Welcome to the year two thousand. We all knew it was coming, but now that it's finally here, and we can say it—out loud—wow! Wow! Sasha's walked. Coffee's brewing. I had a quick bowl of cereal. There're a few of those English muffins you like still left in the fridge. I'm going to see Emily; I'll be back in a couple hours, maybe less. Stay in bed for a while longer if you want."

But now that I'm awake I have no intention of staying in bed, not today. I have to go to Book City to finish clearing out the last of the books that I'm donating to charity; Nick Junior asked Mom and me to come by so he could give each of us a keepsake, a memento of the moments and hours we spent at Martinell's over the years; and Cindy called and left a message last night, five minutes after midnight. I didn't hear my phone, tucked away in the bottom of my purse, and I was too tired to listen to it before we went to bed, but listening to it this morning is number one on my to-do list.

The coffee's hot; the English muffins toasted perfectly, sweet butter and orange marmalade melting across their tops, sliding down into each little crevice; I'm still in my fluffy pink pajamas, the ones with the feet that David gave me for my birthday; outside the fresh snow's blowing across the lawn; the wind creating miniature ballerinas pirouetting madly across the white stage.

If this were a movie, viewers would hear the crisp intonations of a distinguished man in his early 50s saying: "*It's January first in the year of our Lord two-thousand: the first day of the new millennium. Miss Charlie is taking her breakfast in her small, but perfect for her, tidy yellow kitchen, contemplating the day to come. The first day of the next one thousand years, the first day of the rest of her life.*"

I press the 'messages' button. Cindy sounds tired, which isn't unusual. She has four children, one already a teenager; in the last three years she's had a double mastectomy and breast reconstruction; the family will soon be moving into a house still in the construction phase in Thousand Oaks ("Much better environment for the kids than Los Angeles" she'd explained during a phone call three months ago); and she continues to be wracked with guilt over her affair, although it's not something we discuss regularly. But sometimes when we talk and there's a pause in our conversation, those few seconds of sudden quiet that happen between even the closest of friends—I sense that she wants to say something like: "Will this feeling ever go away?" in hopes that I'll respond: "Of course it will, you just need to give it more time", but we never fill up that silent space.

"Hi Charlie. We just watched the ball drop in Times Square, so we know that the world didn't end. Not that we thought it was going to anyway. We let the kids, even the twins, stay up to watch it. Their incorrigible older brother had them scared into thinking that something bad was going to happen, not that they understand the whole concept of what time and a thousand years means or any of that. But they're going to bed happy; we let them have more sugary treats tonight than we usually give them in a month. Matt's upstairs with them now."

Silence—maybe she hung up?

"So, Charlie. Last week I was in Santa Monica, at the Third Street Promenade, having lunch with a woman I met in my breast cancer support group—and—guess who I saw walking out of The Gap with his daughter? Terry—it was Terry. We stopped and talked for a while."

Silence again. I don't think the message recording lasts much longer.

"He's divorced. His daughter's name is Sara, she's eleven. Adorable girl—Terry said that she looks just like her mother. He asked about you, Charlie."

Beep. Message has ended.

It's only 5:30 in California; Cindy probably isn't awake yet. I can't call for at least another hour, which means I have too much time to think, to pose questions in my mind that I can't possibly have the answers to. Questions that I shouldn't even be thinking, anyway, but I am.

"Come, Sasha. I'm going to change clothes and I'll take you for another walk." My year old Golden Retriever shakes her puppyish body from side-to-side as she follows me into the bedroom.

Lucky you—going for another walk already. I sure can't sit around here sipping coffee while I ponder the future. You're so lucky you're a dog. For all you know, your future stretches only as far as into the next ten minutes.

"Hi, Cindy. You were up, right? It's ten here, so I figured—with the kids and all…"

"Yeah, I'm up. Have been for half-an-hour. The kids never, ever sleep in. Not even when the night before they've witnessed something as monumental as the changeover to the next thousand years. Happy New Year. Happy new millennium. Kinda a big deal—huh?"

"That's for sure. So, you and Matt didn't do anything special last night?"

Silence again. I know she hasn't hung up but I wonder if she wishes she could.

"We—we decided to just stay in. I know, I know. Everyone on the planet wanted to be partying last night. But Matt and I—we decided to spend the evening together, just the kids, and us. That's what we wanted."

You needn't sound so defensive, Cindy. I'm sure that's what you wanted.

"Probably a wise move. I had a bit too much champagne last night; I'm paying for it now. David and I slept in a little. He's visiting with Emily now."

"She's the same? Emily?"

"Yeah, she's the same. Nothing much ever changes when you're in a permanently minimally conscious state."

Cindy lets out a sound that's half sigh, half whimper.

"That's such a tough one. I can't imagine…" more of a whimper this time "…how he does it, how he deals with it. He still goes to see her every day?"

"When he can, yeah. If he misses a day, because he's traveling or is sick or something, it bothers him. He thinks that she knows the days that he isn't there. That she'll start to worry that he doesn't love her anymore and isn't ever coming back. I know he knows in his mind that that isn't true—but in his heart…"

"Matt junior! Where are you going this early? I didn't see you eating breakfast. Sorry, Charlie. Listen, I have to cut this short. We seem to have a skateboard-related crisis in the making."

I want to call out: "Oh, please—please wait. Not yet. Don't go yet. There's more I need to know"—but I don't.

"So—about Terry. Matt junior if you walk out that door without giving me an answer you're grounded for the next three days. Sorry—about Terry. I gave him your phone number. Hope that's okay. He seemed a little down. I think he'd like to talk to you. Matthew, I'm not kidding around. Later, Charlie."

"It's January first in the year of our Lord two-thousand, the first day of the new millennium, and Miss Charlie is considering retiring to her bed in the hope that she is having a dream and when she wakes, time will not have passed. But, as we all know, time does march on. And so Miss Charlie will choose to stay awake today. She'll choose to accept what is and what's to come. Lets follow along, shall we?"

Chapter 28

"Hi, Charlie. It's Terry. Is this a good time to be calling? Hope I haven't caught you at a bad time. Have I?" Terry's questions still sound more like statements rather than inquiries.

No, I think, this isn't a good time. I'm preparing for the board presentation tomorrow and in an hour I'm interviewing Samantha for the grant-writing job that just opened up.

Samantha, unlike Derek her husband-to-be, has turned out to be somewhat of a surprise as far as her job choice. Grant writing isn't the career path I'd have guessed she'd choose. A degree in communications perhaps, with her eye on the local weathergirl spot on channel seven, seemed more fitting. When Derek casually mentioned to me the week before New Year's Eve that Samantha had just received her degree in non-profit management and works part-time writing grants for a Catholic charity in Detroit, the vision of her cavorting around Martinelli's at Christmas a year ago, wearing a sexy Mrs. Claus costume, kissing David, Kevin, Sam, Peter, Nick Junior, every man she could lay her lips on, immediately popped into my head, and although I know she isn't going to show up dressed like that today, I almost wish she would. That's the Samantha I know. I can't imagine how I'm going to focus on her grant-writing skills while the picture of her locking lips with an unfazed, and clearly flattered Peter, glows festive and vivid in my mind.

"This is a perfect time—just perfect, "I say as I physically swipe the file folder lying on my desk into a drawer and mentally swipe away at a thought thrusting itself into my head.

Is this the right action to take? Now? Is this where you want to go?

"Well—then—Happy New Year."

Questions race through my mind. How long has it been since we talked last? Fourteen years ago? I don't remember if I called him when Dad died. I think I did. His voice—it's just like I remembered it. Sexy as always, but deeper now: deeper but maybe darker somehow.

I should have told you that this isn't a good time to talk.

"Happy New Year to you, too. How are you? Cindy told me you're divorced, and you have a little girl?"

I hear background noise, glasses clattering and clinking; background noise that, barely, muffles the sigh or maybe it's a groan that he doesn't disguise.

"She left me—yes. Teresa. Teresa and I've been divorced for two years. Two years? Yeah, two, 'cause Sara is eleven now. She wishes her mom and I were still together. Kids have a hard time with that—as I'm discovering. It's not getting better. I thought with time it would. It isn't."

These conflicting thoughts. These questions without answers. I want to get on a plane as soon as I can and go to you—and I want to hang up the phone this second and never talk to you again. What do you expect from me? What do I expect from me?

"I'm so sorry. Sorry about the divorce. Divorce is never easy, even when the couple agrees that it's the best course of action. It's still never easy. But you have a daughter. She must bring a lot of joy into your life."

He doesn't respond to what I've said, doesn't acknowledge that his daughter does, in fact, make him happy. Instead he says, in a whisper that's almost conspiratorial, as if he doesn't want anyone nearby to hear:

"You got married, and then you got divorced. Cindy told me." He sighs, or groans, for the second time, and I wonder if he's sick—or maybe he's just drunk.

On a Tuesday: at 1:00 in the afternoon?

"Well, that was one of those marriages that was most definitely not made in heaven. Not made in hell—it wasn't all that bad. I don't know, made in China? It was all so foreign and strange. Like we were speaking a different language to each other the whole time," I laugh, nervously, but Terry doesn't reciprocate.

I should have told you that this isn't a good time to talk.

"And now?"

Several seconds pass before I realize what he's getting at.

"You're asking what I'm doing now? As far as being in a relationship—is that what you're asking?"

I feel like we've been given a script that's half-finished and we're trying to muddle our way through a rehearsal, ad-libbing, speaking lines based on what we think our characters would say.

"Yes. That's it—exactly."

I should have told you that this isn't a good time to talk. But when would have been a good time?

"I've been seeing someone for just a little over a year. His name is David. He, he's in a difficult situation."

"How so?"

"He's married…"

"God, Charlie. Married? Yeah, so was I—until she found someone else. Married?"

The urge to defend my actions, to defend my life is so strong that I wish Terry were in the room with me, sitting across from me. I want to take his head in my hands, stare into his eyes and say, over and over again: "No, no. You don't understand."

"Terry, it's not what you think..."

"Then why don't you tell me what it is then?"

"Maybe, just maybe if you stopped interrupting me—I could."

"I'm sorry, Charlie. I'm really sorry. I'm being an ass. I'm being a total ass right now..."

He makes no attempt to stifle his crying.

"It's okay. It's okay. Hey, what's going on with you?"

"No, you tell me what's going on with you. You tell me why you're seeing someone who's married. What about his wife? What about his poor wife?

"His wife? His wife, Emily, is in a nursing home. She's been there for nearly five years. Ever since she had a major stroke when she was four months pregnant with what would have been their first child—a girl. She's in what's called a permanently minimally conscious state."

I hear another voice now, fading in and out, barely audible over the sound of sobbing. "Hey—what's—buddy, buddy, hey—call you—I'll call you—want me to—a cab—hey, buddy..."

Although Terry's weeping doesn't appear to be letting up, I finish my explanation.

"David and Emily met in engineering school at U of M. They dated all through college, got married, both went to work for General Motors, bought a house, traveled the world and when Emily was thirty-nine they realized that there was one thing missing from their lives, so she got pregnant.

Unfortunately, things turned out much differently than they'd planned. Terry, are you drunk?"

More clattering and tinkling and what I know is the bartender's voice, a little louder now, more abrupt: "Listen—hey—cutting you off—hey—it man—that's it."

"I'm okay—I'm okay…"

Is he talking to me, the bartender, or both of us?

"I'm okay. But, yeah, I'm drunk—or at least on my way there. But that's pretty much par for the course for me lately…"

No, Terry. This isn't who you are, who you were. Who I thought you were.

"This David, he sounds like he's quite the guy, so devoted and all. Makes my heart melt, just hearing about what a devoted husband he is. Hey! Charlie, did I tell you that my mom's dead? Did I tell you that? Of course I didn't because we haven't talked in years. You've been busy with husband number one and now dear devoted David."

Gloria's image flashes before me. Christmas—her husband and her sons, the angels, her sweet sad tormented face.

"Oh, Terry. Your mom, I'm so sorry. I'm so sorry. She didn't—she…"

"Kill herself? No, but she did die of a broken heart. My mom died of a broken heart."

I hear coughing, then the sound of a glass hitting something solid, hitting wood—hard.

"I'm ready to settle up. What do I owe you?"

"What? What do you mean, Terry? Because of Sara, because of your sister? Your sister died years ago. I don't understand."

"Listen, Charlie. I have to get out of here. Today's my day to pick up the other Sara, my daughter, from school. Have to sober up—you know what I mean? Can't pick her up drunk, that wouldn't be good for her, or for me. Hey—do you think—do you think?"

"What? Do I think what?"

"Do you think that you could maybe come out here sometime to see me? Tell your boyfriend you're going to see Cindy. Do you think you could do that? I'd like it if you could come here. I'd like it very much."

No! No! Don't do this. Don't even think about doing this. Don't do it—don't.

"Yes, yes. Yes, Terry. I'll come."

Chapter 29

One of the good things about flying, possibly the only good thing, is that once the plane has reached cruising altitude and you've explained to the person sitting next to you that you'd prefer not to talk, you have time to reflect on whatever your mindset happens to be at the time. And oftentimes, once your feet touch ground again, your thought are clearer, you have a better understanding of your situation than you did before the cabin doors shut.

But in my case, because during nearly five hours of airborne contemplative time, I've thought solely about lies, lying, making up stories, pretending, and speaking half-truths, my mind is a muddled mess. Not even a flight to Tahiti would have been long enough for me to sort through the stories I've told in the past several days.

Deception. Deceit. Bold-faced lies. Little white lies. Sins of omission. I'm the duchess of dissembling; the empress of equivocation, the princess of prevarication.

David believes that I'm going to visit Cindy ("February's the perfect time for you to visit your best friend in California. We're going to get another late winter snowstorm a couple of days after you leave.") Mom believes that I'll visit with Cindy while I'm in town, but the main purpose of my trip is to talk to the Los Angeles County school superintendent about possibly introducing 'Play Time' into the curricula. Sam believes that because I'm not sure about my relationship with David, I might be thinking about spending winters in the sunny Southland and summers in Michigan, and this is a trial run. Debbie believes that I'm spending a week in California to avoid being her allay in her attempt to convince Richard that the three of them should move to Germany so she can teach math at the American army base in Bamberg.

Each one of them is partially right, but only partially, since Terry's name never came up in any of our conversations, and out of the four only one, Sam, even knows that Terry exists. Sins of omission are much easier to commit when what's being omitted is something that doesn't exist in the mind of the person who's being indirectly lied to. These are complicated times.

The drive to Terry's condo in Santa Monica is as hectic and harried as I'd expected it would be, probably even more so because I'm not paying close enough attention to the traffic surrounding me. Instead I keep thinking about what it's going to be like when Terry opens his door and I see him again for the first time in fifteen years. I probably should have stopped somewhere and got a bite to eat, waited out the afternoon rush hour, which is such a misnomer; there's nothing rushed about driving twenty miles an hour down a five-lane freeway.

But despite the congestion; the tailgating; the constant honking; the middle fingers raised to the sky; the weaving in and out of traffic; the police car that sped by on the shoulder, causing me to wish that I had bought a sandwich and a bottle of water before I left the airport since I might be spending the next few hours trapped in the car, I've arrived.

Terry's condo is on the beach; the building looks like it was built in the sixties but recently renovated. I imagine that at one time, back thirty or so years ago, people used to skulk around here at night, drifting up from Venice Beach, past the pier and the Ferris wheel; some of them drunk, most of them high, looking for a place to crash for the night where they wouldn't worry about getting hassled; migrating to the more upscale neighborhood where they were safe to hunker down and sleep it off as long as they didn't attract attention to themselves by raiding a garbage can or throwing bottles. Now private security guards shoo away anyone lurking around after dark that looks like they don't drive a Ferrari during the day, aren't doing research for an upcoming movie role, or aren't awe-struck tourists from a land-locked state hoping to catch a glimpse through a window of a famous movie star eating dinner.

I should just go back to the rental car, drive a few blocks away and stop and call him and tell him that the flight was delayed and I haven't even left Michigan yet. Sorry, Terry, big snowstorm here. I couldn't get out so I don't know when I'll be there. You dummy. He watches The Weather Channel like everybody else. He'll know you're lying. So what else is new? Lying is all you've been doing lately.

The front door is imposing, carved teak, very Polynesian. The knocker is shaped like a dolphin. There's a doorbell on the wall to the right, in the shape of a hummingbird. I opt for the sea creature.

The sound reverberates from the knocker through my fingers like an electrical shock, traveling across the back of my hand, through my wrist and up my arm.

Maybe he can't hear it inside. It seemed so loud on my side, but that's a really thick door. He probably didn't hear it. I should use the doorbell. Or maybe I should just leave.

As the massive door slowly swings open I feel like I'm being pulled into a vacuum, a place where in another second or maybe three, breathing will be impossible. I need to suck in every last molecule of air now, while I still can. Countless questions race through my mind, faster than the speed of light, questions with uncertain answers, answers that could shape not only the next few hours of my life but potentially the rest of it.

Answers, the answers to life's most important questions, as opposed to—say, history for instance or math, aren't black and white, cut and dried: "Yes you're correct, Columbus did discover America in 1492" or "No, two plus two does not and will never equal five".

The questions we ask about our lives, the things we want, we need to know—are never so easily revealed. There's never only one answer because more than one could be, might be, is—correct.

He looks like I imagined and hoped he would: gray around the temples, bird-feet lines stepping out from the corner of his eyes, maybe a slight paunch underneath his shirt. He's still sexy, still makes my knees weak and my heart flutter. The connection is still there. I feel it, warming and welcoming and remarkable in its simplicity. Yes, I still love you. We're still in love.

That question answered. But what's the one it spawned?

Nothing has changed—everything has changed. The magic of our mouths, our hands, our bodies transforming into one mouth, one set of hands, one body, intertwining. A flutter—a tingling—a pounding—a dance—a coupling—a stillness—a rush—a stillness again.

But there's also wariness in Terry that was never there before. The most important organ, his brain, isn't responding like the others. Our bodies have united but our minds are miles and years apart; they're not sharing the same space.

"Terry?"

"Hmm?"

We've made love twice in the last three hours. Every molecule in my body is energized, pulsing, I'm smoldering—it's a slow, deliciously slow burn. I'm the Charlie of 1984. The Charlie in love with Terry. I liked that Charlie, I liked her very much.

But as much as I liked me then, as much as I liked us then, I like me now, too. I like who I am now.

"Do you want to talk?"

His shoulder stiffens under my left ear, making me even more uncomfortable. I feel like my head is resting on a bony brick with rounded edges.

"About what?"

"Well, I mean—lots of things. There're lots of things for us to talk about. Maybe you want to tell me more about Sara. Maybe you want to talk about your mom? I don't know, Terry. You're the one who wanted me to come out here."

I prop myself up on my left arm and stare into his face. His eyes are closed, his breathing shallow, he looks calm, like he's at peace, but I know that what he's experiencing is anything but a meditative moment.

"Terry—please. Talk to me about something, anything."

His eyes pop open as if he heard an explosion.

"My daughter is wonderful. She's a gift, a gift. She's named for my dead sister, you know. She looks a little like her. You may notice that when you meet her tomorrow, that is if you remember the pictures I showed you of dead Sara. But you won't remember because it's been a very long time since you saw those photos. I'll show them to you again so you can compare the two; I'm sure you'll agree with me. She looks like dead Sara, my sister. "

"That's a good idea, Terry. Tell me more about her. Where does she go to school?"

"Echo Park, a school in Echo Park. It's a small private one. Her mother and her stepfather live there, in Echo Park. Well, at least some of the time, anyway. Her stepfather, I mean. He lives in New York City part of the year. He's a television bigwig. They have two houses, the one here and a townhouse in Manhattan. No, come to think of it, I think they may have another house now, a beach house somewhere on the East Coast. I think he likes it there more than here. Sara doesn't. She likes it here. This is where she was born, this is her home."

"I can understand that. There's something about where we were born and grew up, that even if we leave, if we move far away…"

"Did I tell you that my mom is dead?"

I think suddenly of Dad.

"Yes, Terry. You told me about your mom. Would you rather talk about her instead?"

I expect his eyes to be damp, but they're not. They're dry and vacant, the way they'd look if he were staring at a row of numbers on a computer screen.

"All those years—there was a woman. There was another woman."

"You mean…?"

"Yeah—I mean—good old Dad. Good old Dad, pretending all those years. Such a unique Hollywood marriage, so special, so in love, those two. So in love my ass. All those years he had another woman, a mistress hidden away. What a bastard."

"God, Terry. God, I'm so sorry. I mean—this is hard to understand. I mean—you thought, you believed—what I saw that Christmas—the relationship between your dad and your mom. I can't wrap my head around this."

Terry stretches, his arms and legs elongating like a cat lying in a circle of sunlight on the floor. He shifts, turns his body just slightly to the left, away from me and stares at the wall.

"I need a drink. You want one?"

Before I can answer he's off the bed and walking out of the room, head down, shoulders slumped forward.

He looks so old.

Chapter 30

"Hi. Are you still planning on coming home the day after tomorrow?" Sam sounds like he could, if necessary, teleport his body through the air, across the miles separating us and appear in front of me, smiling and shaking. If he were a puppy, he'd be wagging his entire body from his nose to the end of his tail.

"Hi Sam. I've been thinking about changing my reservation, maybe staying another couple days to finish up some things here. What's up? You sound pretty excited."

"Oh, no! Please, come back when you'd planned 'cause guess who's going to be here the next day?"

The name leaps into my mind, as if it had been crouching there waiting for the right moment to reveal itself. George, its George, isn't it? The past is circling back.

"George? Will George be there?"

"Damn, Charlie! How did you figure that out so quick?"

"Oh, I don't know. A lucky guess that's all. People from the past seem to be making return appearances lately."

"You've seen Terry, haven't you?

"Yes, in fact I'm at his place now. We're leaving in a few minutes to meet his daughter Sara for dinner. She likes sushi. Her absolutely most favorite food ever so Terry says. Eleven and she loves sushi. When I was that age my favorite food was hamburgers, fries and a milkshake."

"Is that the main reason you're there—to see him?"

The lying has taken its toll. It's exhausting being untruthful, exhausting and lonely somehow. Everyone lies but when you do it, you feel like you're the only one in the world being dishonest. And anyway, he's my brother and I can't lie to him and he knows what's going on so…

"Yeah, that's why I came out here. He's dealing with some tough shit. Divorce, his mother dying. He asked me to come—so, I came."

"How's it been?"

"Rough. But hey, tell me about George. My God, after all these years, George. What made him get back in touch after so long?"

"He told me it was because of time—age and memories. He said he needed to set things right."

Action. Inaction. So do I do what's right, or what feels right at this second? And aren't action and inaction the same thing—ultimately? If you don't act, one thing happens. If you do—something entirely different happens. What's right? What's wrong? What feels right? What feels wrong? Does it matter?

"You know what, Sam? I'll come home when I'd planned. I'll be there on Sunday. Wow! George. Do you think we'll recognize him?"

We laugh at the same time, a raucous, deep belly laugh. I can see Sam's face, all skewed up, his eyes closed and his head thrown back as if he were doing a back dive off a platform.

"Well, except for the part about him having an extra leg and arm that I don't have, I'm pretty sure we'll know it's him."

"Yeah. That's why he's coming back, isn't it? I can't wait to see him."

"Me too, Charlie. All three of us together again—wow!"

We've just ordered drinks when Terry announces that Paul and Barbara will be joining us. It did seem a little odd that the sullen-faced greeter, a twenty-something Japanese girl trying without much luck to look a decade older, led us to a table with place settings for five.

"I told my brother that you and Sara hadn't met yet, that I wanted the two of you to have some time to get to know one another but tonight's the only night they could meet us and since you're leaving in a few days—well…"

Terry may want Sara and I to meet but she doesn't appear to share that sentiment. She walks into the restaurant, striding so quickly past the dais at the front door that the morose art house film hopeful has only just looked up from her French manicure when Sara reaches our table. She hugs Terry with one arm, face turned toward me, her pink cheek pressed closely to his torso, her eyes closed. When she opens them I sense the same wariness I felt with Terry five nights ago; a wariness that still lingers like a nagging cough refusing to calm.

"Sara, honey—this is Charlie. Remember? The old friend I was telling you about?"

"Hi Sara," I hold out my hand thinking that she can't possibly refuse to shake it. I'm wrong.

I know she's gone through some rough times, poor kid. But that's no excuse for being rude. This was such a terrible idea. I should have gone to Cindy and Matt's again for dinner tonight.

"Sara, Charlie's holding out her hand so you two can shake, like adults."

I'm embarrassed, standing there with my arm outstretched as if I'm reaching for the hand of someone visible only to me.

"Hey. It's okay. I'll bet you're hungry aren't you Sara? Hungry for some sushi I'll bet. Let's sit down so we can order some."

A shadow darkens Terry's face and I want to apologize for getting in the way of his being a father, for stepping into a situation that I should have avoided altogether.

Shit, you never had a kid, what are you doing? He was trying to get her to behave like she should have. You gave her an easy out, an excuse to not behave like an adult. But, she isn't an adult. She's just a child.

"You know how much I like sushi?"

Her voice is of course a child's voice, not quite shrill but high-pitched and just slightly nasally, and like her father, her question doesn't end in a query; there's no upturn at the end of the sentence. Her eyes mimic her dad's, blue that's soft, yet rich and golden; tiny pinpricks of gilt dancing in the pupils; her hair white blonde, pulled back into a pony tail that hangs down her back nearly to her waist; her skin ivory but reddening in a lip-shaped arc on her cheeks, just at the top of each perfectly sculpted bone. She'll break many hearts and hers will be broken in return. She's beautiful. I both envy her and weep for her.

"Yeah, your dad told me that sushi is your very favorite food. Which kind do you like best?"

Sara smiles, not a wide 'I like you and want to be your friend' expression, but more of a 'maybe you're not so bad, so this is all I can give you now' sort of smile. She slides onto the chair and glances up at Terry who follows suit, then at me. I feel more comfortable seated. She's sitting directly across from me so it's easier to make eye contact at this level.

She takes several seconds to answer. I know she could have answered immediately but I sense that she's stalling for effect, if nothing else.

"Well—right now, as in today—my favorites are California rolls—of course. And cucumber rolls. But my dad has been getting me to try other kinds. I'm starting to like spicy tuna rolls and maybe tonight I'll try a spicy salmon roll. But I will not, not ever eat a spider roll. I don't like spiders. I know there aren't any spiders in there but I don't like the name. No spider rolls for me."

She's most definitely just a kid; a kid with the exquisite face of someone much older and, unfortunately, more knowing.

"I don't like spiders either, so I'm with you there…"

Terry's voice is louder than it should be, as if he's sending out a distress signal: "Paul and Barbara have arrived. I was hoping that maybe they'd be a little late so the three of us could have had some time to talk. Guess that isn't going to happen."

Paul and Barbara also managed to outmaneuver the greeter. He gives Terry a truncated hug, kisses Sara on both cheeks, takes my hand, pulls my body close to his, nestles his lips against my ear and whispers: "I'm so glad you're here, Charlie." When we move apart, Barbara, as stunning, gracious and svelte as I'd remembered, kisses me and then nods as if the kiss were some sort of initiation rite and now I'm in on the secret.

"Uncle Paul. Uncle Paul. I think I'm going to order spicy salmon roll tonight. What do you think of that? But should I get both spicy tuna and spicy salmon? I'm not sure. What do you think, Aunt Barb? I do like spicy tuna. Maybe I should just order that. I don't want to have two dishes so much alike."

Sara's precocious banter should be lightening the mood but it isn't. I feel like I'm sitting in the audience watching master chess players, jousting for the world championship title.

I wish that someone would say something. Paul? Barbara? Terry? For God's sake, respond. The four of us can't behave like this for the rest of the night. If we do, it's going to be one very long evening.

Saved by the waiter. "Here's your Sapporo ma'am, your Jack Daniels on the rocks sir and the hot tea for the lovely little girl. And I see that the rest of your party has arrived. May I please take your drink orders?"

My watch can't be working. Time seems to have slowed down to such an extent that I'm surprised our speech isn't drawn out and distorted as if we've been recorded on a film reel being played in slow motion. Only an hour has passed since our dinners arrived (Sara choosing the safe route sticking with the California and spicy tuna rolls) and even though we've finished eating and Terry is on his third drink while the rest of us nurse our first one, I feel like I've been sitting at this table, surrounded by these people, attempting to make cocktail hour conversation for an entire day.

This is like an old episode of *The Twilight Zone* or a psychological thriller. A film about a woman who ends up somehow in a different world from the one she came from. In one of the worlds, the world she's in now, people aren't who she thinks they are, they aren't who they used to be and time isn't the same as in the other world. In that world people are exactly who they're supposed to be and time's time—it passes by like it always has. But maybe the character doesn't know what's reality and what's not. Maybe this world is the real one. And maybe she can never get back to the other one.

"Charlie, I'm going to the restroom…"

Barbara doesn't have to say another word. She grasps my arm as we walk across the room; the tension in her body palpable, her fingers digging so deeply into my forearm that I force myself to resist asking her to let go.

We're the only two people in the room. Barbara starts talking as soon as she sits down, the urgency of the words flowing from her mouth matching the sound of her urine splashing against the sides of the bowl. She's been waiting all evening to let go.

"Are you going to be okay tonight? Driving back to Terry's place I mean? You can drive if necessary, can't you?"

Suddenly I understand why Sara's mother dropped her off at the restaurant and why she'll pick her up in another half-hour. When Terry told me that Teresa would provide Sara's ride to and from the restaurant I'd assumed it was because she felt uncomfortable meeting me.

"He has had a lot to drink, hasn't he?"

She flushes the toilet and emerges from the stall, face flushed, lips trembling.

"A lot? Hah! Actually tonight's a slow night. Paul and I've seen him put away four, sometimes even five drinks in an hour. I guess he figures he should be on his best behavior since you're here."

She holds her hands under hot running water, and scrubs at them so vigorously she looks like a surgeon preparing to enter the operating room. When she turns to look at me tears are pooling along her lower eyelids.

"It's all so sad. It's all so damn sad. Everything about Terry makes me want to cry now. How are you dealing with all of this? Not like it's his fault. I don't know. Maybe it is his fault. Terry hasn't worked in months, you know."

"I didn't know that. I assumed…"

"Don't assume anything. Never assume anything. Terry did, and look where it got him."

"What do you mean? Are you talking about his mom and dad?"

"Of course I am. What was Harold supposed to do all those years? Gloria on and off medication, sometimes so depressed she wouldn't get out of bed for days. Harold loved her—loves her still—with all his heart. Sweethearts since high school, even when Harold knew then that she was terminally sad."

She wipes her eyes and reapplies her lipstick.

"Terry always assumed that what he saw was real: such a great love between his father and mother. But what Terry saw wasn't entirely real because Harold needed what Gloria couldn't give him. Harold loved her but after awhile, Gloria was incapable of loving back. She was too lost inside herself. Harold did the only thing he could to save his marriage—he had an affair, an affair that lasted twenty-five years. You know, he's still with her today but they'll never marry. Gloria was his one true love."

Two very young women walk in, talking loudly, laughing, already primping at the mirror the second they see their reflections. As Barbara and I walk out I ask: "What did she die of, Gloria?"

"A heart attack, a big one. Harold had taken her on vacation to Maui, every six months he took her somewhere, anything to try to make her happy. They had just arrived, were in their room and Gloria looked at Harold, said his name and fell. It was fast, Harold said, the best way to go."

"Terry told me that she died of a broken heart—a broken heart because she found out about the affair."

"He's wrong. Gloria never knew anything about Harold's affair. Nothing. He couldn't have lived with her knowing…" we're almost at the table, there's not much time left to say more. "But you know, maybe he's right about the cause, just not the reason. Gloria's heart had been broken for a very long time. Love can't fix everything."

Chapter 31

Sam's as animated as a Disney character. This is a Sam who I don't remember ever seeing before; his behavior is exhilarating, exasperating and exhausting all at the same time. Even Peter doesn't know what to make of his partner.

"Charlie, he's driving me crazy. Just crazy. And you know, this Englishman is not driven to such outward displays of emotion all that easily. I haven't seen him this excited since he got his prostheses. No, I retract that statement. He's more excited now than he was then."

"I know. He told me yesterday on what was the fourth or fifth time he called me that maybe he should have had dinner catered tonight. Catered! Can you imagine? You're such a good cook—I mean, how could a caterer be any better than you? And anyway, like I told him, George has been living in the wild country of Alberta for a very long time. I don't think he's expecting a catered meal, he's probably used to eating elk or moose meat, maybe even bear. We've got lots of beer and several decent wines, and your meatloaf's so spectacular. George isn't going to notice that the main ingredient wasn't hacked off the sides of some poor wild animal who should be trundling about in the forest, not mixed together with bread crumbs and mushrooms."

"Thank you my dear for praising my culinary talents. It's good to be appreciated. Sam has come to expect excellence I guess, the meals I create don't seem lately to delight him like they used to."

Peter uncovers the meatloaf and slides it back into the oven. The kitchen smells like a bouquet garni; a rich and savory intermingling of thyme, parsley and rosemary that makes my mouth water in anticipation.

"That smells so good. Dinner is going to be fantastic. I'll open a bottle of wine now so it can breathe. Where's Sam anyway? I've been here for ten minutes and haven't seen him yet."

"At the other end of the house I guess. Making sure that the guest bedroom is still dustless. Or maybe he decided that he had enough time to put a quick coat of paint on the walls before George arrives. Mind pouring me a glass from that bottle you brought? There's a bottle aerating in a carafe on the dining room table, we'll have that with dinner. Might as well start in on this one. If a wine isn't decanted properly, there isn't much point in waiting."

There's a gruffness, harshness in Peter's tone that's off-kilter and out-of-character.

I wonder if he's feeling some jealousy over George's coming back into Sam's life; it wouldn't be unusual I suppose.

"Well, I'll join you then," I fill two glasses halfway and raise mine to toast. "To us—to our lives together—to…"

A glass meeting nothing but air is a lonely and rather pathetic gesture. Peter empties his in two gulps.

"Not much in the mood for toasting right now."

"Peter, what's wrong? Are you and Sam having problems?"

I've never talked to Peter about his relationship with Sam. I've never talked to Sam about his relationship with Peter. I've just assumed all these years that they had something good, something special between them that would get them through tough times. But what was it Barbara said about assuming things? Have I been wrong all this years?

Peter stares at me, his bright blue eyes unblinking.

"We have the kind of relationship that one should expect—no, correct that—that one never expects—between two people who've been together for twenty-eight years. I'm fifty-five, Sam's fifty-one. I know I often wonder, nearly everyday in fact, how we got here. "

Peter fills his glass, to the top this time and smiles.

"I love your brother, and he loves me. The love we feel now isn't the same love we felt two decades ago, or even ten years ago—it ebbs and flows. It's like the tide going out and when it comes back in, it doesn't return in the same way it went out."

"How do you feel about George? About his coming back?"

"Since Sam got George's letter, there's been quite a bit of tension between the two of us. Its partly just plain old jealousy, even though I know it's petty and silly to feel that way. Sam's got something to look forward to and he's so excited about it."

He slowly sips his wine.

"It's a good feeling, having something to look forward to. We all need that, don't we? The thing is if George hadn't been a coward, if he hadn't let your dad browbeat Sam into going to Vietnam, Sam wouldn't have lost his arm and leg. I can't respect George. But if Sam hadn't gone to Vietnam—we never would have met. So, how am I supposed to feel about that? Am I grateful to him? And what kind of man does that make me? Being grateful that the person you love had to suffer so you'd meet?"

"Oh, Peter, I..."

"Charlie! How long have you been here? I didn't hear you come in. I was in the guest bedroom putting some photos around. I hung a few on the wall and sat some on the dresser, photos from the old trunk. Ones of George and me when we were kids—I think George will like seeing them there. I hope he does. Wow! That meatloaf smells delicious. I'm sure he'll love it. Living in Canada, he must eat a lot of meat—eh? Get it—eh? I wonder if George would get upset if I said that. I'd just be being funny—yah know? Oh, I can't help myself, I'm on a roll. What kind of roll you ask? Maybe a Kaiser roll? Dad's not around anymore so I can say that. I sure hope George likes the beer I bought. I wonder if he knows that Stroh's sold out, that the old brewery was blown up fifteen years ago. Shit—if he'd been around then, the two of us would have gone down there, with a big case of Stroh's and watched it happen…"

"Sam—here, not like you need it, but why don't you have a glass of wine while we wait for George to arrive?"

Peter empties the bottle into another glass, hands it to Sam and says, just quietly enough that I know Sam doesn't hear: "Perhaps a strait-jacket would be more appropriate."

As if its been rehearsed for weeks, the doorbell and my phone ring at exactly the same time. It's Debbie calling; I can't ignore her any longer. I know who's ringing the doorbell.

"I have to take this call. Go ahead. I'll be there in a few minutes."

Peter follows Sam out of the kitchen like a man on his way to witness a flogging and Debbie's already leaving a message.

"Debbie. Hey—I'm here."

"Hey back. I'm so glad you picked up. I've got such good news. We're all going to Germany, all three of us. I'm going to teach there. I'm so excited—we're so excited. What an experience this is going to be, for all of us."

"How did you manage to convince Richard?"

"I told him…" she pauses and clears her throat. "I told him that it was his son and his wife, or his mother. I said,

Richard: 'I want our son to have this opportunity, and I want this opportunity. You're a father and a husband now—you're not just a son anymore. Your mom is quite happy in assisted living, she has friends; she keeps busy. You don't have to see her every other day, or even every week. It's our lives I'm talking about Richard, not hers. Besides, she's probably going to outlive us all. When we come back to the states in four years, she'll still be here.'"

If I weren't already on my feet, I'd lay down the phone and give her a standing ovation.

You finally learned how to stand up for yourself, I think. And maybe part of the reason is because I didn't do anything to help. My inaction, forced you into action. I feel like a very wise and trusting mother who let her child go, let her fall down, scrape her knees, get back up, get hurt again and again until eventually that child became an adult and learned how to take care of and protect herself.

"Congratulations, Debbie. What wonderful news. I'm so proud of you for taking a stand. When do you leave for Germany?"

"Not for a few months yet. I start teaching next fall. We plan on moving in early August. In the meantime, there's so much we have to do here. Richard wants to keep the house and rent it out but I'm not too thrilled with that idea. So there's that. And he needs to decide if he wants to teach full-time while we're there, or maybe do something else. Maybe he'll be a house-husband, a stay-at-home-dad." We laugh at the same time.

Peter's come back into the kitchen. He goes to the silverware drawer and takes out a knife, fork and spoon, then grabs a linen napkin from the intricately-carved Belalu wood box Sam bought when they vacationed in Bali not long after Sam got out of the hospital for the last time.

"Debbie—hey—I gotta run. I'm at Sam and Peter's. My brother George just arrived. We haven't seen him in years. I'll call you later. Tell Richard I said hi."

"Peter, I'll be right there. Why another place setting? Sam said that George has been divorced for a long time, but maybe he brought a girlfriend so we could meet her?"

He doesn't look at me as he walks out the door, just turns his head and says:

"Not his girlfriend. He brought his boyfriend. His name is Job."

Chapter 32

I doubt that there's anyone alive who saw *The Wizard of Oz* who wasn't frightened nearly to death by the flying monkeys. L. Frank Baum certainly had a vivid, and somewhat disturbing, imagination. But I wonder how many people were also scared and unnerved by *Alice in Wonderland.* Other than simians capable of propelling themselves through the air, that film in its entirety, and the book, which after I'd grown older I came to appreciate for its hallucinatory drug connections, has always made me uneasy. Uneasy because I realized that Alice's adventures were a 'coming of age' story; that Alice's fall down that rabbit hole was a series of lessons on how to grow up. And one of those most important lessons relates to identity: who we are and what roles we play throughout our lives.

Alice is often asked when she's in Wonderland: "Who are you?" Sometimes she doesn't know, which isn't ideal, not knowing who you are means that sometimes you don't know how you should act in certain situations. But the thing is, we play so many roles in our lives, and each role demands that we behave in a different way, which can be confusing. We spend our lifetime figuring out who we are, and just when we think we know for sure—we realize that we're someone else altogether.

We've finished dinner (George announced mid-way through the meal, to Peter's obvious delight, that the meatloaf was the best he'd ever tasted) and Peter has poured each of us a quarter glass of his favorite cognac. In the last half-hour we: Sam, Peter and I, have learned that George met and married his ex-wife Adrianne shortly after he left Michigan for Windsor.

"I didn't make it very far into Canada initially," he'd laughed, but when Adrianne got pregnant on their wedding night ("We honeymooned in Niagara Falls—where else? The Canadian side's nicer, anyway"), they'd decided it would be wise to move further into the heart of the country. Adrianne had some family in Alberta, she had always wanted to live in a place that was rougher, untamed and wild, and as for George: "I just wanted to get lost, I was running away, hoping that somehow, some way I'd get lost out there. Hah! We can't escape from ourselves though, can we?"

As George tells us about his life with Adrianne, and the two children they raised together until George left the family to be with Job when their oldest child Alan was fourteen, I occasionally shift my gaze to Job's face. Impassive is too mild an adjective to describe his expression. Chiseled out of a piece of granite is more appropriate.

Job is a large, impressively tall and muscular man. He has short dark brown hair exhibiting only a hint of feather-brushed gray at his temples; eyes as dark as his hair; nose long with a bulbous end; reddened skin slightly pock-marked; and the difference in skin tone around his mouth as opposed to his cheeks tells me that most of the time his full lips are surrounded on all sides by a beard—not so tonight, though. He's spoken three, maybe four complete sentences since he and George arrived.

What a serious man, I think. Of course this is all serious, what we're talking about. And it's going to get even more so if and more likely when, we start talking about Dad and the lottery and what happened to Sam. I wonder though if Job ever smiles even when conversations aren't so solemn, and I wonder what did—what does George see in him?

He's so glum. It doesn't seem like there's any way to penetrate that cold exterior. I'll bet if I started singing' I'm A Lumberjack and I'm OK' he might smile. He does kind of remind me of a lumberjack. I've been thinking about that song ever since I first saw him. Nah—he wouldn't smile. He might get pissed-off and leave. But first he'd take a swing at me with his axe. Charlie—get a grip.

"Alan still wants nothing to do with me. He's almost thirty. To this day—he still wants nothing to do with me. But I guess I shouldn't be surprised, should I? Feelings of disappointment and confusion because what you believe should be isn't, don't necessarily abate, not even with the passage of time. Truthfully, it's as if time hasn't passed at all where Alan's concerned. The day I moved out, and he found out the reason why, time stopped for him, at least as it relates to me. There were the fourteen years he and I had shared before that day—and nothing after that." George raises his cordial glass and tips it toward Sam.

I wish Peter, Job and I could just disappear now. Poof! We're eavesdroppers, we don't belong here. Maybe I should suggest that Peter take Elton for a walk and Job and I, we can go sit in the sunroom. We can look at the snow, at the moon shining on the water. It will be still and peaceful and I'll give him a beer to drink because I don't think he's all that crazy about cognac, and then I'll ask him if he thinks it's ironic that his parents named him Job. From the short amount of time I've spent with him tonight, he seems to fit the profile.

"Well, you mattered in Dad's life. Those last few years, as he became more and more confused, he thought I was you about half of the time," Sam says and motions for Peter to refill our glasses. Job covers his glass with his hand and shakes his head.

"I suppose part of the reason is because I used to call him. I called up until eighty-four or maybe it was eighty-five, I don't remember for sure. I made him promise not to tell anyone that I was calling. I said it was our little secret; he seemed to like that idea. The last few times I called he never said my name. I always said 'hi, Dad this is your son George calling', and for a long time he used to say George, and he'd say it over and over while we were talking—as if he wanted to remember it. But he stopped saying it toward the end. I stopped calling when I knew it didn't make any difference anymore, he didn't remember and I didn't believe most of what he was telling me, anyway. I wasn't finding out what was going on with our family."

When he says "family" I feel a catch in my throat, something sticking, and I take a sip of cognac as if to wash it away before I realize that I don't mind so much its being there.

"Yeah, I figured that you'd kept in touch with him over the years. I knew you felt so guilty—about everything. But the thing is—you know how it was…" Sam stops and looks at George, his face expressing an emotion that has no name.

"I know, we agreed. We agreed, but neither one of us had any idea how things would turn out."

Sam chuckles, but it's just a half-sound that barely makes it past his lips.

"When you choose to go to war, to go to *that* war, when you make a conscious decision that you will because you're trying to prove that you're a real man, and then a stranger on TV pulls out of a glass container a plastic ball with your birthdate written on it and your crazy choice is forced on you—when you accept the total irrationality of that decision and that choice that ended up being no choice at all, and what it means for your future—you've got to figure that maybe things might not turn out so well."

Peter sputters out a non-intelligible word at the same time as I shout: "Wait! No, that's not how it happened. I was there. Dad told you that you had to go Sam. He said that you would be the one to go because you were gay. I heard that. I heard him say that."

And then I sink back into my chair and wish again that I could disappear.

"You're right, you heard him correctly. That's what Dad said to me that night, which wasn't surprising to either George or me. We never believed, not in our wildest imaginations that our birthdate would be the first one called, but when it was—we weren't surprised that Dad reacted like he did. I was the gay son, the homo son, the different son and George was the normal one; the one Dad would want to save."

"But the two of you had already decided? You knew what you were going to do if you drew a low number?"

George sounds exhausted, beaten-down, his voice the way I imagine a washed-up, old career criminal on the lam might sound when he finally, thankfully, gets caught.

"I didn't want to go. I wanted to get out of here; away from the phony life I'd created. I was living a lie, had been living a lie ever since I was little. Sam didn't know I was gay. It was all a sham. I couldn't go to Vietnam. That wasn't the kind of getting away I needed. So I went to Canada instead, and ended up still living a lie for a long time, up until I met Job. What a phony I was for all those years. I told Sam I was afraid to go to war and Sam told me he wanted to go—because he wanted to prove to Dad that he was a man. A real man."

Peter sighs, draws breath so deeply, so forcefully into his lungs that I want to say: "Hey, save some air for us", and for the first time all evening Job's up to now inscrutable face shows some emotion. He winces and skews up his mouth as if he wants to speak—but nothing comes out. George reaches out his hand to touch Job's arm, and leaves it there, resting as lightly as if he were cradling a baby bird.

So we sit, the five of us, and no one speaks because at this point in time, what really, can anyone say? I hear my phone ringing from the living room where I left it after I talked to Debbie.

It doesn't matter who's calling; I'll pick up a message from whoever it is later. There's too much I have to deal with to talk now. I'm Alice—and I'm far too busy navigating my way down the rabbit hole.

Chapter 33

It's morning. I know that not because there's light trying to force its way into the bedroom from around the blackout blinds, or because I smell the tantalizing odor of bacon frying, or even because I'm in bed, although I'm still wearing my jeans and sweater. No, the reason I'm quite positive it's morning is because the night that preceded this new day was so surreal, so enlightening yet at the same time so confounding, that I know there was no way it could have continued. It had to end sometime. There'd been more than enough secrets revealed, lives laid bare, memories discounted and assumptions proven wrong for one evening.

Sam apologized to Peter, several times as I recall, for letting him believe all those years that the story I'd told that first Thanksgiving after I returned home, the one about Dad insisting that Sam be the one to go to Vietnam, wasn't the entire truth. All the while he was apologizing to him, I suspected that Sam was also apologizing to Dad. Expressing his shame and asking Dad to forgive him for letting Peter and me believe for such a long time that Sam went to war because he was forced into going, rather than it being his choice, an irrevocable choice thanks to a bouncing Ping-Pong ball.

And George, after first admitting that he had spent his childhood, teenage and young adult years living as someone he wasn't and then finally revealing that he had been scared, as he put it "…Out of my mind that the reality that I was a homosexual man pretending to be straight, would come out if I went over there—to macho land—where men drank and fucked when they could and smoked and got high and killed and drank and thought about fucking and smoked and got high and killed and killed—over and over again…" I came to the realization that Sam and George shared much more than merely a physical likeness, their psychological sameness was startling in its intensity.

After Peter, Sam and George had gone to bed, just before 11:00, all three claiming total exhaustion due to the night's emotional turmoil, Job and I sat in the kitchen, smoked a joint and talked until nearly 2:00.

I don't know if it was the marijuana, the four beers he consumed during our conversation, the fact that my being a straight female made me easy to talk to or if it was all the unburdening that had gone on in the hours before that shook something loose in Job. Whatever the cause (and I tend to think that all four played an equal role in his transformation) the two of us bonded. We confided in one another, we cried a few times and a little after 1:00 we sang the lumberjack song, off-key and missing at least one verse because neither one of us could remember much of the words except for the chorus.

It was the revealing of the joint that surprised me. He introduced it as soon as the others had departed for bed.

"Would you like to get high?" Job asked, as he pulled a tightly rolled roach from his back jeans pocket. "I know I sure as hell would."

A question and a declarative sentence, one right after the other, after a night of monk-like silence, I thought and responded: "Sure. Looks like this night is going to end on a high note, after all."

And Job laughed at my silly play-on-words, which set the tone right there and then, and I decided at that moment that I loved him as much as I loved Peter.

Job spoke first. He told me how he and George had met. How George had showed up at his job-site trailer office one day and told him that he was an excellent carpenter, and that Job, being such a successful and well-respected general contractor, would be a fool not to take him on. And Job said that he knew the minute that George walked through the door that he had met the man he would spend the rest of his life with—despite the fact that George was wearing a wedding ring and told him within the first five minutes that he was supporting a wife and two children.

Talk of George's skills as a carpenter led to my making another breezily clever quip, which unfortunately didn't garner quite the same reaction as the first one. I said something about George's obviously being a talented carpenter because he had nailed Job, but my timing was off. Job was ready to lay down his burdens, to share with me what his life had been like as the homosexual only son of a drilling rig operator and his fervently religious schoolteacher wife.

"So, Dad died without ever meeting George. I didn't go to the funeral. Mom said that Dad wouldn't have wanted me there. I guess I really didn't want to go, anyway. That was the last time she and I talked, it was years ago. Somebody in town told me that she's got cancer. She'll probably die soon. That same somebody will probably let me know when it happens."

That's how Job finished telling me his story. He'd been teary-eyed more than once during that half-hour or so; talking about being bullied in school and his parents not defending him caused him to weep, quietly, for a few minutes, and his eyes were moist when he said that he hadn't wanted to go to his dad's funeral. But I could tell that he was lighter, freer than he'd been when he arrived.

He'd emptied his can of beer and started on another one, and I poured another glass of wine and that's when we began to talk about love, in all its manifestations. Straight love, gay love, love between parents and children, love between siblings, love between married couples, love between non-married couples, love between friends, even the love people have for their pets. We agreed that Sam and Peter's adoration for Elton probably went a bit too far; dressing the dog up like his namesake in gaudy glasses and a big sparkly hat to take him trick or treating being too outlandish.

"That's way too gay, even for gays. Dressing your dog like that would never fly in Alberta, not even among our friends, and every one of them is gay or lesbian," Job said.

People tend to get dramatic, sometimes overly emotional, even maudlin and nostalgic when talking about love, and Job and I were no exception. I cried when I told him that I had fallen in love with Terry the first time I laid eyes on him just like he had fallen in love with George the day George came looking for a job. I cried even more when Job asked me why, if I was so much in love with Terry, I wasn't with him.

"Because of Dad, you know—our Dad. Well, Sam and George's biological Dad, anyway. It's because of him. Things happen, things happened. I had to come back here to take care of him. With Sam, it was always touch and go. Sam needed me."

"I don't sense that you're playing the martyr, although you easily could be," he'd replied.

"You don't think so? Well, thanks for that because there've been lots and lots of times that I have. Lots of times that I've felt really sorry for myself, and then I've hated myself for being such a selfish bitch. I'm not the one who suffered after all."

"When was the last time you saw Terry?"

"A few days ago."

He raised an eyebrow, took another swig of beer but kept quiet.

"I went back to California because—because he asked me to."

"And…?"

"And because I wanted to. I wanted to see him again after all those years. He got married. He has a daughter now, her name's Sara. She's wonderful. And he's divorced."

"Well, that would seem to be a good thing, him being divorced."

"Except that there's someone here I'm seeing. His name's David, he's married, but his wife is in what's sort of like a coma and he goes to see her almost everyday—and—it's all so confusing. It's all so damn confusing."

Job finished off the can, I emptied my glass and it was then that we started singing the lumberjack song.

I hope Peter's making his exquisite pancakes, the ones with walnuts and blueberries. He must be, after dinner last night he has to follow-up with a second act that's just as enticing. A big mug of coffee, pancakes, a couple strips of bacon—my headache is already subsiding just thinking about all the goodness I'm going to ingest soon. But first things first, I have to make myself presentable.

I hadn't planned on sleeping here, in fact I'd told David that after dinner I'd come by his place, and if I'd done that, I'd have woke up in his bed this morning rather than on a lumpy air mattress that Sam uses as make-shift sleeping accommodations in the fourth bedroom. And because this isn't where I'd planned on spending the night, I'm all too aware that there's a distinct odor emanating from my armpits, which is what happens when one sleeps in a wool turtleneck sweater for hours.

I'll just wash up in the bathroom down the hall, Sam's surely got an extra deodorant in there, maybe put on one of his sweatshirts for breakfast. My underwear's a different story but there's not much I can do about that—damn...

My phone's ringing, which reminds me that my phone rang twice last night and I didn't pick up either time.

"David? Hi! I'm so sorry I didn't call you last night to let you know that I'd be staying here. Did you call me?"

"Yeah, I was worried. You didn't check your messages?"

"No, not yet. I'm so sorry. It was a long night—a long and difficult night. But everything's okay. I'm okay, I'm okay."

God—I'm thinking of the lumberjack song. That's kind of amusing, but not really, David was worried.

"Are you coming over later? I haven't seen you since you got back from California."

"Yes, I'll come over later this morning. We're having breakfast, and then I'll leave. I missed you."

"I missed you too, I love you." David ends the call before I have time to respond, no doubt because he knows that my response, or lack of, isn't what he wants to hear, or not hear.

Two messages. Well, you know one's from David so you can delete it. And the other one's from Terry—of course.

"Hi, Charlie. Hope everything's going all right there. It was so good seeing you again. I felt in some ways that no time had passed at all—didn't you? Hey! Sara really likes you. She likes you a lot. Can you come out here again soon? She'd like to see you—and so would I."

And the trip down the rabbit hole is just getting started.

Chapter 34

I leave tomorrow to go to California for the fourth time in the last eight months. The number doesn't seem excessive, considering all I get done when I'm there. I'm accomplishing things: networking; having meetings; having lunch with potential 'Play Time' donors; visiting with Cindy and Matt and their kids; getting stuck in traffic; swearing because I'm stuck in traffic; watching sunsets over the Pacific; luxuriating in the smell of night jasmine and orange blossoms; savoring excellent sushi that can't be found at home; and spending as much time as possible with Terry and Sara. The first year of the new millennium has turned out to be more exciting, exhilarating and equivocal than I could have ever imagined.

I've become practiced all these months at sins of omission, telling David only what I want him to know. There's Emily, after all. She could linger on for many more years. And even when she eventually dies, I don't think David will ask me to marry him. She was—is—the love of his life. He loves me, but not in the same way, and I think I love him, although I've never told him; probably because I'm not really sure how I feel. And the fact that he never asks or seems to even expect me to say the words out loud, causes even more ambivalence in my mind. So, I've convinced myself to not feel too guilty for letting him believe that for nearly a year my primary reason (my only reason) for traveling every other month to Los Angeles has been to bring the 'Play Time' program to the West Coast, which thanks to George's benevolence will happen sooner than I had planned.

Dad left Sam, George and me a considerable amount of money. Despite owning his own company, he'd been somewhat of a miser. The last car he owned, a 1969 Buick LeSabre, that sat un-driven in the garage the final two years of his life, showed nearly one-hundred fifty-thousand miles on the odometer; he neglected the house, often doing make-shift repairs himself, which usually meant that whatever had been broken didn't stay fixed for long; he liked to watch movies, but only on TV (he'd told me on more than one occasion that he wasn't going to pay seventy-five cents to go out to see a movie when he could watch it for free at home); his closet was a throw-back to the early sixties, although he was amenable to purchasing new underwear once a year—buying dinner at Martinelli's were the only times he didn't have a problem parting with his cash.

It took almost a year to settle his estate, at least as far as Sam and I receiving our share. We found out during the process that Maggie and Dad had formally divorced, seven years after she'd left. He'd been reluctant even then to do so, but as his attorney explained: "It's a damn good thing I finally convinced him that he had to. What a can of worms *that* would have been. Him dying and still married to some woman who hadn't been in the picture for years."

Finding George took over a decade. He'd purposely made it difficult to track him down: calling Dad from pay phones; not letting the post office know about address changes; requesting that his customers and Job pay him in cash; paying cash himself for most of his expenses; even going by the first name Howard (the middle name he shares with Sam) instead of George. When the letter arrived, notifying him that he was the heir to two hundred fifty-thousand dollars, he told us that he'd kept it hidden in his sock drawer for weeks, finally telling Job only when his conscience couldn't bear it anymore.

"I started having nightmares, started waking up sweating—sweating bad. It scared me. I started thinking maybe I'd gotten sick. I was paying for what I'd done, and I was going to die because of it. That's when I decided I'd better explain it all to Job," he'd told us.

But it took another four years before George finally called Dad's attorney and asked for Sam's phone number.

"He gave me Sam's number right away, as soon as I said who I was. And I thanked him and said that I'd be calling Sam very soon and was going to hang up and that's when he asked me about the money, what about the money, and I told him that I didn't care about the money—that I didn't want it. But I told him that maybe, once I went back to the island to see my brother and my sister, maybe I'd figure out then what I would do with it."

Luckily for many children, struggling to make some sense of their lives, George decided to give the money to 'Play Time'. It's not that the foundation's hurting financially, not at all, my grandmother saw to that, but additional donations, when you aren't expecting them, are always welcome. And that's one of the major reasons why sometime early next year 'Play Time' will be in the curricula at one or more schools in Los Angeles County. So, my visits are critical, a lot of planning and preparation is happening. Mom can't go with me, her arthritis bothers her quite a bit now and lately her knees have been "acting up"—it's all up to me. No one asks, no one questions.

Why should anyone wonder? I've really got nothing to hide. Not really. So why do I always feel guilty when I leave on one of these trips?

It's early Fall, so I'll need maybe one heavier sweater. I've traveled to California so often in the past several months that I have a suitcase always partially packed and ready to go: toiletries, underwear, something to sleep in; all I have to do is add the appropriate clothing depending on the time of year.

Who's ringing the doorbell? I hope it's not the Jehovah's Witnesses. It was fun though the last time they came by and asked me if I wanted to be saved, and I said that if Wiccans were worthy of saving, then I was down with that and invited them in.

She's very tiny, this grey-haired woman, extending her arm, adorned with silver bracelets, ready to press the button a second time. I notice the bracelets because her deeply tanned arms are bare, surprising since it's November and less than forty-five degrees outside.

I don't think she's from around here, otherwise she wouldn't be walking around sleeveless. And how did she get here, anyway? There's no car in the driveway. I hope she didn't have to walk far with those bare arms.

"Are you Charlie Carpenter?" Her voice matches her body: sinewy and rough around the edges. She sounds like a female lightweight boxer with a bad case of post-nasal drip.

"I am. And you are…?"

"…Hazel Martinez. I know—knew Maggie Carpenter. Mind if I come in, it's a little cold out here."

Hazel doesn't wait for my response. She slides past me, her Western-style boots making a clunking sound as she walks into the living room. Now I notice the denim jacket, a match to her jeans, draped across her arm. There's something white in her hand, I see only the corner peeking out from underneath the jacket sleeve. She scans the room, turning her head slowly as if it's on the end of a periscope, turns to me and says: "Very nice little home you have here, Charlie."

Good god—is there a gun underneath her jacket? No, not a gun, but maybe she's an attorney or something like that, which could be almost as bad. But I haven't done anything wrong. Why would she be here to serve me papers? And what's the deal with knowing Maggie? Why did I ever open the door? I should have pretended I wasn't home.

But I have a feeling Hazel would have stuck around until I did come to the door. She would have camped out on the porch. I've known her for all of twenty seconds and I already sense that obstinate is a good word to describe her.

"Thanks. I don't need anything big. I…"

Hazel isn't listening. After dropping her jacket and what I realize now is an envelope on the sofa, she's quickly gravitated to a sideboard near the doorway leading to the kitchen— the place where I display my favorite family photos. Mom and me having dinner in Greektown; Kevin, Mom and me at Martinelli's the night we refer to as "the big reveal"; a yellowed black and white of Jim not long after he arrived in Vietnam; Kevin, Janet, Alyssa, Mom and me celebrating Alyssa's first Christmas; the five of us plus Sam and Peter on New Year's Eve nineteen ninety-nine at Martinelli's.

"These people are your family I take it?"

Yes—they're my family—damn it. I wouldn't be displaying strangers' photos.

"Yes. My mom, my biological Dad, my brother and his wife and their daughter and the brother I grew up with and his partner. May I ask…?"

"Ah, yes—his partner. That would be Sam then?"

"Yeah. Sam and his partner, Peter."

I feel like we're talking in riddles.

"Peter. Peter. Penis-eater. Hah!"

I'm thinking now of every cliché I've heard spoken in the movies.

"Lady, who do you think you are coming in here like this and causing such a ruckus?"

"I don't know who you are, lady, but for your own good, you might think about leaving."

"Who do you think you are, lady, barging in here like this? Saying all these things?"

But all I can manage is:

"That's not funny. What do you want from me, Hazel Martinez?"

Hazel may be obstinate *and* possibly obnoxious, but she has a conscience, too. Tears are welling up in the corner of her inky black eyes; a skim milk blue circle obscures the pupil of the left one.

Such an awkward moment: Hazel grabs for my fingers at the same time as I'm folding my arms up tight against my chest, hoping to hide my hands under my armpits, as if to ward off something that would do me harm.

"I'm so sorry, Charlie. That was the feisty young dyke in me coming out. I need something to drink, do you have any booze around here?"

And before I can answer she opens the sideboard cupboard door, revealing a few mostly full bottles of Scotch and vodka that I keep around in case a guest wants something harder than wine or beer.

Who the hell is this woman? Booze? It's only 3:30 in the afternoon. And dyke? I should have hid out in the bedroom, waited her out. She would have gotten cold once the sun went down, she would have left once her wrinkled-up old ass started to freeze off.

"Mind if I have a little vodka on the rocks?"

If she makes her way for the kitchen, I'm going to have to tackle her or something. I know she's old but this is insane.

"I'll get a glass and some ice. You sit down, right here on the sofa. It's a little early for me, so if you don't mind, I'm not going to join you. But I'll get you a drink and then will you tell me why you're here?"

"I can tell you now," Hazel says as she sinks down into the over-stuffed sofa, making her appear even smaller. She looks like a ten-year old with gray hair and a pursed-up face, dressed up in mommy's clothes, sitting in daddy's chair. "I have something to give you. It's that letter over there. It's from Maggie—to you."

"How do you know Maggie—from where? Where was she all those years after she left us?"

"Just about all that time, she was with me. We were together, on my ranch in New Mexico, from nineteen sixty-four to five minutes before midnight nineteen ninety-nine. She tried to hang on; I know she wanted to be around for the big changeover to the millennium, but cancer's time-sensitive only as it relates to when it wants to take you. Cancer doesn't give a damn that you want to be part of the biggest fucking celebration in a thousand years."

She starts to cry, really cry—her narrow little shoulders bobbing up and down so vigorously I worry she might break a vertebrae in her back.

I really don't think she needs a drink right now.

"You know—I—I— don't think I need that drink, after all. You—you need to open the letter and read it. And, if—you—wouldn't mind, I'd like you to read it out loud."

Hazel swipes one hand across her face, as she picks up her jacket and the letter with the other, then she pats the empty seat cushion and smiles.

"Please join me on your sofa. The letter will explain it all. You aren't going to have any questions after you've read it. And maybe, if there's time after you've finished—I'll have that drink. And then I'll leave. I'm an old woman, I need my sleep."

She's so short she curls her legs up underneath her, so she's sitting on her feet. I sit with one leg barely touching the floor, the other bent beside me so we're almost facing, she hands me the envelope.

I open it and begin to read.

Chapter 35

Dear Charlie:

Although it pains me to write this, and believe me it does: if you're reading this letter, it means that I'm dead. That's the reason, of course, that there's no date affixed to this missive. I have no idea when I'm going to die, although I don't doubt that it will be sooner rather than later. Multiple myeloma isn't curable and I avoided going to the doctor for months, despite the fact that I knew something was very wrong. So, by the time I paid a visit to old Doc Garfield, the disease had me in its clutches and was hanging on for dear life...mine. Cancer. Try, if you can, to avoid getting it.

But I digress. Having to write that clichéd sentence about my being dead, which is why you're reading this, is overly-dramatic on the surface and reads so trite, but when one thinks about it, and believe me, I have, it's not all that out-of-character for one, being me, to write these words, because for such a long time I was just acting, anyway. Self-preservation, that's all it was.

I was aware from an early age that I liked boys and girls equally—sexually. Hazel tells me it's probably because my biological father, or maybe an uncle, sexually molested me, but that's something I'll never know. Whoever my parents were, they gave me up for adoption when I was less than a year old, so I decided, when I was old enough to make those sorts of decisions, that if they didn't want to keep a child who they'd shared a life with for almost twelve months, then I didn't have any interest in trying to find out who they were, or anything about them. Full disclosure: Hazel is more than a little prejudiced against men. I love her to death (probably not the best choice of words but I wrote them, so they're staying in) but I think she may be a little jealous over the fact that I've been with both sexes, and enjoyed it, something she can't comprehend.

Again, I digress. About my bad acting; it became apparent when I was in foster care that I wasn't disguising my preference for both men and women very well. That's why I lived with so many foster parents. It was different when I was younger, living in the children's home. All little kids engage in 'you show me yours and I'll show you mine behavior.' It's play-acting, kids pretending to be a doctor or a nurse, just so they can get a look at what's underneath the underwear. I don't remember getting in any more trouble than any of the other kids then, but when I got older and had to go into foster care, things changed.

When I was ten I told my first foster mother, Mrs. Roger Grant, that I thought about kissing girls sometimes, as in kissing them right on the mouth, the same way I would kiss a boy. She was horrified—you'd have thought that I'd confessed to thinking about drowning kittens or setting houses on fire. She told me that I needed to "get rid of those thoughts—right now", and on Valentines Day that year she went out and bought a bunch of expensive, very fancy cards and a considerable amount of chocolate candy, which I gave to all the boys in my class. I was a big hit; in fact I was so popular that Chris Baldwin, the first person I ever kissed, and I ended up locking lips in the coat closet. We would never have been caught if I hadn't shoved my tongue down his throat, causing him to gag and scream out at the same time. We were only ten, after all. How I knew to do that, to this day I have no idea. But I did, and that's what set me on the road to perdition, as Mrs. Grant liked to call it. These days I suppose it's referred to as the highway to hell.

I tried. I really tried those next several years to disguise the fact that I enjoyed French-kissing with Chrissie Mitchell as much as I enjoyed it with Chris Baldwin. But the word was out, and I was doomed. Not only was no one going to adopt a teenage girl who was so vile and disgusting that she played dancing tongues with both boys and girls, no one wanted to foster such a foreign and frightening creature for very long, either.

And then, when I was sixteen, living with the Bonkowski's, who turned out to be the best, the most understanding and open-minded of all my foster parents, I met Alfred. We got married when I was eighteen. Mrs. Bonkowski gave me the blue garter I wore that day.

I don't know if Alfred knew when we first met that I wasn't like the other women he knew before. I know that he knew that I was a virgin, sort of, because I didn't believe then that fingers counted, so I never told him about the glorious night I'd spent with Maryanne Thomas. I knew that he wasn't a virgin, which obviously didn't bother me in the least, although he seemed rather ashamed about it.

Like it is with all young lovers, everything was wonderful at first. But eventually of course, life had its way with us. Things changed. Alfred's brother Howard went off to war and got killed, and then, to prove to his father that he was also a brave man, worthy of his dad's affection, Alfred went to war and when he came back, he wasn't the same Alfred who had shipped out with a glint in his eyes and a straight proud spine.

He had failed in the war, hadn't gotten any medals for valor or extraordinary bravery, hadn't returned a hero, and hadn't made his father proud. Instead he'd suffered the pain of failing to do anything heroic on the battlefield other than being injured and returning home a damaged man. Alfred didn't die in the war, and that haunted him as much as anything. You're a hero when you're killed in action, but you're nobody when you're just another guy who comes back different than who you were when you left. Part of Alfred was missing when he returned from the war, but unfortunately it was not a part that anyone could see was gone.

Then Samuel and George were born, and life changed again in ways that neither one of us saw coming. Nowadays I know that parents talk openly, without shame or embarrassment, about how having a child forever alters everything about your life—in mostly wonderful ways but in ways that also aren't quite so wonderful. But back then, in nineteen forty-nine, no one would have dared speak what would have been considered sacrilege.

I nearly died bringing those boys into the world, lost a tremendous amount of blood. I had a hysterectomy before I was discharged after giving birth. Samuel and George nearly died, too. They stayed in the hospital preemie ward for almost three weeks before we could bring them home. Once I was well enough, I went to see them everyday. Alfred came with me once, only once; I think he was afraid of how they made him feel. We never talked about it of course— Alfred and I didn't talk about many things when he came home, but I sensed that he was overwhelmed with his love for them while simultaneously wondering just what that love meant. He had disappointed his father; I often wondered if Alfred worried that his own sons would disappoint him, and then what? Would the disappointment displace the love?

When it became apparent, when they were around six, that my two beautiful boys were gay, I do love that term, it's positive, signifying an innocent happiness and delight unlike the way homosexuals were referred to then, as queer or fag or homo, I knew that as their mother I had to do everything I could to make sure that their father wouldn't be disappointed. But, I wasn't confident that it would work with both of them. I was still struggling with the "who's the real me?" question everyday of my own life. Continually play-acting takes a lot of energy.

So, for what I convinced myself was the noblest of reasons, because I wanted at least one of my sons be the son his father wanted him to be, I arbitrarily chose George as the one who I would encourage to be someone he wasn't; to live a life that was, essentially, a lie—an act— pretending so his father would love him.

Was what I did right or wrong? I will never know the answer to that question, but over the years I've come to realize that it was probably both, and that thinking has allowed me to let go and move on, otherwise I would have gone crazy. I do wonder sometimes though why I chose George over Samuel, that's my only decision that occasionally, to this day, gnaws at me. But I did—I watched the two of them through the kitchen window, playing in the backyard, my two little twin boys and I said out-loud as if there was someone in the room with me: "George." And that was that.

About now Charlie I imagine that you're wondering: what about me? Why did you choose to adopt me? There has to be something about me in this letter, I'm the one you chose to send it to. I told you earlier that I believed that Alfred was afraid of the way he felt about Samuel and George because it wasn't a feeling that was guaranteed to stand up to infallibility. He had offered that kind of love to me, love that I'd never experienced up to that point in my life. A love that was totally unconditional, love that wouldn't diminish if the object of that affection didn't live up to expectations. But I knew that eventually I was going to leave, and that when I did my leaving would totally undermine his belief in the purity of love. I couldn't let that happen. So, we decided to adopt a baby girl, someone Alfred could love always and forever, without reservation.

And then, when you were six, I left. My days of pretending were over. I wasn't ever going to love Alfred the way that he loved me, and that wasn't fair—to him or me.

I know that Alfred thought I was so strong, that I was a resilient tough woman, not some giggling, whining little thing who'd cry for no reason and nag at him to be even better than he was. But Alfred was mistaken: I was a frightened, insecure and confused little girl who grew up to be a frightened, insecure and confused woman, who had learned how to pretend otherwise.

In looking back perhaps the timing wasn't the best, leaving Alfred and the three of you one day after President Kennedy was assassinated. But then, maybe the timing was exactly right. My leaving had nothing to do with someone killing the president; there was no connection between those two events. I suppose that many people in the country, around the world for that matter, who had decided that they were going to do something dramatic, perhaps even life-changing and life-altering, went ahead and did what they had been planning to do all along in the days after his death, figuring that their actions would forever pale in comparison to the enormity and significance of what happened that day in Dallas.

Wives left husbands; husbands left wives; lovers split up; people filed for bankruptcy; supposed best friends told one another that they didn't want to be friends anymore; engagements were ended and marriage proposals were made; students dropped out of college; business partners announced that they no longer wanted to be partners; alcoholics went cold turkey and people who had stopped drinking, started again. Everything we did in those days in late November 1963 we did because we were living our lives, even though we all knew that something had forever changed. But we couldn't let what happened on that big stage conflict with our own intimate personal life stories.

And the day before I left, when I heard Alfred talking to you downstairs in the den, explaining to you why your favorite TV shows weren't on I knew that you would be okay. He was so tender, so sweet, so loving. It's not an easy thing to do—explain evil to a six-year old. Later, after you and the boys had gone to bed and even though it was cold, I heard him go outside. He walked out and sat on the glider, and it squeaked as he went back and forth and back and forth and cried and cried for a very long time. Alfred was a staunch Republican, he didn't vote for Kennedy; we never talked about politics because I learned early on in our relationship that such discussions were verboten, but he cried that night, cried as if there was nothing else left to do.

Alfred and I kept in touch after I left. Every Christmas I sent him money to buy presents for you, Samuel and George. But I made him promise never to let any of you know that the presents were from me, they were always to be from Santa. We talked a few times on the phone in those first years, and each time Alfred would ask me when I was coming back, and I would say: "Never Alfred. I'm never coming back." And he'd answer: "But you will, Maggie. You will and everything will be the same when you do."

Finally, after seven years had passed he called me one day and told me that his attorney had suggested that it would be best if we were legally divorced. Alfred seemed fine with that; it didn't appear to faze him in the least. He told me that his attorney would send all the papers for me to sign, and then, right before he hung up, Alfred said: "This doesn't mean anything, Maggie. You'll come back, and everything will be the same when you do."

Up until then I always knew what was going on in your lives, but once we divorced, I felt that I didn't have a right to know anymore. I had a new life, nearly a decade had passed, I had moved on and I had to let go. There were times when it was very hard to not play detective, to not be a sleuth and find out what I could. I knew that Samuel and George's birthday was the first date drawn in the lottery; there were nights when Hazel and I would watch TV and see the horror that was going on in Southeast Asia and I'd turn to her and say: "Do you think one of them, maybe both of them are there? What do you suppose is happening to my boys?" And she would answer: "What difference would it make if you knew, Maggie? There's nothing you could do for them. Isn't it better this way?" And I would know she was right.

What's that catchy phrase that people like to use these days: 'That's my story and I'm sticking to it?' Well, this has been my story, at least the early part of my story, the first two acts. Hazel will fill you in on the rest. Of course she doesn't want me to die, but she does have a flair for the dramatic, which you'll realize very quickly after you meet her, so I know that there's a part of her that's looking forward to playing a role in this denouement.

I'm old now, Charlie. I'm old and sick and I'm ready to make my exit, but I wanted you to know, before I leave for the final time, that I did what I believed was right. I loved you all, in my own way, and when all is said and done—that's all that's real, isn't it?

Love, Maggie Carpenter

Chapter 36

I didn't fly to California as planned the day after Hazel paid me a visit. As I explained to Terry in what turned out to be a rather uncomfortable conversation a few hours after Hazel's arrival: "She came all this way, all the way from New Mexico. This is the first time in her life she's been east of the Mississippi, the very first time and she's eighty years old. She took a taxi from the airport to the island, and *that* was the very first time she'd been in a taxi. I can't just call another cab to take her back to the airport tonight."

He'd been agitated and unreasonably irritated that I wouldn't be arriving as scheduled.

"I told Sara that the three of us were going to go to Griffith Park the day after you get here. We'd go late in the day, spend some time at the observatory and then look at Saturn through the telescope. Why can't she go back tonight? Doesn't she have a plane to catch?"

His selfishness was upsetting. Why should I have to explain this in detail? I'd wondered.

"Yes, Terry. She has a plane to catch—at five tomorrow evening. She didn't want to 'put me out' in her words, but she didn't know how long she'd be here with, so she figured that she'd spend tonight and most of the day tomorrow in the airport. Crazy woman—she didn't even book a hotel room. 'I'll do some people watching, that'll be a hoot' she told me.'"

"So explain to me again exactly who she is—your adoptive mother's lover? The mother who walked away and left you and her sons, and her husband, just walked away? You don't owe this woman anything, Charlie."

But of course I knew that I did—owe Hazel Martinez something. I owed her the opportunity to tell me her story, to tell me about the woman she had loved for thirty-five years, the woman she'd shared her life with. She'd come such a long way to tell me Maggie's story, and her story, there was no way I was going to let her sleep overnight in terminal A at Detroit Metropolitan Airport.

"She's staying with me tonight, Terry. Tomorrow morning I'm taking her to meet Sam and Peter and we're going to drive by Dad's and Maggie's old house, so she can see for herself where Maggie lived, so she'll no longer have to fantasize about what Maggie's life was like pre-Hazel, at least not as far as the place that Maggie called home. It's not that big of a deal. I'll change my reservation and come out there a few days from now. We'll take Sara to the observatory then."

That seemed to appease him, at least for the time being, but I knew that he wasn't pleased. Terry's feelings' alternate these days between anger and disillusionment, disappointment and denial—negative emotions all. I doubted that, barring a trip in a time machine taking him back twenty years or so he'd start exhibiting more positive attitudes anytime soon.

Hazel, Sam and I spent the next twenty-four hours getting to know one another. We were the last link she had to Maggie's life before they'd met; Hazel needed to reminisce with us in order to bring Maggie back to life—if only for a short time. And all of us knew that when she left, we'd never see one another again.

We learned that Hazel was the oldest of three children born to Carlos Gonzales and his wife, Isabelle. That despite the fact that her siblings were boys and the fact that Hazel was a rough and tumble lesbian born into a culture that expected men to be macho protectors and women to be earth mothers, she inherited the family cattle ranch.

"Those brothers of mine, useless, that's what they were. Useless at least when it came to doing any hard work. They just wanted to sleep with the ladies, go into town to drink—they never wanted to get out of bed before ten. Big on siestas they were, whether they were taking them alone or with one of their lady friends. Neither one of them could rope a calf if their life depended on it. They could reel in some young girl alright, but not a young steer, that's for sure."

Hazel's body type hadn't held her back; rather her tininess was the impetus that inspired and invigorated her. She learned how to ride a horse at age five, to rope a calf at age eight. By the time she was twelve Carlos felt confident enough in her skills that he took her with him on drives and let her assist with calving.

"Daddy knew I was a marimacha, but he also knew that I'd be able to run the ranch when he was gone, and that was more important to him than who I liked to have sex with. His good-for-nothing sons were perezoso, lazy—they'd never amount to anything. When I was fifteen he told me that, if I wanted it and he knew I did, he would leave the ranch to me when he died."

"Did you mother feel the same way?" I'd asked.

"Mama was sad because she knew her first-born, her only daughter, wasn't going to give her any grandchildren. But the good-for-nothings, the two lazy brothers came through. They weren't so lazy in the grandbaby-making department. Henri had three children with his first wife, two with his second wife after the first one died and Juan's wife had six children total. They turned out to be not so much of a disappointment in the end. Henri graduated from law school and Juan started a construction business. They never wanted to be ranchers, anyway."

Hazel's ranch was where Maggie inadvertently migrated to when she left Michigan. She'd been on her way to Albuquerque, thinking that eventually she'd head north to Santa Fe but she got only as far as Santa Rosa, just across the border from Texas, when her car broke down.

"It was serendipitous, her car stalling out like that. I'd just left the ranch in the pick-up, was on my way into Santa Rosa and I saw her, standing by the side of a bright red fifty-nine Chevy Bel-Air with steam rising up out of the hood like Old Faithful. She was beautiful. Tall, long dark hair somehow all fanned out around her, even though I don't remember there being much wind that day. Who would ever have thought? Two lesbians meeting up in the middle of pretty much fucking nowhere; one who'd driven all the way from Michigan. We were meant to be."

Maggie settled into ranch life "...The way you'd cozy down on a cold winter night in an over-stuffed chair with a glass of brandy, your legs and lap all covered up with a woolen blanket and a tabby cat," Hazel explained.

When Hazel turned sixty-two in 1982, she started selling off both land and cattle, and five years later she owned just ten acres; acreage that she turned into an animal shelter of sorts. In the ensuing decade Hazel and Maggie rescued scores of dogs, cats, rabbits, goats, sheep, even a few guinea pigs and a three-legged burro who wandered onto the property one day "Looking for some love, and a little respect." Everyone in Santa Rosa knew that if you had an animal you didn't want anymore, or if you'd found an animal that was lost or injured, you took it to Hazel and Maggie's ranch.

"We were a pair, Maggie and I. Our relationship wasn't perfect, oh no—far from it. We argued, we fought. We fought like banshees, like she-monsters. Two women, two women living together, sharing the same dinner table, the same pots and pans and dishes, the same bed—the same space—day in and day out. I'll tell you, Charlie, sometimes it wasn't pretty. It wasn't pretty at all."

She'd stopped talking for a minute, blew her nose and continued, softer than before.

"But the parts that were pretty—they were exquisite. The thing is…it's not easy for two people to live together, day in and day out. You get all too familiar with someone and you sometimes start taking them for granted, but when all is said and done, it's damn good to have someone you love right by your side when you're helping a first-calf heifer with a breech birth, rescuing a goat who got caught up in a snow storm or consoling a brother who's lost his wife to cancer. The everyday stuff, the petty inconsequential 'you're getting on my nerves with your mouth-breathing' bullshit, doesn't mean squat when you're up against the fucking universe, when you're up against life. It's what you do for each other when it isn't all rosy and wonderful but instead you're worried and scared and cold and tired and depressed—and that someone is there for you, right beside you. Propping you up, telling you that you made the right decisions, that you did what was best, even if they aren't sure that what you did was right, because they love you and they don't want you to hurt. That's when it's exquisite, that's when love's perfect, that's when we know for sure why it is we fall in love."

After I dropped Hazel off outside the terminal, I looked in my rearview mirror as I drove away. She was standing there, one arm raised in the air bent like a goal post, palm flat, looking like a referee wearing denim rather than black and white stripes, doing her own immobile version of a good-bye wave. A woman was walking up behind her; she was much taller than Hazel, hatless, her long dark hair circling around her head like a halo—and for a few seconds I believed she was Maggie, arriving just in time to join Hazel on the trip back to their home.

Chapter 37

"When are you going back to Michigan?" Cindy smiles at me over her latte. The expression accentuates the tiny lines splaying out from the corners of her eyes: "hummingbird feet, most definitely hummingbirds, not crows" she's reminded me every time I've seen her these past few years.

"Tomorrow, the seventh. I want to be back and all rested up from the trip so I won't behave like a zombie at a surprise birthday party on Saturday for one of David's co-workers. This has been a grueling week, in more ways than one." I dip my chocolate-covered biscotti in my coffee and swirl it around, softening it just enough to make it melt when I put it in my mouth.

"I can't even imagine how busy you've been this trip, with 'Play Time' being introduced into two school districts in LA County this semester. You may be all over the country in a few years. I'm so proud of you, Charlie. Really, your foundation is doing so much good for all these kids. Giving them a voice, a way to feel comfortable expressing what's going on in their lives. You must wake up in the morning feeling like a million bucks."

"It's more than just me—everyone, my mom and Derek and Samantha and even sometimes Kevin gets involved. They've all helped make it such a big success. Those kids, Derek and

Samantha. Who would have thought? Derek's turned out to be one of our most valuable board members, and Samantha never ceases to amaze me. Her grant-writing skills have brought in some serious money."

Cindy sits the mug on the table and leans in close to me, as if she's going to whisper and wants to make sure that I'll hear every word. Instinctively I shift in my chair and tip my torso back —her closeness is intimidating.

"So, everything's going well on that front. What about your personal life, Charlie? What's going on with Terry? How much time did you spend with him and Sara this trip?"

"I'm going to get another cup of coffee," but when I stand Cindy takes ahold of my arm and gently guides me back into the seat.

"Your cup's full, Charlie. You don't need another one, unless you're planning on doing some sort of coffee flight, setting up three or four cups on the table so you can do a tasting. We need—you need to talk about what's happening."

"I didn't see Sara this trip. She's on the East Coast with her mom and step-dad. They've got a place near Cape Cod. Sara's flying home tomorrow, we may cross paths at LAX. She's got some charity function on Sunday that her class is involved in, one of those walks or something. She's a very charitable, very altruistic kid. I don't remember being that concerned about other people's welfare when I was her age."

Cindy smiles, flicks out her tongue and swipes away a thin frothy moustache rimming her upper lip.

"Yeah, you were. Don't you remember when we volunteered to read to seniors at the nursing home in Riverview?"

"Yeah, now that you mention it, I guess I do."

I don't, not really. But I seem to recall getting very sick when I was around twelve or so.

"We didn't do it for very long though, a couple weekends I think because I got mono. I do remember that I was really embarrassed—getting mono—the kissing disease. I hadn't kissed anybody but I thought that Dad would think that I had."

"Well, you did have a crush on Tommy Cooksey. I remember you telling me that you wanted to kiss him someday."

Tommy Cooksey. I haven't thought about him in years. He's the only boy, or man for that matter I ever kissed who had red hair. Red hair and freckles: the ultimate nerdy combo. I wonder what he looks like now.

"And—well, I did—kiss him you know. But he wasn't the first boy I ever kissed—that was…"

"…Ray Fisher. Yeah, you kissed a boy before I did, and you told me all about it. How it was kind of 'gaggy' in your words. You invented a whole new word to describe that experience. Gaggy: I never forgot it."

If we can keep this conversation going for the next half-hour or so, I'm home free. Let's reminisce until you have to leave to pick Crystal up from soccer practice.

"So, you didn't spend time with Sara this trip. It was just you and Terry. How was it?"

Amazing how she turns on a dime like that—just like Mom. She's like a laser focusing in.

"It was—he's—I don't know sometimes…" the biscotti's too soft. It crumbled into tiny pieces that bob and weave on the surface of my coffee as I attempt to stir the whole unappetizing mess to the bottom of the cup. I keep talking but I don't look up.

"How do we get people so wrong? It's because we're seeing people the way we want to see them, the way we want them to be—isn't it? We're projecting all the qualities we want in a partner onto someone we met totally at random. We see someone at a party, see him reflected in a mirror—a mirror that reflects his image as well as our own, and we think that what we see, and feel and want to believe in is real. But the thing is—mirrors don't reflect absolutely perfectly, there's always some distortion."

I really wanted that biscotti.

"Hey, I seriously do need another cup of coffee, and another biscotti. This one's all gaggy, floating around in there. I can't drink this."

"My latte's almost gone. Order me another while you're up there. I'm going to call Crystal's best friend's mom and ask her to pick Crystal up. I have a feeling we're going to be here awhile."

The coffee flight, that's not such a bad idea.

Chapter 38

"Sasha, baby I'm so sorry I slept in. Jeez, what time is it?"

There's nothing like the feeling of a fifty-pound dog's paws resting on your collarbone, her silky tongue traversing your face from chin to forehead, to alert you to the fact that you've spent more than your allotted time in bed.

"You need to go out, don't you? Okay, baby. Okay. Just give me a few minutes to get my body in gear and I'll let you out so you can do your business. Wow! I slept like a rock last night."

8:40. I haven't slept this long in awhile. Good thing I wasn't planning on going into the office early. But I needed the rest, that's the best night's sleep I've had since I got back from California four days ago.

Sasha's outside as soon as there's enough space between the door and the frame for her to wriggle her body through. She'd waited as long as she could to wake me; normally I'm up by 6:00.

I've got ten minutes or so before she'll be barking at me to be let back in, enough time to brew coffee and catch some news. It's a slow news day. There isn't much that captures my attention so I settle for watching Matt Lauer interviewing a guy who wrote a book about the always-intriguing Howard Hughes.

"He was absolutely elusive, told you a different story every time you talked to him," the author's saying. "The question's always been: Howard Hughes, who was he? He certainly was an enigma."

Well, I can relate to that. Terry's no Howard Hughes but he's sure turned out to be an enigma to me.

Sasha's right on cue, barking as if she thinks I've surely forgotten that she's out there.

"I'm coming Sasha—I'm coming. You know that I wouldn't leave you outside you silly girl…"

Safe! She's back inside, goes straight for her bowl and I hear Lauer:

"I'm sorry, I have to interrupt you. We want to go live right now and show you a picture of the World Trade Center—do we have it? No, we don't have it. We'll be back with a breaking story."

I pour another cup of coffee, give Sasha, who's almost finished gobbling up what she obviously believes is the last can of Alpo she'll ever receive, a quick pat on the head and sink into the old leather club chair I took from Dad's house after he died.

Back from commercial, Lauer and the perennially perky Katie Couric are in their usual spots on the sofa. Couric leads off.

"As Matt just mentioned, we have a breaking news story to tell you about. Apparently a plane has just crashed into the World Trade Center here in New York City…"

And there it is, the iconic World Trade Center: black/grey smoke billowing from the top and a gaping hole on the side, a voluminous black hole that, as I sit both transfixed and shuddering in terror and disbelief, spreads across the face of the building like the maniacal mouth of a madman—opening wider and wider, revealing incomprehensible malevolence deep inside.

They know, animals do—they know. That "clunk" is the sound of Sasha shoving her empty bowl against the baseboard and now here she is: sweet brown eyes, wet nose against my hand, tail moving back and forth like a metronome. She licks my fingers, gazes up at me and I know what she's thinking: if you'd let me up there, I'd sit on your lap and make you feel not so sad and afraid.

"Sasha, sweetie," my voice surprises me—it's edgy and wet as if I've already been crying for hours. "There's no room for you here, you're too big now. You're a big girl. But you can sit right here by my feet, stay right here, right here by my feet."

I place my palm gently on her forehead, she bows, hind end in the air, tail still wagging, puts her front paws on my feet and slowly lowers the rest of her body onto the floor.

"What is this, Sasha? What's happening?" At the sound of her name she thumps her tail, twice, on the floor and looks up at me.

How long have I been sitting here—watching this? It feels like hours but it's only 9:00, so fifteen minutes, maybe? I can't move; I can't turn away—even though I want to. I wish I'd never turned the TV on.

Couric's talking to a woman who has a front row seat to the horror, she lives in an apartment with what used to be a spectacular view, one I'm sure she paid an equally spectacular price for: the twin towers right there, perfectly framed, right outside her window. The woman's telling Katie about the smoke and fire and how she can hear sirens and there's debris flying about and then:

"Oh! Another one just hit!"

My phone's ringing.

"It's the phone, Sasha. The phone's ringing sweetie—oh, Sasha I have to get the phone. Someone's calling and I have to talk to whoever it is. I have to hear another human voice, another voice besides the ones coming out of the TV."

How many other phones are ringing now—all over the country—all over the world? People frantically pushing buttons because that's all that's left to them—reaching out to those they love is the only thing they have any control over.

"Sam? It's still early there, in Alberta. What time is it? Are you and Peter having a good time visiting George and Job? Are you having a good time?" And as my words begin to collapse and dissipate into the air, the foolishness of my question looms up at me, filling me with embarrassment and shame over its callousness and disregard. I want to take it back, but it's too late.

"Oh, Charlie. We're watching it; we're watching it—what's happening there— in New York. It's a little after seven here. God! Charlie—god—what's happening?"

"Another plane hit, another plane. They're showing it now. Are you watching? Are you seeing what I'm seeing, Sam? That plane? You can see it, now you can, in the video they're showing now. You can see it, Sam. The plane—it's on the right. It's right there in the picture, it's right there. It's happening, right in front of our eyes. That plane—flying right into the building. That plane, filled with people. It just happened, but we can all see it now when it *was* happening. And we can't do a damn thing to stop it. Why can't we just stop time? Why can't we stop it?"

Sam's crying.

"I saw it, Charlie. I love you, little sister. I love you. Let's stay on the phone for a while—okay? Lets talk or—we don't even have to talk. If you don't want to talk, we'll just listen to each other breathe."

Sam and I were still talking, and breathing, when David burst through my front door half-an-hour later with such ferocity that my usually sweet and mild-mannered Sasha bared her teeth at him.

When the South Tower collapsed at 9:59 and the North Tower went down less than a half-hour later, David was sitting at my feet, petting Sasha's head with one hand and rubbing my calf with the other, as if he thought that both of us might disappear into nothingness if he didn't maintain physical contact.

Sam hung up a little after 10:00.

"I'm going to go be with Peter for a while now, Peter and George and Job. I'll talk to you later. I love you."

"There's nothing there anymore. They're gone, the buildings are gone, and so are all the people in them."

David speaks the obvious, but it's so outlandish and unbelievable that even though all we see now on the screen is smoke and empty sky, obscenely blank sky—neither one of us is quite yet willing to accept that what we're witnessing is real.

"It's like a movie. But that's all it is, just a movie. And when we walk out of the theater, out of the dark and back into daylight—we'll see those buildings, on the horizon, rising up into the air—even though we aren't in New York. They'll be there and we'll look at each other and say: "That was the worst movie ever, but that's all it was, only a movie.""

The phone's ringing and I don't want to answer, but I know I have to. Cindy will call soon, but I know that this isn't Cindy. Eventually I'll hear from her, but not now. She's too busy explaining to her kids what she doesn't understand herself.

"You're getting another call." David doesn't look at me; he doesn't take his hand off my leg, just stares straight ahead, immobile.

"Hi Terry"

"Charlie. Charlie. You know, I've always loved saying your name."

"I know, you've told me, numerous times."

Why does he sound so calm and composed?

"Charlie, it would be good if you were here."

"I was just there. I can't come again, so soon. And anyway, I don't think planes will be flying for awhile."

"It would be good if you could come, Charlie. Sara's mom—Teresa—her mom—Teresa, my ex-wife and her husband—they were on American Airlines flight eleven."

The rabbit hole is gaping—wider and wider and I fall, further and further in.

And David doesn't stop stroking my calf, he just stares straight ahead, not moving, listening, watching and not saying a word.

Chapter 39

Five days have passed, and David hasn't yet asked me about Terry, which is only increasing the tension that's been building up over the past one hundred twenty hours. The fact that it's already Sunday night is unfathomable—how could that be? The external world has been ripped apart, and our internal worlds, the individual microcosms that make up our own private universes, have been changed in ways we've yet to understand.

David stayed with me Tuesday night; he didn't ask if he could, and I didn't ask him if he would—he just did. Luckily I'd gone grocery shopping when I got back from California, so there was food in the house, although neither one of us ate much. We sat, me in Dad's old chair, and David and Sasha at my feet for the remainder of the day and into the early evening, only getting up when one of us needed to pee, (including Sasha, who I let out three times), and when I went into the kitchen to pull together a haphazard dinner of peanut butter sandwiches, microwave vegetables, popcorn and two bottles of beer.

I kept the phone in my lap so I wouldn't have to move when it rang. Mom called from Kevin and Janet's at 11:30, relieved to find out that I wasn't alone. Cindy called at 1:00 in the afternoon her time, we didn't talk long; we didn't have much to say. By that time putting meaningful words together had become a monumental task. Terry didn't call again, because I asked him not to, promising him that when I could I'd call him.

A little after 10:00 that night David announced that he was going to bed.

"I can't watch this anymore. We've been sitting here for hours watching the same damn thing over and over again. I'm going to try to get some sleep. Come when you want to—you probably need to return a call."

He didn't sound angry or jealous, just weary. I waited until I heard him brushing his teeth before I called Terry, but there was no answer, so I waited, waited until I thought David might be asleep before I went into the bedroom. But he wasn't—when I crawled into bed he was lying flat on his back, staring at the ceiling as if he were still watching buildings crumble; people covered in what looked like chalk walking the streets as if they were hypnotized; fire engines and police cars stirring up clouds of dust and paper and dirt and all the detritus in the city as they sped by. We didn't speak. We didn't touch. Morning came too soon.

We've become morbidly attached and comfortable with the sameness of the past days. The terribleness and sadness has become so commonplace, that we're finding some comfort in its normalness, as if we're suffering from a bastardized version of the Stockholm syndrome.

We wake up in the morning, after sleeping only a few hours at most, and sit in what have now become our assigned seats. Sasha continues to behave as dogs do, nothing has changed for her, but she understands that something has happened in our world, so different from her own, which involves only eating, playing, and being loved. She sits at our feet, her head resting on mine, and David pets her and occasionally murmurs to her and she thumps her tail, and the silence that sits hulking between us, grows larger and more untenable with each passing minute.

I didn't try to keep my voice down when I called Terry on Wednesday, after David had already gone in the bedroom. Is he letting me know that he doesn't care anymore? If that's the case, why has he stayed over here every night since the attacks? And why did he make love to me last night more passionately than ever before? Doesn't he wonder who this guy is who's calling me, who I'm calling back? I wish there were fewer questions and more answers, about a lot of things.

"You're going back to work tomorrow, right?"

David swivels his head to look at me, and doesn't hesitate to speak, as if he's relieved that this might be the beginning of a normal conversation.

"Yeah, we can't stay home forever. In fact, I'm going to go home tonight. I've stayed here five nights in a row. It's time."

"I think that's wise. I don't think either one of us has been sleeping very well on my full size mattress."

He looks back at the TV, nods his head, then turns to face me again.

"Our poor sleeping had nothing to do with your mattress, Charlie."

"No. I suppose not."

"It'll be a relief to go back to work tomorrow."

"Yes, it will. I'm planning on going in early."

"I guess I can leave anytime. It's close to noon. I'll swing by the nursing home to check in on Emily, and stop at the grocery store before I head back to my place."

David hasn't missed a visited with Emily; terror and turmoil be damned, he's been to see her without fail, including the day of the attacks when he'd gone to the nursing home first before coming to my house.

"I had to make sure that the TV was turned off in her room, she doesn't need to be exposed to all this madness," he'd explained while we were picking at our meager dinner.

The fact that there was even a television in the room of someone in a comatose state had taken me by surprise, a feeling I probably should have kept to myself.

"There's a TV in her room? She can't watch television. She can't even talk. She doesn't even know when you're there."

He clenched his jaw—once, twice—I waited for an angry outburst but he just turned away and faced the screen. He'd muted the sound but it didn't matter, the terrible cacophony we'd been listening to for hours was forever stamped onto our psyche, like grooves on an album stamped in hell.

"How's everyone been—at the nursing home?"

"Do you mean the patients or the staff?"

David's standing and looking around the room as if he's searching for something, his fingers twitching; acting like a just-released prisoner who's not quite sure if he's ready to leave the place that he knows and step out into the world he doesn't.

"Well—everyone. They have to work through all this. I guess that's better for them in the long run. They don't know what's going on. People need their meds and they need turning and beds need changing and..."

God! I'm rambling. Aren't you ever going to ask me about Terry?

"Most of the televisions in the patients' rooms haven't been on these past few days, but there's a small one at the nursing station. Someone's usually watching when I go over. But, like you said, they've got people to take care of, two people died there this week."

In a few minutes he's going to be out the door, I have to say something.

"David?"

When he bends down to pat Sasha, his voice is muffled.

"Yes?"

"Do you want to know anything about California? About..."

"...Terry?"

"Well. Yes. Why haven't you asked about him, not once?"

"Because he's a part of your life that I'll never be a party to or privy to. A part of your life that I'll never understand and probably don't need to."

"Like the life you and Emily had before...?"

"Yes."

"And what do we do about that part of our lives? What came before the here and now? You and me in the present?"

"Well—I'd say that we have to let everything play out, what we've experienced in our past, how that influences our present and what might be our future."

"I think that maybe I might go back to California next week. Planes are flying again. I'm not afraid, we can't be afraid. Like you said—we have to let our past, present and future play out. Maybe my future is out there, in California. That's what I used to think, way back when I graduated from college. Maybe I was right about that all along."

When David takes my face in his hands and kisses first my nose, each cheek and then my lips, I have a sense that something's been lifted from me—the weight of having to perform in a certain way, behave like someone who I'm not always sure that I am. And I sense that he feels the same.

"Go to California, Charlie. Go. Do it now because no one knows what your future holds. Do it now. Go."

David left an hour ago. I turned the television off as soon as he was gone. I took Sasha for a walk. People were out, most of us looking like we weren't sure of where we were going, why we were there, just knowing that we were going somewhere, making an attempt at moving forward into the future while trying to let go of the most recent past, even if it meant simply walking around the block.

We'll take this walk, in a place where we've always walked before and it's going to be just like it was the last time we walked here, even though it really isn't, because our world has changed. But we're going to move beyond that somehow. We're going to get through this walk, and then the rest of the day and the rest of the week and the month and two months and three months and on and on—because we must.

There were a few smiles, tears and hugs between strangers on our walk that were as comforting as the sight and touch of another human could ever be. Sasha was happy, she never stopped wagging her tail and when we got home she made a beeline for the kitchen, making it clear that she was done sitting in front of the television.

"Sasha, okay. I'm tired of sitting in the den, too. I'll make grilled cheese sandwiches, one for me, and half of one for you. But first, I have to make a call."

He doesn't pick up right away, not on the second, third or even the fourth ring.

Please pick up, Terry. Please. Please pick up. Yes!

"Charlie? Are you coming? Are you coming here?

"Yes, yes. As soon as I can—yes."

Chapter 40

Finally—Sara's asleep. She'd been wound up so tightly for the past twelve hours, so animated and frenetic, that I feared she'd never calm down. From the time she and Terry met me at the airport this morning, the three of us have been bustling around the city like gerbils or mice in a maze; scurrying around from place to place, one dead end to another, not staying too long anywhere before scampering off to somewhere else. It's not the destination or the goal realized once the destination's reached that's mattered, but the journey toward it.

She'd insisted when we left LAX that we stop for lunch at a sushi restaurant. After we left there she wanted to go to the Santa Monica pier, despite the fact that, according to Terry, she'd been there at least one hundred times in her twelve years on earth. When we left the pier she told us that she wanted to drive up the coast highway through Malibu, the opposite direction from Terry's condo. Twice she made him pull into a beachfront parking lot, where she jumped out of the car, ran to the edge of the surf, turned her back to the sea and panned her eyes north and south. Each time she returned to the car and announced, with a significant amount of disappointment, that Johnny Depp and Tom Cruise were nowhere to be seen. Even though Terry had promised to grill hamburgers for dinner, by the time we'd crawled our way through rush hour traffic back to Venice Beach, she insisted that she needed to have an ice cream cone. And she chattered incessantly the entire day—mostly about her mother.

"I wish we hadn't had that little fight the day before I left Cape Cod to come home. It wasn't a big bad fight, just a little one. But I know it made her sad."

"Mom liked it when she didn't have to get all dressed up for work or to go to parties. She didn't really like parties. She liked it when the two of us would go to the beach and she didn't have to wear make-up and we'd play in the ocean and drink too much soda and get sand in our hair and the car seats would get all sandy and sticky when we drove home."

"Sometimes I'd lie in bed at night and would think of mean things to say to her 'cause she made me mad. I wish I hadn't done that."

"She let me stay up until midnight on New Year's Eve when we changed over to the year two thousand. She let me have friends over and we all got dressed up and we ate steak and watched *Edward Scissorhands.* That was a fun night."

"Once I told her that I didn't like her new husband and first she got mad but then she got sad and I left then to go to my friend's house and when I got back she was still crying."

"She told me once that I was going to be a very famous person someday. She said that I'd be a famous actress or maybe a famous writer or something like that. I think I was about ten when she told me that. I thought she was being nice. I didn't tell her that I wanted to be a veterinarian or maybe a nurse."

"I try not to think about her plane crashing into the building. But sometimes I dream about it. I think though that it must have been so fast that she didn't know what happened. That's what Grandpa Harold told me when I talked to him on the phone. He told me not to worry, that one second she was flying through the sky in a plane and the next second she was flying through the sky on her own 'cause she was an angel. But then Grandpa started to cry and so did Daddy and then Daddy made me hang up."

It's too quiet now. Silence is supposed to be welcome, 'golden', it's supposed to lead to contemplation and meditation, peaceful and positive states of being but I feel antsier now than I have all day. Without Sara's monologue filling up the space between us Terry and I face an emptiness that's more than uncomfortable, it's foreboding.

He hasn't had a drink yet tonight. Just waiting for her to go to bed I guess. What do I do when he starts?

"I think it's time for a drink. What do you want? Wine, probably, or maybe a beer? Do you want something harder? I've got lots of liquor—been buying even more than usual the past month."

"I'll have wine, thanks. A white, if you've got it."

Watching Terry walk to the kitchen I'm torn between wanting to grab Sara out of her bed and take her someplace far away, or run to him, take him in my arms and tell him that we're a family now and he can stop trying to punish the world because he thinks he's been treated unfairly by punishing, and ultimately, destroying himself. I do neither.

"You know, I wasn't sure that you'd finally do it—come out here to be with us."

Believe me I think, there were times that I wasn't sure, either.

"I knew you needed me, it just took a little while to work it all out. Mom wasn't too happy when I first told her but she came around. I think she'll come out for a visit, maybe at Christmas. Since 'Play Time' is in schools out here now too, it makes sense for me to be here. Mom, Derek, Samantha, the board—the whole team's got a handle on the programs in the Midwest."

"What do I do with Sara? How do I get through this?"

His questions make it clear that he's paid no attention to what I said.

"I think you're doing fine with Sara. I mean—how hard this is, for both of you—you're doing all you can do."

"Am I?"

"Don't second guess yourself, Terry. You're Sara's father. You're a good father. Sara loves you, and she needs you now. She needs for you to be there for her without faltering or showing weakness. You have to be the adult in the room."

"I need another drink, you ready for a refill?" He looks at me over the top of his glass, eyes slit-like, taunting, daring me to respond in a manner that isn't going to set him off.

It really doesn't matter what I say now because he's going to be pissed off with me either way. Anger destroys the mind as well as the body, misplaced anger even more so.

"I don't need another glass, I've barely started on this one, and I really don't think that you need anything more to drink, either."

"Giving me orders now, are we?"

"Please, don't go there, Terry. Please. You wanted me to come back to California to be with you and Sara. How did you think I was going to behave? How I was going to act? What do you want from me?"

I watch as his face turns to putty, as if his skin is slipping off the bones, melting in front of me, everything distorted—the saddest, most conflicted expression imaginable.

"You're wrong. I'm not a good father. I'm a fucking alcoholic. I'm a goddamned drunk, which is why Teresa left me. I'm a mess and I don't know how to help my daughter get through losing her mother. I don't know how to do that. I don't know how—I don't know how."

I don't know, either. I'm forty-four, divorced, never had a child. And now, suddenly, I more or less have one. A child who's hurting and sad and who, for all her seeming maturity, is too young to understand how losing her mother in that way will affect her for the rest of her life. She's changed—forever. No script has been written for this. We're all adlibbing from now on.

Chapter 41

Sara had her first period two months after I arrived in California. Saturday, December 13th. I have no idea when I started menstruating. I'm not sure how old I was and I certainly don't remember the month or date, but for the rest of my life I'll remember when Sara's sojourn as a little girl ended and her pilgrimage to adulthood began.

It was a little after 8:00 in the morning when Sara padded into the bedroom to tell me that she'd discovered blood on her underwear, but assured me that I needn't worry because she had a box of sanitary pads stashed in her closet and she'd already put one on.

"I'm glad that Dad's not here right now 'cause this would be embarrassing if he was. I mean I know he knows all about periods and that kind of stuff, but still—he's my dad. I wonder: do women know all kinds of secret stuff like that about men? They don't have periods but there must be something secret about them that women get to know too, because otherwise it wouldn't be fair, men knowing about personal things that women do in private but women not knowing anything about what men do when no one's watching. Where's Dad, anyway?"

Terry had gone out for a run half-an-hour earlier. I'd managed to convince him during the first week after I'd moved in that if he started running again, it would make him feel better and relieve some of his stress. And of course, I'd also hoped that he would come to realize that running while hung-over wasn't an enjoyable activity, so he'd choose to give up the imbibing as opposed to the exercise. Sixty days later he was running five days a week, but still drinking, albeit a little less, every night.

"He's out on a run."

"That's good. I like it that he's running again. He told me once that he used to run every single day when he was younger and he loved it but then he got married and I was born and he stopped. When I asked him why he stopped doing something that he loved so much he told me that adults have responsibilities, which means that they have to give up the things that they love. I told him that I didn't think then that I wanted to be an adult and he laughed and mussed up my hair and told me it wasn't so horrible because after awhile you make yourself forget about how much you'd loved something. Lets make breakfast, and when Dad gets back the three of us can eat. He's going to be hungry."

We were eating Sara's favorite morning food: French toast with cinnamon sugar, strawberry syrup ("maple's so boring, everybody wants maple", she'd explained the first time we had breakfast together) and whipped cream (but only on hers) when the phone rang. Terry answered.

It was less than ten seconds into the conversation before a pall began to settle over the room.

"What's this about, Dad?"

Instinctively I began talking, too loudly, to Sara who pointed that out to me as she put another piece of toast on her plate.

"Hey—Charlie. Why are you talking so loud? I'm sitting right here..."

There was no camouflaging, no covering up the ugly clamor of hostility and bitterness spurting like vomit from Terry's mouth.

"Are you fucking kidding me? You're kidding me, right? You've got to be fucking kidding me. No, no, no! I really don't want to be having this fucking conversation with you. Not now—not fucking ever."

In almost the same length of time it took me to realize that I didn't know what to do to save Sara from the verbal onslaught, I realized that my concern was unfounded, she wasn't oblivious to Terry's words, but hearing them wasn't fazing her. I watched as she cut the slice of bread into postage stamp size pieces, and then as if she was using a paintbrush, slid each one back and forth several times into the pool of syrup in the corner of the plate before plopping one, or two, in her mouth. She behaved as if she were performing a ritual or was in a trance.

"Well, thanks but no thanks. I'm hanging up now. If you think for one minute that I'm going to watch you get married to that woman—that bitch—the whore. Inviting Sara and me to the wedding? You're fucking crazy."

Sara gobbled up the last piece on her plate and reached for the remaining slice.

"Dad? Is Grandpa getting married to Leslie?"

Terry was shaking as if he had some sort of neurological disease, even his lips were quivering.

"I'd appreciate it Sara if you wouldn't say her name, okay?"

"Why? That's kind of silly, Dad. Telling me not to say her name."

"Well, you may think it's silly but it's my house, so please don't say it out loud in my house."

"When's the wedding?"

Three pieces of bread met their syrupy fate and were summarily consumed.

"I don't know, Sara. I don't care. Sometime soon I guess. I've got no idea, I wasn't listening."

For the first time since she'd told me I was talking too loudly, Sara looked somewhere other than her plate—first at me, then at Terry. She flipped the ends of her hair with her fingers, stuck out her tongue to lick syrup off her upper lip and smiled at him.

"I'd like Charlie to go with me to Grandpa's wedding. You don't have to go. We will. I'd like to meet Grandpa's Leslie."

When Terry walked out the front door, still in his running shorts and singlet, he didn't say where he was going and I didn't ask.

The next call came at 2:00: twenty minutes after Terry had come home, physically cold and psychologically chastened. He'd hurried into the bedroom, stripped off his clothes and taken such a long shower that I thought surely we wouldn't have hot water the rest of the day.

While he was gone Sara and I had cleared the table, done the dishes, taken a walk ("are we doing this because you think we're going to see Dad out here?"), listened to the latest Destiny's Child CD and played three games of Scrabble. She asked me during the second game if I'd go to Harold's wedding with her and I assured her that I would. That was all she needed to hear.

"Charlie, the phone's ringing. What if it's Grandpa calling again? If it is, can I talk to him so I can ask him when he's getting married to Leslie, and tell him that we're coming?"

I'd stubbed my toe on the doorjamb when I came out of the bathroom where I'd stood outside the shower and talked to the disembodied voice inside, the voice that could muster up only one-word sentences.

"Are you okay?"

"Yes."

"Did you get cold?"

"Yes."

"Do you want to tell me where you went?"

"No."

"Are you going to want dinner at six or so?"

"Yes."

"Shall I order Chinese?"

"Yes."

I limped to the phone and didn't disguise my pain, either emotional or physical when I picked up the receiver.

"Charlie? Hey. Is everything okay with you? You sound like you've been crying."

"Oh, hi Sam. No, I'm fine. Klutzy me. Just stubbed my toe that's all. How are you guys? Getting all ready for Christmas? George and Job are coming there, right?"

Talking-on-the phone silences are so disconcerting. The empty air is much more ominous than when you're engaged in a face-to-face conversation and a lull plants itself between words. It's one thing to see a person's expression when they're taking an unusually long time to reply, quite another, less comfortable one when you're imagining what their face looks like.

"Sam?"

"Yeah, yeah—they're coming on the twentieth. Hey—we've got some not so great news here."

Not Elton the Second, I'd thought. Bad timing, the dog dying right before Christmas. No more photos of him wearing a Santa hat and rock star sunglasses.

"Elton didn't die, did he?"

"No, no. Elton will be skulking around under the table as usual looking for handouts at Christmas dinner. No, it's not Elton. It's Peter, he's sick."

"How sick?"

"Sick enough to have a disease with a scary name: chronic lymphocytic leukemia. But the good news is the first word in the name, chronic. He's probably had it for a long time, and just started having symptoms a few months ago. He's on medication. The doc says he could live years, which he intends on doing."

"Is he there? Can I talk to him?"

Peter was ready and willing to talk; he'd been standing beside Sam throughout our conversation.

"Charlie, Peter here. So, all these years I thought that my distinguished English pallor, which plays up my startling blue eyes so well, was one of my most positive physical characteristics. But perhaps if my complexion had been a bit less pallid, if I'd started off pinkish and faded to white, I would have realized sooner that things were amiss with my blood cells. Well, we'll never know, will we? And those blue eyes did attract your brother like a hungry young lad to a Chelsea bun, so it's not so bad, Charlie. Things aren't so bad at all. In fact, they're very good. I'm a lucky man—a lucky man, indeed."

When Terry finally emerged from the bedroom, asking who'd called, I wanted to scream, shake my finger in his face, and then pull him to me and hold him close. But I did neither.

"Sam called. It was nothing. He just wanted to talk."

Chapter 42

"I'm inviting Grandpa and Leslie to graduation. We can have only four people, so I want you and Grandpa and his wife and I think that Dad will come, won't he? It's my high school graduation, and he's my dad. He can't not be there—not even if he doesn't want to be around his own Dad."

He'll be there. And he'll be sober and he isn't going to say something that he'll regret and be humiliated about the next day and he'll treat his father's wife with respect. I've put up with his anger and bitterness and irrationality for far too long. Five years now. If I didn't love him and you so much, I would have left California a long time ago. Sometimes I wish I'd never come back here at all.

"Of course your dad's coming to your graduation, Sara."

"He didn't come to Grandpa's wedding."

"No, he didn't. But this is different."

"Is it? We're talking about family, as in blood relations. Grandpa was so sad when Dad didn't come to his wedding. Remember how he kept saying all during the party afterwards that he was sure that Dad was going to come through the door at any time? He kept looking at the door all night. All night he waited for Dad to show up."

"Your dad's relationship with his father is very complicated, Sara..."

"...Why do you think it's so messed up? Who's at fault?"

Your dad, your dad's at fault. No, he isn't. Harold should have told his sons years ago that he was seeing Leslie. He never should have pretended. Paul and Terry should have always known about her. Who did he think he was protecting? Pretending all that time just made it worse. But Paul, he forgave Harold right away. And Terry never did. Why couldn't he, when Paul could? Maybe it's no one's fault—and maybe they're each to blame.

"Too complicated. Listen, I don't have all the answers, okay? Your dad expects, rightly so, that his Dad should be a certain kind of person, should behave in a certain way. Your dad admired your grandfather, put him on a pedestal. But often, in fact most of the time, people don't turn out to be exactly who we think they are. Come on, Sara. You're a grown-up woman now. You grew up way too fast, way too soon. I know you understand what I'm saying. We never really know who anyone is, sometimes it takes a lifetime just to figure out who we are ourselves, let alone who anyone else is."

"I'm so glad you came back into Dad's life. He still drinks way too much, and is such a royal pain-in-the-ass sometimes, but if you hadn't come back after Mom died, I don't know what we would have done. I was only testing you. I wanted to see what your answer would be—about who was wrong. I knew you wouldn't blame either one, not Dad or Grandpa. Gotta go—meeting some of the class party planning gang. It's either Mexico or New York City. What a choice, huh?"

She plants a noisy kiss on top of my head and, as if sometime during her four years of high school she took levitation lessons at the Hogwarts School, she virtually floats out the door.

"Come on Sasha, let's go in the office. I need to reply to Debbie's email from the other day."

Sasha, who's sprawled out in her favorite spot in the living room—a multi-colored sisal rug Teresa bought on a vacation to Brazil that she and Terry had taken shortly after they married, doesn't open her eyes, just thumps her tail a few times and continues snoring.

"I get it, you're comfy there. Don't blame you, there aren't any rugs in the office for you to lie on." I pat her on the forehead and rub two fingers up and down her nose. When she snores again her moist breath warms my skin.

I love the time I spend in the office. It's at the front of the house so it faces the ocean. I never tire of looking at the sea. It's a distraction I know, but what a magnificent and calming one. And it's not like I'm doing critically important work in here; I do that in the 'Play Time' office near downtown. This room, with its stark white walls; bamboo floors; black and white photographs of California poppies, mustard plant sprouting over hillsides and the sun setting into the sea; minimal and minimalist furniture; and the unadorned windows looking west, is my haven.

Sometimes I sit in the black leather Herman Miller chair and gaze out the window, forgetting that I'm holding on to my laptop; which has resulted in my replacing the screen twice in the last year because it slipped out of my fingers. Occasionally I lay a mat on the floor and do Yoga poses, or sometimes I dispense with the poses altogether and concentrate so hard on my breathing that I fall into a near-meditative state. But I'm not doing those things today—this is a day for reaching out, not looking inward.

Debbie sent me an email two days ago, telling me that she and Richard and Richard Junior are coming back to the states in a few weeks. It was the first time I'd heard from her in three months. Surprising how one of my strongest connections to home, to Michigan, other than Mom and Kevin and his family,

Sam and Peter and Derek and Samantha, is my ex-husband's wife. Over the years I've come to admire her. She may look like someone else, but she isn't that person, she's her own unique self, and that self has managed to create a family from the most unlikely melding of personalities and backstories.

From: charliealways@gmail.com
To: dalexander@yahoo.com
Date: May 20. 2008
Subject: Welcome home!

Debbie: So delighted to hear that you're on your way home soon, although I'm sorry I wasn't able to get over to Germany for a visit while you were there. Would have loved to have seen that part of the world with you as my tour guide, but it wasn't meant to be. I'm glad though that Gertrude was able to, twice, before she died last year. I know that meant a lot to Richard. You're going to get your doctorate now, from the University of Michigan no less? Congratulations, that's very impressive. And I'm happy for Richard that he's decided that writing books about statistics is his calling. This will be his third one, right? (Sorry I didn't read the first two, but I'm sure if you're into math they were absolute page-turners!) I wonder how Richard Jr. will react to being back in the US. He probably thinks that he's German, from what you've written in the past, he speaks the language fluently. I'll be going back to Michigan in mid-summer, so I'll catch up with you in person then.

Love, Charlie

As I push 'Send' I hear Sasha's nails clicking across the living room floor, she knows that Terry's back from his run so she's on her way to greet him.

Perfect timing—Sara isn't going to be back for a couple hours. Terry's always in a good mood when he's finished running, so now's the time to tell him that Harold and Leslie will be coming to graduation.

"Hey, Charlie, you in the office? Of course you are, it's your favorite room in the house."

There are times, like this very moment, when I look at Terry and see the man I fell in love with across a crowded room twenty-two years ago. His skin is flushed from the run, not from alcohol; his soft blue eyes clear, not bloodshot; all the good clean oxygen he's been breathing in for the last hour has softened the creases around his mouth, even the furrow between his brows doesn't appear as deep. I'm ecstatic at the sight of him, like that, the way I remember him being, but I know that memories, no matter how much joy and pleasure they bring can also mock us, taunt us because what we're remembering isn't now.

"Just sent an email to Debbie. She and Richard and their son are coming back to the states soon. She's going to start working on her doctorate at U of M in the fall, and Richard's going to write another book on statistics and Richard Junior will be going to some private school in Ann Arbor for child prodigies. He told Debbie and Richard he wants to be a nuclear physicist, a computer programmer or a composer, as in symphonies."

"Never have quite understood why you're such good friends with your creepy ex-husband's wife, I guess it's a woman-thing, huh?"

I feel a quick stab of cold, like I've been poked with a fork made of ice. What a narrow-minded thing to say. What the hell is he talking about? Did I ever say that Richard was creepy? I don't think so. If I did, I don't remember saying it.

"Richard wasn't—isn't creepy. I never, ever said that. And a woman-thing, what's that supposed to mean?"

He baited me and I took the lure.

He's stretching—palms against the wall, knees bent, staring straight ahead at all that whiteness, as if there's some sort of secret code written there that only he can decipher.

"Okay, maybe I did say once that Richard was a little—eccentric. I guess you might have heard that as creepy. As far as Debbie, I like her. I like her a lot. She's turned out to be her own woman, she finally stood up for what she wanted, for the life she wanted to have and it seems that she won. She's like a younger sister to me. I can't explain it, I just feel close to her. And you know, people are always happy when the people they care for come out on top—you know—when they win."

Terry turns on me so quickly that I crouch.

"She won? So, marriage—relationships are some sort of war? Something's that won or lost? That's what you're saying?"

I don't want to be in this room, not this room, and not now, with you.

"Are you thirsty? Of course you are. I'll make you a smoothie. Come on. Let's go in the kitchen. We'll talk about this after you've had something to drink."

He follows me, Sasha so close on his heels that I feel a little jealous, even when we argue, Sasha seems to take Terry's side against me.

"What do you want in it? The usual? Banana? Strawberries? Yogurt? Protein powder? Orange juice?"

"What is it, Charlie? Are relationships nothing but a series of battles that eventually someone ends up winning, which means that the other person is the loser? The battle of the sexes?"

I switch off the blender, pour the bubblegum pink concoction into a tumbler and sit it on the counter in front of him.

"No. I don't believe that. I shouldn't have used the word 'won'. Debbie didn't win. She didn't beat Richard at anything. She and Richard have a good solid relationship, they've had their ups and downs; relationships are tough, but they're certainly not wars."

He sips at the smoothie, leaving a rosy moustache above his lip.

If this were a different time, if we were in a different place, I would lick it off and then give him a long luscious lingering kiss. But this isn't a different time or a different place.

"She was pregnant, wasn't she? That's why he divorced you and married her."

"Yes, she was pregnant but that's not the reason he married her. He married her because he loved her and because he loved her is why she got pregnant and that's why he married her."

"Teresa was pregnant when we got married. That's why I married her. But you're just finding that out because you never asked me about her. You've never asked me, not once, about my relationship with her. Why's that?"

"Because it didn't matter."

"What the hell does that mean?"

"Because what happened between Teresa and you has nothing to do with you and me. You and I already had a history together. Your relationship with Teresa has—had no relevance to our relationship."

You have to tell him about Harold and Leslie. There's never going to be a good time. You just have to do it.

"Terry—Sara wants your Dad and Leslie to come to her graduation. She's inviting them, along with you and me, of course."

He's defeated and defiant at the same time.

"I knew she'd want him there. He can come, and so can she—but I'm not sitting with them. You can sit with whomever you choose to. I'll leave that up to you."

His body grows smaller as he walks toward the bedroom. He's diminishing right before my eyes.

One day he'll just be gone.

Chapter 43

I cried when I heard *Pomp and Circumstance,* but I always do. Terry cried, too. I knew he was thinking about Teresa when he watched Sara walk across the stage and take her diploma. And if Harold and Leslie hadn't been sitting three rows behind us, I'm sure I would have seen Harold crying as well—crying with joy, pride and deep melancholy for and because of Sara, his only grandchild, named for his beloved daughter whose exit from this world left an emptiness in his heart that never filled.

But our tears have dried, the ceremony's over, and once Sara's finished gabbing with, kissing and high-fiving her friends, she and her boyfriend Troy ("Whoa! Flashback to old-time Hollywood", I'd laughed when she told me his name) Terry, Harold, Leslie, Paul, Barbara and I are having a celebratory dinner at her favorite sushi restaurant.

"I hope she doesn't take much longer, our reservations are for seven." I speak to Terry's back; he's turned away from the stage, surveying the people emptying the seats behind us. "They told me they were leaving as soon as the ceremony was over. They're meeting us at Rising Sun. By the time the four of us get out of here, Barb and Paul will probably already be there too."

"Only three, there's only going to be three of you showing up last."

He's staring down at his feet; I expect at any minute that he'll start scuffing them back and forth, dragging his toe across the floor like a recalcitrant child being scolded.

"Oh, God Terry. Please, please—it's Sara's graduation dinner. This is family, your family. Please."

I'm wasting my time. He could care less what I have to say, what I want, what Sara and Harold and Leslie, what all of us want.

He looks at me, straight into my eyes; his are filling with tears.

"Except for Sara and you, I don't have a family anymore. I'll see you at home, Charlie."

Sara seemed neither surprised, disappointed or upset to learn that her father wouldn't be joining us for dinner.

"At least Dad made it for the ceremony", she smiled and then whispered in Troy's ear as they walked toward the car; Troy holding on to her hand so tightly that I wondered if he was worried she'd otherwise slip from his grasp.

I've continued to wonder throughout dinner.

Troy's a nice kid, he's smart, well spoken, talented, good-looking, but he seems a little overly protective with Sara. She doesn't need protecting, not now. It's a little late for that. What she needs is someone to love her and let her be the woman she wants to be. She'll take care of herself.

"Charlie, Grandpa, Leslie, Barb, Paul—thanks so much for this dinner tonight. It's been a blast, so much fun. Thanks for coming to graduation and thanks for the money. I'll put it to good use decorating my dorm room, and I'll probably buy a new laptop. But hey! Troy and I have to get out of here. We've got a couple parties to go to. We're gonna split."

Kisses all around and they're gone.

"He's a pleasant young man." Paul announces, his eyes moving from person to person around the table.

Do I detect the need for re-assurance and mutual agreement in his voice?

"He is but he seems a little controlling to me," Barbara says. "Maybe controlling isn't the right word…"

"…Possessive, perhaps?" I ask.

"Yes, that's a more appropriate adjective. He just seems to be…"

"…Filling in for her Dad? Trying to protect her somehow? What does he think he's protecting her from? Her mother died in an unbearably horrific tragedy, and her father is an alcoholic who's estranged from his family. Seems to me her days of needing protecting are over, she's well past that phase."

Shit! Talk about a party-pooper. No one mentioned Terry's name at dinner, not once. My frustration is definitely on full display.

Harold speaks first.

"I know my son isn't a perfect man, but he wants to be. And he wants everyone else to be perfect, too. He expects the impossible, a pristine world. Terry's been that way ever since he was a child—too trusting, too romantic and idealistic to believe that people have faults; that they often do foolish things and sometimes they do things that might seem to be wrong. His inability to reconcile reality with what he wants reality to be has been a terrible burden for him to bear all his life."

None of says anything, but the tension is like an electrical current surging through the air. I feel as if we're standing on the edge of a cliff, peering over the side, each one of us experiencing the same irrational and frightening rush of adrenaline shooting through our bodies, all thinking: *It's scary looking down, but there's a part of me that wants to jump off and fly for awhile before the ground comes up to meet me.*

Leslie's the first one to respond, but not before she reaches over and cups Harold's hand with hers. Despite being in her mid-seventies her physical beauty is compelling: short-cropped hair the color of white smoke offset by hazel eyes. She's tall and big-boned, in a Katharine Hepburn sort of way but missing some of Hepburn's elegance, when she went to the restroom earlier in the evening, I noticed that she walked with a child's gait. She looked like she was ready to break out into a coltish trot. A youngster still but now in an old woman's body. A mature woman who knows exactly who she is and what she wants out of a love affair—age be damned. In the last hour-and-a-half I've come to realize that she adores Harold and he feels the same about her. The love between them practically radiates from their pores.

When I'm their age, will I be in love like that? I used to be, or I thought I was but I'm not that sure anymore. What will old age be like if I'm not in love, if there isn't anyone to share the last years of my life with?

"Father and son have both borne heavy burdens. The guilt Harold felt for so many years..." she squeezes his hand and smiles at him, "...that I know he still feels, to this day. The choices we make in life, the choices we *have* to make, so often means that someone's going to be hurt along the way. In this case there's been more than enough hurt to go around. Everyone's shared in the pain."

Harold coughs once, then again and Paul clears his throat. I expect him to say something but Leslie hasn't finished.

"I told Harold that he had to confess to Terry, that he had to tell Terry the truth about our relationship. I remember asking him: 'Do you want your son to think of you as a liar or a hypocrite?' Harold knew that being a liar was the worse of the two choices. Either way—Terry was probably never going to forgive him."

One of us just jumped off the cliff.

"So, what you're saying is that my brother knew about you and Dad before Mom died?

A wide-eyed expression of simultaneous surprise and comprehension seats itself like a mask across Leslie's lovely face, and Harold coughs again, once, then twice before he speaks.

"Yes, Paul. That's correct. As Leslie said, I really didn't have a choice, it was either being a liar in Terry's eyes or a hypocrite, and I chose the latter. I lied to him once, the first time he saw Leslie and I together. It was an accident, we were always very discreet, but he saw us at a restaurant where we were having lunch. It was an unlikely spot, in a strip mall in North Hollywood, cheap little place but that's why we chose it."

He clasps his hand over Leslie's.

"I told him that day that Leslie was a new-hire. I didn't think he believed me, but he never mentioned it. Six months later he ran into us again, at the same damn restaurant. We'd talked about it, Leslie and me—how lightning wasn't going to strike twice in the same spot. We liked it, it was out-of-the-way; people in the business didn't go there. But, it turns out that my oldest son had an affinity for the place. The chances of him showing up there twice were inconceivable—until it happened. I guess karma made the choice for me, karma and Leslie's reasonable argument."

"How long was this before...?"

"Your mother died?"

"Yes."

"Four years."

"God! For four years Terry knew and kept it a secret. He pretended that everything was the same as it had always been. Living with that must have been hell for him."

And there goes Paul—over the edge.

Harold and Leslie's faces contort. Both look as if they're nursing a sore tooth, not wanting to poke at it because it hurts, but unable to keep their tongues away because they derive a perverse pleasure from the momentary blast of pain.

"I asked Terry not to tell you, Paul. Truthfully, I pleaded with him not to tell you. It was bad enough that he found out the way he did, that I had to tell him the truth. But you hadn't seen us. You had no idea that Leslie existed. "

Leslie stiffens, her spine straightening. She appears to have suddenly grown an inch taller.

Everyone's jumping off the cliff. I really need to get out of here—now. I need to be with Terry.

"I'm going to take off. Harold thanks so much for paying for dinner. I know Sara was so happy that both of you were here. I enjoyed talking with you, Leslie. You're a very interesting woman. I can understand how sad your students must have been when you retired. Barb, Paul, it was nice seeing the two of you again. 'Night everyone."

Just before I walk out the door I look back at the table—all four are looking down at their plates and no one's saying a word.

The house is quiet, so still that if I hadn't seen Terry's car in the garage, I wouldn't know he's there.

In two months, when Sara leaves for Columbia, it's going to be quiet like this most of the time. Just Terry and me—together, but alone, the two of us—in this big house. Listening to a lot of nothing. It's going to be so different without her here.

"Terry?"

I still miss Sasha. She'd be at the door now, wagging her tail to greet me. Sara was right: we should have adopted another dog after Sasha died.

"In here, I'm here. I'm in the office."

"Jeez, Terry. It's really dark in here."

He's sitting at the desk, his body barely lit by the low-wattage light atop it, a bottle of what looks to be gin to the right of the lamp.

"I'm just watching the ocean, although at night all you can see is the white foam roiling up on the sand. Otherwise, it's just black; it's so dark out there. It's black and dark stretching out for thousands of miles. I'll bet you didn't know that I like to sit here too, did you? You're not the only one who likes looking out these windows."

I see now that he has a glass in his hand—a glass whose contents he appears to inhale when he lifts it to his mouth.

"My girl, my baby, my daughter. She's leaving, Charlie. She's all grown-up now, so she's leaving."

"Terry my love. That's how life goes. That's what happens; things change. Children grow up. They take on a new role. Sara's a remarkable young woman; you can be so proud of her. And she isn't going away forever."

What a ridiculous thing to say: of course she is. Your little girl isn't a little girl anymore. She's gone to you forever in that way, the way you most want her to be.

I'm sitting at his feet now, watching as he pours more gin into the tumbler.

"Why did she have to choose New York City? She never liked it there. She hated it, in fact. At least that's what she told me when Teresa married Alan. 'I don't like it there, daddy. I hate it. I miss you, and the ocean and the mountains and the palm trees.' That's what she told me. Then she applies to Columbia University School of the Arts, and of course she gets accepted. She knew she would. She wants to get away from me.

I'm all she's had ever since her mother died, but that doesn't matter, she still wants to get away from me."

Yes, a part of her does.

"She loves you. But there's a woman, an artist that she's destined to be. She believed that Columbia would help her fulfill that destiny."

"Oh, Charlie. You're always so optimistic, always so sunny now, aren't you? You weren't that way in the beginning, not when we first met. I was the one cheering you up, telling you to look on the bright side. How our roles have reversed, haven't they?"

He downs what's left in the glass and fills it halfway with what's left in the bottle.

"So, how was dinner? What did you think of Leslie?"

"She's a lovely woman."

"That's it?" Another gulp and the glass is emptied again.

"What am I supposed to say, Terry? That she's an old ugly hag and I have no idea what your father ever saw in her to begin with? Is that what you want to hear? That's a lie. It would be a lie for me to say that, so I can't. She's a lovely woman; she and your dad are in love. I'm happy for them."

The second the words leave my mouth I realize that I've created, perhaps sub-consciously but more than likely consciously, deliberately, the perfect segue way to what I need to say next.

"Terry, I had no idea until tonight, until it came up at dinner, that you found out about your dad and Leslie several years before your mom died. I'd always thought that you and Paul found out months after your mom's funeral. That's what you led me to believe."

"I guess I led you to believe a lot of things that turned out to be not true, didn't I?"

What I would give to go back. If we could just slide back through time, slip through a black hole in space—go back to what once was. If I'd been with you when you found out about your dad's affair, if I'd been here, with you, things would have turned out differently. Together we could have worked through it. You, me, the two of us—we'd be in a different place than where we are right now. That's ridiculous, Charlie. You know it wouldn't have made any difference if you'd been here. Would it?

"Please, don't say things like that."

"Why not? What's that old saying—the truth hurts. Of course it hurts. The truth hurts like hell. I'm the poster boy for taking a big old ugly dose of truth right on the chin and then dishing it right back out."

Why am I suddenly cold?

"What do you mean—dishing it out?

"Well, I couldn't keep all that truth bottled up inside of me, could I? Dad made me promise not to tell Paul. The old man didn't want both of his sons to know what a liar and a hypocrite he was."

He starts to get up from the chair, but I push him back down.

"Please, Terry. You don't need another drink. Finish explaining what happened. What you did."

"What I did? I did what any good son would do. I'd found out that my father, my mother's husband, first lied to me with impunity and then turned out to be a fake, a phony. Pretending to be a loving husband, pretending to care, while all along he was spending whatever free time he could carve out of his busy schedule with another woman. A woman who he said he loved. He told me that, Charlie. He told me that he loved her. 'Oh, not the same way I love your mother, your mother gave me you and Paul, we have a long history together, we've made memories that I'll have forever, but I do love Leslie.' That's what he said to me."

He did what any good son would do. His mom wasn't a wife anymore, not in his mind, but she was a mother—his mother. He felt an obligation to tell her the truth, no matter how convoluted and misguided that thinking. He would be the man in her life who wouldn't betray her. He'd be honest with her.

"You told your mother, didn't you?"

"Yes."

"When did you tell her?"

"The day after I found out."

"How did she react?"

He's turned away from me, swiveled the chair so far to the right that I'm no longer looking at his profile, all I see is the back of his head.

His beautiful head—the head that I used to love to wrap my fingers around when we kissed.

"She didn't." His words are muffled, he sounds like he's speaking from underground—mistakenly buried in a coffin but still alive, calling out to those above.

"You mean she didn't say anything or do anything? Nothing at all?"

"Nothing."

"And I'm guessing that you never brought it up again."

"Never."

"Terry, did you eat any dinner?"

"No."

"Let me make you something. Come on, come in the kitchen with me and I'll make you a grilled cheese sandwich. How's that sound? You need some food."

I should have listened to Sara. I wish I had a dog.

Chapter 44

Watching Cindy walk through the door at Starbucks I'm struck, as I am whenever I see her and whenever I look in the mirror, by how we've changed. Two years ago she cut her chemo-curly hair short ("At least I'm not bald again", she said at the time. "If you're going gray, this is the only way to do it. Cut it all off and let it grow in naturally.") Those lines extending from the corners of her eyes have grown way too long to be hummingbird feet; her neck has some folds that weren't there a year ago; her jawline, particularly seen from the side is a bit droopy, while the rest of her face is thinning out. Under each cheekbone is a hollowed-out space that's a mismatch to the emerging jowls, and occasionally she remarks at the odd dichotomy between the ninety percent of her aging body and her torso, where the implants have yet to concede to the downward pull of gravity.

As for me, nightmarish haircuts in my thirties (primarily self-inflicted) have made me reluctant to shore off my auburn locks in favor of letting nature have its way. Unfortunately, hair with red and gold tones loses its hue and luster on an aging head, so for the past few years I've paid a ludicrous amount of money every five weeks to have a colorist ("I specialize in color only, darling. Just color. Nothing else. I'm a master, an artiste, this is what you pay for, your hair is now a work of art," Stephen reminds me each time I pull out my credit card) transform my tresses back to a shade that looks like it belongs sprouting on a human head rather than wrapping a mummy. I've always been heavier than Cindy, particularly in my face, so I've yet to develop any unpleasant creases. Lucky for me, I inherited Mom's beautiful skin. However, my lips have grown thinner, but as Cindy, in her usual brutally honest fashion, pointed out to me on New Year's Eve last year: "Glopping up your lips with gloss isn't appropriate for those of us over fifty. Use a nude lipstick, and play up your beautiful eyes."

"Hey, Cindy."

"Hey. I'm going to grab a latte, I'll be right there."

Dressed in black tights, an over-sized red and black striped sweater and black leather boots, Cindy looks like she could be a model for the front cover of the *AARP* magazine bearing the headline: *Fifty-Five is the New Thirty.*

This is the first time we're seeing each other in a few months. Although we do talk on the phone every other week or so, scheduling conflicts have prevented us from getting together during the day, and the four of us haven't spent an evening together in almost a year, since the New Year's Eve party when besides giving me make-up advice, Cindy navigated me into the bathroom ten minutes before midnight and said: "It hurts me seeing that the love that makes you so happy also makes you so sad."

"So? How's things?" She asks as she slides across the booth seat. "Last time we talked you said that Sara's coming back to California when she graduates?"

"Yeah, you know just like Matt junior, she took flight, high-tailed it to the East Coast for college but she'll be back in late May. I think she may already have a job lined up at one of the studios. I'm really not too sure about that, though. She's being a little tight-lipped as far as her future other than the fact that she'll be here, back home."

"When Matt junior told us that Cornell was his first choice, Matt and I made a bet. Matt said that he'd stay in the east for only a year and would transfer to UCLA. I said that he'd not only stick it out, he'd probably get his masters. Of course I was wrong on that account, when he was offered that job with JPL he couldn't turn it down. And now since he decided to get his masters at UCLA, and let JPL pay for it, it turns out that we both lost, and won, the same bet. There was no fair way we could settle-up."

She smiles and sips her latte. "It's never a good idea to make a bet as to what your child is going to do with their life, or anyone else, for that matter. You didn't think Sara would come back to California, did you?"

"I don't know. No—well, maybe—yes. Yes, I did. She loves her dad and this is where she grew up. She needed to get away for a while to realize the significance of that reality."

As if her face was a chalkboard and someone swiped it with an eraser, Cindy's smile disappears.

"Well, of course, she loves her dad—but what about you?"

"Me? Yes, I still love Terry. I'll always love him, in a certain sort of special way. I mean—I love who he was—once—in a different time."

Don't cry. Don't start crying, not here. You're well over forty. You're sitting in a Starbucks on Colorado Boulevard in Santa Monica surrounded by beautiful people most half your age. If you start crying you'll look like a sad pathetic, maybe even crazy old lady.

"But…"

"That's a mighty big word."

"Sara's coming back home and I'm going back home. I'm going back to Michigan in a few weeks. I'd hoped I could stay at least until she graduated and moved back here, but Mom needs me. She's having hip replacement surgery the first week in April. I want to be there for that. I miss seeing my two nieces. You know how it is, kids grow up really fast, visiting with them a couple times a year isn't cutting it. And I miss my brothers…all three of them. It's time to go home—for good."

Cindy's eyes are filling with tears.

Oh, please Cindy, don't you start to cry. You'll embarrass both of us.

"Remember when we left Michigan and moved to California? We had such big ideas, such high hopes. Not that I don't love my kids, and Matt and my life and all of it but sometimes I wonder—how did we ever end up here? How did we get to this place?"

"We drove across country in your VW?"

"Don't be glib, Charlie."

"Sorry, I was just trying to lighten the mood. I know, I know…"

What are all these lovely twenty-something's worrying about now? Am I going to get that callback? Is he really going to spend the weekend with her instead of me? Why did she tell me that she was sick and then I saw her at the bar with him? I know I used to think those things, but it was such a long time ago, and was it really all that important? Yeah, of course it was, because it was my reality then and it mattered. Damn it—it mattered. Youth and all its superfluous silliness, it matters. You can't grow old without having been young. You'll never be mature and wise without first having been impetuous and foolish.

"I'm going to miss you, Charlie. Yeah, I know that we don't get together much anymore, but—I don't know, there's something about your going back to Michigan this time. I know you aren't coming back. When I call you from now on, it's not going to be the same. You'll be twenty-five hundred miles away, not thirty-five."

"I'm not leaving forever, I'll come back occasionally."

"Not to stay, you aren't going to come back to live here, to stay here."

No, I'll never be a permanent resident here again. Not physically, anyway.

"Have you told Terry you're leaving?"

"I told him last week."

"And...?"

"He knows I'm going back for Mom's surgery."

"And...?"

"That's all I've told him, that I'm going back to Michigan because Mom is having surgery and I need to be there."

"So, he thinks that you'll be coming back to California?"

"I suppose he does..."

"I repeat: don't be glib."

"I'm not. I suppose he does because I'm choosing to be a coward rather than telling him the entire truth. It's ironic—when I went home after Dad got sick, I knew I'd eventually come back but I don't think Terry thought so, he didn't think he'd ever see me again. Now I'm leaving again and this time I know I'll never come back but Terry believes that I will, just as soon as Mom recovers from her surgery."

We can make ourselves believe anything to be true, and in the long run does that make us more or less happy, more or less willing to trust? When what we believed to be true turns out to be so, do we even consider what might have happened if it went the other way and wasn't true at all? And when what we thought was true, isn't, do we begin to lose faith in ourselves after awhile, in our ability to distinguish what's reality, what's true from what's false?

"I guess that sometimes in life it's best to do that, to avoid causing pain by fashioning the truth to fit the situation—isn't it?"

Cindy looks at me in a way that she never has before, not in the fifty years I've known her. Her face isn't displaying anger, or disappointment or bitterness, not sadness or remorse. What I read there instead is a two-sided expression of introspection—she's looking inward and out at the same time, my emotional state reflected back at her when she looks at me and vice versa.

I wait, just long enough, before answering: "Yes, but it's a good idea not to make a habit of it."

"I'll drink to that," she raises her cup and we toast our lattes to truth, no matter what form it takes.

David and I haven't talked since Christmas, a little over three months ago, so the fact that he's calling tonight, the same day that I told Cindy that my upcoming change in venue will be permanent, is a turn-of-events that I didn't envision. We've kept in touch over the past eleven years. I've seen him nearly every time I've been back in Michigan. The first year we slept together at every visit, but after awhile our coupling became uncomfortable, for both of us, so we settled for conversations over a glass or two of wine and an occasional dinner. Each time we parted David told me that he loved me; each time we parted I said: "Goodbye, I'll see you again in a few months."

"David, hi. Wow! I sure didn't expect you to be calling. How are you? What's happened in your life since we last talked?"

I know exactly what's happened in his life, why he's calling. What's happened in his life is death.

"It's Emily, isn't it?"

A sickening silence that stretches out across two thousand plus miles—like throwing out a rope with an anchor tied to the end but the rope just keeps sinking and sinking deeper into the water until you want to scream out: "Touch bottom. I need to feel secure and tethered to something substantial."

"Yes, Emily. She died two days ago. She managed to survive pneumonia twice but unfortunately the staff didn't realize that she had developed Legionnaire's disease until it was too late to save her."

Save her? Oh, poor David. Save her so that she could spend another five or ten years virtually comatose. Save her so she could spend the next five to ten years being fed through one tube and peeing through another one. She left you years ago but as long as her body was still there, you couldn't let her go. And Legionnaire's disease of all things? I thought that it was conceived and subsequently died out in the late seventies, about as long as discos lifespan.

"I'm sorry, David. I'm so very sorry. These past years have been hard on you, I know. You were so devoted to her, visiting every day."

"She knew that I was there. I know she did. The doctors and nurses tried to tell me that it didn't make any difference if I came to visit her or not. They told me that she might as well been dead, that I might as well have been going to her grave and standing over it, talking to the ground. But I knew she knew I was there. Emily was still inside that body; she was inside. I know she was."

Is destroying a person's reality, taking away their hope, what they believe to be true, part of a job description?

"David, I'm coming back to Michigan very soon, in the next few weeks."

"How long are you staying this time?"

"Indefinitely. The timing's perfect, the renters who've been in the house for the past two years are ready to buy a place of their own, so I'm moving back into my bungalow. Mom's having hip surgery April fourth, and once she's up and around I'm getting another dog. I've missed Mom and Sam and Kevin and Kevin's daughters and Peter…"

"And me, you've missed me haven't you?"

"Of course I have. Twelve years, that's how long we've known each other and yet we've been apart for most of that time. I'd say this is a long-distance relationship that's held up pretty well."

"I'll never ask you anything about Terry. You don't have to worry about explaining anything to me."

"It's alright. Someday, if you'd like to know something—anything— I'll tell you. Whatever you want to know."

"I don't want to know, so I'll never ask. I'm glad you're coming home, Charlie. I'm so glad you're coming home. I love you."

"I'm glad I'm coming home, too."

Don't make him wait too long for the anchor to settle…

"Bye, David."

But yet…

"I—I—will see you soon."

Chapter 45

It doesn't seem right, Peter showing up at my house this afternoon, without Sam. I seldom see one without the other.

"Peter, hi. What a surprise, the middle of the day. You're usually seeing clients now, aren't you? I don't think I've ever seen you like this, you know, without Sam and at two o'clock in the afternoon in the middle of the workweek."

"I only had two patients between two and four. I canceled them until tomorrow. I felt that my time would be better spent conversing with you. Sam's sleeping, he does a lot of that in the daytime lately, but since he's asleep does it matter what I'm doing? I think not. So, I decided that since he's blissfully unaware of my itinerary, I'd come over here to visit with you."

"Well, you picked a good day and time for a visit. I saw Mom this morning and I had no reason to go into the office this afternoon. In fact, I was just thinking that Bailey needs her second walk of the day. Please join us. We can talk while she's trying to catch squirrels. It's such a beautiful day, isn't it? I did miss springtime in the Midwest. In California it's not always easy to distinguish one season from another."

Bailey's already in the kitchen, she heard her name and "walk" and that was all she needed to rouse her from her favorite napping spot: Dad's old leather chair. It's worn and creased and cracked—like the skin on the face of a very old man. When renters lived here Sam and Peter took the chair to their home to keep is safe, and Peter plied it with waxes and conditioners. Along the armrests the leather's stretched thin, like tissue paper and the seat cushion is split nearly apart, so I try protecting it from further damage by covering it with the ugly red white and blue checkered quilt. Even when Bailey's too big to sleep there, which will be in another few months, the quilt's not coming off. Both chair and quilt comfort and ground me.

"Tell me again why you have a female dog with a male's name?" Peter says, watching me fasten Bailey's leash to her collar.

"Because I love the name, and I thought maybe I'd end up getting a male but when I went to the shelter and saw Bailey, of course her name wasn't Bailey then—the people who'd had her for all of one month had given her the name Miley, which is so inappropriate for a Golden Retriever. Just for that reason alone those people had no business being dog owners. Anyway, I fell in love with her and when I got her in the car I told her: 'Your name's Bailey now.' Besides, I've spent my entire life answering to a man's name. Dogs do take after their owners."

"I should have brought Elton the Third with me, it would have been fun to watch them play together."

Bailey's already pulling on her leash so hard that it's wound out as far as it will go, and we aren't even on the sidewalk yet, but she's sure there are many squirrels available to be captured that haven't yet entered her line of sight. They're probably all hiding, they've left their scent behind though, she's a wily puppy, she knows they're out there.

"Next time bring him along. Maybe you and Sam could come over for dinner next week, before you go to Canada. Aren't you visiting George and Job over the Memorial Day weekend?"

"Yes, if all goes as planned."

A cold jab like I'm being stuck with a fork made out of ice pierces my breastbone.

Stay calm.

"So, Peter. To what do I owe this teatime visit on such a lovely May day?"

"I want to talk to you about Sam, not in his presence."

"What's wrong with my brother? Is he sick?"

"He's been better. When he was sixteen, he was doing much better than he is now, but then again, so was I."

We've stopped walking. Bailey has decided that rolling around on the grass on her back, eyes closed, tongue hanging out and paws curled inward like a baby's hands is more fun than chasing critters she'll never catch anyway, so we're watching and goading her on, as if she needs our encouragement to behave like the two-month old Golden Retriever she is.

"Go, Bailey. Go. That feels good, doesn't it?"

"Bailey, you're so cute. That's it, roll around, girl. Go, Bailey."

She's creating a nice diversion, but we need to get back to the conversation at hand.

"So, you're saying that he is sick?"

"Sick, as in physically ill? No, nothing physical. His cholesterol is a little high and so is his blood pressure but those maladies don't concern me as much as what's happening with him psychologically. The nightmares, the inability to sleep at night, the moodiness, the flashes of anger—all that is getting worse."

Worse?

"Peter, I don't understand; I don't understand at all. What do you mean getting worse?"

Bailey's taken up the hunt again; we're on the move.

"Oh, Charlie. Your brother's battled his demons for so many years. He's suffered so. What you see when you look at him: the missing arm, the missing leg—he's missing so much more than his limbs."

"I never knew. I never had any idea."

The squirrel Bailey just lunged for continues taunting her as it scampers up a tree trunk, chattering all the while.

"Sam's always seemed so, so normal, so in control of his life, considering all that's happened to him. I never knew, Peter. Never. How did I not know?"

Peter grabs hold of my shoulders, pulling me in close to his chest, so he can look at me full on, straight into my eyes. Bailey's leash stretches out at a right angle to my torso. She should be tugging, pulling at it so she can sneak up on another pesky squirrel, but once again she seems more content to lie down on the neighbor's lawn to explore that spot of greenery from a puppy's viewpoint—on her back, paws swimming through the air.

"You didn't know because Sam has been taking anti-depressants and anxiety medications ever since he returned stateside, all those years ago. You didn't know because you've been living your own life, as people do. And you saw what Sam wanted you to see. What he wanted you and your dad to see. What he wanted everyone to see, but mostly your dad and you. Sam's strong and he's stubborn, but eventually even the strongest, and the most stubborn, succumb to pain. That's inevitable."

"Is he—is he going to be okay?"

Of course he isn't going to be okay. That's what Peter's here to tell me.

"His doctor put him on some different meds for the anxiety and depression. We should know in a week or so how well he responds. And the doctor put him on another medication, something Sam's never taken before. Galantamine. It's for another disease altogether. Alzheimer's, mild Alzheimer's, is what it's prescribed for."

"Sam? No! Not Sam. Dad and now Sam? No! No! No! Come on Bailey, it's time to go back to the house, enough rolling around on the grass for one day. Lets go."

I pull on Bailey's leash so hard that she lets out a little yelp.

"Charlie. Your brother is in the very early stages. There's so much research being done now, new medications being introduced every year. It will be many years before he..."

Peter's voice trails off while he follows Bailey and me as we head back to the house. I don't want to hear him. I don't want to look at him. In fact, I would prefer that he go away. This visit and this walk are officially over.

"Charlie. Sam and I are getting married when we go to Canada. I'm going to be your brother-in-law, or another brother, which is a nice thought. I feel like a brother to you anyway."

Poor Bailey. Our walk has ended a third time. She sits at my feet, tail thumping and limpid brown eyes questioning: "Are we coming, going or staying?"

"Getting married? Michigan doesn't recognize gay marriage. What's the point?"

Ever the gentleman, Peter ignores my callousness.

"Because Sam and I love each other, and we want to be married in the eyes of God and under the law, at least in Canada. One of these days we hope that the good citizens of not only Michigan, but the entire country, will realize that there's nothing at all frightening, unnatural or damaging to society about two old homosexuals marrying, or two young ones for that matter."

Bailey has had enough—she stands on her hind legs and paws at my thighs, her black puppy lips displaying her white puppy teeth.

"Can I come to your wedding?"

"Of course you're invited, don't be silly. Bailey looks like she's ready to go back to the house. Come on Bailey, come on."

Peter takes the leash from my hand and leads both of us home.

Chapter 46

It's strange, knowing that in less than an hour I'm going to be seeing Sara again, in Michigan, here in my house. The idea of her being in this setting, visiting me in the place her father never made it to, makes me alternately sad and elated. Since she called me a week ago, the day after I returned from witnessing Sam and Peter's wedding in Montreal, I've been thinking about Terry more than usual, second-guessing my decision to leave California, waking up after a few hours of restless sleep wanting to call to tell him that since Mom's recovered from the surgery and my extended visit with family is drawing to a close, I'm coming back. I suppose my feelings are directly related to the emotional impact the ceremony had on my psyche, reinforcing the stark reality of my life. I'm in limbo when it comes to love. My love life is so complicated, so confounding, and Barbara's words from all those years ago echo in my mind a lot lately: "Love can't fix everything."

The wedding was everything one expects, and wants, a wedding to be: traditional marriage vows (reliably stoic Peter became blubbery when he repeated the words: '…in sickness and in health, 'til death do us part'); copious tears from the rest of us and equally as many titters of joy and outright laughter; a bouquet of roses (held by me who, after the ceremony gave it to the first little girl I saw on the street when we left the church); one minor flub: the minister mistakenly calling Sam George; something old: Peter's mother's wedding ring, which Sam now wears on a gold chain around his neck; something new: Peter's underwear (Sam assured us this was accurate); something borrowed: the sport-coat George lent Sam; and something blue: a robin's egg blue linen shirt Peter bought especially for the occasion, which he sweat through on the warm late spring day.

Sara's call woke me from such a deep sleep that at first I didn't recognize her voice.

"Charlie? Hi. I didn't wake you did I? It's six-thirty here, I figured you'd surely be awake by now."

I'd been so groggy that it took a few minutes, during which I managed to drop my phone in the space between the headboard and the mattress, before I spoke coherently. Even after I realized who I was talking to, I was confused about the time difference ("What are you doing up, Sara? Isn't it three in the morning there?), and twice I asked her if she'd received the check I sent her for graduation.

It was the dream I was having that accounted for my discombobulation. I was running through a forest, a forest with so many trees that sometimes it was hard for me to keep moving, because the trees grew so close together. And every so often a figure popped up from behind one of them: Mom, Maggie, Dad, Jim, Sam, George, Kevin, Sara, and when each one appeared, like an apparition, I would run toward the figure and then they would disappear again. But I knew they were there, all of them, even if I couldn't always see them.

Eventually the forest began to thin out, the landscape was becoming more desolate and arid, more like a desert than a forest, and that's when I realized that I was nearing the edge of a cliff, and Terry was standing, right there, just an inch away from going over and I called out to him, and when I did, I heard someone coming up behind me and it was David and he called my name and I looked back at him and turned to look at Terry again and he was still standing there, right at the boundary between earth and air and he was looking at David and then he looked again at me and David called out my name once more—and I woke up.

"Sara, it's so good to see you, so good to see you." I grab Sara's face in my hands and plant a kiss on each cheek. "And this, of course, is Ben. I'm very happy to meet you." When I hold out my hand, he grasps it tightly, and then pulls me in close to his chest—I'm a sucker for strong affectionate hugs. I wonder how he knows.

Ben, Benjamin Morales, is as handsome as Sara described him. He's tall and thin, but muscular and with his caramel-colored skin and licorice black hair, he and pale, azure-eyed riveting blonde Sara look like two ideally mismatched bookends, striking opposites that somehow make a perfect pair.

I'm so glad she and Troy broke up their freshman year, not only was he too clingy and over-protective, they didn't even look good together.

"Come in, come in. Did you have a hard time finding your way here from the airport?"

Sam and Ben follow me into the living room and as I gesture for them to have a seat on the sofa I notice Sara eyeing the photographs on the sideboard and, like Hazel years before, she sweeps her hand forward in a rainbow arc and says: "These people are your family? I can't wait to meet them, all of them."

Before I can respond Bailey makes her entrance—her tail wagging to a wild rhythmic beat only she hears, her nails clicking on the hardwood as she scampers toward Ben, holding her favorite toy: a mangled pint-size teddy bear, which she drops daintily at his feet before sitting back on her haunches and staring at his face.

He's not only handsome, my dog loves him; I like this guy more and more.

"So, you want to play, do you? What's her name?" Ben asks.

"Her name's Bailey, and yes I know that's a name better-suited to a male dog but that's what I named her and the second you try to pick up that bear, she's going to grab it and will run—well, I see you've already learned her game," I say as Ben, after making a feigned attempt at picking up the bear, begins to chase her, teddy safely snagged in her mouth, around the sofa.

"What do you and Ben want to drink: iced tea or lemonade? I made both. Come in the kitchen with me while those two play. Ben will want something to drink once he's done racing around after Bailey. He's a lovely man, Sara—very handsome, just like you said, and Bailey took to him immediately. You've got yourself a keeper there."

She nods her head several times, as if she's a child being told that she's been a very good girl and her mother is proud of her.

"Oh, Ben's a keeper alright, Charlie. You have no idea."

Bailey is exhausted, fast asleep on her outside bed in the corner of the patio. We've finished off the pitcher of iced tea; I've made a salad that's crisping in the refrigerator; the salmon is marinating, ceviche-like, on a platter; and I've poured us each a glass of wine. We have another hour until dinner and I sense the chitchat that's filled up the last thirty minutes ("How was your flight? Did you have trouble making your connection in O'Hare? What are you going to miss the most about being in college? Are you going to move back in with your dad for a while? How's your dad doing anyway? I haven't talked to him in two weeks") is coming to an end.

The ending begins with more small talk.

"Ben, where are you from?"

"I'm from here, right here in Michigan. Well, I mean I'm not from the island but I'm from near here. Detroit, the southwest side, off Vernor."

"Mexicantown?"

"Yeah, with the last name Morales I wasn't brought up in Corktown!"

"So, that's why you and Sara are here, because of your family. You want her to meet them."

Sara, sitting across from me, leans over and touches my knee.

"And you, Charlie. You and Ben needed to meet, you had to meet."

Ben clears his throat and reaches for Sara's hand.

"Actually there isn't much of my family left for Sara to meet. My dad died of liver cancer my sophomore year at Columbia. I can't believe he lived as long as he did. Mom, who was a white girl Dad met on a high school outing on Bob-Lo Island, is still around but she doesn't want much to do with me. Neither does my sister, Carole. Both of them think I embarrassed the family by airing our dysfunctions in public. And my brother Ed, he was the youngest..." his voice trails off as if he's turned his back, leaving me struggling for a few seconds to make out what he's saying.

"Ed served a tour in Afghanistan and then another one and then another one and after the third one he put his service revolver in his mouth and pulled the trigger when he was home on leave at Christmas in two-thousand eight. Ed was a good soldier, in more ways than one. He protected Mom and Carole from Dad's drunken rampages. Even though he was the youngest, he was bigger than me, taller and stronger. I didn't think that the best way to combat violence was by more violence. But one time Ed broke Dad's jaw and that was the last time Dad ever tried hitting Mom, so maybe violence works—sometimes."

I'm struck by how calmly he speaks. He could be reading a list of things he needs to buy from the grocery. He's certainly had practice at telling this story, this isn't the first time and it isn't going to be the last.

Sara fills the quiet, her voice tinkling with love and pride, like fingers playing over piano keys.

"But violence was never going to work for Ben, not even when he saw something good come out of it. Ben chose another outlet to deal with what was happening in his home—he wrote a play about it. He wrote a play because he was one of six kids in his ninth grade class, the only boy, who were chosen to take part in the 'Play Time' program. Your foundation Charlie, yours and your mom's and your grandmother's, what you created— may have saved Ben's life and it certainly made his life turn out to be much different, much better, than it could have been."

I feel as if I've been punched in the stomach, like all the air has been knocked out of my lungs, but in a good way, because the getting punched part didn't hurt, it just made me very aware of the fact that I'm alive, and that life is fascinating and beautiful and surprising and sometimes—magical.

"Wow! Ben—I'm nearly speechless, which is unusual for me because I tend to rattle on and on, but not this time."

Sara and Ben respond in unison, parroting each other, as if they've rehearsed their dialogue again and again.

"It's all thanks to you, Charlie. You and your mom and your grandmother."

"This is unbelievable. You have to meet my mom. Tomorrow. I want you to meet her tomorrow, before you go to Detroit."

The smiles on their faces tell me that another punch is on its way.

"Well…" Sara's smile grows even wider, "…we were thinking that if it's possible, we'd like to meet Sam, too. We have a project we're working on that we'd like him to be a part of, if he's willing, of course."

"We're making a documentary. Sara and I met in Screenwriting One first semester. I always knew I wanted to be a writer. She was still making up her mind."

"By the second term I knew though that that's what I wanted to do. So we started collaborating then on a concept, an idea, and now that we've graduated, it's time to turn it into reality."

Considering his background, and hers, I know from firsthand experience that living with Terry wasn't easy. I'm guessing that they're making a documentary on how children cope with, and overcome, having a parent who's an alcoholic. But Sam's sixty-three now, he's a little old to be a subject.

"Sure, I know Sam would love to meet you. He's heard enough about you over the years, Sara. As for this documentary, of course I can't speak for him. What's it about, anyway?"

As if he's a proud expectant dad describing his yet unborn child, Ben doesn't hesitate to answer.

"It's about what war does to people—violence, killing, what it does to people when they're forced into doing what they've been taught growing up was wrong—to kill another human being. No matter how just the war, how much it needed to be fought to save the world from tyranny, I'm speaking of course of World War II, the damage that's done to the psyches of those who did the fighting is the same. It's ironic: little boys are given toy guns to play with, and when they get older they play violent games on Xbox, usually some kind of war game where they attack and kill their enemies, and the behavior is justified as 'boys being boys', even as those same boys are learning at home, in school and through the religious community that killing is a travesty, a sin, an immoral act."

"Sara told you that my brother lost an arm and a leg in Vietnam, that's why you want to interview him?"

"Yes, if he's willing. Losing limbs is not only physically traumatizing, it's psychologically damaging, as well, as I know you're aware. Too many veterans aren't getting help for the wounds they've suffered that no one can see. My brother is testament to that. Maybe if someone had known what Ed was going through, if he had felt comfortable talking about his conflicted feelings, he wouldn't have made the ultimate sacrifice—by his own hand. We want to get vets on camera, we want them to talk to us about the way they feel, how they see the world once they've come back from war. The world is different for them than it is for everyone else, that's a very isolating way to live."

I know Sam will be honored to be part of this. He understands what it's like to love a brother, and to believe that he's lost forever.

"We'll talk to him about it tomorrow, but I'm ninety-nine percent sure he'll want to be involved."

Bailey is giving notice that it's time for her pre-dinner walk. Like a stealthy Ninja, without us even realizing that she was on the move, she's managed to climb onto the sofa next to Ben, where she sits, looking at him as pitifully as if she were a shelter dog, sitting in a cage giving potential adopters the 'please take me home' look.

"Seems Bailey would like you to take her for her before dinner walk. Would you mind? It's amazing, the internal clocks animals have. It's as if she knows that the salmon's finished marinating. Sara, you can help me, and Ben, you and your new best friend can go for a walk. I'm letting you know now though, that she gets another one after dinner. She's one spoiled dog."

The front door closes and I ask:

"How's your dad, really? You were a little vague when I asked you earlier."

"He's okay. Just okay. At least I'm back now, so I can see him more often, he's happy about that. He likes Ben. He told me that he was worried that I was going to end up marrying Troy. Dad didn't like Troy very much. He's really excited about the documentary. He's very proud of me already and we haven't even started filming yet."

The salmon sizzles, a burst of butter and dill-scented steam rising up from the pan.

"He's still drinking?"

"Yes." She neatly slices the skin off a cucumber. "You're staying here aren't you? You're not coming back to California to live, are you?"

"Yes and no."

"I don't blame you. I know you love him but I know how hard it is for you to love him. I went away to school, as far as I could go, because I had to—because I love him—he's my father. And I came back home for the same reasons. The day I left for Columbia, I knew I'd be back. But it's different with you, I understand that."

"But he doesn't think that, does he?

"He believes that you're going to come back, like you did after you left the first time. He needs to believe that, Charlie. There's nothing wrong with him believing it, in fact, everything about it is right."

The salad's ready, the salmon's skin crisped golden, the wine's decanted; we're waiting for the door to open. It's time we talk about something else.

"Are you planning on interviewing World War II vets?"

"Yes, we're hoping to. Problem is, they're dying off at a rate of nearly five-hundred a day, and many of the ones who're still alive have dementia or Alzheimer's that's progressed so far that no longer remember anything."

"What about letters? Letters that they wrote when they were overseas? Would those be of any use to you?"

"I hadn't thought of that, it's a good idea though. That could work."

"I was thinking about my dad, Al. He wasn't my biological father, but he might as well have been. I loved him as if he was. Dad fought in the war. He was injured physically, he had a limp, but the war affected him psychologically, too. He couldn't remember how to balance his checkbook or what he'd had for lunch, but he'd talk about the war, sometimes I think he thought he was still there. After he died I found letters he'd written to Maggie—his wife. Letters from boot camp and letters from when he was overseas. I'll never forget the first line of one of them: 'Our dreams are all nightmares now.'"

"Charlie, that's not just a good idea, it's a wonderful idea. Are there photos of him in his uniform?"

"Yeah, I've got photos, too. So does Sam."

"Perfect! Ben's going to love this…"

Bailey slides into the kitchen, all four legs splayed wide apart as she rounds the corner and heads for her bowl. We hear Ben before we see him.

"Hi! We're back. Bailey and a blue jay got into a little spat, I had to break it up, but no one got hurt and Bailey's ego remains intact. She fancies herself as quite the hunter. It sure smells good in here."

"Honey! Charlie gave me a really good idea for '*Letting Go.*' Reading letters World War II vets wrote from the front, letters to their wives and girlfriends. Charlie's going to read letters her dad wrote."

" '*Letting Go*', you already have the title?"

"Yeah, Ben came up with the name. Do you like it? 'Cause that's what it's about: letting go. Feeling safe enough to express your feelings. Letting go of what haunts you, what brings you pain rather than pleasure and happiness; freeing yourself from what's holding you back, so you can move forward. We may have a sub-title, "*Voices From War*", something like that, but I don't think we'll need it. '*Letting Go*' gets the point across quiet well, I think. What do you think?"

"The title's perfect, just perfect. Now lets eat while the salmon's still hot."

There are many ways to let go. Have I chosen the easiest way or the hardest? Have I chosen the most loving and caring or the most cynical and cowardly? Will I ever know the answer? And if I knew right now what the right answer is, if there's even a right one, would I do things any differently anyway?

Chapter 47

Terry had his first and final heart attack three weeks ago. Sara gave me the news in an early morning phone call.

"He'd started running again, I convinced him that it was good for him, that he needed to get out there at least a few days a week. I told him that if he didn't want to do it for himself, he should do it for me."

Oh, God I'd thought, how will she live with that guilt?

"He'd gone out for a run, when he came back he told me that he was a little tired but he wanted to do some work before he took a nap, so he took a shower and went in the office. I had a meeting with Ben and one of our producers, so I was gone from the house for about two hours, and when I got back it was so quiet I thought Dad was still napping. But his bedroom door was open and he wasn't in bed. That's when I walked in the office and he was sitting there, sitting in the chair, and his head was just slumped over to the side a little, so I thought that maybe he was asleep, and I didn't want to scare him awake by coming up behind him so I walked around to his side and his eyes were open, they were wide open, as if they could still see the ocean."

My tongue had gone numb and I'd felt a hard knot rise up in the back of my throat when Sara told me that he'd been sitting in that chair, looking out at the sea. I remembered the night of her graduation, when I came home and found him, staring into all that blackness. I heard his voice: "I'll bet you didn't know that I like to sit here too, did you? You're not the only one who likes looking out these windows."

"I can't believe he's not here anymore." She began to cry.

His voice was stronger then, sorrowful and heartbreaking in my head. Terry could have been right beside me, talking into my ear: "My girl, my baby, my daughter. She's leaving, Charlie. She's all grown-up now, so she's leaving."

And I'd thought: now you're the one who left.

"I'll come right away, Sara. I'll leave early tomorrow…"

"No, don't come now. You were coming out for the Oscars anyway. Dad's been cremated. When you're here in February, we'll have a ceremony on the beach and we'll scatter his ashes then."

"Oh, Sara I'm so sorry he didn't live to see *Letting Go* win an Academy Award. He was so proud of you, and Ben, when your documentary was nominated. Seeing you win would have been the second biggest thrill of his life, the first one being the day you were born."

"You're way too optimistic. Word on the street is that the film about the NSA listening to our phone conversations and monitoring emails is a sure bet. Dad would have ended up being disappointed and angry, that we didn't win, which means he would have gotten drunk at one of the after-show parties and it would have been a disaster. Of course, he would have gotten drunk if we won, so I suppose it wouldn't have mattered one way or the other. He took Ben and I out for dinner when *Letting Go* was nominated and had so much to drink that the valet wouldn't give him the keys to his car. We ended up driving him home, we left his car at the restaurant overnight."

I'd started to say "I'm sorry" again but stopped because once you've said them enough times those words tend to lose their impact. Instead I said: "I'll see you in February. I love you, Sara."

First I called Cindy to let her know, and then I called David, who upon hearing the news, insisted that he'd come over right away, which is what I hoped he'd say.

Bailey greeted him at the door and led him to the tiny office space I'd created out of a room off the kitchen that at one time must have been a pantry or root cellar of some sort. It doesn't have vents but in the winter a space heater is all I need to keep me warm. That day I'd turned the heater to the highest setting, wrapped myself in a down comforter and, until she retrieved David, Bailey had lain on my feet, which I'd covered with two pairs of wool socks. Since Sara's call, I couldn't get warm.

"Charlie, I'm so sorry." He said it only once. "When's the service? Are you leaving for California right away?"

"No, Terry was cremated. I'm going back as scheduled, for the Academy Awards show. We'll scatter his ashes sometime during those days I'm there."

"You're cold. The heater's blazing away, you're wearing a sweater, the slippers I gave you for Christmas but your cheeks, your nose, your fingers, everything's cold. You need to get out of this room. I'll build a fire and make us some hot toddies, and—we'll talk."

And we did. We talked and David built a fire in the fireplace and we drank another warm wintry concoction and we talked more and we ate a dinner consisting of boxed macaroni and cheese, which I'd bought for Kevin's youngest daughter when she comes to visit, and we talked some more and David put more logs on the fire and we opened a bottle of wine and each had a glass and then another one and we talked more and at some point during the evening David told me that every time he went to visit Emily he always believed that when he walked in the door of the nursing home a doctor was going to come up to him and shake his hand and say: "Congratulations, your wife has had a miraculous recovery, she's asking for you."

And then I told him that for the past three years I thought every morning when I woke up that it would be the day that Terry would call me and promise me that if I came back he would stop drinking, forever, and then he'd ask me to come back to him and I would because I knew that everything he said was true because he had made a promise and then David told me how much he loved me and when I replied: "David—I..." he had taken my still cool hands in his, held them to his warm cheek and said: "You don't have to say it, you don't have to say anything."

Chapter 48

Letting Go didn't win Best Documentary of 2014 at the Academy Awards yesterday. As Sara had predicted, along with almost everyone else in Hollywood, the Edward Snowden film took home the honors. But the afternoon and evening were still exciting and glamorous and ultimately, quite tiring.

We learned that documentary filmmakers are assigned to the 'nose-bleed' seats, but Sara had brought opera glasses, so for four hours we shared them back and forth, ogling from the balcony. By the time the show finally ended, we'd had our fill of watching people, even beautiful people, blowing air kisses and women tugging at the bodices of their gowns to avoid an embarrassing reveal. We also learned that if you're involved with a documentary, and it doesn't win, your chances of being invited to any of the fancy after-the-show parties that the media obsesses over are dismal, but we did attend a party in North Hollywood hosted by the *Letting Go* producers, where Gary Sinise, a long-time supporter of the military, made an appearance to thank the team for making the film. Sara and Ben were simultaneously honored and exhausted.

Twenty-four hours have passed, but for Sara, Ben and me nothing has changed as far as our states-of-mind—we've exchanged one surreal day for another one. Two hours ago

Barbara, Paul, Leslie, Cindy, Matt, Ben and I stood at the stern of a boat and watched as Sara lowered a basket of ashes mingled with rose petals over the side.

We didn't say much as the captain steered the small cabin cruiser past the Santa Monica Pier out to the open ocean. Not long after we pulled away from the dock Leslie, much older and weaker than the last time I saw her, said that it was a blessing that Harold had died before his son since "...there's nothing worse than burying a child", but when she saw the look on Sara's face she'd started to cry and apologized for making it seem like she was somehow minimizing Sara's grief, that certainly losing one's father at the age of twenty-five was a tragedy. The rest of us just sat, silently, and looked at the two of them, not knowing who we should feel sorrier for.

The captain cut the engine when we were two miles off shore. It was quiet on the open water, all we could hear were the waves gently pushing against the sides of the boat, like the sound of a beating heart. When Sara picked up the basket we all took in a deep breath, and didn't let it out until Sara said "Good-bye, Dad", and the ashes and petals began to spread out over the surface of the sea.

"We're going to go, Charlie. We'll see you before you head back to Michigan. Matt Junior and Meghan are coming over tonight, with Collin. He's six weeks now, we haven't seen him since he was a month old. Babies do change so much, even in a few weeks. Sorry you didn't get to see him this time, but when you're out here next, we'll make that happen."

Cindy kisses me goodbye and whispers in my ear: "I know he was the only man you ever loved. Now you have all those beautiful memories that will live in your heart forever, and you can let the bad ones go."

Matt hugs me, kisses the top of my head and they walk away. They aren't holding hands, but their bodies are close together, close enough that their arms collide when they swing them and I see, even from the back, that Matt laughs at that and he circles his arm around Cindy's waist and she leans her head to the side and even though I can't see her face, I know she's crying.

"I'm going to go settle up with the captain. Paul, Barbara, Leslie, please join Charlie, Ben and I for dinner."

"We're going to go. Barb's not feeling too well." Paul looks at his wife who nods her head in affirmation. "Come over next week for dinner Sara, Ben. We'll call you. And Charlie, next time you're in town, we want to see you, too."

The awkwardness settles over us like an invisible shroud.

"I'm going to go too, then. I'm tired, and in this weekend traffic it's going to take at least an hour for me to get home." Leslie says, and Sara, Barbara and Paul step forward to receive their hugs.

"Come on, Sara, I'll walk up to the office with you," Ben says as Barbara and Paul head for the parking lot, leaving only Leslie and me on the dock that moves slightly from side-to-side; it's as if we're still in the boat. I didn't notice it while we were on the water, but I realize now that I'm nauseous.

"Charlie, I'm glad we have a few minutes alone. Would you walk with me to my car so we can talk?" Leslie asks and takes ahold of my arm as if to get her balance.

Am I experiencing prescient nausea I wonder, as I place my hand over hers and her fingers cling to mine—they're clammy and cold and the tips are as rough as sandpaper.

"Sure, lets get off this dock and back on truly solid ground. I don't know about you, but I'm feeling a little sick. I thought Sara held up quite well, didn't you? She's such a remarkable woman. Terry was so proud of her, rightly so."

Leslie's fingers tighten around mine as we sit down on a bleached-out teak bench. I sense that she wants to hold on as long as she can.

"Sara, yes. She's an amazing young woman. When you think of the tragedies she's endured…"

Leslie's head drops forward and she slumps down before speaking again, her fingers tightening like a vise.

"I so loved Harold. I loved him more than I can ever begin to explain. He was honest with me from the very beginning, he told me that he loved me but that he loved Gloria in a way that he'd never love anyone, not even me, and I understood that."

I understand it too I think, as she squeezes even harder.

"When I convinced him to tell Terry the truth about us, I thought I was doing the right thing. I believed he had to be honest with his son, the same way he was honest with me. And Harold agreed with me. He told Terry because he believed that I was right."

"You were, Leslie. It wouldn't have been good if Harold had continued to lie to Terry. It was the most respectful and loving thing to do."

She makes a noise, a sick-like groan, from deep in her throat.

"Harold was on morphine the last few weeks. The medication made him talk crazy. Sometimes he had hallucinations. I'd been told to expect that. But two days before he died he told me that he was sorry that he had told Terry the truth."

"That's all he said?"

"Yes, then…but don't you think that was enough? He was regretting being honest with his son. He was regretting it because he never considered the consequences of telling Terry, and neither did I. We never could have imagined that Terry would tell his mother."

"Of course you and Harold didn't think that Terry would tell Gloria. How could you have known? Don't beat yourself up over that, Leslie. It was right, what Harold did. We aren't mind readers. None of us knows for sure how someone will react to our actions. If we did, I don't think our lives would be nearly as interesting, or complicated."

"But—it's what he said on the last day, on the day before he died. I was sitting on the bed. I had my head on his chest. I'll never forget the sound of his heart. I could hear the blood rushing through his arteries; the sound was so loud and so strong, vibrating against my eardrum that I didn't believe that a heart beating like that could ever stop. He was stroking my hair and I was listening to his heart and I believed at that moment that everything his doctor said about him dying was a huge mistake and then Harold said: 'It wasn't a heart attack.'"

"Leslie, I..."

She lets go of my hand, stretches out her long legs, pushes her body upright and off the bench and turns to face me for the first time since she started talking.

"Don't, Charlie. Don't try, there's nothing you can say. I just wanted you to know. I can't tell anyone else, not Sara, certainly not Paul or Barbara. You're the only person I could share this with. Thanks for listening. I'm going home now."

I watch her shuffle toward the parking lot; the coltish trot long gone. Before she disappears into the row of cars she turns back and waves, just once, and then she moves on and out of my sight.

Chapter 49

"I'm surprised you chose Chinese over sushi," I say as Sara and I walk into the restaurant with the sign in the window proclaiming that diners should prepare themselves for the best dim sum in the greater Los Angeles area.

"Mom and Dad introduced me to sushi, which is my favorite, but the truth is Dad always preferred Chinese. I thought it would be more appropriate to eat here today," she replies as we follow a tiny gray-haired Chinese woman to a table set for four.

"More coming?" she asks as we sit.

"No, this is it. It's just the two of us," Sara says and the woman smiles and motions for a server to bring a pot of tea.

"It would have been nice if Ben had joined us, but…"

"But this is better, isn't it? That's why he decided not to come. He thought that you and I needed some time alone together, and he's working on a new project, another documentary. This one's about a child prodigy, an amazingly talented ten-year-old who plays jazz piano so well now that by the time he's twenty, he may be the new Thelonious Monk. The kid's from East St. Louis. No dad in the picture, six or seven siblings, mom's been in and out of jail for prostitution over the past few years. But there's a grandmother, who just happens to have a piano that Marcellus learned how to play when he was four. It's a great story, one that needs to be told."

"Ben's a wonderful man, Sara, but of course I'm not telling you anything you don't already know. You're working with him on this film, aren't you?

The waiter sets the teapot in the middle of the table and as Sara reaches for it, she knocks over the cup in front of her. Memories surge through me like a jolt of electricity: real, vivid, in living color.

Hi, Terry. Nice to see you back in your body, although it seems a little strange considering that your daughter scattered your ashes, mixed in with some very lovely rose petals, over the ocean only two hours ago.

Sara, not surprisingly, seems oblivious to the fact that her father has appeared at our table, but then she says:

"No, not this one. I'm going to try my hand at writing a screenplay, a drama. It's going to be about a woman's life. She loses her mom on nine eleven, and that changes everything about what comes after. How she withdraws at first, and her dad tries to draw her out but it's hard for him to do that, to be the strong one for her when he's so broken inside. So he withdraws, into a bottle, and although he wants to, he's never able to find his way back out."

So, she knows you're here, too, but we're seeing you from our own perspectives.

"But this isn't going to be overly melodramatic—not that people aren't going to cry at certain points, they will. I mean, life's happy and sad, comedy and tragedy. I don't want people coming out of the theater, providing I can sell this and get it made, all glum and depressed because that's certainly not the way my…her life has been. "

"Does the story end in the present?

"Oh, no. She's going to age; she'll be a very old woman when the credits start to roll. A very old woman who lived a very extraordinary, and ordinary, life."

The elderly Chinese woman must be working in the kitchen. A sullen-faced boy with short spiky black hair and a starched white shirt is leading a family of four to a table in the corner: mother, father, teenage son and a daughter who looks no older than six. When they're seated the girl and her mother are facing me. I smile at the girl and she smiles back.

"Will you let me read it when you're finished?"

"Of course. I'll probably have Ben read it first though. Let's order; being on the water always makes me hungry, even on a day like today."

We order shrimp dumplings, pot stickers, meatballs, ribs and noodles (taste in food must be genetic) and for the next hour Sara and I eat and laugh and cry, but we cry just once, and only for a few minutes, when she says she was surprised at how heavy the ashes were in the basket and how weightless they seemed when they were airborne: "I thought for a second or two that they might never drop into the water, that they'd sail around on currents of air until Dad decided where in the ocean he wanted to rest."

And we talk. We talk about how Sara hopes that she'll see Leslie again, and how she's going to reach out to her although she thinks that today was an ending, but she believes that today was a beginning as far as her relationship with Barb and Paul.

"I'm their surrogate daughter now. I always sort of was anyway since they never had children, but now that I'm an orphan, our connection is more real than ever. You know, Barb tried over and over again to carry a baby to term, she miscarried five times so they decided that they didn't want to be disappointed anymore and they filled up that emptiness with even more love for one another."

She tells me that even though he left it to her, she's not keeping Terry's house on the beach. "Dad has two mortgages on the place. Those in-between jobs years, he drew money out of the house. The market is hot now. I should be able to sell it, pay off both the first and the second and still might make a little profit. It's too big, anyway. Ben and I want to get a little condo in Studio City; we don't need all that square footage."

And she tells me that the Academy Award nomination is helping thaw Ben's relationship with his mother and sister. "His mom called the day before the show, before we left for the airport to pick you up. She was excited. Ben said that she used the word 'proud' more than once. Then he talked to his sister, who told him that she wants to come out for a visit sometime soon. And he told her that she has to bring their mom and she said 'sure thing.' He was so happy, and I told him not to feel guilty about being happy since Dad had died only a few weeks before, because I could tell that he didn't want to smile too much, and we agreed then to keep supporting each other, in good times and bad, but not at the expense of hiding our own personal feelings."

While Sara's talking I watch the young girl across the room. I'm paying attention to Sara, I'm not pretending to listen; I hear every word she says. If I had to, I could repeat what she's been saying, verbatim. But still, all the while I'm listening, I'm also thinking.

That little girl I saw on Christmas Day over thirty years ago, at a Chinese restaurant just like this one, at a time when everything in my life seemed to have come together, when I'd finally found someone I loved, someone I could eventually bare my soul to, someone who'd never stop loving me because I was fallible, as was he—what happened to that little girl—for that matter, what happened to me? She's close to forty now, I'm almost sixty and that man I loved turned out to be much more fallible, and human, than I'd ever expected, as did I, and now he's gone.

And what about this little girl, the one sitting across from me now? I know that there will be times that her life will be so beautiful, so exquisite and perfect she'll wish for nothing to ever change, and there will be times when she'll feel like she's gone down the rabbit hole and even though she'll learn a lot about herself, and the world and why she's alive while she's fumbling around down there, hoping to find out the answers to her questions, things will change, and she'll suffer disappointment and heartbreak. But even though I know what her future looks like, because all of our futures are the same, in many ways, I'd never tell her, and she wouldn't want me to. Who wants to go to a movie, or a play, and have the usher hand you the screenplay or the script when you walk in the door?

She waves at me and when I wave back I wonder if somehow she's reading my mind.

"Charlie, what's up with you and that little girl? Do you know her or her family from somewhere?"

"No, I have no idea who she is, she's a cutie though, isn't she? Maybe I remind her of a favorite aunt or a teacher she likes."

"Or maybe kids just like you. Are you ever sorry that you didn't have kids of your own?"

"No—yes—no, I'm not sorry. It's not like I made a decision at some point in my life not to have children, I just never did. Biologically I'm sure I could have but there's more to creating and nurturing life than just biology. I don't think I was—sorry, it's David, do you mind?"

"Go ahead and take the call, I'm going to the restroom and then we should probably get the check. You've got an early flight tomorrow."

When Sara walks by the girl waves at her too and then sticks out her tongue. Sara laughs, sticks hers out and the child convulses in giggles.

"David. Sara and I are just finishing eating. We're heading back to the house soon so I can pack. Early flight tomorrow, I have to be at LAX by five-thirty."

"How was it today? I've been thinking about you all day."

"Can we talk about it when I get home? I'd rather talk about it then."

"Sure, I understand. I just don't like thinking being of you being so sad and I'm not there to comfort you."

"It's okay, David. It is, really. I'm sad but being sad is a temporary condition. I'm not going to be sad forever."

Terry's gone. He's not sitting at the table anymore. I didn't see him leave, so I don't know if he waved or maybe blew a kiss when he walked away.

"I can't wait to see you, Charlie. While you were gone I had a contractor come to your house. He thinks it's possible to get heat in that root cellar, there might be a way he can add on to it and run wiring and vents without destroying the structural…"

"David, we can talk about it tomorrow. There're a lot of things I'd like to do with the house, that's just one of them."

"I can't wait to see you, sorry, I already said that. I love you, Charlie. I love you."

"And I love you, David."

That was so simple.

Sara and the waiter arrive at the table at the same time. We both pull out our wallets, but I grab the check and motion for her to put her money away.

"No, I'm paying for this dinner. It's my small way, very small way to thank you Sara, for everything. You have no idea how much joy you've brought into my life because you made Terry happy, you brought joy to his life. And I thank you for that. I'll thank you for that forever."

As we walk away from the table I grab ahold of her hand and say:

"You know, I was thinking—maybe after I've finished packing we can go sit in the office for awhile. We'll have a glass of wine and look at some of those photos of you and your dad and your mom the first time they took you to the observatory. And then before I go to bed, I think, if you don't mind, I'd like to sit by myself and stare out the window at the sea. I don't have a view like that in Michigan."

And off we go into the cool Southern California night. It's time to go home.

Acknowledgements

Many thanks to Stevan Nikolic, editor at Adelaide Books who after publishing *Ambivalence A Love Story* in *Adelaide Literary Magazine,* told me that if I had a completed novel manuscript, he'd like to read it. I did, I sent it, he read it and a month later sent me a contract.

Thanks also to the people who read the manuscript in its early drafts, sometimes a chapter at a time. They are: Mary Hausch, Susan Buxton, Scott Hubbard, Richard Rutherford and Sara Badertscher Wisener. My apologies if I've forgotten anyone.

About the Author

Claudia Piepenburg spent much of her career as a copywriter and editor. *Letting Go* is her first novel. Her short story *Where Do We Go from Here* won Honorable Mention in the *Glimmer Train* May/June 2018 Short Story Award for New Writers. In 2019 her short stories were published in *Adelaide Literary Magazine, Writer's Block, Literary Yard* and *Potato Soup Journal.* She is currently working on her second novel as well as a non-fiction book about for-profit Alzheimer's care facilities.

Made in the USA
Las Vegas, NV
03 November 2020

10535262R00206